UNLEAVENED DEAD

By Ilene Schneider

Oak Tree Press   Taylorville, IL

Oak Tree Press books may be purchased for educational, business or sales promotional purposes. Contact Publisher for quantity discounts

First Edition, November 2012

ISBN 978-1-61009-198-5
LCCN 2012939146

To my family: husband, Rabbi Gary M. Gans, for never nagging me about surfing the 'net or watching TV instead of writing; and to our sons, Natan and Ari Schneider-Gans, for . . . well, just for being.

ACKNOWLEDGEMENTS

I'm going to quote from myself, from the acknowledgement page in *Chanukah Guilt*: "A reminder: this book is a work of fiction. The characters, the town of Walford, the plot all came from my imagination. None of the characters are based on anyone I know." So please, don't stop me in the street, or the store, or the synagogue, or the office, or wherever you may see me, and say, "I know who you based that character on." I didn't. At least my conscious mind didn't. I don't take responsibility for what my subconscious may have done.

My heartfelt thanks to the staff of Oak Tree Press, who have been so supportive and helpful: publisher, Billie Johnson; acquisitions editor, Sunny Frazer; PR manager, Jeana Gartshore-Thompson; office manager, Suzi Yazell. It's been a pleasure working with all of you to produce this book.

My gratitude to those who gave freely of their expert advice: my "in-house" lawyer, my brother-in-law Jeffrey R. Gans, Esq., who confirmed the answers I found on my internet search about suicide clauses in insurance policies; Jim Doherty, Jr., a fellow member of the Mystery Writers of America, who answered my questions about the Witness Protection Program; and David C. Knott, Deputy Chief Fire Marshal of Evesham Fire-Rescue, who patiently and in detail described what happens when a gas dryer vent is blocked, the effects of the carbon monoxide buildup resulting from such a blockage, and regulations concerning CO detectors in homes.

Here's to the members of New Jersey Birding who answered my questions about which birds are apt to nest in dryer vents and when. I didn't quote every posting, but did read them all. I knew I could count on you to help me out. My thanks go to Trina Anderson, Margaret Bossett, Theodore Chase, Carol Flanagan, Michael Gochfeld, Claus Holzapfel, Barbara Jones, Susie ("kraziezoo"), Laurie Larson, Fred Lesser, Karen Swaine.

Thank you to my first readers: my parents, Esther and Marshall Schneider, who are completely unbiased when they say they love my writing. And to writing teacher, journalist, and novelist Stacia Friedman, who gave me a lot of valuable criticism and advice, none of which I followed. She tried, but I'm stubborn.

And special appreciation to all the fans of Rabbi Aviva Cohen who kept asking when they would "see" her again. Here she is.

Ilene Schneider
Marlton, New Jersey
November, 2012

UNLEAVENED DEAD

Chapter One

I love weddings. I even enjoyed my own. Both of them. Too bad the marriages weren't as successful as the weddings.

While it's true that I cry at weddings, at least as often as I do at funerals, it's not because I'm recalling the outcomes of my own. Instead, it's because there's something so hopeful about weddings: the optimism that love will remain strong, commitment will continue, happiness will be forever; that there will be a future.

Unfortunately, though, sometimes you just know the couple will be headed for divorce within a few years. The respective parents barely acknowledge the others' presence. The bride and groom smile with their mouths, not their eyes. The surface is there – the ritual, the flowers, the dinner, the dancing, the toasts – but the substance, that intangible sense that these two people are *beshert*, destined to be together, is noticeably absent. The guests are having a good time, but not a great one. There's no joy, no atmosphere of celebration.

When I officiate at those weddings, I seldom have to struggle to keep my composure.

No matter how soulless a wedding may be, though, no one equates it with untimely death.

Maybe I'm not being fair, maybe the deaths would have occurred anyway. But all the trouble did seem to start with two weddings, one that took place under deceptive circumstances, and one that was almost cancelled before it was even planned. Then there was the third wedding, the one at which all the pieces began to come together. But I'm getting ahead of myself . . . .

It all began on a normal day in August. In a synagogue, a normal day in August means there's very little for the rabbi to do. Maybe a few board meetings, a couple of hospital visits or funerals. But religious school isn't in session; no one wants to stand around in what feels like tropical heat and humidity for the unveiling of a tombstone; the synagogue sub-groups – men's club, sisterhood, adult education classes – are on hiatus for the summer; kids are at camp, so bar and bat mitzvah ceremonies are postponed until the fall. In other words, it's the perfect time for a rabbi to prepare for the High Holy Days and research sermon topics. Which explains why, when Florence Fisher burst into my office without knocking, I was working diligently on my laptop, checking movie schedules.

"She's getting married!" Florence shouted with exclamation points, throwing her satchel-sized purse on the couch and flinging herself after it. "Audrey's engaged! I can't believe it! I'm so happy!"

Florence was anything but subtle, in vocal volume or appearance. In her mid-seventies, she had bleached blonde hair, wore lots of makeup and jewelry, heels, and a pair of shorts and a sleeveless top made of some kind of purple silky material; it probably was silk. Maybe she once had the figure to carry off the ensemble, but now she looked like a plum. A plum that had been in the fridge too long and had begun to shrivel and wrinkle. Her varicose veins were color-coordinated to match her outfit.

I closed the top of my laptop, so she wouldn't see that I was checking the International Movie Database, not working on sermon notes, and came around my desk to sit in the chair facing the couch. "Mazel Tov! Who is she marrying? Tell me all about him."

Florence hesitated before speaking. "His name's George Rivers. He's a few years older than she is, divorced, adult children. They both work for the same community college, but they actually knew each other casually in high school. I think he dated one of Audrey's friends, but I never knew him. His family moved when he was in tenth or eleventh grade. We haven't met him yet, but have spoken to him on the phone. He seems nice. Very polite. Jack and I are flying out next weekend to meet him and talk about the wedding."

The Fishers' only child, Audrey, forty-one years old and never married, had moved to the West Coast after college, much to her mother's chagrin, and had lived in all three Pacific states in the lower forty-eight. Actually, Florence was probably more upset about her daughter's marital status, or lack thereof, than she was about the distance between Walford, New Jersey, and Eugene, Oregon, her latest home. No marriage, to Florence's way of thinking, meant no grandchildren. No grandchildren meant fewer opportunities to criticize and meddle.

Florence continued, "We were hoping to have the wedding here, but they want to have it in the Eugene area. Audrey said all their friends live there – not that she's ever had that many friends, not like we do, and she couldn't care less that *our* friends will be inconvenienced. She never did think about anyone but herself, or she would realize we would want to invite our friends, too. Well, that's our problem, not yours. Here's why I'm here: they don't belong to a synagogue and don't know any rabbis, so if you're willing, we would fly you out to Eugene and put you up in a hotel for a couple of days."

"I would be honored to officiate." Great! Oregon! I had never been there and the opportunity to increase my bird life list with the addition of western species was irresistible, even if it did mean spending time with Florence.

Then Florence did something I was surprised to see – she blushed. "There's a problem."

"He doesn't have a *get*?" I guessed. A civil divorce isn't sufficient under Jewish law; a Jewish divorce is also required. Some liberal rabbis don't require one, but my feeling is that the *get*, the Jewish divorce decree, parallels the civil divorce, just as the *ketubah*, the Jewish marriage contract, parallels the civil marriage license. I like the symmetry.

"Not exactly. He never had a Jewish wedding, so he doesn't need a *get*, right?"

"His first wife wasn't Jewish?"

Florence now was definitely embarrassed. "Well, no. But neither is he."

I took a deep breath before responding. "Florence, you know I don't perform intermarriages."

Now she got angry. "But you're a woman! You're already breaking with tradition! What difference does it make to you?" It was an argument I had heard before. When I was first being considered by my synagogue, Mishkan Or, there were members who were upset that I wouldn't officiate at intermarriages. They were outvoted by others who were pleased I didn't, but I had noticed recently that some of my supporters were beginning to switch sides as their children found non-Jewish partners. Florence and her husband Milton weren't active enough members at Mishkan Or for me to know where they stood in the controversy.

She tried another tack. "It shouldn't really matter, anyway, because they won't be having children, so there won't be any arguments about Christmas trees. Audrey's never been interested in becoming a mother, and he already has his first grandchild. And even if she did want children, she's too old. Audrey didn't come along until I was in my thirties . . . my *early* thirties, that is . . . and I was ten years older than all her friends' parents." I decided not to tell her that my niece Trudy, who had just turned fifty, and her partner Sherry, only three years younger, had a biological eight-year-old son and a newly adopted baby daughter.

"Children are not the only reason I won't officiate, Florence. I really believe that as a rabbi I am authorized to perform only Jewish ceremonies." I emphasized the word Jewish. I continued, "If the marriage is between a Jew and non-Jew, it's not a Jewish ceremony."

Florence sighed in resignation. "Oh, well. Audrey and you have hardly even met, so it won't matter if you're there or not. Do you know any rabbis in the Eugene area who do perform intermarriages?"

Glad to know I'm so highly regarded. My day dream of increasing my life list evaporated as quickly as a sleeping dream. "Sorry, I don't." I thought for a minute. "Well, I do know someone who's in the area, Ben Bronfman, a classmate of mine from rabbinical school, but he doesn't officiate at intermarriages either. He may know someone who can help you, though."

"So what should they do if they can't find a rabbi?"

"I'm sure Rabbi Bronfman knows a Jewish justice of the peace who can do a nice ceremony and incorporate some Jewish symbols."

"But I had my heart set on a Jewish wedding!"

So Audrey and George have no say in the matter? Out loud, I cautioned, "I'm sure they can find someone. But you need to be careful who you find. I know there are several rabbis who do intermarriages, and they do so because they really are committed to outreach and believe it's best for the Jewish community. But there are others – not many, but they exist – who'll marry the proverbial bird and fish if the price is right. I doubt if Audrey and George want a rent-a-rabbi."

I had no idea what they wanted and I was sure Florence didn't either.

I looked up Ben's phone number and gave it to Florence. I then forgot all about the incident until I bumped into Florence at Trader Joe's several months later and she told me he had officiated at the ceremony. I was surprised as I remembered him as having been adamantly opposed to intermarriage.

And then a few weeks after seeing Florence, Ben and I both attended the annual conference of the International Rabbinic Alliance, and I found out what had really transpired.

CHAPTER TWO

"Aviva? Is that you?"

Oh, great. I thought. *Someone else I haven't seen for a while. Someone else who isn't sure if this dumpy, middle-aged lady with the frizzy graying hair long overdue for a cut and color is the same petite, perky red-head with the sleek pixie cut from thirty years ago. Well, guess what? People change over the years. Or decades.*

I turned to see who was calling me, and was pleased and surprised to see it was Ben Bronfman. We had been great friends during rabbinical school. He was one of the only guys who didn't assume I was there to find a husband, and he believed men and women could be pals. His wife didn't, but I really didn't care about her opinion. Ben and I liked each other and were able to spend time together as study partners without his wife's interference. I had lost touch with him, though, after he had moved to the West Coast. He seldom came back East, except to visit family, and neither my conference budget nor my personal finances stretched to cover plane fare to the West Coast when the International Rabbinic Alliance conference was there.

But this year the IRA, the oldest and largest inter-denominational professional organization of its kind, was holding its conference in Philadelphia, only fifteen miles from my home in Walford, New Jersey. It was well within my budget, especially since the conference venue was only a short Hi-Speed Line ride away. The problem was the timing. The week before Passover is probably the worst time to schedule an annual conference for rabbis. Or for any Jews.

No, I'm wrong. There's no "probably" about it. It is the worst time. The timing is a holdover from the days when all rabbis were male, all their spouses were women, and the congregation was the prime focus of their lives. The synagogue wasn't the mistress; the legal wives were. A mistress knows, if she's seen any Lifetime movies, she'll always come second to the needs of the wife and family. A rabbi's wife and children in the past always knew they would be ignored in favor of the congregants. It was the rebbetzin, the rabbi's wife, who took care of home and children, and sometimes worked as an unpaid teacher, sisterhood advisor, and marriage counselor in the synagogue. Rather than be underfoot and hinder the rebbetzins' Pesach preparations, the rabbis would decamp to a luxury hotel for four days of seminars, schmoozing, and boozing, far from the eyes of judgmental congregants or resentful wives.

I'm not sure why I go to the IRA conferences, except one of the only perks I get from my synagogue is a budget line for conventions. (Well, for one convention. And only if it's fairly local. It's not all that large a budget.) And if I don't use a budget line, chances are it will be deleted from the following year's budget. Plus, it's a chance to get away and have a break. I don't do much for Pesach anyway – my townhouse is too small to host a seder, which my niece Trudy and her partner Sherry hold at their mini-mansion on the first night. We have a community seder at the synagogue on the second night. I come away from both events with much more than a week's supply of leftovers, so I'm able to survive the holiday with a minimum of cleaning and cooking.

The other reason I go to the IRA conference is to see my old classmates. And I mean "old" both as an age and as the length of time I've known some of them. Many of us are now beyond the point of middle age, unless we live long enough to approach Moses' one hundred twenty years, but we're not about to admit we're senior citizens. Actually, in the eyes of most retailers and organizations (AARP being the exception, grabbing us six months before we turn fifty), we're in a nether world, too old for student discounts, too young for senior ones.

As I said before, this year's conference was in Philadelphia, so I didn't stay at the hotel. After I arrived there the first afternoon, I picked up my registration materials, checked the schedule to see which sessions (most of them) I would skip, and still had plenty of time to hang out in the bar off the lobby looking for friends, knowing from experience it was the most likely place to find my colleagues. And there was Ben.

"Ben, hi!" I gave him a kiss on the cheek. "It's been forever! How have you been?"

He laughed and gave me a bear hug. "Great to see you, Aviva. You look ... er ..."

"Yeah, I know, old and fat. But you look great! What's your secret? A moldering portrait hidden in your attic?"

"Must be good living. You remember Sandy, don't you?"

"Of course, how are you?" I turned to his wife, whom I wouldn't have liked even if she hadn't mistakenly thought I had the hots for her husband. She was tall and thin and buff, with perfect features and long, silky, blonde hair. She was the kind of person who looked elegant even in jeans, which she always wore, even when staying in five-star hotels. But that wasn't the reason for my dislike. After all, Ben was also tall and thin and buff and blonde, but I liked him. It was her abrasive personality, her air of arrogance, her insistence that she knew better than professionals how to do or fix anything, her refusal to listen to anyone else's opinion or even consider that she may be mistaken about something that caused me – and quite a few others in our rabbinic circle – to avoid engaging her in any conversations. Although I have to admit that she did once give my car a hot shot when the battery died, for which I was indebted to her. But first she had scoffed at me for considering the idea of calling AAA, and ever afterwards, she would remind me that she knew more about cars than anyone else of our mutual acquaintance.

"I'm fine," she said. "Actually, I'm great. We're moving back East. To your neck of the woods, in fact."

If they were moving to my area, they were literally coming to my neck of the woods. Walford was at the edge of the Pine Barrens, over one million acres of pine, oak, and cedar forests, active and abandoned cranberry bogs, wetlands, vernal ponds, sugar sand roads, and endangered flora and fauna. This ecologically unique area was protected by local, state, federal, and United Nations laws, and straddled several of the southern counties of the most densely populated state in the Union.

I looked at Ben questioningly. "Yeah," he nodded, "I'm about to sign a contract with Temple B'rith Abraham. That's why we came to the IRA this year: I was coming East anyway to meet with the congregation and finalize the details, so I – we – decided to combine both and then spend Pesach with Sandy's family."

I knew B'rith Abraham well. It was established when a group of members left my congregation, Mishkan Or, in protest over my being hired. They might enjoy shrimp scampi when they went out to eat, but they weren't going to allow a woman to be their rabbi. B'rith Abraham was a "Conservadox" synagogue, one that would be Orthodox except they allowed men and women to sit together in services and to drive to *shul* on Shabbat. Until now, their rabbis had been retirees who wanted a part-time pulpit to supplement their pensions.

"I didn't realize they were hiring someone full time."

"It's part-time, but one of the members is arranging for me be an adjunct at Walford U. in the Cultural Heritage program. Another member knows someone who owns a couple of investment condos and is renting one to us at lower than market value. And I'm sure Sandy won't have any problems finding a nursing job in the area."

"It will be wonderful to get back to civilization again," Sandy interjected. "You wouldn't believe what a backwater Eugene is." I wondered if others living in her area agreed with her assessment. Plus, despite its proximity to Philadelphia and the presence of a university, Walford was a definite backwater. I knew better than to dispute her word, though, so I just gave a slight smile and turned back to Ben.

"Guess who else lives in the area now? Remember Steve Goldfarb?"

"Your husband? I mean, ex-husband. Of course, I remember him. How could I forget? I co-officiated at the wedding."

Oops. I was the one who had forgotten. I don't know how I could have – after all, it's not often the rabbi drops the wedding ring, which then rolls under the front row of seats. Maybe Steve and I should have considered the ring mishap an omen. It would have saved us the expense of a divorce.

Ben continued, "Didn't I hear he remarried? And wasn't he teaching somewhere in North Jersey? What brought him to Hicksville?"

"Careful. You're insulting my home. We've got electricity and indoor plumbing now. Besides, we're not hicks. We're Pineys. Anyway, it's a long story about Steve, but he's been the acting police chief in Walford for the past year-and-a-half. His wife died not long after he took the job. And, no, before you ask, we're not back together."

"Why not? You're both available. And you always did make a great couple, even if you couldn't agree whose career came first."

"Ain't gonna happen." I quickly changed the subject. "I meant to tell you, Ben. I heard very nice things about the wedding you performed for Audrey Fisher, the daughter of one of my congregants. I bumped into her mother, Florence, a couple of weeks ago, and she told me how great you were."

"They did say you had recommended me. Thank you. How did you happen to think of me for the wedding?"

"Florence asked me if I knew a rabbi in the Eugene area who performed intermarriages. I said I didn't, but that you might know someone. I was surprised when she told me you had done the ceremony. Have you changed your views?"

Ben visibly blanched. "Intermarriage?"

Uh-oh. Not good. "You didn't know? Audrey's mother told me that George wasn't Jewish."

"I need to sit down." Ben looked sick.

"How could you?" Sandy was clenching her fists, as though she wanted to hit me. "How dare you recommend Ben? You know he doesn't perform intermarriages."

"I do know. All I did was suggest they contact him to find out if he knew anyone to help them."

She turned her ire on her husband. "You *putz*," Sandy sneered. "Can't you do anything right? If you screw this up, I swear I'll leave you. After I cut off your balls, not that you have any."

Whew. Sandy was being a bit harsh, even for her.

Sandy stomped off, while Ben and I found two easy chairs in a dark corner of the bar.

"I can't believe he's not Jewish. He never said."

"Didn't you wonder when he didn't have a Hebrew name? Or when you met his kids and realized they weren't Jewish?"

Ben shook his head. "He said he grew up somewhere in the Midwest, where there were no Jewish families, so he had no Jewish background. And he said he was an orphan and an only child of only children, so there were no aunts or uncles or cousins at the wedding. He said his first wife wasn't Jewish, so I wasn't surprised that his children weren't. I had no reason to doubt his word." He thought a moment. "Now that I think about it, he never said he was Jewish. He just never said he wasn't." He put his head in his hands. "I can't believe I was such an idiot."

"I don't see why it's a problem. I mean, no one knows but us and the couple, and they're in Eugene. Oh, and Audrey's parents, but they wouldn't tell anyone – they would be embarrassed if any of their friends knew Audrey had 'married out.' In fact, I doubt if they even told the rest of their family. Oh, wait, they couldn't – Florence told me they don't have any family."

"You don't understand, Aviva. B'rith Abraham will never hire me now. I had to assure them that I've never performed an intermarriage and never will." He was practically in tears. "Sandy hates living so far from her mother, who's not well. She wasn't kidding about leaving me. B'rith Abraham's my last chance. She's made it clear she's moving back to the Delaware Valley with or without me."

Ben was one of those rabbis who are better suited to academia than the pulpit, but he never finished his doctorate. Since ordination, he has bounced around from congregation to congregation. He would stay a few years, but then he would forget to visit the synagogue president in the hospital or he would repeat his Yom Kippur sermon from a previous year or he would decide he didn't need to be involved with the religious school, and his contract wouldn't be renewed. The synagogues he went to became smaller and less prestigious each time he relocated. At least coming to Walford would be a lateral step for him rather than a demotion, even in a part-time pulpit, as he would now be in a metropolitan area with a sizable Jewish population. But even so . . .

And he wasn't exaggerating that it might be his last chance, and not just for his marriage. There's a subtle form of age discrimination in the rabbinate. Rabbis in their mid-fifties who leave a congregation often find it difficult to be hired by another one. Younger rabbis are expected to move around the first few years, relocating to progressively larger and more prominent synagogues. But a synagogue isn't interested in a rabbi who will probably retire in a few years. And if the rabbi is so good, the argument goes, why wasn't the contract renewed? By a certain age, many rabbis have a long-term or even life contract. Mine wasn't set to run out for another fifteen years, barring my getting caught doing something immoral or illegal. (I could do something immoral or illegal; I just had to be discreet and not get caught.) By the time the contract expired, I would be lucky if I hadn't also expired. At the very least, I would be seventy and moribund. (True, I know a lot of seventy year olds, and eighty year olds, and ninety year olds who are active and busy. But I don't plan to be one of them. I haven't felt like being active or busy since I hit forty, which was why I left a large Philadelphia synagogue for the more laid back lifestyle and scaled down expectations of Mishkan Or.)

"I really think you're worrying unnecessarily," I said. "I doubt if B'rith Abraham will find out."

"But I can't take that chance." His face suddenly brightened with hope. "Maybe I can sue the Fishers for fraud."

"Don't be ridiculous." I hadn't heard Sandy come back. She was standing right behind us. "If you sue then everyone will know."

"But at least they'll know I didn't do it willingly. They'll know it was inadvertent."

"No, all they'll know is that you're incompetent."

Ben put his hands back over his face. "I'll think of something," he muttered.

"You had better, or I will." Sandy stomped off again.

I really didn't know what to say or do, so I murmured something inconsequential and went off to look for other old classmates. I knew I wouldn't say anything, but despite what I had told Ben, I didn't know whether or not the Fishers would. They weren't involved with the social side of Mishkan Or and generally came to services only to say *Kaddish* on the anniversary of their parents' deaths. Sometimes they didn't even come on the High Holy Days. With any luck, they didn't know anyone at B'rith Abraham or hang around Walford University (known as "Triple-U"), so they would have no reason to let everyone know of Ben's "transgression." But then again, poor Ben never did have any *mazel*, and I had no reason to think his luck would change.

CHAPTER THREE

Early spring in southern New Jersey. Crocuses pushing through the remnants of snow. Forsythia buds beginning to swell. A tinge of warmth cutting through the late winter chill. The smell of springtime rain rather than autumnal chill. So, what am I thinking about? Migrating birds returning from warmer climes? What I'll plant in this year's garden? Finally being able to shed my heavy coat and panty hose? No, I'm thinking about cleaning, cooking, and generally going *meshugana* trying to get ready for Pesach.

Don't get me wrong. I like Pesach. So do a lot of Jews. Along with Chanukah, it's the most observed of all the Jewish holidays. Even non-practicing Jews do something to recognize our journey from Egyptian slavery to American-style malls and coffee bars on the beach in Tel Aviv. True, for some it may mean having a ham sandwich on matzah instead of white bread, but at least they make the effort.

But the preparations can be brutal. Every tiny scrap of leavened food must be removed from the house. It's spring housecleaning on steroids. Pesach is proof that God is male, as no woman would ever have come up with a holiday with so many regulations about cooking and cleaning.

It was only Monday, though, and Pesach didn't start for a week. I had plenty of time to finish cleaning, shop, make a couple of kugels to take to my niece's on Monday night, prepare for the community seder. I work best under pressure, and I didn't feel pressured – yet.

Monday is my day off, so I slept late before getting myself ready to go back to the IRA conference. There was an afternoon session on small, unaffiliated synagogues I wanted to attend. Several of the other sessions were educational ones which afforded some of my colleagues the opportunity to use the big words they assume in their hubris (look it up) their congregants wouldn't understand. I had to endure listening to them bloviate (look it up) all during our classes in rabbinical school, when I had no choice in the matter. I wasn't going to listen to them voluntarily. Other sessions were geared toward subjects that didn't interest me, even if they should, on topics such as fund raising or budgets; or were irrelevant, such as how many associate and assistant rabbis were needed for congregations with over two thousand members. Mishkan Or had never cracked one hundred fifty.

As it was my day off, I was surprised when my cell phone began to play "Hava Nagilla," the ring tone I use for official business. It was my secretary Liz Smithers, a retired middle school librarian who had brought all her organizational and research skills with her to help the synagogue run as smooth as . . . well, as a middle school library in a top school district. "Hi, Aviva," she sounded contrite, which was unusual. "I'm sorry to bother you at the conference."

"No problem. We're between sessions." Okay, a fib. I was still driving to the Hi-Speed Line, and before you lecture me about using my cell phone in the car, I was in the parking lot at Dunkin' Donuts, about to indulge in a pre-Pesach iced coffee (extra cream, no sugar) and glazed donut. Or two.

"Your niece called here looking for you. She said she left a message on your land line and you weren't answering your cell."

"Hold on." I took a quick look. Sure enough, there was a missed message icon.

"I had the phone off and didn't feel it vibrate." The truth was, when I had run into Dunkin' Donuts, I had forgotten the phone in the car, where it was plugged into the recharger. I have a tendency to forget to charge it overnight. Fibbing was becoming second nature. I would have to do an extra *al het* prayer during the High Holy Days to beg forgiveness. But I really didn't feel like listening to Liz lecture me about playing hooky from the conference. And I really, really didn't feel like listening to all the one hundred twenty pounds of sinew and muscle in her seventy-year-old body lecture me about my eating (too much of the wrong kinds of food) and exercising (too little of any kinds of physical activity) habits.

"She said it wasn't important," Liz continued, "but she did want to reach you ASAP. Give her a call."

"Thanks for the message. I'll call her right away."

"Make sure you do. I'll see you on Thursday in the office. In the meantime, I'll forward any emails that come in for you to your home computer, and send you any other phone messages that seem important."

Liz is very good at making sure I keep my commitments and serve my congregants well. That's why I fib.

I called Trudy on her main number, knowing it would track her down no matter where she was. After being one of the first few women graduates of MIT, Trudy went to the University of Pennsylvania, where she was in the forefront of computer geekdom. I don't pretend to know how she does what she does, but she is successful at it, and, as a consequence, very wealthy. Her mother, my older sister Jean, still blames me for influencing Trudy to become a software whiz instead of a high school math teacher living in the suburbs with a husband and two kids. Instead, she lives in the suburbs with her same-sex partner and two kids. In the past year or so, Jean has claimed that she no longer blames me for her daughter's being a lesbian, but I don't believe her. She fibs, too. It's a family trait.

"Hey, Auntie Aviva! Whazzup?" Trudy never says "hello," and she's adopted an appalling habit of using out-of-date teenage slang, probably so her eight-year-old son Josh will be impressed. But Josh has Asperger's Syndrome and doesn't impress easily.

"You called me. 'Whazzup' on your end?"

"I know you're at the IRA this week, but could we get together? Sherry and I have something to discuss with you, and want to do it in person."

Trudy sounded upbeat, but that didn't stop me from being worried. "Is it a health matter? Are you okay? Are the kids?"

Trudy laughed. "Everyone's fine, *Mother*. It's something good. More than good. Fantastic. But we don't want to tell you on the phone. And we want to tell you before we announce it to everyone at the seder next week. Can you come for dinner tomorrow or Wednesday?"

I mentally reviewed the conference schedule. "Wednesday will be better. The closing banquet is tomorrow night, and the conference ends around two o'clock Wednesday. What time?"

We agreed on seven o'clock, after the kids had been fed and plunked in front of a DVD (eight-year-old Josh) or in bed (seventeen-month-old Simi). Then Trudy hit me with one of her techie pieces of magic, which she knows infuriates me. "Drive carefully. Don't spill your coffee. And aren't you missing the morning sessions? I mean, you're not even in Philadelphia yet."

"How do you do that? How do you know where I am?"

Trudy hummed the opening bars of the "Twilight Zone" theme, cackled, said, "I'll never tell," and clicked off. Damn. I hate when she does that.

CHAPTER FOUR

I was surprised when I went to the seminar on small synagogues that Ben wasn't there.

"He said something about going to look at his new apartment," Shoshana Landon, rabbi at a congregation in Oklahoma that was even smaller than Mishkan Or, said when I commented on Ben's absence. She shook her head, obviously thinking the same thing I was – Ben really didn't have his priorities straight. His apartment could wait, but this seminar had the potential of being helpful to him in his new position.

"I'm surprised Sandy didn't go by herself to check it out. She's the one who knows whether everything is in workable condition or not. Ben can barely use a microwave. But I guess he wanted to see where he'll be living the next couple of years, or however long his contract runs." Shoshana had been ordained several years after Ben and me, but even she knew his reputation as a *luftmensch*, someone with his head so far in the clouds he has no idea what his feet are doing.

"Has he officially signed his contract then?"

"I think he's meeting with the search committee, or maybe it's the full board, tonight. All I know is he said he would be gone all day today and not back until late tonight. You know the synagogue, Aviva. Do you think Ben will finally find a place to stay until he retires?"

I made a face. "I don't know. It's a funny place. The members want everything at the synagogue to be as traditional as possible, until it inconveniences them. So they want services both days of holidays, but if they go at all, it's only for the first day or for *yizkor*. They insist on a daily *minyan,* but they never get ten men. And they refuse to count women in the *minyan* or call them to the Torah, and then complain when they can't hold a service, even if there are eight men and fifteen women. They don't want to be held to the same standards as their rabbi – they expect him to keep kosher and Shabbat, but he had better not give a sermon about how important it is that they do. He has to be above reproach, but they don't. So far, the rabbis have been retirees, so they haven't cared much about the congregants' opinions, but if Ben wants to stay for any length of time, he's going to have to walk a tightrope – and we both know he's got a pretty lousy sense of balance."

Thinking about the Fisher-Rivers intermarriage, I added, "I have to admit, I have my doubts. I don't think that congregation is a good match for him. But I'm not sure what congregation is. Maybe he'll do well enough at his teaching job at Walford U. that it will become full-time." And maybe I'd become a super model.

The seminar, or, rather, the support/discussion group, was beginning, so Shoshana and I didn't have time to explore Ben's troubles any further. Instead, we talked about the problems we all had with resources, financial and human, and how to offer a full range of programming with a limited budget and a limited number of lay leaders. There were no new ideas, no "solutions" that we hadn't all tried at some point, but at least we had the comfort of knowing we weren't alone. As the ubiquitous they say, misery loves company. I don't mind the company, but I could do with less of the misery.

CHAPTER FIVE

I wasn't particularly interested in the evening program, so I got home at an early hour; fed the cat, named Cat; watered the plants, unnamed; cleaned the litter box and put the odiferous contents into the trash can, which I wheeled out to the curb for pickup the next day; flipped through the newspaper; and finally noticed my phone message alert was blinking. I really should get a machine with an audible signal. Otherwise, I never think to check.

The first message was the one Trudy had left in the morning; I deleted it. The second was from my ex-husband. My first ex, that is. There was a second, but I never hear from him, probably because he lives with his wife and kids on the other side of Philadelphia. I had seldom heard from ex number one, who used to live with his wife and kids on the other side of New Jersey, either until he had moved to Walford to become the interim Director of Public Safety; the interim had lasted sixteen months so far, and the township council was dragging its feet to hire someone to replace him. He was juggling his job with the police department and his responsibilities to his graduate students at Crescent State, up near Princeton, who had been counting on him to shepherd them through the dissertation process. I had gotten used to having him around and hated to admit it even to myself (and never would to him), but I would miss him when he finally did leave.

"Hey, Aviva. Guess who I saw today? Ben Bronfman! Remember when he dropped the ring at the wedding? He's moving in next door to me. He acted really weird when I told him we have the same landlord – can you believe he didn't even know who he was renting from? Anyway, give me a call when you get the chance. Nothing important. Just want to chat, catch up on what's going on with you, maybe go out for dinner or something. I figure you'll be at Trudy's for Pesach. I'll be at my oldest daughter's, so I'll be out of town for a couple of days. Call."

Dinner? Was he asking me out on a date? Yeah, right. And Cinderella and Prince Charming lived happily ever after, and never argued about her hair clogging the drains or his leaving his dirty socks on the floor. (Well, maybe they didn't – they probably had servants to take care of those things. But I still didn't think Steve was suggesting a date.)

I decided to call Steve before I overanalyzed his invitation and read a lot more into it than he had intended. He picked up on the first ring, but sounded groggy.

"I'm sorry, Steve, did I wake you? I didn't think it was all that late."

He audibly yawned. "I fell asleep on the couch. Big mistake. I'll probably never fall asleep again now. Wait a sec . . . I needed to mute the TV . . . how's the IRA? The one thing I don't miss about being married to a rabbi is being schlepped to those things."

"I never had to schlep you. I remember you always liked going, so you could make fun of all of us." I was trying not to think about "the one thing" he doesn't miss – did he mean he did miss other things about our marriage? *Stop it, Cohen. You're reading too much into things again. And what's gotten into you? You couldn't care less about getting married again, especially to Steve. Couldn't you?*

"So, how about dinner this week? I figure your cupboard's bare, this close to Pesach."

"I haven't done enough clearing out yet. I hired a cleaning service to come in on Friday morning and scrub out the kitchen. I figure I'll eat on paper plates in the living room for the weekend."

"Don't you anyway?"

"Very funny. I'll have you know I do eat at the dining table. Sometimes. And even use real dishes. Sometimes."

"Hah! I happen to know your townhouse is so small, the dining table is in the living room. And your 'real dishes' are plastic."

"It's a great excuse not to entertain."

He chuckled and changed the subject. "So, what's your schedule like?"

"I'm going to the conference banquet tomorrow night and to Trudy's on Wednesday night, which leaves Thursday night. Let's make it early, though, so I can finish emptying out the kitchen before the crew comes to disinfect it on Friday. I'm afraid what I'll find lurking in the back corners of the fridge."

"Okay, Thursday it is. How about five o'clock at that hub of haute cuisine, the Walford Diner? Maybe we'll be in time for the Early Bird Special and practice for when we retire to Florida."

"Sounds good to me, except for the retiring to Florida bit. Any place I don't have to dress up for sounds good to me." (*"When we retire?" Did he mean a generic "we" or a specific one? Stop it right now, Aviva. You don't even have the excuse of being pre-menstrual or even peri-menopausal. You're just being plain silly.*)

"Great. I've got several things I need your opinion on. If nothing else, you always were a good listener. See you Thursday at six."

Now, what did he mean by that? I would have three days to figure it out.

CHAPTER SIX

The final message was from my older (much older) sister, Jean, who lives in south Florida with her latest dog, a Scottish terrier called Two, as in Bobby II. Bobby I, named in honor of Robert Burns, had finally succumbed the year before to old age and diabetes caused by over-indulgence.

My sister was the product of my parents' youthful ardor, born at a time when people looked askance at married couples who didn't have children within two years of marriage. I was the product of their "old age," when my then thirty-nine year old mother mistook her unplanned pregnancy for menopause. Mom is now ninety-four, and just beginning to show her age. Jean, in her early seventies, has looked and acted far older than her age for years. To say we've never had a close sisterly bond is an understatement.

Jean's dislike of technology, which she fortunately did not pass on to her daughter Trudy, caused her to be succinct, to prevent invisible rays from reaching out from the answering machine and giving her brain cancer. "Call."

I really didn't feel like talking to her, especially since she was coming for the seders and I would have several days to see her. But it was better to call now than to wait and get a lecture about how Mom and Dad were obviously senile while raising me, or they would have instilled better manners and I wouldn't ignore messages. If I tried to use the excuse that I had gotten home too late to call, I would have to listen to her other favorite complaint, that if I didn't waste time gallivanting around, maybe I would still be married. It was easier to call.

But I decided to multi-task and start clearing out my fridge at the same time. It really was too soon to start cleaning for a holiday that didn't begin for a week, but I now had plans for all three nights leading up to Friday's mega-cleaning, which needed to be done before I could make the dishes I had promised to bring to Trudy's. Besides, if I cleared out the perishables tonight, I would be able to dump them into the trash for pick up the next day. I didn't want to think about what the smell would be like if they had to sit in the trash can for another week.

I decided to do the freezer first, as it would be easier than the refrigerator. I had been eating weird combinations of foods (blintzes and pizza, barbecued chicken and cold Thai noodles – actually not that bad together – vegan egg rolls and spanikopita) for weeks, so all that was left now were stale ice cubes (yes, they can get stale), heels of freezer-burned rye bread, and Friendly's Candy Cane ice cream, left over from the previous December. There was also a large plastic storage bag of fresh cranberries I had been hoarding since the fall, when I had bought them right off the back of a farm truck at the Chatsworth Cranberry Festival, but those I could use to make a cranberry-orange relish to take to Trudy's; it's so much better than the gelatinous goop from the cans. I had finished the previous June's fresh-picked blueberries a few days earlier in my Cheerios. The milk froze when it hit the fruit.

I closed the freezer door, and as I opened the lower one to the refrigerator, I hit the speed dial for Jean's number. "Hello?" her deceptively sweet voice greeted me.

"Hey, Jean. It's me, returning your call. What's new?"

"Why, yes, thank, you, I am feeling fine. So nice of you to deign to call. Do you have any idea how many hours ago I left the message? And why do you call only after I call first?"

"I'm always afraid you'll collapse from shock if I make the first call. And I called as soon as I could." I was fibbing again. "I was at a conference in Philadelphia all day and just got home." This time I crossed my fingers and held my hand behind my back. Somehow, my sister always made me feel like a pesky six-year-old kid again. Which I'm sure was exactly how she still thought of me.

"Hmm, yes, well, be that as it may. I just wanted to let you know

I've changed my travel plans, so you don't have to pick me up at the airport."

I was supposed to pick her up at the airport? Someone forgot to tell me. I bet that was the important, gleeful news Trudy had for me – I was appointed to meet her mother instead of Sherry, who probably refused. I certainly couldn't blame Sherry, who until last year Jean had insisted was Trudy's roommate, not partner. No wonder Trudy was going to ply me with food first.

Jean continued, "My original plan was to fly to Philadelphia for the seder first. Afterwards, I was going to drive back to Boston with Larry to spend some time with him and, of course, Mom, and then fly home from Boston. But now I've decided to fly both ways from Boston so I can have a few extra days there. *(Why am I not surprised she would prefer to spend extra time with her son, the prince, than with her daughter, the disappointment?)* And even with the fee for changing the tickets, it's still cheaper to travel to and from the same airport. Did you know Mom's not coming to New Jersey?"

"Yeah, Mom told me last time I spoke with her that she wasn't up for the long drive. I feel terrible about it. I haven't seen her since December and I'm not sure when I'll get there again."

"Don't you get a spring break?"

"No, Jean, I live in a university town, but I don't work on a school schedule. In fact, I'm busier than ever this week – regular services Friday night and Saturday morning, a wedding Sunday afternoon, Pesach services Tuesday and Wednesday mornings, then Shabbat again the following Friday night and Saturday morning, and Pesach services again Sunday and Monday mornings. Plus the community seder on Tuesday night. And in the meantime, I'm trying to clear out my fridge before the cleaning service comes on Friday."

"You complain you can't afford to visit me, but you have the money for a cleaning service?"

I tried, I really did, not to get exasperated. You would think I would be used to her after all these years. "I've told you before, it's not the money, but my schedule. You know my work time is other people's leisure time."

"You have the month of July off. Visit me then. Believe me, we have air conditioning."

"I'll think about it when they figure out how to air condition the outdoors. Oh, yuck."

"What?"

"I told you, I'm cleaning out the fridge. I just looked inside a container and I'm not sure what the contents were in a former life, but I think I may be brewing a cure for cancer."

"Why am I not surprised? Your room always was a dump. I'm not sure why the EPA didn't declare it a toxic waste site."

"Probably because that was forty-five years ago, before there was an EPA." I wasn't sure about my facts, but reasoned that she didn't know either. I was right, as she didn't challenge me.

"And I suppose you're going to spend your money eating out instead of at home the rest of the week. Why are you cleaning so early? You always waited till the last minute. If you bothered at all."

"I always clean for Pesach. And I told you, the cleaners are coming on Friday. Tomorrow is the closing banquet for the conference, Wednesday night I'm going to Trudy's for dinner, and Thursday I'm meeting Steve for dinner." I mentally kicked myself as I said that last bit.

"Steve? Steve Goldfarb? Your ex? Are you seeing each other? It's been over a year since his wife died, so he's done mourning. Now's your chance. I always liked Steve."

No, you didn't. But I saw no point in reminding her that she thought I was jumping into marriage with Steve too soon after the breakup of a long-term relationship I had with a pseudo-hippie/ organic gardener who later made a fortune when he sold his flash-frozen organic vegetable company to a mega-corporation and now owned one of the most successful organic Kosher wineries in California. And I especially didn't want to remind her that her hesitation about our marriage proved to be right.

"No, we're not seeing each other, as in 'seeing each other.' It's just a friendly meal."

"I wish you would stop having boy friends and find a boyfriend."

"I'm happy by myself. After all, who would put up with me and my schedule? And I didn't notice you running out to find someone after

Harold died."

"That was different. Do you know the ratio of single women to men in my age bracket down here? It must be ten-to-one. And I was much older than you were when you and Keith divorced. Now that was a good catch. I can't believe you let him go."

You didn't think my second husband Keith Rubenstein was such a good catch when we first married and he worked at a poverty law center; you didn't like him until he became a big bucks corporate drone. "It wasn't working, Jean. We wanted different things out of life. I wanted a partner and he wanted an accessory. Oh, double yuck."

"What now?"

"I don't know. I think it's a new life form. It just winked at me. Listen, I'll see you soon. I really have to concentrate on this refrigerator. I'm not sure, but I think some old pickles just spoke to me."

"How can pickles go bad? They're already preserved in vinegar."

"I don't know, maybe they hung out with a rough crowd of slimy lettuce. Give my love to Mom."

"And to Larry?"

"Of course, to Larry, and to Karen. And to the kids. Are they coming, too?"

I already knew the answer. My nephew's kids were in college and unlikely to take off from classes on a weekday, especially to travel to South Jersey from New England. "No, they already had spring break. They're staying at their colleges for the holiday. But they promised to come home this weekend to see me and to look in on their great grandmother. Such nice boys." Unspoken were the words, "Unlike Josh," who, it's true, was only eight and she had only gotten to know him for the past year or so. But, to be fair to Jean, something I seldom am, Josh is what is known as a "high maintenance" child.

"Well, give my love to all. See you soon."

I finally could give all my concentration to the refrigerator. It was even worse than I had thought. After dumping all the unidentifiable objects, I kept a couple of containers of yogurt, a jar of peanut butter, and some milk not yet past its sell-by date so I would be able to eat at least something at home the next few days. By the time I had emptied tins half-filled with green tuna, bottles of fuzzy tomato sauce, and jars of mutated olives into the garbage disposal, my recycling bin was overflowing with glass and metal. Some of the leftovers got thrown out directly into the trash, along with their storage containers; I was afraid I would unleash poison gases if I opened them. I turned on the lights in the rooms facing the back of the house and opened the shades so I could find my way through the dark backyard to the composter, where I added the fruits and vegetables that had begun to morph into creatures that any director of horror films would love to use. Everything else went into giant black plastic trash bags, which I dragged to the curb and added to the trashcan. Being green has its limits, and if I hadn't gotten that stuff out of the house, I would have been turning a very unflattering shade of green.

The non-perishables would take more time, so I would save them for another day. I would have to sort out the opened and unopened boxes, storing the former in the garage and bringing the latter to a food bank. The peanut butter in the fridge would get mixed with some corn meal and flour and remnants of trail mix and then frozen until I put it out for the birds.

I slept the sleep of the righteous that night, knowing I had begun the odious task of making the house kosher for Pesach. Thoughts of Ben and Steve and Trudy and Jean and my mother didn't disturb me at all. I can be selfish when it comes to sleep.

CHAPTER SEVEN

I may have slept soundly, but I had gone to bed far too late, so when my clock radio turned itself on the next morning, I wasn't ready to get up yet, and I ignored it. Or tried to. I keep the radio tuned to KYW, the Philadelphia all-news station, and was listening to it while not absorbing what I was hearing. I thought I heard something about Oak Glen Road, a street of single-family homes in an "active adult" section of my development, but I would have to wait for the reports to cycle back around to know what I had missed. And I would have to concentrate or I would miss it again.

Of course, I could get up and check on line, but that would take too much effort. I snuggled back under the covers, but couldn't fall back to sleep, not because I wanted to hear the news, but because my bladder woke up before the rest of me. At that point, I figured I may as well brush my teeth and take a shower, so my hair would dry somewhat before I had to leave for the IRA. And by the time I had finished all my morning ... what's that quaint word? ... ablutions, the perky announcer was talking about the daily traffic backup on the Schuykill Expressway, not so affectionately known as the Sure Kill. Nor was it the express way to anywhere.

There were a couple of interesting speakers scheduled for Tuesday, plus a business meeting. I usually skip the business meeting, but one of the agenda items was a discussion of whether to change the conference date. The issue comes up every few years, and the decision is usually to keep it as it's always been, since there's no date that is convenient for everyone. But an increasing number of our members now worked in secular colleges, and the conference always seems to be either right before or right after spring break. I had gotten drafted into the subcommittee studying the issue again. We attempted to figure out how to come to a compromise; i.e., a decision that everyone can live with but no one likes. Once again, we had failed. Somehow I had been appointed to deliver our report to the organization. I knew I shouldn't have left the meeting early that day.

While driving over to the Haddonfield station of the Hi-Speed Line, I was listening to KYW when the report I had missed earlier came back on. A couple who lived on Oak Glen was found dead in their bedroom of carbon monoxide poisoning. The investigation was on-going. The names had not yet been released.

I did a quick mental inventory, but couldn't think of anyone I knew who lived on the street. Just as I came to that conclusion, my cell phone rang. There was a cop car behind me, so I signaled and turned into a parking lot before answering. I'm a good citizen and safe driver when at the risk of getting a ticket.

The caller I.D. listed Steve's number. "Hey, Steve."

"Hi, Aviva. Listen, I wanted to tell you before you hear it on the news. A couple you know died of carbon monoxide poisoning over night."

"I just heard the report on the news, but no names. Who was it? I was just trying to think if I know anyone on Oak Glen."

"You do. It's Florence and Milton Fisher. We were just talking about them, sort of. They're my landlord, and were going to be Ben's."

"Wow. I hardly ever see them and suddenly they're everywhere. What happened?"

"The Fire Marshal is still investigating, but a blocked dryer vent seems to be the culprit. The houses on that street have had problems with the vents for a while, and the owners are suing the builder for negligence. Most people got them fixed. At the very least, they had CO detectors. You have one, right?"

"Um, no."

"Why the hell not? I know you can be a bit . . . casual at times, but it's not like you not to take simple precautions."

"Steve, I don't have gas in my house. It's all electric. And, before you ask, I did have the place tested for radon, and it's clean. I mean, it's a mess, but there's nothing toxic. Except the contents of my fridge, and I cleaned that out last night." I was babbling, which I tend to do when I'm stressed. The news of the Fisher's deaths disturbed me more than I expected. Even though I knew them, I didn't really know them.

"Didn't the Fishers have a detector?" I asked. "I thought they were required by law."

"They are required, but only the past few years. Houses built before then are supposed to have detectors, but we've no way to check on compliance unless the owner has applied for a building permit for renovations or a house is sold or rented. The Fishers didn't have one. Want to hear something ironic? They were found by their son-in-law, who stopped by with a CO detector for them. He said he was worried because the dryer wasn't working well, and they had both been complaining of being dizzy and headachy. They thought they were coming down with the flu, but he finally convinced them they should get a CO detector."

"What a shame. Their daughter just got married a few months ago, and now this."

"Ah, newlyweds. That explains why she and her husband were staying at a hotel instead of at her parents' house. Remember when we visited your folks shortly after we got married and your mother insisted we stay at a hotel? She was always cool, but I think your father was mortified at the idea his little girl was having sex."

It was a good thing he couldn't see me through the phone. I blushed at the memory of that visit. Or, rather, at what went on in the hotel room. I changed the subject. "Wonder if I'll be doing the funeral. It'll be a tough one."

"The daughter said something about how they're from Connecticut originally and have plots there."

"I didn't know that. They were already living here when I moved to the area. I still might be doing a chapel service in the area. They've lived here a long time and their friends are unlikely to travel three hours or more each way for the funeral. Unless, of course, the Fishers left a directive and they requested a graveside ceremony only, or if Audrey decides that's what she wants. Well, in any case, if they use

Ruben Funeral Home, then Caryn will get in touch with me." My best friend, Caryn Rozen, was a funeral director in the family business founded by her grandfather. "I guess I had better keep my cell phone on."

"We still on for Thursday night?"

"Yup, unless I have to meet with the family. I'll let you know. And keep me informed if anything else comes up."

"And what do you expect to come up? Once upon a time, you investigated whether a natural death and a suicide weren't, so now you're looking at an accidental death as though it wasn't?"

Huh? It took me a second to figure out what he had just said. "That's not what I meant, but come to think of it . . . well, it is a coincidence that their deaths solve a major problem for Ben Bronfman. Maybe their daughter and son-in-law should be extra careful, too. I'll fill you in when I see you."

"Can't wait. Don't let your imagination get the better of you. Can you really picture Ben as a cold-blooded murderer?"

"Not really. But when it comes to Sandy ...."

I was joking, I think. But the more I thought about what I had just said to Steve, the more sense it made. Sandy certainly had been angry enough at the conference when she heard that Ben had unwittingly officiated at an intermarriage, but was she also desperate enough to save Ben's job – and their marriage – to kill? Maybe I was letting my imagination run away with me. Or maybe not.

CHAPTER EIGHT

The business meeting was every bit as boring as I had expected. Also, as I had expected, the proposal to change the date for the conference went nowhere, mainly because the people who would benefit the most – those working in non-pulpit positions – weren't there to lend their support or vote in favor of a change. We did have a minor victory for them, though, in passing a decision to mail the membership a survey with a few alternative dates. Knowing what I do with such questionnaires – add them to the recycle bin unanswered – I didn't foresee much hope for a change. It annoyed me, because a different date wouldn't inconvenience those of us in pulpit positions and would actually be more convenient than just before Pesach. Tevya was wrong: tradition isn't always a good thing.

After the meeting, Shoshana Landon, who had also been on the subcommittee, and I plunked ourselves down in the bar area and held court. Most of our cohorts were skipping the rest of the afternoon sessions, too, so we had a mini-reunion.

"Anyone seen Ben today?" I asked. I hadn't seen him at the business meeting, but if I hadn't been drafted to deliver the report on changing the conference date, I wouldn't have been there either.

"I haven't seen him since ... let me think ... Sunday night maybe, or was it yesterday morning? I need to get out of this hotel; I'm losing track of the days." Shoshana was the type who got up at five o'clock every morning to jog, no matter the weather, so I was surprised she hadn't been outside. The only time I see five o'clock in the morning is if I haven't gone to sleep yet. Or my bladder wakes me up.

Shoshana answered my unasked question. "I've been using the hotel gym instead. I really don't like jogging in the middle of city traffic."

I don't like jogging anywhere. "Back to Ben, I know he had some meetings with his new board last night – you told me that yesterday, Shoshana – and Steve Goldfarb saw him at his new apartment. Weird coincidence: they're going to be neighbors. It's strange that Ben's not around. Maybe he had to go back to Walford today. Or they went to see Sandy's parents and stayed there overnight." I didn't add that Ben's potential problem had disappeared with the Fishers' deaths. I wondered if Ben had heard about the accident yet.

"I doubt if they're with Sandy's folks – they're staying with them after the conference for a family wedding on Sunday and then for the seders."

"He said something to me about staying here for Pesach. Things must be worse with his old congregation than I realized if they don't need him there for Pesach services."

Yankel, another of our classmates, was listening in. He took a swig from his bottle of Samuel Adams and added, "Yeah, they're hiring one of the guys graduating in May. He's going there this week to 'audition,' but it's pretty much a done deal. I heard they're paying him about double what Ben was getting."

We all sat in silence for a while, sipping from our drinks of choice (mine was a Diet Coke with lime), contemplating what it meant to be able to command a larger salary with less experience. Of course, the newer grads also had many more debts than we did. My school loans had been paid off years earlier.

Yankel's seat was facing the entry, so he saw Ben enter the room first. "Ben! We were just wondering where you were. Come and join us. Where's Sandy?"

"Thanks, guys. Sandy's upstairs packing. She's going to her parents' tonight, to help prepare for Pesach. They're making a big deal of it because of our moving back to the area. Unfortunately, her mother's heart condition's getting worse, and it may be the last time she has the strength to make a seder. Oh, and Sandy's also got a job interview at Walford Community Hospital later this afternoon."

Ben sounded very upbeat, almost manic, especially compared to his depression the last time I had seen him. Was it because he was free of Sandy for a couple of days? Or because Sandy had a lead for a good job? Or because he didn't have to worry about the Fishers?

"Um, Ben, could I talk to you for a second? In private?" I smiled my apologies to the others and motioned Ben to join me in a corner of the room. He looked puzzled, but came with me.

"Did you hear about the Fishers?" I asked.

"No, what about them?" His normally pale complexion blanched even more. "Oh, no, don't tell me they've told B'rith Abraham about the wedding? I met with the board last night and no one said anything. We even finalized the contract and it's all signed. I thought I was safe."

"No, they didn't say anything. At least not that I know of. And now they won't be able to tell anyone anything. They died last night of carbon monoxide poisoning. Probably a blocked dryer vent."

Either Ben was a great actor or was truly shocked at the news. I hoped it was the latter. "How awful! I hope they didn't suffer."

"What's awful about it? It's a peaceful way to die, and now we don't have to worry about anyone finding out what an idiot you are." Neither of us had heard Sandy coming up behind us. For someone so tall, she really walks lightly. It must come from her nursing experience. I hate to think of what her bedside manner must be like, though. And I certainly wouldn't want to be on the receiving end of any thermometer she was wielding.

"Unless," she turned to me and narrowed her eyes, "you plan to say something, Aviva."

"What possible reason would I have? Ben made an honest mistake. I'll be happy to have Ben – both of you – in the community."

"Yeah, sure you would." She narrowed her eyes again, but this time in thought rather than suspicion. "Shit, I just thought of something. What's going to happen now with the apartment? Ben and I were supposed to meet with them to sign the lease on our new place tomorrow. Talk about lousy coincidences: did you know they were supposed to be our new landlords? Oh, and Steve Goldfarb lives next door."

I just thought of something? What did she mean? Why would she have thought of it earlier, unless she already knew they were dead?

Maybe she had heard the news on the radio. Maybe she had been the cause of the news. I wasn't about to give voice to my suspicions, especially after she had just looked at me like a cat eying a particularly succulent goldfish. Instead, I said, "Steve told me he saw Ben at the apartment. As for the lease, I don't know what will happen. Their daughter is here, so if she has power-of-attorney for her parents, she might be able to sign. I'm sure there's a lawyer at B'rith Abraham who can help you."

"Oh, great, the daughter's in Walford, too. And what's to keep her from blabbing the truth about her 'Jewish' wedding?"

"Maybe the fact that she'll be arranging her parents' funeral?" I was getting really tired of Sandy's narcissism. In fact, I was getting tired, period. "I'll see you at the dinner later. I'm going to Shoshana's room to change."

"You won't see me," Sandy wrinkled her nose, as though we were going to have a picnic at a landfill instead of a catered gourmet Kosher meal in an overly ornate banquet room. "I'll be with my parents. But Ben will be there. Won't that be cozy for you?"

I had given up a long time ago trying to convince Sandy that I had no romantic interest in Ben at all. She persisted in believing all single women, and several married ones, lusted after him. "Very cozy, just Ben, me, and a couple of hundred other rabbis and their significant others. Enjoy your visit with your parents."

Shoshana had given me a key to her hotel room, so I could change there for the banquet later. My pants and sweater, although nicer than I usually wear to the office, weren't dressy enough for the event, so I had brought a dress with me. I stopped by the table to let her know I would be going to her room. When I got there, I took off my shoes, with a sigh of relief, and plunked down on the king-sized bed, turned on the TV, found nothing to watch but CNN, and promptly fell asleep. I'm a lousy napper, and woke up feeling more tired than before. I splashed some cold water on my face, which worked better in theory than reality. I knew I'd be okay as soon as I got downstairs again, so I changed and thought some more about Sandy's reaction to hearing about the Fishers. She hadn't sounded in the least bit surprised at the news.

CHAPTER NINE

Tuesday night's banquet was as interminable as I had known it would be, with a lot of congratulatory speeches and self-congratulatory ones from both the incoming and outgoing officers. If I had realized the installation was part of the evening, I would have stayed home with a pizza and DVD instead. But at least I had a good time with my table mates as we made fun of the speakers, who at one time would have joined us in the ridicule if they hadn't been on the dais. What is it about power, real or imagined, that makes people so pompous? At least the food was half-way edible for convention food.

I decided to go back on Wednesday mostly because the Women's Rabbinic Network was getting together for lunch. Okay, I'll admit it. Lunch was an excuse to engage in the time-honored tradition followed by groups of women whenever they reach a critical mass of, say, two: male bashing. It was a chance for us to air our grievances about the male elite that still controlled so much of Jewish life, even though women had been ordained for over a generation. Some current students hadn't even been born when the oldest of us were ordained and had never lived in a world without women rabbis. Things were certainly not as restrictive or sexist as they had been when I had been ordained in the mid-seventies, but I always thought it was my duty to remind the "kiddies" of the bad old days. They complain about not being able to break the glass ceiling protecting the mega-synagogues and being stuck in a congregation of "only" five hundred members. I remind them that the only time my cohorts and I got anywhere near a glass ceiling is if we had a bottle of Windex and a wad of paper towels in our hands.

"Did you hear what happened to Wendy?" Rivka grabbed a seat

and joined the other six of us who were already perusing the menu. "I just got an email from her. She's furious."

Rivka stopped to take the menu from the waiter and sip from her water glass. "Stop drinking and tell us, already, what happened?" It sounded like something juicy, and I was in the mood for a good piece of *lashon harah*, aka gossip.

"She didn't come to the IRA this year because her synagogue had the ground breaking for their new building on Sunday. When she left the house, the weather was nice, so she wore a lightweight suit and a thin blouse. By the time the ceremony started, it had clouded over and gotten chilly. She didn't realize it, but the cold wind popped out her nipples and they could be seen through her blouse. To make it worse, she didn't find out about it until the rabbi emeritus, the senior rabbi, and the synagogue president called her into a meeting this morning and chewed her out about her inappropriate attire and unprofessional demeanor!"

We all instinctively crossed our arms in front of our chests protectively, the way men's hands shelter the front of their pants during a circumcision. And undoubtedly, we were all thinking the same thing: would a male rabbi have been reprimanded for getting an inadvertent erection in public?

"Wait a minute, isn't Wendy's senior rabbi the one who pulled a Newt Gingrich on his wife?" Shoshana asked.

"You're right," Rivka answered. "He did." She turned to one of the youngsters, who was looking puzzled. "The senior rabbi's wife was in the hospital, having just been diagnosed with pancreatic cancer, and he told her he had been having an affair with the sisterhood president and wanted a divorce to marry her before the baby was showing! He was worried his wife would respond to the treatments and live too long for him to be free unless they divorced. Geez, he survived that scandal, but an errant nipple might get Wendy fired. In any case, she's so pissed off she's about to quit."

"And do what? Go where? It's late in the year to start looking. And isn't her partner beginning a surgical residency? She can't just pick up and move somewhere else." Shoshana always put practicality before principles.

"I don't think she's planned that far," said Rivka. "This whole thing just happened. Maybe it'll blow over."

"As long as the wind isn't nippy!"

Our food arrived, and we were quiet while masticating not just our sandwiches but the news. Unemployment is something that worries everyone, but women rabbis, no matter how much experience they have, are particularly vulnerable. I don't know what the others were thinking, but I began worrying about what I would do if I lost my job. There really wasn't anything else I was trained to do, nor did I have the experience. Maybe I could teach, but without certification, my options were limited. Limiting, too, was the fact that I'm not crazy about teaching kids, and, since I don't have an earned doctorate nor have I published any scholarly works, I wouldn't be able to teach on the college level, except as an adjunct. I don't enjoy the idea of living below the poverty level, so that wasn't a realistic goal. I suppose I could try my hand at counseling – I do enough of it in my job – but I'm not credentialed. I began to get scared, so I turned to that tried-and-true technique of avoidance and denial and gave my full attention to my grilled salmon and pasta.

CHAPTER TEN

I got home with a couple of hours to spare before going to Trudy's for dinner. Not that I was hungry, but Sherry's a great cook, so I was sure I would manage to stuff my face anyway. And I was certainly hungry for whatever news it was they wanted to tell me.

But first I had to attend to more important things, like cleaning out my pantry closet. I also had to read the morning paper, clean out the litter box (how does a ten-pound creature manage to produce so much waste?), and take a nap. Not necessarily in that order.

Cat greeted me with an angry scowl and hiss, so I knew his food dish was empty. It's a good thing I had never had kids or they would have either learned how to use a microwave by age two or would have been malnourished. Or both, considering what they probably would have put into the microwave. (I had a sudden vision of microwaved Cat.) On my way back to the kitchen I noticed the one plant I had forgotten to water the other day, the new gardenia that I had sworn to myself I would remember to water and mist *this* time, unlike the other umpteen times I had succumbed to temptation at the Philadelphia Flower Show and brought one home. The leaves, the ones that hadn't gotten crispy and dropped off, were droopy. I sighed. Another addition to the composter.

I looked in the storage closet I use as a pantry, realized I had eaten more of the non-perishables than I had remembered, and decided it could wait until I got back from dinner with Steve the next night. I sorted out the sports and business pages of the newspaper, tossed them into the brown paper shopping bag I use for recycling newspapers, junk mail, and catalogs, took the rest with me into the living room, and scooped up Cat, who had finished eating, on my way to the couch. He favored me with a purr and curled up on my chest after I stretched out prone on the couch. He licked my nose, curled up, and went to sleep. So did I, minus the nose lick.

Big mistake. Two naps in two days were two too many. I woke up an hour later with cotton wool in my brain and my mouth. Although it may have been cat fur in my mouth. Cat was still asleep on top of my chest, his backside in my face. I unceremoniously dumped him onto the floor as I got up from the couch. I went upstairs, washed my face, brushed my teeth, shook my hair into some semblance of order, changed into jeans and a sweatshirt with pictures of raptors on it, and left to see Trudy and Sherry.

My niece, Trudy Meisner, lives with her partner of several years, Sherry Finkel, and their kids, Joshua Meisner Finkel and Simone Finkel Meisner. Last names are confusing when same sex couples can't marry, and when Josh was born they had a big fight about which name would go first if they had hyphenated it. Then they decided the resulting name would be too long and mess up databases (a problem Trudy could make a second fortune by solving), so they gave Josh his biological mother's name, with his "other" mother's name in the middle. They adopted Simi seven years later. Trudy was the primary adopted mother of record, so, in the spirit of egalitarianism and the Jewish value of *shalom bayit* (peaceful household relationships) gave Simone the Meisner last name. They comforted themselves with the notion that their family surnames were no more convoluted than those in many heterosexual blended families.

Their huge "soft contemporary," whatever that means, house is in an upscale development in Medford, not far from Walford. It was in an area that the developer had manipulated so it didn't fall under the Pinelands regulations, which limit development in the New Jersey Pine Barrens. Therefore, he was able to tear down the trees, forcing the owners to spend a bundle on new ones. Trudy and Sherry's house was one of the few that was fully landscaped; even better, to my ecologically conscious mind, they had used all native plants. I thought it was my green influence; it was actually laziness, as neither Trudy nor Sherry liked to garden and figured, correctly to some extent, that native plants would require less maintenance. Whenever the poison ivy or pokeweed began to take over, they hired someone to clear it out for them.

The house is so large that they keep the front door unlocked when expecting company, so they don't have to trek in from the back of the house, where they spend most of their time. I walked in, sniffed the air to get a hint of what was for dinner, and was greeted with the aroma of ...takeout pizza? Accompanying that familiar smell (familiar in my house but not theirs) was the sound of ...raised voices? Uh-oh. Trudy and Sherry never fight, at least not in public. Trudy spends too much time in her own head figuring out what new killer app she can devise to make her next million, and Sherry is too laid back and mellow. The only time I ever heard Trudy raise her voice to Sherry was to tell her to cut out the "psychobabble crap," and then she had laughed when Sherry responded with a characteristic, "And how does it make you feel to call it psychobabble? But I agree it may be crap."

"Oh, hi, Aviva. I thought I heard the front door open. Lock it, will you? No one else is expected tonight." I looked up to see a head leaning over the railing around the second floor balcony. It was attached to their nanny Lynda, a graduate student in special education at Triple-U who lives with them for free in exchange for keeping Josh happily involved with whatever his latest Asperger's induced obsession was, and for keeping Simi's prying fingers out of the electrical sockets.

"Where are the kids? I hope they're not witnessing World War Three in there."

"Simi's asleep, or pretending to be while figuring out how to escape from her crib, and Josh is reading a Star Wars novel. And they've already finished with Three; I think it's World War Five now."

"What's it about? I've never heard them fight before."

Lynda shook her head. "I'm trying not to eavesdrop. I didn't succeed, but I think you had better hear it from them. I like this job too much."

"I understand. Okay, I had better get to the trenches."

"Good luck. I don't think they've gotten to the throwing dishes stage yet, so you won't need a helmet. Anyway, they're using paper plates tonight."

Paper plates? Things are more serious than I had realized.

I gave Lynda a wave, took a deep breath, and made my way to the kitchen. It's a kitchen that would have given Julia Child wet dreams. Move a bed in there, and I could happily live there the rest of my life. It even has a TV (fully equipped with DVR, DVD, and VCR) and a computer.

Trudy and Sherry were sitting at opposite ends of the table, glaring at each other. Since eight people could sit around it comfortably – twelve if they use the leaf – it wasn't surprising they needed to raise their voices.

"You know," I said during this pause, "if you would sit across from each other in the middle of the table, you might not have to scream."

"I have to scream to get this knucklehead to listen to me," said Trudy.

"Knucklehead? What are we, back in grade school in the fifties? I'm being completely rational. I cannot – will not – marry you until we're on an equal footing and I find another job. Period. End of discussion."

"Discussion? What discussion? You've laid down ultimatums. Here are my ultimatums: I don't give a shit about your job, I love you, and we're getting married. Period."

Wow. If this were Hollywood, they would have run to each other in slow motion and embraced. But it's not, so Trudy had to ruin her effect by adding, "Besides, we were never equal financially. You know my earning power is much more than yours."

I thought Sherry was going to blow a gasket. Instead, she burst into tears. "I know. Don't you think I know? Don't you think I've always known? Don't you think it's always bothered me? Why do you think I take on more than my share of the cooking and child raising?"

"Because you enjoy it, you're good at it, and I'm not. So, it all equals out!"

"Then why did you bring it up?"

"I didn't, you did!"

It was time for me to interject again. I had a feeling the "discussion" had been going in circles for a while.

"Um, back up a minute. I'm new here. Remember me? The elderly auntie you invited for dinner to tell her something important? What's this about a wedding? And about needing a new job?"

"It doesn't matter," Sherry pouted. Now, Sherry is tall and solidly built. She pumps iron, has no nonsense short gray hair, and wears chinos and button-down shirts. She's the director of the Student Counseling Center at Triple-U, where she deals with student problems ranging from home sickness to eating disorders to suicide to how to explain to parents that Einstein, Jr. is flunking all his courses. But never have I seen her pout.

"And why doesn't it matter?" I put on my best rabbinic counseling demeanor. I've absorbed a fair bit of psychobabble in my day, too.

"Because I was just fired today, so we won't be getting married."

"Getting married? Since when? I didn't know you were getting married. Besides, this is New Jersey, not Massachusetts. You can't get married, unless you move back there." I stopped at the thought. "Oh, shit, don't tell me you're moving back to Boston! What will I do without you here? You're the only family I've got in the area."

"Thank you for your empathy, dear Auntie Aviva," said Trudy. "So nice of you to think of someone besides yourself."

"Sorry, sorry. That was insensitive. Are you moving? I think it's wonderful that you want to get married, now that you can. But I will miss you."

"Yes, we're getting married. Or want to. No, we're not moving."

"But I thought you have to be a Massachusetts resident to marry there? Are you going to use Larry's address? You can't use your grandmother's – neither of you is old enough for Assisted Living. And even if you were, the kids aren't."

By now I had taken a seat, snagged a piece of Papa John's pizza (boy, Sherry must really be depressed to allow anything but her own hand-thrown pizza enter her kitchen) and a paper plate (yup, she's depressed) and was stuffing my face. I got up to rummage in their room-sized (a normal room, that is) refrigerator and retrieved a bottle of Diet Coke, while Trudy explained to my back.

"Okay, here's the story. From the beginning. Sherry, blow your nose. You're sniffling in and will get an earache. Anyway, we asked you here to find out if you would do a Jewish wedding ceremony for us. We know we can't register it, but it would mean a lot to us. This September will be eighteen years since we moved in together, twenty since we met. We liked the idea of finally solemnizing our commitment to each other with a public ritual, even if it's not a legal one. And then genius here quit . . ."

"I didn't quit. I was fired. Well, I was as good as fired. They didn't give me a choice. It was either leave or be humiliated with a demotion and a new boss and per diem status."

"Whatever. She left her job, and now has decided she can't marry me unless she finds another job and can contribute to the household. As if she doesn't contribute enough just by her presence. Besides, she carried Josh for nine months. That's certainly above and beyond the call of duty. I know; I had to live with her those nine months, not to mention the fifteen hours of labor. Geez, grow up. You don't have to keep fighting the feminist battles of the seventies. We're equal. Okay?"

Sherry sniffled again. "No, not okay. Why can't you accept my feelings? I feel worthless, and you're trying to downplay my emotions."

Time for more intervention. "Sherry, I'm sure Trudy values your emotions. But you need to hear what she's saying, too, and validate her feelings."

In sync, the two of them turned to me and yelled, "Shut up." They looked at each other then and burst out laughing.

"Glad I could be of help. Pizza anyone?"

CHAPTER ELEVEN

"Okay, now that you're both human again – you are, aren't you? – let's try this again. I get the bit about wanting to get married. But I take back what I said before: there's no way in hell I'm going to conduct a ceremony for the two of you until you meet with me – or someone neutral if you prefer – and hash out your obviously divergent views on what makes a partnership. I can't believe it's never come up before now."

"There was never any reason before now," Sherry said. "When Trudy and I met, neither of us had any money. I actually made more than she did and subsidized her while she was getting started in the computer business. When she made all those mega-bucks, I felt I had helped contribute to her success. I mean, I'm making – was making – *bupkes* at Triple-U, but my salary was enough so I didn't feel I was totally dependent on Trudy. But now, I won't even be able to buy a pair of pantyhose without feeling I need her permission."

"Smart woman. I would never give you permission to buy pantyhose. When did you ever wear them anyway?"

"Come off it, Trudy, you know what I mean. I'll have no money of my own at all. Remember what Emma Goldman wrote about marriage being legalized prostitution? Well, I don't want to feel like a kept woman."

"But I won't feel that way about it, so why should you?"

"Because it's me, not you! And how would you feel if the situation were reversed? Would you want to live off my salary if you had no independent income?"

"It wouldn't bother me."

"Like hell it wouldn't! You hated it when the rent on that rat hole in West Philly came out of my graduate stipend because all the money your mother gave you for rent went to buy more ... whatever it was you needed."

"I only hated it because I felt guilty lying to my mother."

"Since when? You managed to commit a lie of omission for years by not correcting her when she referred to me as your roommate!"

It was time for me to intercede. "You guys are getting off topic here. Stop glaring at each other and try to figure out why you're both so angry. Sherry, you start. What happened? How did you lose your job? I thought you were tenured. Oh, wait, no, you're not. You're not in an academic position, are you?"

"No, I wasn't tenured. I had a year-to-year contract. I don't have a doctorate, and the Counseling Center's not part of any academic department. But that's about to change. Not the doctorate part, but the academic part. Merwin Carruthers, the dean of the psychology department, is nominally my boss, but never interferes. We would meet once or twice a year, he would ask if everything was going okay, and he would sign off on my job assessment evaluation, which was always 'outstanding.' If I had a question or budget problem or whatever, I spoke with his secretary, who ran the department anyway. But Carruthers is retiring at the end of the semester, and the newly hired dean has decided to clean house and take over the Center – and me. He wants the Center to be part of the graduate psychology program, so the students can intern there."

"That's sounds reasonable."

"In theory, it's great. In fact, I've suggested it myself for years, but the administration was afraid of privacy issues. They hire undergraduates to answer the phones and do the scheduling – as if that's not a violation of privacy – but until now didn't want graduate students to do the actual counseling, even with supervision. Anyway, John Quincy Moorhouse shows up, having been headhunted away from his private practice, and decides to put my idea into practice, taking credit for it himself. Then he tells me that since I don't have a doctorate, I can't do the supervision. In fact, I can't even be the Center director. Instead, he wants me to do the administrative work part-time. Oh, and if I want, I can continue to work per diem with students I've got a 'rapport with,' but only if I report directly to him and let him see my case notes!"

Sherry had started to cry again and stopped to grab a napkin and blow her nose. "I was so angry, my blood pressure spiked and I almost fell when I stood up. I told him what he could do with his so-called offer and slammed the door on my way out. And that bastard of a soon-to-be-sitting-in-retirement-heaven Carruthers just sat there looking uncomfortable and said nothing. He wouldn't even make eye contact, just mumbled something about how the Board of Trustees of the university had approved the Academic Council's recommendations, and there was nothing he could do."

She blew her nose again. "I'm so angry I could kill Moorhouse."

"Don't bother," Trudy said. "I can hack into the university computers and bring them down. And I can even make it look like Moorhouse was responsible."

"I would rather run him over. And then back up and do it again."

Those words would come back to haunt us.

CHAPTER TWELVE

Nothing was solved that night. Nothing that serious could be solved that quickly. I decided to meet with Trudy and Sherry separately and then together. The problem was the timing: they had hoped to announce their wedding plans to the combined families at the seder on Monday, but since the plans were now in limbo, they weren't sure what to do. I couldn't tell them what to do – I was sure the wedding would take place, but wasn't so sure they could bridge the gap between them in time to plan a September ceremony – so I left it to them to decide what and when to tell the rest of the family.

Sleep didn't come easily that night. The DVD in my brain kept playing back the employment problems I had heard about all day – all week, actually, beginning with Ben's worries, now conveniently resolved. Sherry would probably be okay, and not just because she has a wealthy partner. She had state licensure and could open her own practice, something she had long planned to do as a way to keep busy after retirement. And Wendy would weather, so to speak, her wardrobe malfunction. But I really didn't know what I would do if I lost my job. I had been coasting along, not making waves, thinking it was all smooth sailing. I wasn't sure if my queasy stomach was from anxiety or sea sickness.

To add to my concerns, I was meeting on Friday with Meryl Felsner, the synagogue president, and Len Krasner, a lawyer who handles all the personnel issues for Mishkan Or. It was time for my annual job evaluation. My contract might still have fifteen years to go, but, even though in the immortal words of Chico Marx, there's no such thing as a Sanity Claus, there were escape clauses for both sides.

I opened one eye and squinted at the clock. The neon green

"three" stared back. I had some options:

1. Keep fighting my overactive negative brain waves while trying to get to sleep.

2. Get up and troll the Internet on the chance it would fog up my mind so much that I would forget my (I hoped, imaginary) worries and be able to sleep.

3. Get up and chew a few antacid tablets and wait for the dull ache in the middle of my chest to go away so I wouldn't add (not so imaginary) health fears to my list of woes.

I chose a combination of numbers two and three, which worked well enough that number one became a possibility. By then, the "three" on my clock had morphed into a "four."

When the radio blared out the KWY theme, annoying at the best of times, which this definitely wasn't, I hit the snooze button so hard the clock radio almost fell off the night stand. *Ten minutes*, I thought, *just ten more blissful minutes of oblivion. That's all I need to feel human again.* Ten minutes later, I discovered how wrong I was.

By then, though, I was awake enough to know I wouldn't be able to fall asleep again, so I gave into the inevitable and got up. The brisk morning shower didn't do its job, nor did my customary bowl of Cheerios. It was the end of the box, so I figured I was doing a *mitzvah* by finishing up the *chametz* (non-Kosher for Passover food), but I hadn't planned well enough and had no idea what I would eat for the next four mornings. My sour stomach came back when I remembered the breakfast meeting with Meryl and Len the next day. Okay, so I only had to worry about three more breakfasts. I topped off the cereal with some more antacid.

I actually got to the office before Liz, an event that occurs so seldom that I couldn't recall the last time. She kept things running so smoothly that I wondered why I was needed. (*Careful! Remember tomorrow's meeting! You're indispensable. Keep repeating it and maybe it will come true. Faith worked to bring Tinkerbelle back, although the Cowardly Lion didn't have as much luck with his mantra. Doesn't hurt to try. Take a deep breath and close your eyes: "I do believe, I do believe, I do, I do, I do."* Shit, my self-actualization pep talk didn't work. I still felt sick when I thought about the evaluation meeting.) Liz had returned important phone calls and left me detailed notes about them. She had set up the automatic "out of office" reply on my e-mail that I had forgotten to do. The snail mail was opened and sorted into categories: meeting notices, professional journals, listings of new Jewish books. The pure junk had been recycled. She had confirmed with the caterer and the committee chair that all was in order for Tuesday night's community seder. She had gone to the printer and picked up the "interpretive" (i.e., abridged) Hagaddah for the service before the Passover meal. She had contacted the Triple-U Jewish Students Union to get a final count of how many students we could expect on Tuesday. She had even watered the plants in my office and polished my desk and dusted the bookcases. I should give her a key to my house and let her take over there, too.

There was one thing she could not do for me, though, and that was put together a discussion for Friday night's service. And Saturday morning's. And my remarks to the couple at whose wedding I was officiating on Sunday. And fill out the commercial *ketubah* (the customized one was filled in by the calligrapher). And finish cleaning my kitchen and do the cooking I had promised Trudy and Sherry I would do for Monday night's seder. And plant some winter-hardy pansies in the boxes on my front porch and back deck. Okay, so there was a lot more than "one" thing she couldn't do for me.

And she certainly couldn't go out to dinner with Steve that night, or resolve Trudy and Sherry's dispute. On second thought, I was sure she could solve my niece's pre-marital troubles as well, if not better, than I could. If it weren't for clerical privacy ethics, I would ask her advice. I wondered if there were a way I could disguise their identities, maybe make them sound as though they were a heterosexual couple. Nah, wouldn't work. Liz was much too astute and intuitive. She would guess who I was talking about right away.

"Well, look who's back! How was the convention?" Liz came in carrying a Dunkin' Donuts bag. She handed me an iced coffee with extra cream and no sugar, and took a sip of her decaf with skimmed milk and no sugar. That's why she weighs the same as she did when she got married forty-something years ago, while I wouldn't be able to get my wedding gown – either of them – over my shoulders.

"It was . . . interesting. Thanks for the coffee. What's in the bag?" I knew it was too much to hope it was a Boston Kreme donut. I was right.

"I got a bran muffin for myself and a low-fat blueberry for you. And do you mean 'interesting' as in 'informative and educational,' or 'interesting' as in 'she has an interesting face'?"

"The second," I laughed. "Although more as in 'she's got a nice personality.' It was good to compare notes with colleagues, though, and find out Mishkan Or is doing pretty well for a small synagogue. I also found out that a former classmate has been hired by B'rith Abraham as a part-time rabbi."

"He must have been a 'mature student.' You're too young to retire. Unless he's independently wealthy."

"Neither. I guess B'rith Abraham decided to hire someone who wasn't going to spend three months in Florida every winter. Ben's a nice guy – his name's Ben Bronfman – but has never had good luck with jobs. He'll also be an adjunct at Triple-U."

"Well that will make him lots of money. Is he married? Have kids?"

"His wife's a nurse. In fact, she's already interviewed at Walford General Community. I have no doubts she'll get the job; she's got a lot of experience and I'm sure her references are good. No kids. They just moved here from Eugene to be closer to her family. You'll like Ben."

"And his wife?" As I said, Liz is intuitive.

"Sandy's not one of my favorite people, but I'm sure you'll get the chance to decide for yourself. Oh, and talk about coincidence – they're moving next to Steve Goldfarb and Ben's the rabbi who officiated at our wedding."

"He's not the one who dropped the ring, is he?"

"Yup, one and the same." I had forgotten I had told Liz the story. In fact, I had a sinking feeling there were very few people in the area who hadn't heard it. Poor Ben. Again.

Just then the phone rang. Liz picked it up almost before my auditory nerves had registered the sound.

"Shalom, Mishkan Or. Liz Smithers speaking. How may I help you? Oh, hi, Caryn ... I'm fine, thank you. And you? ... Oh, good. And how's that delightful grandfather of yours? ... Ha! Sounds just like him! And your boys? ... That's wonderful! Even when they were raising hell in my library, I always knew they had the potential to succeed! Send them my love ... Yes, she's here. Hold on."

Liz pushed the hold button and handed me the phone. "Caryn Rozen."

"Gee, I think I guessed." I took the phone off hold. "Hey, Caryn, have I got gossip for you! Remind me to tell you about Ben Bronfman. Oh, and the story of the wayward nipples. And ... lunch today? I'm not sure. I mean, I don't think I have any appointments," I looked at Liz, who was realigning the mail I had thoughtlessly messed up, for confirmation, "but I've got a million things to do ... No, I'm not exaggerating ... Yeah, you're right, I do need to eat, but I'm going to dinner with Steve tonight." I held the phone away from my ear as she yelped. "It's no big deal. It's just to the Walford Diner. But I don't want to eat too much too often or I'll have indigestion and I'm running low on antacid (*Note to self: stop at CVS on way home.*) ... Okay, I guess Salad Works at noon won't ruin my appetite for the diner's haute cuisine. See you then."

"Wayward nipples? This is a topic for a rabbinical conference?"

By the time I finished telling her the story, Liz was spluttering with a combination of mirth, disbelief, and indignation. Her mirth won out: "At least she wasn't on national TV at the Super Bowl when it happened."

CHAPTER THIRTEEN

Much to my surprise, I actually got a fair amount of work done before meeting Caryn at Salad Works. I would have to return to the office after lunch, but at least I had gotten enough accomplished that I wasn't paralyzed by despair. That's because I deliberately blocked my kitchen from my mind.

Caryn and I had become friends during her short-lived plans to become a rabbi. Those plans were derailed when she married Alan Rozen and decided to become a preschool teacher instead. It was a good thing she had some income, as little as it was, as Alan developed into a chronically unemployed hypochondriac. Caryn embarked on her third career plan after Alan decided he needed to find himself and could only do so alone. Alan had never been much of an earner to begin with, but Caryn knew she would need a larger income to support herself and their two college-bound kids, Dan and Jon. Her grandfather was the founder of the Ruben Funeral Home, so Caryn got her mortician's license and joined her father and two brothers in the family business. The fact that the job came with a free apartment was a plus; the fact that the apartment was on the second floor of the funeral home was a minus.

Caryn was already at the restaurant with her salad when I got there. I got my lunch and joined her at the table. As she put away the book she was reading – a new cozy mystery, a pleasure we shared, along with old movies – she started in without a greeting, "Okay, spill. What's this about wayward nipples?"

"Why, hello, I'm fine, thanks. And how are you? Oh, shit, I'm channeling my sister!"

"We already said hello on the phone and established that we're both still alive and kicking. Well, alive anyway. I've been trying all morning to figure out what you meant, and finally gave up."

For the second time that day, I related the hazards of thin blouses and cold winds. Caryn didn't find it as amusing as I had thought she would. "To tell you the truth, Aviva, I've supervised a couple of graveside funerals and had the same thing happen. It's pretty embarrassing. I've been able to hide it by holding my notebook against my chest. I finally went out and bought a couple of black jackets that button high enough to camouflage any 'popage.'"

Caryn raked her hand through her curls, somehow not disarranging them. She has the kind of wash-and-wear hair I dream of; mine is wash-and-frizz. "So," she said, "tell me about Ben Bronfman. What's his latest *tzuris*?"

"Things may finally be going his way for once. He's the new rabbi at B'rith Abraham. But two people had to die to ensure he would get the job." Caryn looked startled and I quickly filled her in on the inadvertent intermarriage, the apartment rental, and the convenient deaths. To my way of thinking, telling Caryn was not tattling. She was a friend, had no personal connections with B'rith Abraham, and wouldn't spread the word about Ben's Blunder.

"Wow, that's almost too convenient. Any chance that it wasn't an accident? I can't imagine Ben doing anything like that, but I wouldn't put anything past Sandy."

"You know, it's interesting that was your first reaction. It's exactly what I said to Steve on the phone last night, and he politely but firmly told me my imagination was running away with me. The more I think about the Fishers' deaths, though, the more I have to wonder. But how do you asphyxiate someone and have it look like an accident?"

Caryn shrugged. "Maybe you can clog up the dryer vent from the outside. Or leave a car running in the garage. Or ... I don't know ... turn off the automatic pilot light on the stove."

"But don't they add something to the gas in stoves so it has an odor? I know when I had a gas stove in my first apartment, there was always a faint smell. And car exhaust certainly isn't odorless. I wonder if the carbon monoxide from a gas dryer has an odor. I'll have to check it out on the Internet. Too bad I've got no time to do it."

While buttering her roll – I hate that she can eat things like real butter and never exercise and still stay slim. Curse genetics! – Caryn asked, "Have you ever met the Fishers' daughter? She came to us to make the arrangements."

"Years ago, maybe. I don't really remember her, but I think she came to services once or twice when I was first here. I have no memory of her or what's she's like or even what she looks like."

"She's sort of nerdy: bad skin, bad glasses, bad hair, bad clothes. Her husband's the same, but he's tall and scrawny while she's tall and 'big-boned.' They both have washed out looking hair. She wears hers short but still has a lot more of it than he does."

"As my mother always says, 'There's a lid for every pot.'"

"No, it's my mother who says that. Although she thinks Alan and I came from different sets. Anyway, I was even less impressed with Audrey when she said she wants to have her parents cremated, no ceremony, no shiva, no memorial service, nothing. She doesn't even want the cremains back. She asked if we could sell the cemetery plots her parents bought in New York for her, but we have no jurisdiction to do that, particularly in another state. I suggested she advertise the plots in the Jewish papers, but I think she's listing them on E-bay."

"How much do cemetery plots go for?"

Caryn shrugged. "Depends on location, how popular the cemetery is, how filled it is. Anywhere from a thousand to five thousand each, maybe even more. That plus the house, plus the car, plus whatever other assets and savings they left her will add up to quite an inheritance, especially as they're going for the cheapie, no frills funeral. She definitely showed no sorrow about being left an orphan. I have to wonder what her parents did to alienate her so much. She seems a more likely candidate for a murderer than Ben. Or even Sandy."

"How many cases of parricide have you come across professionally? Or personally?"

"None."

"Ditto. I think I'll mention it to Steve tonight. He already thinks

I'm on the edge of dementia, so it won't do any harm to my reputation."

"So, *nu*, tell me about this date of yours!" Caryn in her eagerness leaned so far across the table toward me that she almost wound up wearing lettuce on her boobs.

"Why does everyone insist it's a date? It's just two old friends getting together for dinner and to catch up."

"Two old friends who happen to have once been married to each other."

"You should talk! What about you and Alan?"

"Exactly my point. We've gone beyond being old friends. I'm not about to marry him again, but we're definitely together. Sort of."

Caryn and Alan had become a couple again after Alan landed a job as manager of a health store, where his years of experience as a hypochondriac gave him an advantage.

"What do you mean 'sort of'?"

"He wants us to live together, but I think it's because he wants to save money on rent so he can work fewer hours at the store and work on his 'holistic healthy eating' cookbook. I'm afraid he's about to fall back into his old habit of relying on me to subsidize his fantasies. And I refuse to be an enabler again."

"Good for you."

"If he keeps up the pressure, though, I might have to break up with him. I would miss the sex, but not necessarily the package that goes with it." She stopped and looked at me speculatively. "Have you and your 'old friend' Steve slept together?"

"Of course we have. The last time was ..." I quickly did the math in my head ... "um, twenty-two years ago."

"Very funny. Wait a minute, didn't you get divorced twenty-three years ago? I remember because I was pregnant with Jon at the time."

"We filed for divorce twenty-three years ago, but the final papers didn't come through for a year. We decided to show how civilized we were about the whole thing and went out to dinner. One thing led to another and ... do you really need all the details?"

"I think I can fill them in for myself. So when is the last time you had sex?"

"When did Keith and I separate?"

"Don't tell me it's been over fifteen years!"

"Okay, I won't tell you. Do you have any idea how hard it is for a woman rabbi to get a date, especially in a small town? And, quite honestly, I'm just not interested. Casual sex is just not safe, and I'm too set in my ways and too independent to have a relationship."

"Bull. What are you going to do for companionship when you get older?"

"Get a second cat. No, really, stop worrying about me. I'm fine with my life the way it is. Look at my sister. She lives over a thousand miles away from her kids and grandchildren. She's been a widow for years. And she loves her life, has a ton of friends, is active in all kinds of things. I'll be fine."

"So you're going to move to Florida, buy cute little outfits for your dog, and learn to play mahjong?"

"I prefer backgammon. I can take Florida in small doses only. I only like dogs when they belong to other people, and cats have too much dignity to allow themselves to get dressed up."

"Joke all you want but methinks the lady doth protest too much."

I thought so, too. In truth, the idea of being alone was starting to frighten me, especially when I thought about friends. I know a lot of people, but Caryn is one of only a few I can really call a friend.

"I love you, Aviva, and will do anything – almost – for you, but I refuse to prepare your corpse after your cats have devoured it because no one checked to see how you were doing."

Yup, a real friend.

CHAPTER FOURTEEN

I called Steve when I got back to the office and made our "date" for seven instead of five, to give me time to finish up in the office and work on my kitchen. I didn't want to think anymore about Ben's sudden spate of good luck, about my single status, about what I could do to earn a living if I lost my job, about my lack of friends or future plans or retirement, about Trudy and Sherry. If, as Samuel Johnson said, "The realization that one will be hanged in the morning concentrated the mind wonderfully," so does the realization that it's important for one's mental health to avoid thoughts of unsolvable problems. So I concentrated instead on what I could accomplish. I finished my notes for the sermon-dialogues for Shabbat, got the material together for Sunday's wedding, reviewed the plans for the community seder, and got home in time to finish up my kitchen and take a shower.

Steve and I arrived at the Walford Diner at the same time and pulled into adjacent parking spaces. My car was a lot nicer than his, but that's because it was newer. My decrepit one had been totaled in a "deliberate accident" about sixteen months earlier. Because the Blue Book value was almost in the minus column, I'm lucky the insurance company gave me any money at all to replace it, but the unplanned expense certainly hadn't improved my savings balance.

"Glad you could tear yourself away from your Pesach preparations," Steve said as he enveloped me in one of his characteristic bear hugs. The increasing years and hairiness had made his resemblance to a teddy bear even more pronounced, but it's a look I like. Unfortunately for him in his present employment, it's a look that fares better in an academic environment than in a law enforcement one, but he's basically an administrator, so he hasn't taken too much flak from his underlings. They were more concerned about his lack of practical experience with any police force than with his facial hair, and he still hadn't convinced some of them that his "liberal-egghead-ivied-tower" theories may have real life applications. And I had a feeling that his experiences with the real world were making him rethink some of his theories, too.

"Thanks for meeting later. Those extra two hours gave me the chance to catch up on the work I didn't do during the IRA and to finish fumigating the kitchen." We walked into the diner.

"I seem to recall that keeping house was not one of your talents."

"Oh, I can do it, I just don't like or want to. But I did feel a little bit like your mother, who, if I remember correctly, would clean the house before the cleaning lady came. And then she would clean it again after she left. If I hadn't gotten the kitchen emptied out, though, there's no way even the professionals could have done anything with it tomorrow."

"Yeah, my Mom did always make a face when she came to our apartment."

As we were seated at a booth and handed our outsized menus, I made a face of my own. "And how is she these days? Still celebrating our divorce?"

"Hey, come on, that's not fair. She didn't think much of you as a housewife, but that's not what I wanted for a wife. She may not have been torn up about the divorce, but she wasn't happy about it either. And, if it makes you feel any better, it took her a long time to accept Ellie, too. After all, her darling boy was marrying a law professor who was a widow with three daughters. Let me count the number of strikes against her. Anyway, she and Dad are doing okay. I've been trying to convince them the house is too big and too old for them to stay there, but they're not interested in moving. I worry about what will happen if one of them falls and breaks a hip."

"I know what you mean. I'm glad my mother's in an assisted living facility so I don't have to worry as much about her safety."

The waitress came over and we realized we hadn't even looked at the menu yet. Not that either of us needed to. I had my usual Greek salad, (wow, two salads in one day!) although I knew the sodium would make it impossible for me to remove my rings later, or get them on again in the morning. And Steve ordered a tuna melt and fries and a chocolate milkshake. No wonder he was getting more rotund. Not that I was a good example of nutritious eating: I had passed *zaftig* at least thirty pounds ago.

As soon as we got our drinks, I leaned forward eager to impart all my *lashon harah.* "Wait until I tell you what's been going on. First of all, I saw Caryn for lunch today, and when I told her all about how Ben's problems had been solved by the Fishers' deaths, her first thought was that Sandy had something to do with it. And you know Caryn doesn't go in for conspiracy theories or anything fanciful. So maybe I'm not so crazy. Okay, so maybe I am, but not about this."

"Hold it." Steve interrupted. "You haven't told me the whole story. What deep, dark secret of Ben's did the Fishers know? They're from Connecticut, have lived in Walford for years, their daughter lives in Eugene – oh, I forgot. Wasn't Ben in Eugene for a while?"

"Right. It was his last job. Well, his current one, but his contract hasn't been renewed."

"What a surprise."

"Yeah. A recurring pattern with Ben. Anyway, it was kind of my fault, but not really. Last summer, Florence asked me to do the wedding for her daughter in Eugene. I would have loved to since I've never gone birding on the West Coast and could have really added to my life list. But she blurted out, or maybe I guessed, that the daughter's boyfriend wasn't Jewish. So I gave her Ben's number to call and ask if he knew any rabbis who did intermarriages. But when the kids ... they're in their forties, so they're not kids ... anyway, that's not the point, when, um, Audrey and George? ... well, when they went to talk to Ben, they didn't bother to tell them George isn't Jewish, and Ben, being Ben, never asked, so he agreed to officiate. Then he found out his contract wasn't being renewed, Sandy wanted to come back to the Philadelphia area because her mother's not well, and the job at B'rith Abraham opened up. They hired Ben part-time, arranged for him to rent the place next to you at a discount, and found him another part-time job at Triple-U. But – and here's where it gets really interesting – B'rith Abraham won't hire a rabbi who does intermarriages. So Ben was in a sweat that the Fishers, whom he didn't know were going to be his landlords, would tell the synagogue board that he conducted the wedding and he would be out of a job before it began. Oh, and Sandy was furious when she found out. She had already threatened to leave him if he messed up this job, but now she warned him she would cut off his balls if he didn't do something to stop the Fishers from talking. Or she would do it herself. And neither of them was seen at the hotel on Monday night. In fact, I don't think anybody saw them until Tuesday afternoon."

I finally stopped to breathe and spear a slice of hardboiled egg. Steve was already done with most of his sandwich, half his fries, and the entire milkshake.

He put down his fork. He's the only person I know who eats fries with a fork, not his fingers. "Aviva, it was an accident. Fortuitous for Ben perhaps, but still an accident. The fire marshal said they pulled a wad of twigs and grasses and trash out of the dryer vent. Birds must have been nesting there for years. It's amazing they hadn't had trouble with carbon monoxide before now. In fact, they probably did and that's why they were getting headaches."

"So why did it happen now, when Ben and Sandy were in town? For that matter, how come it happened while the Fishers' daughter was in town and conveniently not staying with her parents?"

"Don't tell me you suspect her, too? If there's anything to your theory about Ben – which I greatly doubt – I would think she would be the next victim. And her husband. And, for that matter, you."

"I swore to Ben and Sandy I wouldn't tattle. But I don't think Sandy believed me. Besides, I told you, I have an all electric house"

"But you have a car that you keep in the garage. And it's right under your bedroom."

Steve may have thought he was being flippant, but his comment got me thinking. "I know the layout of those houses on Oak Glen Road. I looked at the models when they first went up, but they were too pricey for me. Their garages aren't under the bedrooms, because, unlike my bedroom which is on the second floor, all the ones on Oak Glen are on the first floor, even in the two-story houses. So the carbon monoxide wouldn't have far to travel. Did you check the car instead of the dryer, or did you go for the obvious again?"

"Don't be nasty." The last time I had challenged the official findings in two deaths, I had shown that the obvious solutions weren't. "First, the fire marshal is in charge of the investigation and, yes, he checked the car. It was in the garage, the engine was cold, and the tank was full. And their bedroom is on the first floor, but it's also right next to the laundry room."

"Pretty noisy if you throw a load of wash in late at night."

"Not everyone does household chores at weird hours."

"But if the dryer was running while they were asleep, then they must have. And it would have been noisy. They make quiet dishwashers now, but I've never heard of a quiet dryer." Of course, what did I know? I was still using the same appliances that came with the townhouse fifteen years ago.

"Who said they were asleep? They were in bed, but the TV was on and the newspaper was on the bed. They may have been waiting for the load to finish before turning off the lights."

"I'm still not convinced. It just seems too convenient. Do you think the fire marshal will talk with me?"

"I'm sure he would be happy to. Okay, not happy, but willing. But you really should drop this wild notion of yours. It's getting obsessive. Excuse me." He took his cell phone from his pocket and glanced at the screen. "I have to take this." He got up and walked to the outside of the restaurant.

I made a small dent in my salad when he walked back in looking perturbed. "I have to go. There was a hit-and-run fatality at Triple-U. Someone coming out of the Student Counseling Center stepped off the curb, and was hit by a speeding car. A witness said it looked deliberate." He stopped a second and stared at me. "Isn't that the building where Sherry works?"

My face must have paled because Steve put on his solicitous look. "Do you want to come with me? In case ... well, in case we need an identification? No, never mind. I couldn't put you through that."

"It will be better than waiting for you to call me, if you even remember to. Let's go."

CHAPTER FIFTEEN

By time we got to the scene, I was a wreck. I had made the mistake of calling the Meisner-Finkel home. Lynda picked up. "Hi, Aviva. No, Sherry's not here. She and Trudy had another fight – but don't tell them I told you – and Sherry stormed out to drive around and cool down. It's what she does when she has to think or decompress or just get away from the madness here or at school. Do you want to talk to Trudy?"

"No," I managed to choke, "that's okay. Just let them know I called, okay? I'll call later."

Steve glanced over at me, his eyes filled with the kind of concern that first attracted me to him over a quarter of a century ago. "She's not home, is she?"

I didn't trust myself to talk and just shook my head.

"Maybe it wasn't her. I didn't think to ask if the victim was male or female. The report just said someone was run down by a speeding dark colored SUV while leaving the Student Counseling Center. And would Sherry have been there this late?"

"She would have if she wanted to clear out her desk when no one was around. And Lynda said she was upset when she left the house, so she might not have looked before stepping off the curb."

"Why was she clearing out her desk?" I didn't realize until Steve asked me that question that I hadn't told him what I had learned the night before.

"We were so involved in talking about the Fishers at dinner that I didn't get a chance to tell you about Trudy and Sherry. They were going to announce that they're getting married – I know," I responded before he could protest, "they can't marry legally in New

Jersey, but they can still have a Jewish ceremony. But then Sherry got herself forced out of her job – the administration wanted her to go part-time, hired someone else to work full-time as her boss – and she had a big fight with Trudy about not wanting to get married if she had to be financially dependent on her. And I told them the wedding is a moot point until they resolve these differences." I heaved a big sigh. "It's been a hell of a couple of days."

Steve looked pained. "What?" I didn't ask so much as demand. "What are you going to say to add to all of the things on my mind?"

"It's not important. It can wait."

"I was married to you, remember? I know that look. You're feeling guilty about something, aren't you?"

"Not guilty. More like conflicted. We're almost at the crime scene." We could see the emergency vehicle lights a block away. "Really, it can wait."

Steve pulled up behind the ambulance and flashed his ID. It should have been raining. In movies, it's always raining. It had been raining earlier, but now the sky was starting to clear, and the almost full moon was starting to shimmer through the haze. And Steve should have been wearing a worn out trench coat, an old suit, and wingtips, not a well-worn parka adorned with an old ski lift pass (*When did he start to ski? And why do I care right now? Or at any time?*), jeans, and non-trendy sneakers. As for me, I shouldn't have been there at all.

"I'll wait here, Steve. You go look and tell me." I'm not usually squeamish, but the taste of regurgitated feta was making me feel even more ill than I already was.

Steve conferred with his officers, briefly lifted the cover on the body, and sauntered back to me, giving me a thumbs up. I had no idea if he meant it was or wasn't Sherry, but the slight grin on his face gave me a clue.

"Sorry to have brought you out here and frightened you, Aviva. It's a man. The driver's license in his wallet is in the name of John Quincy Moorhouse. Don't tell anyone until we've confirmed his I.D. and informed his family. What's wrong, Aviva? Do ... did ... you know him?"

I shook my head. "No." It wasn't a lie. I had never met the man. But I knew the name. In fact, I had heard it for the first time last night. He had been the psychologist who had humiliated Sherry by replacing and demoting her and demeaning her accomplishments.

Steve called over one of his officers, a kid who looked as though he should be planning how to get a fake I.D. in time for the prom, not carrying a gun. "Please take Rabbi Cohen back to the Walford Diner to pick up her car. Here," he tossed him his car keys, "take my car. I don't think we need the Walford gossip line buzzing with speculation about why the Rabbi was seen in the back seat of a police cruiser."

Steve gave me a peck on the cheek and a quick hug. "Go home and unwind. I still need to talk to you before I go home for Pesach, so I'll give you a call tomorrow or Saturday."

I couldn't help but notice that he still referred to the North Jersey house he had shared with his second wife as "home." It made me realize again just how temporary his stay in Walford was. I wondered if I could change his mind. I wondered why I wanted to change his mind.

I nodded at Steve, still unable to trust my voice. I was relieved, of course, that the body wasn't Sherry's, or anyone else that I knew, but the last anyone had seen Sherry, she had been angry. And she blamed John Quincy Moorhouse for making her lose her job. And for her refusal to marry Trudy. And for her fights with Trudy. And she was going for a drive. And she had more than one traffic ticket for speeding. And her car was a dark green SUV. Plus, her words of the previous night were so loud in my head that I was afraid they would leak out, like too-loud music seeping out of headphones: *I would rather run him over. And then back up and do it again.*

CHAPTER SIXTEEN

I directed The Kid to my car, thanked him, and got behind the wheel. I was sitting there thinking when I realized Steve's car was still parked next to me. The Kid must have been taught never to leave a helpless female in a nearly deserted, poorly lit parking lot late at night. I waved, put the car in gear, and drove off on auto pilot, the car pointing itself in the direction not of my house but of Trudy and Sherry's.

The front of the house was dark, except for the outside security lights. I wasn't surprised, as they usually were in the back of the house. I pulled into the driveway, which curved around to the three-car garage tucked away on the side of the house, out of sight of the sidewalk, giving the house a nicer "curb appeal" than a front entry garage would. One of the bay doors was open, the light was on, and Trudy and Sherry were examining the front bumper of Sherry's SUV.

As I got closer, I could see rain drops polka dotting the car's shiny surface. "What happened?"

"Oh, hi, Aviva," Trudy answered. "Lynda told me you had called, but didn't want to talk to me, only to Sherry. Should I be relieved or insulted?"

"Um, neither." Damn, I hadn't thought up a good excuse for why I had called. "I just wanted to see if she was feeling any better about what happened at Triple-U." The reason sounded lame even to me, and I was the one who said it.

"Thanks, Aviva, but, no, I don't feel any better," Sherry said. "Now I've got another reason to be angry at Moorhouse. I went out for a drive and then it started to pour. It was so bad, I could barely see, so I pulled into a strip mall lot, hydroplaned, ran into a concrete light pillar, scraped the bumper and broke the headlight. If I hadn't still been so upset, I would never had gone out driving on a night like this."

The fact that it had only been lightly raining in Walford didn't mean anything. There seem to be microclimates all over the place in the Pine Barrens. One street could be dry and a mile down it could be flooded. I don't know anything about damage to a car involved in hitting a pedestrian, but the radio reports on hit-and-run accidents always seem to include a plea to the public to be on the lookout for a car with front end damage.

Could Sherry have used her car to kill the man she held responsible for her current problems and then deliberately hit the light post to cover the damage? Could the heavy rain have washed away any forensic evidence, like blood and DNA? Had it even rained that heavily where she was, or had she come home and used a garden hose to wash away the gore? Was there any gore to wash away? And why was I even thinking this way? I've known Sherry for years; she's my niece's partner. I consider her my niece, too. She may look like a "typical" (whatever that is) dyke, but she's as gentle and warm and caring as anyone I've ever met. Trudy, with her soft, curvy, Earth-mother looks, would never run anyone over either; she would use a knife to eviscerate him instead. It's much more personal.

I walked around to the front of the car and tried to look knowledgeable. In truth, the only intelligent thing I know about cars is how to contact AAA and how to find a trustworthy mechanic. But even my untrained eye could see Sherry had really walloped that light post.

"Wow. What does the other guy look like?" I mentally cringed as I realized my choice of words may not have been the most prudent. But Sherry didn't seem to react to them guiltily.

"I didn't look. It was raining too hard to get out of the car. I just backed up, sat there until the rain let up and my heart settled down, and came home. At least I hadn't pushed the fender into the tires, or, worse, the engine. The damage seems to be cosmetic only. I hope. I didn't hear any funny noises while I was driving, and I got back okay."

"Let's go in and warm up," Trudy said. "And call the insurance company."

"I could use a hot drink, maybe with a shot of something alcoholic in it. We can call the insurance company tomorrow. They're not going to do anything tonight."

"Did you call the police?" I asked as we made our way indoors.

"No need. There was no other car involved."

Yeah, I thought, *but what about a pedestrian?*

"Will the insurance pay off even if there's no police report?"

"I've no idea. But I'm not in the mood to call them now. I want a drink and all I need is for some cop to come in here to get a statement and smell booze on my breath. I'll call tomorrow and if they ask why I waited, I'll say I was too shaken up to think straight. It's true."

But what else have you said is true? I was really feeling guilty thinking such thoughts about Sherry, so I decided I had better leave before I said something I would regret.

"Are you sure you don't want something before you go?" Trudy asked as she filled two mugs from the always ready coffee maker.

"No, thanks. I really do have to get going. I've got a long day tomorrow. In fact, a long next five days. I won't be able to relax until after services Wednesday morning. Unless you decide I should take your mother to the airport."

Trudy tried to look innocent. "I would never ask you to do that. Anyway, she's driving back to Boston with Larry. I swear my brother is a saint."

"Well, it's easy for him to be. He always was your mother's idyllic child, and could do no wrong. Of course, he never did do anything wrong, which is what makes him so insufferably dull. Well, good night. I'll stop by with the kugels Saturday night. Assuming I get them made in time."

"You had better. We're counting on them. And make some meringues, too. They're always a hit."

I looked at Sherry, who was pouring a hefty slug of whiskey or brandy – I know about as much about alcoholic drinks as I do car mechanics – into her mug, and at Trudy, who was drinking her coffee straight, no milk, no sugar, just lots of caffeine. "You two okay now?"

They looked at each other. "I guess so," Trudy said, as Sherry said at the same time, "Maybe."

"Well, Monday night will be here sooner than you think, so you have to decide what to tell the family. And I meant what I said last night: I'm reluctant to officiate at any ceremony for you two until you stop arguing and figure out what's really important in your relationship and makes you partners."

"Stop being a rabbi and be an aunt for once, will you? You know you're going to do the ceremony. And please trust that we're grownups and can work out our own problems."

I was skeptical, but kept my thoughts to myself as I let myself out through the garage, got into my car, and went home to my cat. My only cat. So far.

CHAPTER SEVENTEEN

I was surprised I had been able to sleep, but it had been a tough day, and no one had jumped out and yelled, "April Fool" to make it better. My response to stress is to sleep, and I was snoring (or so I've been told in the past when there were witnesses to my sleep patterns) within seconds of getting into bed. I didn't wake up until a rusty lawnmower started to rumble next to my ear. It was Cat, who had pounced on my stomach and was pawing at my chest trying to get it to lactate, while snurfling at my ear. "Get off, I'm not your mother!" I pushed him away and squinted at the clock. "Shit!" It was later than I thought. "Sorry, Cat, you were right to wake me. I must have forgotten to set the alarm." Why was I apologizing to Cat? He had no idea he was doing me a favor. He just wanted breakfast. Maybe Caryn was right and I should find someone to talk to in the morning besides a cat. If I weren't careful, I would be buying cute little matching sweaters for Cat and me.

I took a quick shower, brushed my teeth and hair, gave up on my hair, found some reasonably clean pants and top, pulled on a blazer to make the outfit look more professional, and got downstairs in time to let in the cleaning crew. It didn't take me long to show them what to do – it was the same crew who had done the kitchen for me the previous couple of years, and gave the house a thorough cleaning monthly the rest of the year. I made it to Walford Diner just before Meryl Felsner, Mishkan Or's president, and Len Krasner, the chair of the personnel committee, arrived.

We ordered our breakfasts and, in his no nonsense lawyerly way, Len got right to the point. "As you know, Aviva, we sent a confidential questionnaire to the congregation members to assess their perceptions of the job you're doing. I won't keep you in suspense – you passed." *(Whew!)* He allowed himself a grin. "But there were a few concerns that came up more than once that you need to be aware of." *(Uh-oh.)* He pulled a piece of paper from his briefcase and put on his half-moon reading glasses before continuing. "Some of them are what the committee, quite honestly, found frivolous. We particularly got a kick out of the complaint from someone who drove by your house on a Sunday afternoon, and saw you doing some gardening in the front yard wearing a pair of torn jeans and a dirty T-shirt." *(So, nu, hire a gardener to take care of the yard for me.)*

"And don't forget," Meryl interjected, "the complaint that she wore the same dress to two different bar mitzvah receptions." *(They're lucky I had checked to make sure my shoes matched – each other, not the dress.)*

Len chuckled. "I wonder what they would say if they knew I wear the same 'lucky' tie every time I'm in court."

Meryl took up the narrative. "There were also a couple of comments that you spent too much time 'fooling around' in matters that didn't concern you. They questioned whether you had neglected your work while poking your nose into police matters and if it was right to let you still collect your salary while you were recuperating from your injuries. We ignored those, too." *(Only time in fifteen years I had taken off more than a day at a time for sick leave, and they think I'm a slacker?)*

"More seriously, though," said Len, "there was a group that decided you had become too ... how to put this? ... set in your ways, that the services were predictable and routine. *(What do they think the meaning of 'ritual' is?)* So we will be making a recommendation to the Ritual Committee to look into some new, creative ways to spend Shabbat together, maybe once every month or two."

"It just so happens," I interrupted, "that I picked up a folder of ideas for 'revitalizing, rejuvenating, and re-imagining Shabbat' at the IRA this week." *(Good thing I hadn't tossed the materials, but had left them on my desk to look over at another time.)*

"Great, that's just the kind of thing we're looking for," Meryl said.

"We even heard rumors that a small group had decided to look into replacing you *(Again!?)* – don't worry, it's not about to happen. They called a couple of the seminaries and found out that the new grads with no more than student placement experience were getting starting salaries higher than we're paying you. *(I could have told them that.)* Their plan backfired – the personnel committee voted to give you a raise above the cost-of-living one provided for in the contract." *(Nice of them, but I doubt if it will be enough to put me in a higher tax bracket. I'm not about to turn it down, though.)*

When they mentioned the amount, I knew my thoughts had been correct. I could probably afford a milkshake-disguised-as-a-coffee-drink at Starbucks an extra day a week. But I put on my most sincere smile as I said, "Thank you. I appreciate the vote of confidence."

Len smirked, "Maybe now you can afford to buy another fancy dress. And get your hair styled and buy some makeup. Yup, those were some other complaints. *(Blame genetics. In the shtetl, there was a good reason hair like mine used to be shaved or hidden under a wig.)* Another recommendation we're making is to suspend these questionnaires and find some other assessment tool. It really brought out all the loonies." *(I could have told you that, too.)*

"But," Meryl cautioned, "there were some thoughtful suggestions, in addition to perking up services. Some felt you weren't involved enough with the younger kids or in doing fund raising and recruiting new members. I know you're not interested in any of those activities, and I'm not even sure the rabbi should be involved with fund raising or membership drives, but we should take a look at how you can take a more proactive role in the religious school. I know you supervise the principal, but you may want to get into the classrooms more often." *(I really, really had hoped no one had noticed my lack of involvement with the school. Oh, well.)*

I nodded in agreement and tried to look thoughtful, but truthfully I would rather have root canal without Novocain than face a class of school-aged kids who would rather have root canal without Novocain than be in that class. "I'll talk with Ron" – the school principal – "and see what we can work out." Ron Finegold, who doubles as our cantor, and his wife Brenda Fishman, a literature professor at Triple-U, were good friends. I felt sure he would come up with a painless way for me to participate. More painless than root canal anyway.

Business out of the way, we finished eating our breakfasts while chatting aimlessly. I gave them a broad enough outline of the IRA so that they had no idea I had skipped most of the sessions. And I filled them in a bit about Ben – well, only that he was going to be the new rabbi at our "rival" synagogue and that we had been classmates. "I'm hoping our friendship will help the two congregations find some common grounds for cooperation, maybe even help us plan some joint programs."

"Don't count on it," Meryl replied while shoveling in pancakes dripping in butter and syrup. Another one who doesn't need to worry about dieting. In Meryl's case, though, I didn't think it was genetics but running after three kids, one a tween who had just started middle school and a set of twins in the second grade, plus owning a craft shop, plus working countless hours as president of Mishkan Or that kept her in fighting trim. "Some of their members are really intractable. There's still a lot of bitterness that we hired you – nothing personal, you understand. It's just that they don't want to see any changes in Judaism unless the tradition inconveniences them. And having a male rabbi isn't an inconvenience, like keeping kosher or not working on Shabbat would be."

Len finished up his English muffin and wiped his hands and mouth before finishing his coffee. "I agree. I don't see them wanting to have anything to do with us. You'll be lucky if they allow their new rabbi even to socialize with you. I was sorry when they split away, but not sorry when I realized the depths of their intransigence." He shook his head. "You would think the fact they've lost almost all their members, either to death or Florida, and haven't been able to attract new ones would tell them something. Anyone who still wants to be traditional is going to join an Orthodox shul."

"But the closest one is in Cherry Hill," I said, "and if they're that traditional they're not going to drive on Shabbat. Even the Orthodox *minyan* at Triple-U is too far for most."

"A group of young Orthodox families, who couldn't afford Cherry Hill, have moved into that new townhouse community off Route

Seventy – Pinewoods, I think it's called – and meet at someone else's house every week."

"Reminds me of the *chavurah* movement in the late Sixties," I reminisced. "We weren't Orthodox, but we were ... what's the word I'm looking for?"

"Nuts?"

"Quiet, Meryl, you're too young to have known what it was like back then. We were idealistic. No, that's not the word I want. These senior moments are becoming senior hours. Intense? No. I mean, yes, we were idealistic and intense, but ... I know, earnest. We really believed in what we were trying to create."

"And where are all of you now?"

I sighed. "Some became ultra-Orthodox and renounced their 'youthful indiscretions.' Some made *aliyah* and joined the settlers' movement. Some are rabbis in large, traditional synagogues. Some work for establishment Jewish agencies. But others who made *aliyah* are working for human rights organizations in Israel. And others have gotten their Jewish agencies involved in ecological issues. And others have transformed their synagogues."

"And you?"

"Me?" I laughed. "What you see is what you get. Old, fat, and lazy. A human Garfield."

Len hadn't participated much in the conversation, but now he added, as he stood up and grabbed the bill before either of us could, "I'm not too young to remember those times. In fact, I was a bit too old to have participated. But, boy, did I envy those of you who did. Don't sell yourself or the Boomers short, Rabbi. After all, Mishkan Or did hire you and we're doing okay, while B'rith Abraham is barely surviving."

He threw down some bills as a tip, waved, and left. Meryl and I just looked at each other. "Where did that come from?" I asked.

"I don't know. I've never heard him say anything that wasn't part of the Republican line. He's the last person I would suspect of being a closet hippie."

"I'm not sure I would go quite so far, but I would have expected him to have railed against the excesses of the Sixties, not extolled them. There's hope for all of us."

We talked for a few more minutes, but I had to get over to Mishkan Or and Meryl had to check that the Triple-U business major she had hired part-time for the craft store hadn't decided to give all her friends deep discounts. And I was worried that if I spent any more time with Meryl, I would tell her all about my suspicions that Sherry and Ben were involved in two separate murders. I wasn't willing to share those thoughts with anyone. Even myself.

CHAPTER EIGHTEEN

I sat in my car for a few minutes trying to organize my day. I needed to get to the office, check messages, make sure the memorial lights on the plaques were lit next to the names of those whose deaths were being commemorated this week, put my notes for tonight's sermon dialogue on the podium, and check that the pastries delivered by the bakery for tonight's Oneg Shabbat, the reception after the services, were of good quality. (Tough job, but someone's got to do it.) I also had to do all my shopping so I could prepare the kugels and cookies for Monday's seder. Oh, and I had better take care of the *ketubah*, the wedding contract, and put it in my car, along with my Rabbis' Manual, or I would forget them on Sunday. At that point, I pulled out my phone and started entering notes into the "to-do" list. I had learned the hard way not to rely on my memory.

I was about to start the car when my phone rang. It was Steve. "Hi, Steve," I answered. "You caught me just as I was about to leave Walford Diner and go to the synagogue. Any news on what happened last night?"

"You know better than to ask me that, but you'll keep asking anyway, so I'll just say we've got some promising leads. So don't ask again." He paused, then resumed, "Listen, Aviva, I still need to talk to you before I go to my daughter's tomorrow. What's your schedule like today?"

"Hah. I was just trying to figure out when I would be able to go to the bathroom. It's crowded. Can't you tell me on the phone?"

"I would rather not." He paused again. "What time will you be home from services tomorrow? It's not that long a drive to my daughter's, so I could leave in the late afternoon and still be there before dark."

"Depends. If we get a minyan, and no one wants to talk to me after services, about twelve-fifteen. If someone needs to talk, who knows? And if there's no minyan, then around ten-thirty." I looked at my watch. "I need to spend a couple of hours at the *shul*, then I'm going food shopping. I'll be home by four or so, and don't have to be at Mishkan Or until eight. Do you want to come by later today? I can't offer supper, though. I was going to grab a quick bite out before sundown, and then pig out at the Oneg to get me through the rest of the night."

"I'm pretty busy later today, since I want to make sure everything's taken care of before I leave. I'm not planning to be back before Wednesday. The only time I can really free up is now. Tell you what, I'll stop by tomorrow, early afternoon, and bring us lunch. I wouldn't want you to starve."

"Don't worry about that. I'll be cooking in the afternoon – great way to spend the Day of Rest, right? – and I'll have to sample my dishes to make sure they can be served to others. And if I time it right, I'll be done in time to go to the movies Saturday night and fill up on popcorn."

"Your nutritional choices are astounding, Aviva. Not that I can talk. Anyway, I'll see you tomorrow."

I listened to the radio on my way home, and the news about John Quincy Moorhouse's hit-and-run death was one of the lead items. Earlier, the accident was on the news, but not the identity of the victim. Obviously, the police had notified his family.

I had just pulled into my parking spot at the synagogue (the "Reserved for Rabbi: Thou Shalt Not Park" sign was a lot more polite than the "Don't even think about parking here" signs I had seen elsewhere), when my cell phone rang again. If I didn't need the calendar function, I would dump the damned thing into the nearest trash compactor. I knew I was always on-call, but I hated not even having the excuse that I wasn't near a phone. I know, I could turn it off or claim there was no reception or my battery was drained, but lying makes me feel guilty. Not often, but sometimes.

The caller I.D. said, "Meisner-Finkel," and my cheerful, "Hey, there" was answered by a growl.

"You knew, didn't you? You knew when you came by last night that Moorhouse was dead, and you thought I had done it, didn't you? That's why you were so interested in how my car got damaged, wasn't it? How could you? How could you suspect me, Aviva? I thought you knew me better. I'm so angry and hurt I can hardly talk. In fact, you're the last person I want to talk to." And, to punctuate the point, she slammed down the phone. If I hadn't known from the caller I.D. that she had been using a land-line, I would have known by my sore ear. Cell phones can't be slammed. Well, maybe they can, but they're not usable afterwards.

I stared at the screen on the phone, as though my thoughts would penetrate it and fly through the ether into Sherry's brain. I didn't realize my mouth was open until my throat became dry. I shook my head and blinked (and closed my mouth) and dragged myself into the building. No one was there, which was fortunate because there's no way I could have pretended to be okay. I slumped into my desk chair, which skidded backwards and banged the wall. I decided it was my punishment for having thought exactly what Sherry thought I had thought.

I had to put a good spin on what had occurred last night, or I had a feeling I wasn't going to be welcome at the seder. My kugels and cookies would be, but I wouldn't. I decided to be a coward and call Trudy instead of Sherry.

"What the hell do you want?" Trudy has my office phone on her caller I.D., and she didn't even bother to pretend to be polite and say "whazzup" when she picked up the phone.

"Listen, Trudy, I came over last night because I was worried. I knew someone had been run over in front of Sherry's office, and I thought she had gone there to clear out her stuff and she was the victim. And then I called and Lynda said she wasn't home, so I came over to see what was happening."

"Good try, but the only way you could have known is if Steve told you while you were having dinner together. There's no way it would have taken you so long to get from the Diner to our house. If you had come over right after finding out, you would have been at our place within fifteen minutes, not ninety. You went with Steve to the scene, didn't you? And you knew exactly who was dead before you got to our house, right? And your first reaction was to suspect Sherry. How could you, Aviva?"

I don't know why I even try to fake out someone who got into Mensa with one of the highest scores ever. "You're right, Trudy. Almost, anyway. I never believed Sherry would deliberately run someone down. Even if she had threatened to the night before." I would have bitten my tongue to keep myself from saying that last sentence if I hadn't blurted it before thinking.

"And did you tell Steve all about that little off-hand comment?"

"Of course not! All I told him was that Sherry had gotten forced out of her job, and that the only reason I knew Moorhouse's name was because he was the one who had done it. I would never say anything to endanger Sherry. You know that."

"But revealing even that much was putting Sherry on their radar. And why wouldn't you say something to Steve? After all, you and your ex-hubby are getting awfully chummy again."

"No we're not. We're just friends. We never stopped being friends. It's just that we never saw each other when he lived in Princeton Junction. (*And was married.*) Listen, different topic – well, maybe the same one – I'm making the kugels and meringue cookies tomorrow. When should I bring them over? That is, if I'm still welcomed in your house."

"Do you swear you didn't suspect Sherry?"

I crossed my fingers, a distinctly non-Jewish symbol, but I'll do anything to get back into my niece's good graces, especially when food is involved. "Yes."

She sighed. "Okay, then, I guess you can still come to the seder. But give Sherry a chance to calm down. Stop by Sunday."

"Saturday night's easier for me – I have a wedding Sunday afternoon."

"Who gets married the day before Pesach?"

"Someone whose honeymoon is on a cruise ship that includes a seder."

"Sounds nice. Okay, come over on Saturday then, but call first."

"Am I forgiven?"

"I thought you said you hadn't done anything wrong."

"Am I forgiven for what you thought I had done?"

"We'll see. Hang on a sec." She must have put her hand over the mouthpiece because all could hear was a muffled, "Josh, stop screaming. I'm on the phone. What's so important that you came into my study without permission? You know you're not allowed in here when the door is closed."

Josh's voice was so loud that I probably could have heard it even without the medium of a phone. "But MomT, you've got to come out right away! MomS said so. There's a police car! And two cops! With guns and everything! Well, one has a gun. One is wearing a suit like a regular guy, but he has a badge and told MomS he's a detective somebody. Come on!"

If I didn't know Trudy so well, I would have thought she was angry. But I could hear the fear in her voice as she got back to me. "Okay, Aviva," she said softly, "what did you tell Steve? The truth now. Why are the cops here?"

"I swear, I didn't tell him anything except Moorhouse had fired Sherry. That's all." I think that was all. I really didn't remember. My emotions had been in such a state at the time, first thinking Sherry had been run over and then finding out it was someone she had wished dead only the night before.

"If you're lying ..." I've no idea what dire threat she was going to utter, as the line went dead.

CHAPTER NINETEEN

"You fucking coward!" I screamed into the phone. "Stop hiding behind your voice mail. You know it's me. Pick up." I waited. "Fine, be like that. 'Promising leads?' Why didn't you tell me one of them was Sherry? Never mind, I know why. Because you knew one of the courses at the seder would have been your head on a platter. Don't worry. I would have figured out how to slaughter you so you were kosher. Don't bother to call back. I'm too mad at you. And forget tomorrow. I really am not interested in whatever it is you have to say. Unless it's an abject apology, coupled with ... I don't know what. I'll think of something appropriately expensive. And you had better think of how you're going to make it up to Trudy and Sherry. *Shmuck.*"

I couldn't believe Steve hadn't warned me. Okay, I could. At least rationally I could understand that he couldn't tell me they would be questioning Sherry. But emotionally, I meant every word I had said in the message.

"Well, you certainly told him off." I hadn't heard my secretary Liz come in. "Although your language was certainly un-Rabbinic, I'm sure you got your point across. Want to tell me about it?"

"What are you doing here? I thought you had left for the day."

"The bakery called to say they were going to be late with the delivery, so I came back to let them in. Now, don't change the subject: what's happening?"

I sighed. I do that a lot when I'm upset. Or frustrated. Or thinking. Or tired. Okay, I just sigh a lot. "It's a long story. And I've got a lot to do."

Now Liz sighed. I guess it's as contagious as yawning. "No you don't. I mean, you do, but it's just routine stuff you can finish in a few minutes. You know you always feel better after you talk out a problem."

I sighed again and leaned back in my chair. "I'll try to condense it. Sherry got fired yesterday. Well, downsized anyway. Her job's being taken over by a new dean, a Ph.D. in psychology who used to work in the field. They told her she could stay on as a part-time administrator and as a per diem, which means lousy pay and no benefits, so she walked out. Last night, the guy was killed in a hit-and-run and now the police are at Sherry's door."

"That's not the Reader's Digest version. It's the short abstract version. I suspect there's a lot more to the story or you wouldn't be so angry at ... who were you leaving the message for? Dr. Goldfarb?" Only Liz would use Steve's professional academic title. Most people in Walford call him the "Chief," even though it's not his official designation. He's the Interim Director of Public Safety. "Chief" is simpler.

"Yes, it was him. And, yes, there is a lot more to the story, but it's too complicated to go into. Let's just say that Trudy and Sherry think I said something to Steve to tip him off."

"Tip him off to what? And did you?"

"The only thing I told him is that the victim had fired Sherry. I didn't tell him that Sherry was angrier than I've ever seen her. She loved her job, and she was good at it – better than good, and has the annual job review evaluations to prove it. She was really hurt that they treated her like ... like ... I don't know ... like a temp without even a GED."

Liz stared at the wall over my shoulder, a sure sign she was trying to recall something. "Wait a minute. I think I heard about the hit-and-run on the news. Moorhouse, right? I thought I recognized the name, but they didn't say what his profession was. If he's who I think he is, there should be no shortage of suspects. He used to have a practice around here, oh, maybe twenty-five years ago. Adolescent psychologist. He left the area under a cloud. There were vague rumors of some kind of improprieties, maybe sexual abuse, but never proved. It was the talk of the teachers' lounge – the high school and middle school shared the same building back then, and the schools used him as our in-house counselor. ADHD was the trendy diagnosis, and he positioned himself as an expert. Yes, it's coming back to me now. And it wasn't ADHD – his specialty was eating disorders, so most of his clients were young women. Skinny young women who thought they were fat, with the occasional fat one who thought she could lose weight by throwing up. He was in his mid-thirties then, very good looking with that devastating combination of dark hair and blue eyes. And dimples. The teenage girls all had crushes on him and, according to the scuttlebutt, he knew it and took advantage of the impressionable ones. Which at that age is all of them."

"I wonder why Triple-U hired him with that background."

"As far as I know, he was never charged with any crime. In fact, when some girls came forward with their accusations, the parents refused to believe them, saying they were acting out. I found one of the young women crying in a back stack. She told me her mother had slapped her for making things up and her father refused to talk to her. Then Moorhouse spoke at a teachers meeting and said he had heard the rumors and the 'truth' was the girls had a classic case of transference and when he rebuffed their advances, they colluded to accuse him of abusing them. I wasn't the only one who doubted his version, and at the end of the school year, he left Walford and relocated, I think to California. I guess he thought enough time had passed that it was safe to return." She took a breath and continued. "After all this time, you would think I wouldn't be upset, but I am. Whenever I'm upset, I use run-on sentences. And I didn't even know any of the young women, so imagine how they must still feel."

"I wonder if the police know about his background. It might take the heat off Sherry if they look at who around here has a long memory. When I see Steve, I'll suggest he check and see which of Moorhouse's teenage patients are still in the area. Sexual abuse is a better motive than being fired."

"After that message you left Dr. Goldfarb, do you really think he'll want to talk to you?"

"Yeah, he's used to my tirades. You should have heard the things I called him when we were still married."

"Probably why you're no longer married." Liz said under her breath but just loudly enough for me to hear. When I looked at her, she gave me a beatific smile.

"Don't you have filing to do or whatever it is you do that makes you so invaluable around here?"

She grinned broadly, gave a wave, and left my office. Actually, she left the building, which meant the bakery had delivered the pastries before Liz came into my office. I stared at my phone, then at my computer screen. Neither of them could answer my questions, and I wasn't in the mood to have people hang up on me or ignore my emails, so I went to light the *yahrzeit* board and raid the evening's goodies.

CHAPTER TWENTY

I quickly finished what I needed to do (the pastries passed inspection), and left to take care of my errands and pick up the perishables I would need to do my cooking on the weekend. I thought these would be mindless tasks that would help me zone out and forget what was going on, but, of course, my mind wouldn't switch off. It didn't help when I bumped into Janet Brauner, Mishkan Or's resident yenta, at Produce Junction. Without her, I would know only a fraction of what I knew about my congregants' private lives.

"Rabbi Cohen, cutting it pretty close to the beginning of Shabbat, aren't you?"

"Oh, hi, Janet." I pretended I had been engrossed in examining the various bags of dried fruit, hoping she wouldn't notice me. It's amazing how fascinating the different types of apricots can be when you want to avoid talking with someone. Once Janet got started, I would be lucky if I got out in time to get to the supermarket and make it to services by eight o'clock.

I glanced at my watch. "It's only two o'clock. I have plenty of time before Shabbat starts," I said, actually dismayed at just how late it was.

"Well, you know best, I suppose. I'm glad to see you, though. There's something important I need to talk to you about."

Oh, great. I may not finish up in time. I grabbed a bag of raisins and got into line to pick up the onions and eggs; I would then have to move to a second line for the apples. I really wasn't interested in hearing about whose child had been caught cheating on a test, or whose spouse had been caught cheating, period. But I was still leery after the morning's meeting about my job performance, so I was gracious. I hope. "I hope it's not bad news, Janet."

"Well, I don't know how 'bad' it is, but it is distressing. You know, don't you, that the Fishers and I are – were – best friends?"

If everyone Janet claimed as a best friend really was, she was the most popular person on the planet.

"No, I didn't realize you were close. I'm sorry for your loss."

"Thank you. I'm very distressed about, well, about everything. Nothing makes sense about their deaths. The news report said they didn't have a carbon monoxide detector, but I'm sure they did. In fact, I know they did – we bought ours at the same time and talked with them about the best types. And I know their dryer worked okay. The vent on mine got clogged, and I called and told Florence to get hers checked out. She said she had someone look at it just a few weeks before after her clothes wouldn't dry. Turns out the vent was fine: she had set the temperature dial on low and forgot to reset it to medium. This whole thing is odd."

Ah, hah! I knew it was. "Did you let anyone know? The fire marshal? The police?"

"No, but I did say something to their daughter. And that's another thing – Audrey is acting abominably. I mean, I know she and her parents had their disagreements, but I thought she had gotten over her adolescent rebellion. After all, she's in her forties! But she's having no funeral, no memorial service, no *shiva*, and she's having them cremated! Can't you talk to her and let her know that even if she's not mourning her parents, their friends are?"

"I don't know Audrey. She moved out of the area before I got here, and we have met maybe once or twice. I don't recall her at all. And I can't imagine that she would listen to anything I have to say." I looked at my watch openly this time. "I don't want to be rude, Janet, but I have to stop at the supermarket on the way home and, as you said, it's getting late." I paused to give my order to the clerk. As I was paying, I said to Janet, "I would like to talk to you more, but it may have to wait a couple of days, what with Shabbat and a wedding on Sunday, and then Pesach."

"The Caplan-Pinsky wedding? I'll be there, too. Maybe we can talk during the reception. That is, if the band's not too loud."

Somehow, I managed not to roll my eyes. I hope. "Great. I'll see you then, Janet. *Shabbat Shalom.*"

"Oh, you'll see me before then. Phil and I will be at services tonight and tomorrow. You know we always attend."

"I do know, Janet, and it's wonderful to know that we can count on the two of you to help make a *minyan.* Pun intended."

She looked puzzled, but wouldn't admit she didn't understand my reference. I explained, "We count ten for a *minyan* and we can count on you to be there. Don't worry. It was a pretty weak joke. Anyway, I'll see you in a few hours."

Very few hours. I still had to get to the supermarket to pick up Passover yogurt, milk, cheese, non-dairy margarine, and whatever else struck my fancy, or my stomach. I knew I still had Sunday, either before or after the wedding, and Monday until sundown to finish my shopping, but I needed the margarine for the kugels. I may as well save myself another trip and get everything today.

The supermarket was as crowed as usual for a Friday afternoon, but I somehow got what I needed and made it home in time to make a couple of calls before taking a shower and stretching out on the couch to read the morning paper. I don't know why I bother to get the paper, as by the time I read it, I've already heard most of the news on the radio or read it on the Internet. But there is still something satisfying about getting through the whole thing and turning to the back pages to read the comics.

The first call I made was to Steve. Or, rather, to his voice mail. I strongly suspected he was screening his calls. Considering the message I had left him earlier, I didn't blame him.

"Steve, listen. I promise I won't yell this time. I found out something important today about John Quincy Moorhouse, something that might set you and your bloodhounds on a scent other than my niece's life partner. When he had a practice here twenty-five years or so ago, he worked with the schools and treated a lot of teenage girls. According to a very reliable source – okay, it was Liz, and you can't get more reliable than Liz – it was common knowledge that he was sexually abusing his adolescent female students. At least I think it was only the females. And it was more of a suspicion than actual knowledge. Anyway, I'm rambling here, but I think you guys should check and see if any of the women who accused him of rape then are still around. Apparently, none of them were believed, so they would certainly still have a major grudge against him. And the schools. And their parents. And ... okay, I'm rambling again. Bring tuna hoagies and fries for lunch. Forget the fries; get chips instead. And get the hoagies from Lee's. They know how I like mine. We'll have a picnic in the living room, unless it's warm enough to sit on the deck. Which it won't be. I know – rambling. *Shabbat Shalom.*"

The second call was to Trudy and Sherry. All I got was a busy signal. They have both call waiting and an answering machine, so they must have pulled the plug on the landline. Calls to both of their cell phones went to voice mail, and Sherry's was full. I wondered if the press had heard she was a suspect. No, I didn't wonder; I knew. Fortunately, I had a number I doubted if any of the media knew.

"Lynda, hi. It's Aviva ... yeah, I know I'm *persona non grata*, but I doubt they would fire you if they knew you had taken my call. I couldn't get through on the other phones. Listen, I've got some important information, so put one of them on the phone, please. Preferably Trudy, because it will involve a computer search."

I heard Lynda grumble something about not getting paid enough as she went to find Trudy. Her family was far from wealthy, and I hoped she didn't decide to sell her "first-person-from-the-inside" story to a tabloid in exchange for tuition payments. Grad school's not cheap, even at a state university.

"This had better be important. You're not entirely forgiven yet."

"You mean I'm partially forgiven?"

"Well," Trudy sounded very reluctant to continue, "it turns out the police got their tip from Triple-U. Sherry's co-workers were very eager to let the police know that she had been stomping around the department telling everyone she saw that she was ready to commit murder, but only after slow and extremely painful torture. She didn't specify the victim, but everyone knew she had been meeting with the dean and Moorhouse just before she knocked over the wall of a cubicle she punched. If the dean shows up dead, Sherry's really in trouble."

"You mean she's not in trouble?"

Trudy hesitated so long I thought the connection had dropped. "I don't know. The police took Sherry's car. It fits the description of the one seen by the witnesses. Aviva," Trudy's voice dropped to a whisper, "I'm really scared. What if Sherry was lying about how the car got damaged?"

"Now, stop it, Trudy. You know Sherry would never do anything to hurt someone else." I wondered if Trudy realized she and I had just reversed roles, with her being doubtful and my assuring her that Sherry was innocent.

"You're right. I know you are. But ... Lynda said you had something important to tell me. What is it?"

"Get on the computer and use some of your illegal or quasi-legal or sources not available to mere mortals and find out everything you can about Moorhouse. Liz told me that when he left Walford in the late seventies or early eighties, he had been accused by some patients of sexual improprieties. By teenage patients. Any of them still in the area would have plenty of reason to want revenge. And, yes, before you ask, I did call and leave a message for Steve."

"Steve wasn't the one here. It was Lieutenant Merino. Maybe they feel Steve knows us too well. Not that it makes any difference. Merino knows us, too. Anyway, I'm sure Steve will pass your message along."

Unless they've already decided Sherry's guilty and don't investigate further. Trudy didn't need me to voice my concern. I'm sure she shared it. And we both knew the Walford police had a history of making up their minds and ignoring contradictory evidence.

"I'm sure he will, Trudy, and I'll make sure of it when I see him tomorrow. If I see him. I left him a pretty scathing message for having even considered the possibility Sherry could have anything to do with the hit-and-run."

"Seeing him tomorrow? Oh, never mind. You'll tell me about it when we wake up from this nightmare. In the meantime, thanks for the lead. I'll check it out. And if I find out anything, tell Liz I owe her lunch. In fact, tell her I do anyway. Even if it doesn't pan out, it's another direction to search."

We ended the call on a good note, with my promise to stop by on the weekend with my contributions to the seder. I really hoped we would be having a seder.

My third call was to the Walford Fire Chief. It went to his voice mail, and I explained I wanted to discuss the Fishers' deaths and that I would call him again on Monday.

I took my shower and made the mistake of stretching out on the bed instead of the couch to read the paper. I fell asleep somewhere in the middle of an article about how the army was recruiting video gamers. I was dreaming about how the war in Afghanistan now going to be called *Ender's Game* when Cat pounced on my stomach, having discovered the Philadelphia *Inquirer* covering it made great crinkling noises that reminded him of mice. I've no idea how he would know what a mouse sounded like, since he had never seen one. Recognition of mouse squeaks must be hardwired into the feline brain.

I couldn't yell at Cat for waking me, though, for, once again, he had prevented me from being late. Despite my brain's being in its usual post-nap muddle – it was now three naps in three days; maybe it was time to call the doctor for a checkup – the admonitions about my choice of clothing were vivid in my mind as I stood in front of my closet. I chose a dark skirt and subtly patterned sweater. How boring.

I was looking forward to services, hoping the familiar ritual would lull me into a sense of peace. I needed to meditate myself into a place where Trudy and Sherry could get legally married, where Sherry had a job she loved and wasn't a murder suspect, where daughters loved their parents when alive and gave them respect and dignity after their deaths, where all my friends and colleagues made the right decisions and were happy in their personal and professional lives, and where I could wear jeans to work.

It wasn't to be.

CHAPTER TWENTY-ONE

Services were fairly well attended, mainly because it was the first appearance of one of our cantor Ron Finegold's experiments to encourage group participation in the service. It was called "*Mishpachot Shirot*," Families Sing, but it wasn't a traditional choir: no one stood in front of the congregation performing, there were no solos or microphones, and a good singing voice was not a requirement. Anyone who wanted could join: we defined "family" very broadly, figuring everyone had parents at some point, so everyone was part of a family. The only criteria were a loud voice and enthusiasm. He then scattered the singers throughout the room, with the idea that everyone else would join in when they heard the others singing. I thought it was a terrific idea, but I still planned to mouth the words. I did have a microphone, along with the world's worst singing voice. Ron may not mind off-key singing, but I do, when I'm the one doing the singing.

We – or, rather, they – were well into a rousing rendition of *Lecha Dodi*, a medieval mystical song welcoming the Sabbath Bride, when the door opened and a couple quietly took seats in the back. I had to squint to make sure – I was past due to visit the optometrist – but it was definitely Ben and Sandy. I caught Ben's eye and nodded to let him know I had seen them, but my curiosity about their presence would have to wait until the service concluded.

Up until then, I was beginning to relax and temporarily blank my mind to all but the service, but Ben and Sandy's presence jolted me out of my peaceful reverie. Why were they here? Were they spying on me to find out how much I knew, or suspected? Were they (or Sandy at the very least) going to make veiled threats to keep me from talking about the wedding? Was I becoming increasingly and irrationally paranoid?

Ron's experiment was a success, but I never did get into a state of bliss, or whatever. Instead, I was edgy and distracted. I doubt if anyone noticed – I had been doing the services for so long, I was on autopilot. But my discussion that evening on the origins of April Fools' Day and its connections with Purim (yeah, I was a month late) and the popularity of vernal equinox celebrations in many cultures was too much fun for me not to enjoy. I particularly liked the story about the history professor who, in nineteen eighty-three, publicized his theory that April Fools' Day originated when Constantine allowed his court jester to rule the empire for the day. The punch line is that the professor's story was itself a hoax, a perfect example of an April Fools' Day joke. And the Jewish connection (and probably a tipoff that the story was a fabrication): the jester's name was Kugel.

During the announcements following the Mourners' Kaddish and before the closing hymn (*Adon Olam*, which despite its serious meaning, is often sung to the melody of a pop tune), I publically welcomed Ben and Sandy to our community. I noticed Janet looked startled when she heard the name and then looked around to match it to a face. After the services, she stood impatiently waiting for the others who wanted to greet me to leave, then took me aside. I looked longingly at the table with the rapidly disappearing éclairs and was glad I had sampled one (okay, two) earlier.

"Why do I know the name Rabbi Benjamin Bronfman? I've heard of him before, and not in connection with B'rith Abraham."

"I'm not sure, Janet. We were classmates, but he hasn't lived on the East Coast in a while. His current pulpit is in Eugene, Oregon."

Whoops. Janet's face is pretty readable and the satisfied nod she gave told me she had figured out how she knew the name. "Of course. Eugene. I heard about him from Florence. He did the wedding. I wonder if he'll pay a condolence visit to Audrey and convince her she's making a mistake not to have a full funeral and sit *shiva*."

"I really don't think he'll have the time. I think he's going back as soon as Shabbat's over. And I doubt if he had any connections with Audrey except for the wedding." I did know they were staying until after the seders with Sandy's parents, but I didn't want Janet to have the chance to let them realize just how many people locally may have heard about the wedding. Although it still wasn't clear if anyone knew George wasn't Jewish. From the little I knew of Florence – and the even less I knew of her husband, Milton – as thrilled as she had been that Audrey had gotten married, she hadn't been thrilled that Audrey had "married out."

Janet's next words let me know I had underestimated Florence's acceptance of Audrey's marriage to a non-Jew. "Florence was overjoyed they found a rabbi. After you said you wouldn't do the ceremony – and, by the way, I don't care what anyone else says, you were right – she was worried they would have to use a justice of the peace. It's just not the same, though, without a *chuppah*."

"What anyone else says"? After today's job assessment, I was sensitive to every nuance of every criticism or even casual comment. But I had bigger worries. I caught a faint gasp to my left and looked over to see a pale Ben and glaring Sandy standing within earshot. I didn't know how much they had overheard, but obviously it was enough. Or, rather, too much.

I tried to act nonchalant. "Ben and Sandy! *Shabbat Shalom*! What a surprise to see you here tonight! I'm honored."

"I did a service tonight at B'rith Abraham. It was an early one – a lot of the congregants don't like to drive late at night – and it was over early enough for us to be able to come here and see you." Ben was talking to me, but he kept glancing at Janet, who stood expectantly by my side.

"I hope you enjoyed our service," said Janet. I should have known better than to think she would leave without my having to introduce her to Ben and Sandy. I didn't have to introduce them, though; Janet introduced herself. "Janet Brauner. And you must be Rabbi Bronfman and this is ...?"

"Oh, um, this is my wife, Sandy." The three shook hands. Janet was oblivious to their body language, Ben broadcasting discomfort and Sandy defiance.

It didn't help when Janet added, "I know all about you from Florence Fisher. Such a tragedy. I'm sure you heard all about it?" She continued after Ben and Sandy nodded. "You know, Florence was my best friend. We lived next door to each other for years, until they bought the house in Serenity Acres – dumb name, sounds more like a cemetery than an active-adult community – oh! That was an insensitive comment." Janet giggled nervously, but recovered quickly. "It was strange not to live next to them, and the people who bought their house, well, a lovely young couple, but so *young* and with two toddlers who make an infernal racket all day with their Tyke Trikes or whatever they're called. I've been thinking Phil and I should move to Serenity Acres. Our house is really too big for the two of us, and I wish Phil would stop fixing things and just take it easy. Plus, a house a few doors down from the Fishers just went on the market – the husband died of a stroke and the wife moved to Chicago to be closer to her son – and, talk about coincidences, my sister Charlotte – you remember my sister Charlotte Silver, don't you, Rabbi Cohen? Oh, of course, you do. She used to live next door to Marilyn Phillips, the one who lost her daughter, and she went with you to clear out Madison's dorm room during that whole unfortunate incident last year – um, where was I? Oh, yes, Charlotte bought the house across the street from the Fishers only a few months ago. In fact, I was staying there the night the Fishers ... er, died .... The sound of the emergency vehicles woke me up only a couple of hours after I had finally fallen asleep. I hadn't slept well. I never do in a strange bed, but Charlotte's husband went to some kind of convention or something and she doesn't like to stay alone ...."

Janet must have realized she had been rambling on too long, because she suddenly stopped. I thought at first she had remembered something, but if she had, she would have just tacked on another sentence. Maybe she had just run out of breath.

If she had, she quickly replenished her lungs. It was surprising that Janet, after years of smoking, didn't run out of breath more often. I realized I hadn't seen her sneak out for a smoke the whole evening; Shabbat or not, she still managed to feed her addiction. Maybe she had finally quit. She claimed she had after a bout of lung cancer followed by a heart attack, but I had my doubts. I stopped the needless speculation to focus in on what she was saying. For some reason, she had changed the topic.

"So, Rabbi Bronfman, what did you think of Cantor Finegold's choice of tune for *Adon Olam?*"

"Interesting. I don't think I've ever heard it sung to "Yellow Submarine" before."

"You'll find we do a lot of things here they don't do at B'rith Abraham." Janet paused. "Although Rabbi Cohen is a lot more traditional in some ways than people realize."

Janet gave Ben a seemingly innocent smile, but I knew what was behind it. So did he, judging from the way he gulped. Sandy's glare was so icy it could have caused frost bite. But then Sandy did something unexpected: she smiled. To anyone who didn't know her, the smile seemed gracious. To me, it seemed predatory. Then she launched surprise number two. Looking straight at Janet, she said, "I'm going to get some coffee. May I get anyone something to drink?"

"Why, thank you, dear," Janet answered. "I do believe I would like some coffee. We serve only decaf, though, so if you're looking for high octane, you're out of luck. Please put a largish amount of skimmed milk in it for me." She looked at the rest of us. "I would much prefer half-and-half, but my doctor has me on a strict regimen. If it tastes good, I can't have it." She giggled at her own joke, but after her heart attack last year, it wasn't a joke.

"Nothing for me, thanks," I answered. Sandy ignored me. Ben didn't seem to have heard Sandy, or maybe she already knew her husband's answer.

While Sandy went to get the coffee, Ben and Janet made small talk. Or, rather, Janet did. Ben just smiled and nodded. I looked over at the table where the coffee urn was, and thought I saw Sandy put her hand into her pocket and add something to one of the coffee cups she had filled. I mentally shrugged; we had probably run out of artificial sweetener again and she used her own. I thought nothing more about it. Then.

"Um, Janet, excuse us, please. I want to introduce the Bronfmans to Meryl before she leaves."

As we walked away, Sandy hissed in my ear (she had to bend almost in half to reach it), "I thought you said you hadn't told anyone."

"I didn't. Didn't you hear Janet say she had heard about Ben from the Fishers? I had no idea they were such close friends. And, no, before you ask, I don't know who else they may have told. My suggestion is don't volunteer any information; in fact, just smile and avoid answering any questions or comments others make. It will blow over. It's no big deal."

"Yes, it is a big deal, Aviva. Ben's professional reputation is at stake." *What professional reputation? As a screw up?*

If B'rith Abraham had done its research properly, which was doubtful, they would have known that Ben wasn't the best candidate out there. But maybe he was the only one desperate enough to accept them.

"Aviva's right, Sandy. Let's not make a big deal of it, and maybe it will blow over."

Sandy turned her glare on him now. If she kept this up, no amount of Botox would ever erase her scowl lines. "Right, blow over, just like every other time you've done something stupid."

As we walked across the room, I tried think of a way to get Ben by himself so I could figure out if he had been involved with the Fishers' deaths, or if he knew anything about whether Sandy was involved. "What are you doing tomorrow?" I directed my question to Ben, ignoring Sandy.

"I'll be conducting services at B'rith Abraham."

"They're getting a free weekend out of Ben. But at least we got them to agree to pay for our transportation for this visit, as well as our moving expenses this summer." I didn't tell Sandy it was fairly standard for a congregation to pay moving expenses. One of the reasons I didn't tell her is because I wasn't sure it was standard. I had never moved farther than fifteen miles to change jobs, and didn't have all that much to move in any case, with the exception of a back breaking number of cartons of books. Members of Mishkan Or hired a U-Haul and helped me schlep everything from my Center City apartment to my new townhouse. I had no idea what it would cost to move a household from Eugene to Walford. The other reason I didn't say anything is that if I were wrong, Sandy would know and counter with statistics about rabbinic contracts.

"That's great." I glanced briefly at Sandy and turned back to Ben. "Why don't you come by my place for lunch after services? It will give you a chance to see Steve again. He's coming by with tuna-cheese hoagies, not exactly a traditional Shabbat luncheon, but all I can offer this close to Pesach."

"I'll be at my parents' house helping them clean for Pesach," Sandy interrupted. "Ben will just be in the way, so he can go alone." I guess I was too subtle in addressing the invitation to Ben only. And the poor guy – after thirty-plus years of marriage, he still needed her permission. Maybe Sandy saw him as the substitute for the children they had never had. When I had the time, or interest, I would try to figure out how much Sandy's childless state had influenced her brash personality. Probably not at all, as she had always been obnoxious, even as a newlywed.

"I'll take you up on the invitation then, Aviva, especially if it will get me out of washing the dusty Pesach dishes. It will be nice to talk with Steve."

"Be sure to ask him about the condo. I don't want there to be any surprises, like a leaky roof or noisy neighbors. Or nosy ones."

"Sandy, I really would prefer not to discuss business on Shabbat. I'm sure those questions can wait until another time."

We reached Meryl just as she was going to the coat room. "Meryl, wait up. I would like to introduce you to B'rith Abraham's new rabbi and his wife. Rabbi Benjamin Bronfman, Sandy Bronfman, this is our president Meryl Felsner."

"Oh, hello, I heard about you from Rabbi Cohen. We're looking forward to your joining our community. I hope our two synagogues will be able to cooperate on some programs."

Meryl is certainly diplomatic when necessary. After all, she was the one who had put the kibosh on that same idea when I had suggested it at breakfast. But it's good idea for Mishkan Or's morale to think we had made overtures and been turned down by the narrow-mindedness of B'rith Abraham. I doubted if it would ever get to that stage though. Chances are the idea of joint programs would never be broached again.

Meryl had to get home to her kids – the eight-year-old twins were too rambunctious to take to services, her husband was away, and the twelve year old's babysitting skills were just enough to keep her from being hog-tied and dumped into the basement by her younger siblings. I took Ben and Sandy around and introduced them to a few others Ben needed to meet. Knowing him, though, he would have forgotten their names immediately even if he hadn't been distracted by worries.

Ben was chatting with Ron about various tunes for *Adon Olam*, when Janet pulled me aside. "I need to talk with you. There's something I forgot to tell you and I think it's important. And it's private. Let's go into the kitchen."

The kitchen was far from private, but the chatter of the volunteers as they cleared up after the Oneg, plus the clatter of the dishes they were washing and the rush of water into two sinks provided enough background noise to drown out any private conversation.

"Remember I said I was staying at my sister's the night the Fishers were killed? I mean, they died?"

I nodded. Nothing else was required of me.

"And I said I had trouble sleeping? Well, at about one in the morning, I decided to look out the window. No particular reason why. I just did. Charlotte and Marty bought a two-story model, which seemed crazy to me at the time. Why downsize and go into an active adult community if you're going to buy a two-story house? But they said they needed the extra space upstairs for when the grandchildren visit. So far, I'm the only one who's stayed there, but Charlotte and Marty haven't lived there all that long. Anyway, the guest room is in the front of the house, and I was looking out the window. Oh, I already said that didn't I? Well, the Fishers' garage door was open and their car was in there. Which was strange because they never put the car in the garage. We always joked with them about why they had a garage filled with boxes instead of cars. And it's not as though they have lawn mowers or snow blowers or kids' toys taking up space. The homeowners' association takes care of the lawns and the snow clearing and kids under nineteen aren't allowed. So I noticed there was a car in their garage. I thought maybe it was Audrey's. I couldn't see it clearly, and I don't recognize car models in any case. Too bad Phil hadn't come with me. He would have figured it out. I was worried the door was open so late at night, and debated if I should call the Fishers and let them know or if they'd be angry I had woken them. But if they got robbed, I would feel guilty I hadn't. So I wondered if I should call the police. But then the garage door closed – someone must have pushed the button for the automatic opener from inside the house – so I didn't have to worry about it."

I wanted to look at my watch without her noticing, but she wasn't taking her eyes off mine. I stifled a yawn. I was sure the story had an end, but I wasn't sure how long it would take. Or what the point was that Janet was trying to make.

"So, I went back to bed (*Lucky you. I wish that's where I was right now.*), but now I feel guilty that I didn't call. Maybe whoever put the car in the garage so late at night was too tired to remember to turn off the engine. Maybe the Fishers wouldn't have died if I had called. Do you know what time they died?"

"No, I don't. I know George found them when he stopped by with a carbon monoxide alarm for them – ironic, huh? – so that must have been late enough in the morning for him to have gotten to a store to buy one."

I stopped as I thought of something that didn't make sense. "But I heard the news early Tuesday morning. Maybe he bought it on Monday and didn't get a chance to bring it over then. Talk about feeling guilty! I can't imagine what he must be feeling."

"If Audrey's behavior is any indication, he's not feeling much of anything. She certainly isn't grieving."

"The timing just doesn't make sense. I'm going to have to think about it some more when I'm less tired."

"Why don't you tell the police and let them know what I saw. Let them figure it out."

"Why me, Janet? Why don't you tell them?"

"Because they already know you. Me, they'll ignore as a silly old lady. But you, well, you've already shown them that they make mistakes."

"Precisely. I'm not sure I'm exactly their favorite person. Besides,

I think it's the fire department, not the police, who is in charge of the investigation. If there even is an investigation; I think they've decided it was accidental. And nothing you've said indicates it wasn't."

"The car in the garage does. I told you, they never kept the car in the garage. Obviously, someone drove it in there and left the engine running to kill the Fishers."

"But the investigators found the car engine cool and the tank full."

"So figure out how it could have been done. You're good at that. Then you can get the fire department to change its mind. You got the police to change theirs."

It was getting crowded in the kitchen as people came in to pack up the leftovers. Beginning at sundown Saturday and lasting all day Sunday, the kitchen was going to be emptied out and scrubbed for Passover.

"Let's go back into the social hall, Janet. People may be looking for me. I'll think about what you said and get back to you."

As we walked back into the social hall, Janet grabbed my arm and pointed her chin toward the door. "Looks like you'll be able to get things rolling now."

There at the door was my old "friend," Lieutenant Joe Merino, Steve's second-in-command. I had come to like Joe, but I wasn't sure the feeling was reciprocated. Actually, I was sure it wasn't, and his presence wasn't a good sign. I didn't think I had done anything to be arrested for, but I couldn't be certain that Joe hadn't come up with something. He had never really forgiven me for having, as Janet put it, changed his mind.

CHAPTER TWENTY-TWO

"Lieutenant Merino, hello. What brings you here this evening? I'm afraid services are over, but I can probably get you something from the kitchen, coffee or cake, if you would like. And for you, Officer ...?" Sindone was it? Or Ryan? I had met him before, the previous year when the police had responded to two separate burglar alarms on the same night, but I couldn't remember which of the two officers he was.

"Um, Ryan, Ma'am. And it's Sergeant now. I took the test last month and passed. First try." He looked as proud as a high school kid who had gotten a date with the prom queen. And he looked about the same age.

"Congratulations, Sergeant Ryan. So, may I get anything for either of you gentlemen?" I was being on my best behavior. My sister would have been proud of me. My mother would have been appalled that I was cozying up to, as she would put it, "the pigs."

"We're not here on a social visit, Rabbi." Merino gave Ryan a look that warned he wouldn't be a sergeant much longer if he accepted my offer. "Sorry to bother you on your Sabbath, but is there some place we can talk in private?"

"Can't it wait until tomorrow night? It is the Sabbath, as you said, and it's late. I've had a long day and was about to go home."

"No, it can't wait. You know we're investigating a hit-and-run murder and you may have some information we could use."

I acted innocent. "I did hear something about a hit-and-run, but murder? I mean, wouldn't it be vehicular homicide or manslaughter or something?"

"That's for the District Attorney to decide, but don't try to sidetrack the subject, Rabbi. I'm well aware of your knowledge about the case." He barely suppressed a smirk as he continued, "I heard the voice mail you left the Chief."

"Yeah, well, he deserved it. I mean, he knows Sherry better than to suspect her of killing someone. Okay, so he doesn't know her all that well, but he's known her partner Trudy, my niece, since she was a college student. In fact, you should know better, too. You even went to their daughter's baby naming."

"That was the only time I met with them socially, and I believe I can be objective in this investigation. That's why I'm in charge of it. Steve ... the Chief ... has recused himself as he's too, um, intimately involved with the family. And he's going to be on leave for a few days."

"Does that mean you're the acting chief until he gets back? Or the acting interim director of public safety? Or ... oh, whatever the title is ... head honcho, maybe?"

"Right, whatever. So, can we meet in your office? Or would you like to come to police headquarters?"

"'Headquarters'? Doesn't that mean there must be other quarters?" The look on Merino's face told me he wasn't in a joking mood. Not that he ever was. "Wait. Am I a suspect? Do I need a lawyer?" I looked around to see if Len Krasner was still around. Or some other lawyer.

"You need a lawyer only if you did something wrong or want to confess. Don't look so worried. I don't think your three warnings for speeding give us enough of an excuse to lock you up. And, yeah, I did check to see if there was anything we could use if you became stubborn. By the way, you're lucky most of the officers know your relationship to Steve, or those wouldn't be just warnings." He didn't smirk this time. It was a full grin. He still wasn't joking, though. Despite the grin, he was serious. But he was also enjoying himself too much – at my expense.

"Okay, I give up. You've got me dead to rights. I invoked my ex-husband's name to get out of some tickets. And, yes, I'll be a good girl and not speed again when there's a speed trap nearby." I sighed – it was one of those occasions – and said, "Come on. I have to go to my office anyway to get my coat. You may as well come along."

I looked around the room again and spotted Len. "Excuse me a minute, though, I have to talk with my lawyer first."

As I made my way across the room, I could sense the curiosity in the room. Janet, of course, had to waylay me and find out what was happening. "Janet, I really don't know. They just want to talk with me."

"Is it about the Fishers? I knew it wasn't an accident."

"No, it's about the new dean at Triple-U who was killed last night in a hit-and-run."

"Why do they want to talk to you?"

Oh, good, if Janet hadn't heard anything about Sherry then it wasn't yet common, or even uncommon, knowledge. "As I said, I don't know. I want to talk to Len for a second and then I'll find out."

I took Len aside and quickly filled him in. "How should I handle this? Do you think you should come with me? I don't want to say anything to implicate Sherry, but I don't want to lie either. Well, not too much anyway."

"I could come with you, if you would like, but I don't think it's necessary at this point. Don't lie. Just don't volunteer anything other than direct answers to their questions. And, whatever you do, don't invoke the Fifth Amendment. You've done nothing that could incriminate you, but they will think you have. And they're not a Congressional committee."

"How did you know that was exactly what I had planned to do?"

"Because you're a drama queen with no experience being questioned in an investigation. And, no, before you protest, the situation last year doesn't count because you're the one who instigated it. You, if the news reports got it right, were the one interrogating the police."

"I hate to ask this, Len. It's late and you've had at least as long a day as I have." It seemed longer than the thirteen hours that had passed since breakfast. "But would you please come with me? Just sit in the back of the room and listen, but it will make me feel better."

Len agreed and while he arranged for his wife to get a ride home with a neighbor, I went around the room and made my goodbyes. I had no idea how long the "meeting" would last, but I had a feeling it would be more than a few minutes.

"Ben, Sandy, I hate to abandon you, but I have to meet with some people." I wasn't about to tell them it was the police and I doubted I they would believe me when I said it had nothing to do with the Fishers. "It was great of you to stop by. I'll see you at my house tomorrow after services, Ben." I gave him directions, which I knew he wouldn't remember, but Sandy would. "Sandy, it was nice to see you again. We'll have to get together when you move here." No, we wouldn't, but I was still being on my best behavior.

"Who are those men, Aviva?" I should have known Sandy wouldn't let go so easily.

"Nothing to do with B'rith Abraham, I promise you."

"Come on, Sandy, it's time to go. We've a long drive back to your parents' house." Ben had practice in knowing when Sandy was about to overstep the bounds of decorum. Not that he was ever able to stop her. But she did give up after one final frown at me and suspicious glance at Merino and Ryan. We said our goodbyes and I doubted if I would hear from Sandy before they left to go back to Eugene. At least I hoped I wouldn't.

I collected Len, introduced him to Merino and Ryan, and we headed for my office. "I hope you realize, Rabbi," he murmured, "this consultation is going to lose me money. Not only won't I be charging you a fee, but my wife is far from pleased with me and I will have to come up with an expensive apology gift."

"Sorry, Len. Is my appreciation payment enough?"

"No, but it's the best I can hope for."

In the office, Len and I took the couch, while Merino and Ryan sat on the uncomfortable wood straight backed chairs I reserve for my most annoying congregants.

Merino took charge while Ryan took notes. "Rabbi, why were you worried last night when the Chief got the call about the hit-and-run?"

"I already told him."

"But he's not here and you are. And he's not involved in the investigation. I would rather hear it from you."

I glanced at Len, who nodded his assent. "I knew the location was outside the building where Sherry ..." I looked at Ryan. "That's s-h-e-r-r-y, like the liquor; last name Finkel, f-i-n-k-e-l."

"Rabbi," Len interrupted, "remember what I said about only answering what you're asked."

"Sorry. Okay, I knew Sherry worked there and I was worried she might have been the vic."

"The 'vic'? Rabbi, you're watching too many bad TV shows. And what made you think the deceased might have been your niece's, er, partner?"

"I didn't think. I was just concerned. I mean, it was where her office is. Was."

Merino's eyebrow lifted at my correction, which I could wish I could have unsaid after seeing his reaction.

"'Was' her office? Isn't it still?"

"Come on, Joe," I deliberately used his first name to equalize the power situation here. "Don't play games with me. You know she was fired. Or quit, or forced to quit, or whatever. So, yes, 'was.' And I didn't know if she would have gone at night to clear out her office when no one was around. Sherry hates it when people fuss over her; she can be very private sometimes. And you know she was angry, so don't bother asking me about her mood the last time I had seen her before the, um, incident."

"Rabbi," Len warned again. "TMI." I was surprised he knew the acronym referred to anything other than Three Mile Island.

"Excuse me, Joe, while I confer with my lawyer." I whispered to Len, "Maybe it wasn't such a good idea to have you here, after all."

"To the contrary. It was an excellent idea. Just be careful you don't give them any new information. You really don't know just what they already have."

I turned back to Merino. "Really, Joe, I have no idea what I was thinking or why. I was worried that it might have been Sherry."

"As the 'vic' or the 'perp'?"

"You know I was afraid she was the victim. I never ever thought she had been the driver!" Okay, it was a lie, but I hoped my indignation was genuine.

"Yet once you found out who the deceased was, your first action was to drive to your niece's house and check out her partner's car."

"No I didn't! Okay, I did go there, but it was only to make sure Sherry had gotten home okay. And I needed to talk with her and Trudy about ... another matter."

"Why would Sherry not be home?"

"You know from Steve that I called and found out she had gone out for a drive. It's what she does when she needs to think. I do the same thing. A lot of people do."

"But do they go out for a drive when they're angry? And it's raining? And don't you think her anger was a bit over-the-top for just a lost job? She shouldn't have trouble finding another one."

"Maybe she doesn't want another one. And how can you judge when the reaction to losing a job is disproportionate? Have you ever been in a situation where you've done a great job in a career you love and then they bring someone in from the outside who immediately dismantles what you've been doing and demotes you and ..." Whoops. Yes, he had been in that situation. He had been given every reason to believe he would be named the new chief of police when the former one died. And then the Township Council went and appointed an inexperienced academic with no practical real life police skills, namely Steve, to reconstruct the police force.

Joe just stared at me for a few seconds while I felt my face flush. He otherwise ignored my faux pas as he asked, "And what was this 'other matter' you needed to discuss with them?"

"Clergy privilege."

Len looked at me in surprise. "That's one I didn't think of."

"Well, it's true. I've been doing pastoral counseling with Trudy and Sherry, and I promise it had nothing to do with the murd ... I mean accident." *Nothing directly connected with it, but I was really reaching here. If they knew the topic of our conversations, it would have given them more reason to suspect Sherry. Losing a job may not be a good enough motive to kill someone, but losing a job plus a mate might.*

Merino took a deep breath before he asked, "And what about Ms. Finkel's car?"

"What about it?"

"What condition was it in when you saw it?"

"I don't know. I'm not a mechanic. It had been raining, so it was wet. There was a dent on the front bumper, passenger side, but I don't know how long it had been there." Technically, I didn't. It could have been there for ten minutes or a couple of hours.

"But didn't Ms. Finkel or Ms. Meisner offer an explanation?"

"It would be hearsay if I told you." I preened a bit as I looked at Len, who winked at me. "Ask them."

"We have. And they said you were there last night and could corroborate their version."

"Well, I can only confirm what they told me. Tell you what, you tell me what they said and I'll let you know if it's the same story."

Merino shook his head. "Now I understand why you never remarried."

"Oh, I did. But he was a typical male, too, convinced his way was the only one."

"Let me guess. You divorced. Or he had himself committed."

"Both. He married a lawyer who quit her job to become a party planner while he made partner. That's commitment to a vision."

Merino stood up and, after closing his notebook – I noticed he had stopped taking notes a while before – so did Ryan. I would have to find out his first name. I might be able to get away with calling Merino by his first name, but not if I simultaneously called his subordinate by his title.

"Chief Goldfarb asked me to pass on a message to you. We will likely have to question Ms. Finkel again, this time as a formal interview at the station with her lawyer ..." he glanced at Len, "present. He said he'll be seeing you tomorrow afternoon, and requested that you not, and I am quoting here, 'kill the messenger.'" He nodded goodbye to Len, then added, "And, Rabbi Cohen, we may need to speak with you again. Please cooperate." He nodded again. "Good night and ..." he hesitated, "Shabbat Shalom."

I let them walk out by themselves, hoping someone had set the alarm and it would go off, embarrassing them. Unfortunately, no one had.

CHAPTER TWENTY-THREE

"So what do you think, Len?"

"I think you handled it well. Not the way I would have, but it doesn't look as though you gave them any information they didn't already have."

"Good. But that's not what I meant. Do you think they still have an open mind about the investigation, or have they already decided Sherry's guilty? Are they looking into other possibilities, or just focusing on finding evidence against her? ... Oh, no! I forgot to ask him if Steve gave him my message about the sexual abuse allegations!"

"You've lost me there, Aviva. But you may be right about their having tunnel vision when it comes to Sherry. What's this about sexual abuse?"

"This morning, Liz told me that Moorhouse, the guy who was killed, had been in private practice in the area about twenty-five years ago. The school referred a lot of teenagers to him, particularly girls with eating disorders. Several of them accused him of sexual abuse, but he was able to deflect the suspicions and say the girls had come on to him and, when he rebuffed them, had conspired to have him arrested. The authorities, and the parents, believed him, but he still left Walford and relocated to California. Until now. I have Trudy checking to see if any of the accusers are still in the area. It seems to me they have a stronger motive for getting rid of Moorhouse than Sherry."

"Interesting theory. And it would give the police another lead to follow."

"Merino has probably left by now. I'll call when I get home and leave him a message."

We made it to the entry foyer, where someone was waiting. Guess who? "Oh, Janet, hi, I thought everyone had left."

"No, I stayed to find out what you talked about. Did you tell him my doubts about the cause of the Fishers' deaths?"

"I'm sorry, Janet. The subject was entirely different and I didn't think of it at the time. I have to get in touch with the Lieutenant again anyway, and I'll tell him then."

"Okay, thank you. Let me know what he has to say."

"Janet, come on. It's late. Let the rabbi go home already." Janet's husband, Phil Brauner, was one of the nicest – and most patient – men I had ever met. As well as handy.

"Phil, I forgot. When you get the chance, the sliding closet door in the kindergarten room is off the tracks again. Could you please fix it when you get the chance? I'm worried it will fall on one of the kids."

"No problem, Rabbi. I'll get here on Sunday before classes and take care of it before the kids get here."

"No rush. There's no school for the next week. Spring break."

"I'd rather get it done sooner than later."

There were two things I could count on with the Brauners: Janet would gossip and Phil would do whatever needed to be done around the synagogue, from substituting for Ron – or me – to plunging the toilets.

When I got home, I called Merino's office number – in a moment of weakness, he had actually given me the number to his direct line – to leave him a voice mail and was surprised when he picked up the phone. "Working late, aren't you?"

"When it comes to a murder investigation, there's no time clock. What can I do for you, Rabbi? And it's just as late for you."

"I was going to leave you a message before I forgot. I already did forget once. Did Steve give you my message about the sexual abuse accusations a group of teens brought against John Quincy Moorhouse when he worked in Walford twenty-five years ago?"

There was a pause. I couldn't picture the Marine-trained, ramrod straight, never-let-'em-see-you-sweat Merino hitting his head on his desk, but he probably considered it. "Yes, Aviva, I did get the message. We're looking into it, but, frankly (*my dear, I don't give a damn?*), there may not be anything to find after all this time. Do you really think a woman in her forties would still be holding a grudge after all these years?"

"Spoken like a man. Yes, I do. No one believed them, and, if they were telling the truth, they have never been able to trust again."

"You said it, Aviva, not me: 'if.'" He paused again. "We are checking it out, really. But I have to tell you, the circumstantial evidence against Sherry is beginning to pile up."

"And you said it, Joe, not me: 'circumstantial.' Even if it were substantial, I would have trouble believing it. Oh, and another thing."

"What now?"

"A different topic entirely. One of my congregants is convinced there was something, er, fishy about the Fishers' deaths – the carbon monoxide case earlier in the week. She told me quite a few things that don't jibe with the official findings. Who would I contact about it?"

"What is it about you, Aviva, that makes it impossible for you to accept the obvious?"

"Obvious doesn't mean true."

"On this one, you can bother someone else. Call the Fire Marshal, Bob Jeffers. And, Aviva? Do me a favor. Don't tell him I sent you.

CHAPTER TWENTY-FOUR

I glanced at my watch and was surprised it was only a quarter to eleven. It felt as though it should be at least three in the morning. I knew it wasn't too late to call Trudy, but it wouldn't be too late in fifteen minutes either, so before I called her, I called Steve. I decided to call his cell, hoping he was at home with the cell turned off. Of course, his cell phone was turned on, as it was his lifeline to the police dispatcher.

"Goldfarb."

"Hi, Steve, it's Aviva. Bring an extra hoagie tomorrow. Ben Brofman's coming, too."

"With Sandy?"

"Fortunately, no. I'm hoping between the two of us we can eliminate him from our inquiries."

"Please stop quoting cop shows. And what's this 'we?' Besides, I didn't know there were any inquiries to eliminate him from."

"I'm still not so sure the Fishers died accidentally. And Ben and Sandy had the motive."

"But what about means and opportunity? Now you've got me spouting jargon. I'll be happy to see Ben and warn him the roof leaks when there's a nor'easter (*Is Sandy psychic now?*), but I'm not about to interrogate him about a crime I'm not sure even was committed."

"Who said anything about an interrogation? We'll just casually bring up the subject and see how he reacts."

"You bring it up. I'm off-duty as of three hours ago."

"I thought a cop is never off-duty."

"I'm the Chief. I just rewrote the rules. Good night, Aviva. I'll see you tomorrow."

I called Trudy then. She picked up on the first ring, so either she was expecting a call or she wanted to grab the phone before the ringing woke the kids. I had dialed the house land line without thinking.

Her disinterested "hello" indicated she was deep into something – I hoped it was computer research on Moorhouse's background – and was so absorbed in what she was doing that she hadn't looked at the caller identification.

"Hi, Trudy, it's Aviva. I hope I'm not calling too late."

"Oh, hi, um, no. I don't know. I've no idea what time it is. Oh, only eleven. No, not too late. Why are you calling?" Sometimes Trudy's lack of social skills made me wonder if she weren't Josh's biological mother instead of Sherry. There's supposedly a strong genetic link in autism spectrum disorders.

"Several things, Trudy. First, how's Sherry?"

"I don't know. How is a murder suspect supposed to be? Angry, scared, indignant, depressed? Take your pick. She's been all of them, sometimes simultaneously."

"And the kids? How are they coping?"

"Simi's too young to know, but she can sense the tension in the house and has been crankier than ever. Josh is too immature to understand the implications, so he thinks the whole thing is cool."

"And you?"

"I'm doing what I always do under stress – work."

"Have you been able to find out anything about what I told you about Moorhouse?"

"That's why I'm working instead of researching the information. I came up against a blank. The event, if it was even in the papers, was so long ago the articles haven't been archived on-line. And none of my usual sources panned out."

"I wonder if those papers are on microfilm or microfiche at the central library?"

"Probably, but I don't read anything unless it's on a monitor. And the screens on those readers don't count as monitors as far as I'm concerned. And I don't have the time. In case you've forgotten, we have forty people coming for a seder on Monday night. Sherry's been bipolar all day, cycling between mania and catatonia. And I keep going back and forth between thinking we should just cancel, and then thinking we shouldn't. It might be good for Sherry to have a task that has to be completed by Monday night. And I'm sure it will be good for her to have her family and close friends around. And there's my mother and brother to worry about. Plus, I don't know what we should tell them about the whole thing, or if we should just pretend everything's fine."

I heard Trudy take a deep breath. She paused so long I wasn't sure if she had disconnected. But then she whispered, "Aviva, I'm scared. What if they arrest her? And, no, before you make some snarky comment, I'm scared for her, not for how I would manage to put together a seder meal by myself."

"I know that, Trudy. I wasn't even thinking such a thing." I was, only because I know how much she hates to do anything domestic.

I wasn't sure this was the best time to pass on Steve's message that Sherry was going to be questioned again, so I didn't. My excuse for not telling Trudy was that Merino said the message had been for me, and implied Steve had sent it only so I would let him into the house the next day without putting myself at risk of being arrested for assaulting the police chief. Instead, I went back to what we could do about Trudy's futile search for information about Moorhouse that could help take the attention away from Sherry.

"Trudy, I won't be able to get to the library to look through the old newspapers until ... I don't know when. I could go tomorrow after services, but I have to cook and bake and Steve's been trying to tell me something for a couple of days and is stopping by tomorrow with lunch before he goes to his daughter's house. Ben Bronfman is coming for lunch, too. And the library opens too late on Sunday for me to get there before the wedding I'm officiating at and closes too early for me to get there afterwards. So, Monday morning, at the earliest ...." I stopped as I had a brainstorm. "I won't be able to go, but I just thought of someone who can. I've got to get off the phone and call her before it gets any later. I'll talk to you tomorrow."

I was already checking the contact list on my cell phone for Leesa Monaghan's phone number and didn't even wait for Trudy to say goodbye before I pushed the flash button to get a new dial tone.

CHAPTER TWENTY-FIVE

I had met Leesa years earlier when she had studied with me for her conversion to Judaism. She was engaged at the time to a Jewish guy, and we became so close during our sessions together that she asked me to officiate at the wedding, too. The marriage didn't last, but the Judaism did. In fact, after the divorce, Leesa refused to date any guy who wasn't Jewish. Her last name was a definite hindrance, but she had not taken her ex's name. As she explained, it wasn't only for feminist reasons or professional – she was just beginning to make a name for herself as an investigative reporter in the local area – but because his last name was Lesser. "Leesa Lesser? Uh-oh, no way." Being an African-American probably didn't enhance her chances of meeting too many Jewish guys either. She denied that racism had a role in the breakup of her marriage, but I always wondered. From what I had observed at the wedding, neither family was too thrilled with their respective kids' choice of mate.

Leesa was quite a bit younger than I am – I could have been her mother – yet she and I had stayed in touch off and on over the years. I had followed her career as she went from free lancing for small weeklies to full-time reporting on a small daily to writing a muckraking column on a midsized daily. She had recently been hired by the Philadelphia *Gazette*, a fairly new publication that was trying to break the hold of the *Inquirer* and *Daily News* by printing synopses of the articles in a small-page format on recycled and recyclable paper, easy to read over a latte or on the subway, and posting the in-depth analyses of major stories, with frequent up-dates, on line. She was a night owl, so I knew she would still be up. I hesitated for a moment wondering if she might be on a date, or if I would be interrupting the post-date happenings. But I called anyway.

The cacophony in the background told me she was either on a date or trolling for one. "Yeah, who is it? This better be a tip for a story that will get me my much-deserved and overdue Pulitzer, or I'll be royally pissed."

"Leesa, it's me, Aviva. Get yourself to a quiet spot. You play this story right, and who knows what awards you'll win."

Leesa put her hand over the receiver, but I could still hear her bullhorn voice. "Hey, guys, don't leave without me. I have to take this call. It's my rabbi." She spoke back into the phone. "Aviva? You there? I'll call you back as soon as I find a place where we can talk without my screaming."

Leesa kept her word, as any good journalist would. Within five minutes, my phone rang. She sounded much more sober (in the sense of "not drunk," as well as in the sense of "serious") than five minutes earlier. "Okay, Aviva, I'm guessing that since you called me on Shabbat you need to tell me something that will save a life. Spill."

"Where are you? It's much quieter than when you answered my call. And it's too cold to stand in the parking lot."

"I'm in the women's bathroom. Erase your mental picture. I'm in the anteroom on a comfy settee, not in a stall. I was in the process of charming a very cute and very young guy, and Jewish, too, so you had better have a great story. I'm still the newbie at the *Gazette*, and if I don't come up with something spicy I'll be writing obituaries and wedding announcements until I retire. I'll be forever in your debt if you get me out of the back pages."

"I'll collect on that debt now if you'll run with this story. But you have to promise not to reveal you got the info from me."

"You? Who? Never heard of you. Oh, you mean that short, *zaftig* old lady rabbi? The one who hasn't figured out yet that unruly frizz went out with the Sixties?"

"Hey, if you want to know what I have to say, you had better be nice to me."

"Sorry, I meant, that erudite rabbinic scholar who has her own unique and eclectic style."

"Better. Okay, here goes. You know about the guy who was run over in front of the Student Counseling Center at Triple-U? Is anyone covering the story?"

"Just tangentially. The police haven't been too forthcoming, and Triple-U is bush league – or should I say piney league? – in Philadelphia. Talk around here is that it was some underage teens who were out for a joy ride and lost control of their speeding car in the rain."

"Well, the talk around here is that my niece's partner – female, not that it matters (*So why did I add it?*) – deliberately targeted the guy."

"Why? Do they have any evidence?"

"Circumstantial only. She drives the same kind of car that the witnesses saw, a dark-colored SUV. And it got some front end damage that night. Worse, she'd had an altercation with the guy the previous day and everyone in the Counseling Center – she was the director – heard her say she could kill him. It's an expression we all use, but … well, you can see how the police would view such a statement."

"You said she 'was' the director." One of the things that made Leesa such a good investigative reporter, instead of just a good reporter, is that she paid attention to details.

"Yeah, the guy – his name's John Quincy Moorhouse, by the way – had just been hired by Triple-U to revamp the Center. His first act was to oust Sherry – Sherry Finkel, my niece's partner."

"The reception's not great. Did you say 'out'? Triple-U has a reputation for being pretty liberal. What difference would it make that she's a lesbian?"

"No, I said 'oust,' as in 'get rid of.' Not that it was couched in those words. It was more like, 'I'm a Ph.D. in psychology and you're only a licensed clinical social worker, so I'm in charge. You can stay here on a per diem basis as a secretary.' Or words to that effect. Sherry was furious, told him and the Dean what they could do with their offer, and then punched out a cubicle wall after threatening to torture the bastards. Those words plus the damage to the Sherry's car, which happened, according to Sherry, when she skidded into a light post in a parking lot – a deserted parking lot – the same evening Moorhouse was killed have made Sherry the odds-on favorite. Well, to the police, not to anyone who knows her."

"Do you think there's a gay bashing angle going on?"

"I've no reason to think so. As you said, everyone around here is pretty accepting, particularly for a semi-rural area."

"Then I'm not sure what you want me to do with the story. I can understand that you want to help Sherry, but there's no scandal here. It seems the police are just doing their job."

"I haven't gotten to that part yet. My secretary used to be the librarian at Walford Middle School, which twenty-five years ago was in the same building as Walford High. The two schools shared the same staff lounge. John Quincy Moorhouse was in private practice then, specializing in adolescent psych and eating disorders. He was also an outside consultant for the school district. According to Liz – Elizabeth Smithers, my secretary – a group of teenage girls accused Moorhouse of taking sexual advantage of them. When they tried to tell the authorities, including their parents, no one believed them. Moorhouse used some psychobabble about transference and accused the girls of fabricating the accusations to get revenge for his having rebuffed *their* advances. According to him, the young women were in a conspiracy to frame him and get him fired and ... whatever the equivalent of being disbarred would be. He was believed, but he still left the area and relocated to California. Until now."

"Interesting. I wonder if anyone at Triple-U was aware of the allegations when they hired him. Statute of limitations would have run out by now, I'm sure, but still, why would the university take a chance with its own reputation by hiring someone like him? I bet they didn't know." She stopped. I could picture her chewing off her lipstick while trying to think up different scenarios. "Aviva, am I right in thinking that you suspect one of his accusers – discredited teenage accusers – ran him over in revenge?"

"Exactly what I'm thinking."

"Have you told the police?"

"Yeah, and they claim to be looking into the issue, but I doubt it. They weren't even aware of it until I told them. And I'm afraid that now that they have Sherry in their crosshairs, they're not even looking for other prey."

"Those girls would now be, what, forty or so?" She paused again. "I wonder if any of them still live in the area."

"That's what I've been wondering. My niece is a computer whiz of the first order – she made millions during the dotcom heyday and cashed in before the crash, that's how good she is – and even she couldn't find anything on line. Any newspaper articles were too long ago to have been digitized. I'm not sure when I'll have the time to get to the library to check the microfilm or microfiche, and time is the one thing Sherry doesn't have. I'm really afraid – and so is my niece – that they're going to arrest her soon."

"I don't suppose the police would give you access to their files. No, why would they? A civilian with an ax to grind. And I'm guessing you're not exactly flavor of the month after you made a fool of them last time."

"Right. And it's not fair. All I did was figure out who might have dunnit. They were the ones who told me the why. I couldn't find a motive at all."

"Yeah, they found the motive – after the murderer confessed. The fact is, the case was closed and you forced it open. And your ex can't be seen as giving you any preferential treatment. Okay, I can see why you need me. If it turns out this Moorhouse scumbag was run over by a victim of past sexual assault, then I've got the story I'm looking for. And even if I can't prove he was murdered in revenge, I can do an expose on Triple-U's hiring practices and lack of background checks. Of course, the story would be even better if I can show the university knew about his past and hired him anyway. Hmm, even if it turns out your niece's partner was guilty – don't get in a huff, I don't know her, so I'm completely neutral, which is what you need right now – Triple-U will still have some explaining to do. If I find anything, Aviva, I'll even forgive you for having dragged me away from the jailbait I was fishing for. I'm going to go back to the bar to see if he's still there, and tomorrow I'll hit the newspaper morgues and the police, and get back to you as soon as I can. Fair enough?"

"More than fair, Leesa. And I will still owe you, even if you do get a Pulitzer out of this story. But watch your metaphors – you use bait to catch fish, you don't fish to catch bait."

It was a lot later than eleven now, but I wasn't tired. Too much adrenalin. And I still had one more task to do before going to sleep. I turned on my computer and, after waiting much too long for it to boot up, logged onto the New Jersey Birds list. I posted a message: "I know that birds sometimes nest in dryer vents. But what birds (wrens, chickadees?) would build a nest in a dryer vent? And which (if any) would build one by the beginning of April?" If anyone would know the answers to those questions, it was the members of the group. Some of them have been known to use the Latin instead of common names of birds. Some of them even can tell the difference between a Cooper's hawk and a Sharp-shinned hawk at a glance. I can't differentiate them unless they're sitting next to each other and I have a bird guide with pictures of those particular individuals. In other words, I can't.

CHAPTER TWENTY-SIX

I woke up to another dreary, chilly, rainy day. It was early April but felt like – well, like early April. At least it wasn't snowing.

It was an understatement to say I hadn't slept well. I wasn't sure I had slept much at all, but I must have because I didn't remember looking at my clock any time between four and seven. *Oh, well, sleep is overrated anyway, and three hours is more than enough.* Yeah, right. So why couldn't I stop yawning?

I stumbled into the bathroom, almost fell asleep standing up in the shower, and somehow found a pair of clean, run-free panty hose. As I walked downstairs, I glanced at my feet and realized I was wearing one black shoe and one navy blue one. Properly dressed in matching clothes (I hoped), I finally got to the first floor. I was staring into my nearly empty and incredibly clean refrigerator, trying to figure out how I had forgotten that I had bought a new one and why I hadn't stocked it yet, before I woke up enough to recall I had put the Cheerios and paper bowls in the living room. I grabbed the remnants of a quart of milk and a banana that would be more at home in a cake batter than a cereal bowl, put them on the coffee table in the living room, and went outside to get the paper, where it had landed on the wet lawn instead of the relatively dry driveway. I definitely had to remember to tip the deliverer this Christmas. Maybe Easter, too, as then I wouldn't have to wait another eight months until I got a newspaper that wasn't soggy.

I sorted out the sections I don't read – business, sports, classifieds – when I noticed the lead headline in the South Jersey section: "Local therapist leading suspect in hit-and-run death of her new boss." Oh, shit. Sherry had made the news.

I quickly skimmed the article, which was, unfortunately, fairly factual and accurate. But there was no mention of Moorhouse's cloudy past. In fact, the reporter didn't seem aware that Moorhouse had ever been in Walford before being hired by Triple-U.

It was early, and I was sure that even if Leesa had gotten much more sleep than I had, which wasn't difficult, my call would go straight to her voice mail. It didn't.

"Leesa Monaghan, ace reporter." She sounded chirpier than anyone should at that hour, especially someone who had been bar hopping the night before.

"Leesa, Aviva here. Any luck last night?"

"If you mean with the hottie, no. But it didn't matter anyway, because I decided to go to the paper and check out the morgue."

"In the middle of the night? Oh, right, nothing will stop you in your pursuit of fame, fortune, and a Pulitzer. Well, here's something for you. Have you seen this morning's *Inquirer* yet?" Stupid question. Of course she had, probably while I was sleeping. Or not sleeping.

"Stupid question. Of course I did, as soon as it was published. I always check all the local papers first thing, followed by the nationals. And if I've got time, the internationals. So, yes, I did see the article about Sherry, and, yes, I did notice they didn't mention the sexual assault accusations. In fact, I've already written an article about it. The only problem is that I don't have any evidence yet to back up what I wrote. But I'm working on it. That's why I'm in the morgue, sneezing from all the musty papers and newsprint."

"Why are you a journalist if you're allergic to newsprint?"

"I thought it would all be digital. Anyway, let me get back to my research. I really hope I find what I'm looking for. I hate to do rewrites, but I don't think the legal department will let us run the article unless I can corroborate my information. And my editor's kind of a stickler for facts: 'If I want to read fiction, I'll buy the *National Enquirer*!' Besides a libel suit will do nothing to get me out of the back pages."

"Not to mention that you want to be the one to break this news. I have to leave for services soon, but leave me a message on my home number if you find anything. And be sure to include the Internet link to the article!"

I thought I would be the first to arrive at Mishkan Or, but Phil Brauner had beaten me there. He was in the hallway, leaning against the wall and making notes on a scrap of paper with a tiny golf pencil. "Oh, um, *boker tov*, Rabbi." His already florid face reddened more as he put the paper and pencil into his back pocket. "Sorry, I just wanted to jot down some numbers before I forgot – I wanted to look at that sliding door in the nursery room as soon as possible, so I could save some time. It's a good thing I did. The door's not just off the track; the track is bent. I'll have to get to a hardware store to pick up some supplies. But I'll get it fixed, don't worry."

"I'm not worried, Phil. And don't you worry, I'm sure you'll be forgiven for working on Shabbat. After all, it's in a good cause – I hate to think of what would happen if the door fell on a child. And you know that the kids tend to hang out in here when they're supposed to be in services."

"I know, you know, the parents know, but I don't think the kids know the adults know. Ah, let them have fun. At least they're in the building. And the door won't fall. I took it off the track and put it flat on the floor."

"Phil, I've said it before – this place would disintegrate without you. Please, don't tell me you're thinking of moving to Florida."

"Nope, Arizona." He laughed when he saw my face. "Just joking. We're here for good. Been here too many years to think about moving, although Janet's making noises about getting a place in Serenity Acres. I wouldn't be surprised if she decides we should buy the Fishers' place. If fact, she probably will. She figures it will go cheap, since most people won't want to live where a couple died or where there's a problem with carbon monoxide."

"How do you feel about it?"

"I don't believe in ghosts and I know how to check to make sure appliances work okay. But I like our place. Those houses don't have a basement and I doubt if there's enough room for a workshop in the house. Janet would never let me use one of the extra bedrooms for one. And we would want to use the garage for the cars so we don't have to clean ice off the windshields in the winter."

"Makes sense. Where is Janet today?" It wasn't like her to have let me get in the door without accosting me.

"She said she had an upset stomach and felt like sleeping late. I wouldn't be surprised if I get home and find she went to her sister's so she can snoop around the Fishers' house. I just hope she doesn't make any decisions without me."

"Would she dare?" I laughed. Before he could think of a rejoinder, I heard some voices in the lobby and excused myself to get ready for services.

Nothing unusual happened during services, giving my mind time to wander. I wondered if Phil was right that the house would be sold for less than market value. And if that lower price would fit my budget. Not that I have much of a budget, but I try not to spend more than I have in the bank. Or much more. I don't like the idea of an age-segregated neighborhood, but I dislike the steps in my townhouse more. Maybe it would be worth looking into.

Looking at Phil, I suddenly recalled he had been a physical education teacher and coach at Walford High School until his retirement only five or six years ago. And sports need cheerleading squads. And most cheerleaders are girls. And they need to be thin, so they might be prone to having eating disorders. And Dr. Moorhouse treated – and if rumors were to be believed, mistreated – Walford High students with eating disorders. Okay, maybe I was stretching the point, but I made a mental note to ask Phil if he remembered anything about the Moorhouse incident all those years ago. Even more importantly, if he remembered any of the names of Moorhouse's accusers.

After services, Phil was enjoying filling up his plate with the goodies that Janet would never let him have when she was around. When I first met Phil, he was still working at the high school and was in great physical condition. "It's important," he once told me, "for the coach to be a good role model. Why should the student athletes take advice from someone who doesn't care about his own body?" After retirement, though, he indulged in all the pizza and high caloric soft drinks and pastries he had denied himself during his teaching career.

"I've got forty years of junk food to catch up on," was his excuse.

Janet tried to curb his appetite but it was difficult for her to act the role of the noble and self-righteous health nut when she used to smoke like the proverbial chimney. A chronic cough, osteoporosis (some kids called her "Hunchie" behind her bowed back), and a husky voice didn't stop her. Nor did the fact that a pall of smoke hung around her, perfuming her clothes, hair, car, and house. It took a lung scan last year that showed stage one lung cancer to finally stop her. She got through the chemo and radiation, and was in remission, when she had a mild heart attack, the reason she was now drinking skimmed milk in her coffee. While recovering, she told me that the very thought of a cigarette made her feel physically ill. She didn't catch the irony that because of the cigarettes, she was physically ill. Unfortunately, she regained her craving after she finished recuperating. Although she claimed she had quit, a telltale whiff of tobacco sometimes accompanied her.

But without Janet to monitor him, Phil decided to indulge himself. He knew there was probably a salad awaiting him at home for lunch. Since I was planning on pigging out on a lunch consisting of a tuna hoagie and potato chips, followed by movie popcorn for dinner, I was in no position to say anything. So I joined him, but I put a few grapes onto my plate of brownies and miniature cream puffs. Everyone knows that fruit negates calories. But just to be safe, I also added a glass of Diet Coke.

"Phil, could I pick your brain for a minute? In exchange, I'll tell Janet you had only fruit during the Kiddush."

"Rabbi, for shame. Lying? Okay, it's saving a life – she would kill me if she saw what I'm eating. Let's sit down over there and I'll help you if I can. And you didn't even have to blackmail me. I always enjoy talking with you."

Did I mention that Phil is a gentleman? And a flirt?

"Does the name John Quincy Moorhouse mean anything to you?"

Phil took a big bite of a brownie while thinking. "Wasn't he the guy who was run over at Triple-U the other night?"

Damn. I had hoped he would jump up and say something like, "That bastard. Everyone knows what he did to those girls, but we couldn't prove it."

"Yes, he was. But I'm thinking about further back, like twenty-five years ago, at Walford High."

Phil shook his head slowly, then he sat straight up and his eyes widened. He looked like a caricature of someone who had just had a brain storm. He just needed lightning bolts to complete the image. "Moorhouse! Yeah, I remember now. Wasn't he involved in some kind of scandal back then? It's coming back to me now – something about having sex with patients – but I have to think about it some more. It happened well before you were in the community, though. How would you have heard about it?"

"It's a long story."

"I have time. The only thing waiting for me at home is a salad – and maybe a contract for a new house."

I told Phil what I had learned from Liz, without using her name. I also omitted the information about Sherry. I didn't want that story to spread even further than it already undoubtedly had.

"Is there any chance, Phil, you knew any of the girls involved? Or that you can remember their names now?"

"Sorry, I just don't remember. Don't forget, I was a coach for the boys' teams. There weren't too many girls' teams then, and the coaches were either new male teachers or women. Small towns like Walford then were slow in implementing Title IX. Let me give it some more thought and get back to you. Is it okay if I ask Janet? She's got a better memory for detail than I do."

Really? I hadn't noticed. "Sure, you can ask her. And even though it's Shabbat, call if you or Janet can think of any names."

"Yeah, I will." He narrowed his eyes in concentration. "You know, there was something … it's tickling the back of my brain … I won't think about it and maybe …. Ah, who am I kidding? I'll never remember. But I bet Janet will."

It was a bet I wasn't going to take.

CHAPTER TWENTY-SEVEN

The first thing I did when I got home was change into jeans and a T-shirt. The second thing was check the New Jersey Birds. Even though I had posted my question late at night, there were a slew of replies, just as I had hoped. I suspect many of the respondents had checked the messages at dawn before going out on their daily jaunts into the wilds of the local preserves and parks, or even their backyards. I was flattered they'd put down their binoculars long enough to answer my question. More experienced birders love helping out newbies. I had been birding for fifteen years now, but still considered myself a rank amateur.

The answers confirmed that nests in dryer vents are dangerous and that there are birds nesting this early in the season. There were three main suspects: European starlings, House sparrows, and Carolina wrens, all of which stay in the area the whole year. Someone suggested House wrens, but they migrate and don't show up in the area (or, at least, in my yard) until later in the spring. Only the last of the three choices is a native species; the others are illegal immigrants. Unlike the human variety, they don't contribute much to the improvement of our society. I doubt they ever even applied for Green Cards or social security numbers.

"Starlings love my dryer vent!"

"House sparrow, of course. They nest early and in such places."

"Carolina wren would be my vote. Year round residents who start nesting early. They've been nesting since March in my air conditioner. They build bulky nests and like houses, garages, etc. Another possibility would be Starlings, who love heat and are often guilty in chimney blockages. They nest year round, not being native

Americans or migrants."

"How about House Sparrow? Carolina Wren might do this as well."

"I have had Carolina Wrens nest in weird spots, like the clothes pin bag, a wreath on my door and one year in my garden gloves I had hanging on the line. They often breed early here."

"Carolina Wrens seem like a likely choice to build a nest in a dryer vent (they often build in garages, etc.); and they may be nest building by now."

"The only ones I think would nest in a dryer vent would be House Sparrow or European Starling."

"I've seen Starlings build nests in openings in homes, attic vents, spaces like that."

The clinching argument was a posting from an ornithologist: "Several years ago I was called to a bird problem in a gas dryer vent. Upon investigating I found several Starling nests going back several years stacked in the vent pipe. This was confirmed by removing several Starling carcasses dried up between the nests. There must have been three to four feet of stacked up nests – the dryer couldn't have worked for years!"

So now that I knew it was possible for birds to nest in vents this early, I could turn my attention to my third task: emptying out all the supermarket bags, putting the ingredients I needed right away onto the kitchen counter, and storing the rest in the utility closet I had fitted out with shelves to use as a pantry. (Okay, so it was the third, fourth, and fifth tasks.) I have yet to see a kitchen that is large enough for a Kosher household. It's not just junk that expands to fill the space allotted to it, but double sets of dishes, pots, pans, cooking utensils, silverware, cutlery ... the list seems endless. There were times when I was tempted to keep "Biblical Kashrut." Nowhere in the Torah is there any mention of separate dish towels and sponges.

Before starting on the kugels, I separated three eggs and put the whites in a bowl on the kitchen table, covered with a paper towel. I knew from sad experience that even the slightest bit of water would prevent the whites from beating up firmly enough for meringue cookies. I hesitated about the yolks, as I hate to waste them, but I couldn't think of how to use them. I wasn't planning to make a challah soon, so I didn't need them as a glaze. Even if Pesach weren't about to begin, I wouldn't be making a challah soon. Not that I ever will bake one as long as there are perfectly good ones available at every grocery store in the area. Reluctantly, I put the yolks down the drain. I put the shells aside to clean, heat, and crush for the birds. At this time of year, they need all the extra calcium they can get to make sure they could lay eggs of their own.

I did some mental arithmetic (never a strong subject), figured out I did have enough eggs for the rest of my baking, and separated three more eggs. The meringue cookies I make are so popular, they need to be hidden, or they would get eaten before the meal, mostly by me. I wanted to make sure I had enough in case I got hungry before I delivered them to Trudy and Sherry's. I would decide later whether to make a frozen mousse cake (aka, a flourless chocolate cake). It would depend on my energy level.

Whites safely out of the way of wayward water drops, I turned my attention to the kugels. The boards of matzah soaked in a large bowl of water while I chopped up onions. Lots of onions. Lots and lots of onions. My eyes were stinging and streaming with tears by the time I finished. I've tried every trick there is, but nothing works. Even the most mild onions irritate my eyes. Of course, just as I was applying paper towels saturated with cold water to my eyes, the doorbell rang.

I stumbled to the front door barely able to see out of slitted eyes, and somehow managed to open my right eye enough to look through the peephole. It was Steve. Early.

"You're early," I said, opening the door and sniffling.

"No I'm not. You probably lost track of the time again. Besides, you left the garage door open so I could see your car and knew you were home. It's a good thing, too, or I would have yelled at you for leaving the garage door open when you weren't at home. You're crying, you know. Onions? Either that or you're upset at having left me that rather intemperate voice mail. I'll make sure to close my office door from now on before listening to messages – the whole building heard your rant, including the mayor on the second floor. Didn't do much to enhance my reputation, but you're now the new darling of the department."

"Don't flatter yourself." Now I was snurfling in addition to sniffling and crying. "I'm not in the least upset. I meant every word." In truth, I couldn't remember what I had said, but I was sure I had been justified. "Come in but don't put the *chametz* in the kitchen. It's *Pesadik* and I've got out the ingredients for the kugels."

"Which explains the bloodshot eyes and dripping nose. Have you tried cutting the onions under cold water?"

"Yes, and I've frozen them, stored them in the refrigerator, put vinegar on the chopping board, breathed through my mouth, chewed gum, and held a piece of bread between my front teeth. Nothing helps. I'm just very sensitive to the enzyme in onions."

"Well, at least you're sensitive to something."

"Ha ha. Let me get this first batch mixed up and in the oven, then we can eat."

Steve took the newspaper and went into the living room. If I wanted, I could have still talked to him, or him to me – the kitchen and living/dining room have only a half wall between them. But I wasn't in the mood for small talk and needed to concentrate on what I was doing to engage in any serious topics. Like why he was persecuting Sherry. I also didn't want to mention the subject of the Fishers before Ben arrived. He was, as usual, late. I had given him precise directions, which Sandy memorized, saying she would write them down for him later, but he probably had gotten lost.

Actually, the kugel is so easy to make that I really didn't need to concentrate on it; but I did need to concentrate on the conversation I was about to have with Steve. A tuna hoagie and chips would be less distracting than remembering to add salt to the kugel mixture, so I decided to wait.

While I melted margarine (*parve*, of course, so it could be served with either a dairy or a meat meal) in the microwave, I squeezed out the excess water from the softened boards of matzah, crumbled them up and added them to the bowl with the beaten eggs, chopped onions, and salt. I coated some aluminum lasagna pans (the perfect size for kugel) with the melted margarine and added the rest to the mixture, combining it all well. Then I divided it into the pans and stuck them into a pre-heated oven. As I said, easy. After Steve, Ben, and I ate lunch – and, I hoped, talked – I would make a second double batch and then start on the sweet kugel. Instead of onions, I would add chopped up apples and raisins to the matzah and eggs. Also easy. It's not as popular as the onion kugel, so I would make only one double batch instead of two. By then, the egg whites would be room temperature, and I could make the meringue cookies. If I timed it right, I would have time to catch a movie after dropping everything off at Trudy and Sherry's. If, that is, I didn't feel too guilty about enjoying myself while they were worrying about a murder charge.

The doorbell rang as I was bending over to put the kugel pans into the three hundred fifty degree oven (or an approximation thereof; the stove was a "builders' special" and had outlived its life expectancy, a side benefit of eating out so often). Steve opened the door and I heard him and Ben exchanging pleasantries.

"Hi, Ben," I called out. "Make yourself comfortable in the living room. You and Steve start eating and I'll join you as soon as I clean up here." Despite my sister's disparaging, and mostly true, comments about my house cleaning skills, I can't work in a dirty or cluttered kitchen and tend to clear up as I cook.

"So," I began, plunking myself onto the couch next to Steve and reaching for a Lee's Hoagies bag. "Why are you so convinced Sherry killed Moorhouse that you won't look at any other suspects?"

"First of all," he said, pulling open the extra large bag of Lay's Potato Chips, "I told you, I'm staying out of the case. I'm too close to the family – not that anyone believes that after hearing your message – and I'm going to be out of town for a few days. Second, show us some suspects. Third ... there is no third. Talk to Merino if you have anything concrete."

"Don't worry I will. I mean, I will talk to him and I will have something concrete. Just give me time. I've got people working on it."

"'People?' What are you, a one-woman detective agency? Let the experts handle it."

"And let Sherry get railroaded for something she didn't do? No chance. And what about the Fishers?"

Steve gave a shake of his head that I interpreted, undoubtedly correctly, as "This is what you call 'casually' bringing up a subject?"

"What about them?"

"Janet Brauner is convinced it couldn't have been an accident and is *haking mir a tshaynik* about it."

"If she's bugging you, it's a good reason not to interfere. From what I've seen of her, it will just encourage her if you buy into her theories. Why don't you just tell her you've investigated and all evidence points to an accident?"

"Tell you the truth, some of the things she's told me make me wonder. She's convinced they did have a detector and had their dryer vent checked recently. And she saw a car in their garage in the middle of the night, and they never put the cars in the garage. I know..." I stopped Steve before he could interrupt. "... go talk to the Fire Marshal. I will. I just don't know when I'll have time. I guess I'll have to make the time somehow on Monday."

In the meantime, I was surreptitiously checking out Ben's reactions. At least, I thought it was surreptitious, until Ben said, "Why are you looking at me like that, Aviva? You certainly don't think I was involved, do you? I know it was convenient for me they died – no, erase that, nothing about death, even an unexpected one, is convenient."

Steve saved me from having to answer. "Believe me, Ben, no one suspects you of anything." I noticed he didn't mention Sandy. Was that because he did suspect her? Nah, he probably just didn't want to introduce another reason to put Ben on the defensive.

"Aviva's just being her usual interfering self," Steve continued. "She's yet to meet an innocent death that she believes was innocent."

"That's not fair, Steve. I only got involved in a police case once. And it wasn't even a police case until I pointed out the discrepancies to you."

I turned to Ben. "That's all I'm doing here. I've heard several puzzling things from Janet Brauner – you met her last night at the Oneg," I reminded him. Ben nodded his recognition, but I wasn't sure he remembered the name; I wondered if he remembered the account he had overheard Janet telling me.

"What kinds of things?"

"Just what I told Steve: inconsistencies between what the family – the daughter and son-in-law – told the investigators and what Janet told me last night."

"So ask the daughter. I don't know anything about the Fisher's house or garage or dryer. I don't even know where the house is. Why are you singling out Sandy and me? You've known me long enough to know I'd never kill anyone. And even though you never liked Sandy – don't deny it; you don't exactly hide your feelings – I assure you she would never do anything to hurt someone. For Goodness' Sake, she's a nurse! She's devoted her entire life to healing, not harming. I admit it was to my advantage that the Fishers can no longer tell anyone I officiated at their daughter's wedding to a *shay...* non-Jewish guy." He stopped himself before using the Yiddish word *shaygitz*, the male version of *shiksa*, but even more derogatory. "But from what I heard last night, the Fishers had already told people, so their deaths didn't help me after all." So he did remember what Janet had said, and had understood the implications of her veiled remarks. But he didn't have that information before the Fishers' deaths.

I tried to put on a hurt look as I apologized. "Ben, I never suspected you or Sandy of doing anything like that." (*Oh, boy, was I going to be in trouble when God looked over my ledger for the year.*) "I was thinking out loud, speculating, not accusing anyone specific. And I still doubt if anyone at B'rith Abraham has heard anything."

We sat in an uneasy silence for a few moments while eating, then engaged in some inconsequential chitchat, including Steve's mention of the leaky roof. He made no mention, though, of noisy or nosy neighbors, so maybe there weren't any.

Ben glanced at his watch, stood up, and said, "Thanks so much for lunch, Steve. It was great to see you again. We're leaving on Thursday. Any chance we'll see you again before we leave?"

"I'm leaving from here to go to my daughter's house in Princeton Junction, and am taking some time off so I can check in with the administration at Crescent State. That's where I was teaching full-time before my six-month Sabbatical that's now stretched to eighteen months. But I'm sure I'll see you when you move in next door."

As I walked Ben to the door, I asked him their seder plans. "We'll be spending the first one at Sandy's parent's house. I'm not sure about the second one, yet. It may be at Sandy's sister's house."

I hadn't even known Sandy had a sister, which shows how disinterested I'd been in her all these years. "We're having a community seder at Mishkan Or on Tuesday night, beginning at six o'clock. Why don't you join us? Even if it's without warning, I'm sure we can find seats for you. The food is served buffet-style and there's always more than enough."

"Thanks. I doubt if we'll take you up on the invitation, though. Sandy wants to spend as much time as she can with her family. If we do, it will be a last minute decision." His tone was chilly, and I knew not to expect him at the seder.

We made our goodbyes. I had learned exactly nothing about his or Sandy's involvement with the Fishers, and had alienated a former friend and jeopardized our professional relationship.

When I returned to the living room, Steve put the rest of his hoagie on the coffee table, wiped his mouth with his napkin, and leaned forward with a serious look on his face. "Aviva, we need to talk."

Uh-oh. This can't be good. "I thought we were talking."

"I mean about us."

Us? What us? Is there an "us"? "Is there an 'us'? I mean there used to be, but ... well, we've been divorced a long time. And you remarried and had an instant family. Whom you are about to go visit for Pesach." *Leaving me here all by my lonesome.* Where did that thought come from?

"I'm glad to hear you say that, Aviva." He cleared his throat, a habit whenever he was nervous. *Double uh-oh. What does he have to be nervous about?* "I, um, I've met someone."

I hoped I didn't look as stunned as I felt. "That's great. When? I mean, you seem to be working all the time. And this is a small enough community that I'm sure I would have heard from someone if you were seen on a date. Not that I'm keeping tabs on you, but ...

well, you know what I mean."

"I do. Jenna, my oldest daughter, the special ed. teacher – oh, I don't think I told you: she's pregnant with my first grandchild! – anyway, she introduced me to her supervisor one weekend when I was at Jenna's for a barbecue this past summer. Mitzi is the head of the district special services department where Jenna works. She's been divorced for several years, has a couple of grown kids. We went out a few times when I visited Jenna, and hit it off. She'll be at the seder Monday to meet the rest of our family, and Tuesday night I'm going to her family's seder to meet them. I don't know if anything will come of it, but I felt it was only right for me to tell you, before you heard from someone else. Oh, and I'll probably be moving back to Central Jersey and resuming my work at Crescent State."

Wow. Two bombshells for the price of one. He's seeing someone and he's leaving Walford. Not only is he leaving Walford, but moving closer to where this Mitzi lady lives. He could have moved back to Central Jersey any time in the past year, once his initial agreement with Walford Township ended, but he kept renewing his contract. In fact, Crescent State had been giving him a difficult time about being away so long after his sabbatical was over. So why the sudden rush? Coincidence? Yeah, right. And Colin Firth is going to convert to Judaism and ask me to witness his *bris*.

"I can certainly understand why you would want to get back to your old job and to move to be closer to, um, your future grandchild, not to mention the woman you're dating."

"You're taking this better than I expected."

"Why wouldn't I? I have no claims to you. Although I have to admit I've gotten used to having you around. And what will you do without my leaving obscene rants on your voice mail?"

"I'll still have a phone. You can leave me messages whenever you want."

"And when will all this be taking place?"

"I'm not sure yet. Maybe not until June. I'm hoping my announcement that I'm leaving will finally get the Township Council to get off their butts and appoint Merino the new Public Safety Director. He deserves the post, and I've been recommending him at every job evaluation. I'll send in my official letter when I get back after the seders."

"And when's the wedding?"

He looked puzzled, and then realized what I was asking. "It's a bit premature. We've only gone out a few times. I have no idea if I'll like her family, or them me. Or, for that matter, if she and I will still like each other after we've spent more time together. Quite honestly, I'm not sure I want to marry again. Ellie was special. Not," he amended, "that you weren't. In your own inimitable way."

"Gee, thanks. I think."

I needed time to process everything I had just heard. I went into the kitchen for a trash bag and brought it back to the living room, where I gathered up our lunch debris and put it into the bag. "Don't you need to get going soon? Do me a favor on your way out – put this into the trash can."

"Sure, but I still have time. And the house is beginning to smell great. I forgot that you're a good cook, when you decide to be."

It did smell good. The onions may bother my eyes, but only when they're raw. When they're cooked, the aroma is divine. Forget the smell of chocolate chip cookies or cinnamon. To me, the best scent is onions and garlic sautéing in olive oil.

"Well then, take this out for me, please, and then you can keep me company while I make the rest of the kugels."

He did, and we talked about "safe" matters – my sister and mother, his younger daughter Rebecca's decision to go to law school instead of graduate school in sociology, the progress of Jenna's pregnancy – while avoiding the elephant in the room. Or, rather, elephants: his new woman friend, his moving out of Walford, and Sherry's possible imminent arrest.

CHAPTER TWENTY-EIGHT

By the time Steve left, I had four pans of onion kugel cooling on the counter and two apple-raisin ones in the oven. The egg whites were room temperature, but I didn't want to whip them up too early. They would need to go into the oven right away or they would collapse or be sticky. So I made some calls.

The first was to Leesa Monaghan. "Brenda Starr, ace reporter."

"Hey, Ms. Starr. How's the mystery man? Any black orchids been delivered recently?"

"I wish, Aviva. Actually, I just want her hair."

"Me, too. Guess we're stuck with what Mom Nature and genetics gave us."

"Speak for yourself. I've never seen anyone as salon-phobic as you." Leesa wore her hair, dyed a variety of colors, in elaborate braids. She kept trying to convince me to "lock" my hair, but I could imagine the reaction of congregants who had problems with my wearing torn jeans and a dirty T-shirt while gardening on my day off if I showed up for services with shoulder-length, graying dreadlocks.

"How's your research?"

"Tough. I've found enough articles to confirm that what you told me isn't rumor. But the girls were under eighteen, so their names weren't published. I'm checking out the reporters, though, to see if any of them still have their notes and are willing to talk to me. That is, if any of them are still around – it was twenty-five years ago, so a lot of the reporters have retired, relocated, or died. But I think I've got one lead that will pan out. I'll call you when I have something else to tell you. In the meantime, though, I did get the approval to run my column. It will be on the website soon, and in tomorrow's print version."

"Great. Even without the names, it might get the police to look at suspects other than Sherry. Email me the link when you have it. I really do owe you. Lunch sometime after Pesach?"

"How about lunch during Pesach? At your house."

"Deal. Call me and we'll compare schedules."

I decided to try the Brauners next. I was sure I would regret involving Janet, but maybe they had some ideas.

Phil answered on the first ring. "Joe's poolroom."

"Hey, Joe, got any open tables?"

"Rabbi Cohen? I'm sorry. I thought it was my daughter calling," Phil laughed. "I haven't asked Janet yet if she knew anything about Moorhouse. She was asleep when I got home and is still napping. I guess she really wasn't feeling well." He sounded worried, and I knew he was thinking about her bout of lung cancer and her heart condition. "I'll have her give you a call when she wakes up. I know there was something about Moorhouse and ... and someone we were friends with. But I can't think of who or what."

"That's fine, Phil. Don't worry about it. Tell Janet I hope she feels better. I know she's looking forward to the wedding tomorrow."

"You better believe she is. She even went out and bought a new dress for the occasion. Not that she needs a special reason to shop. I think it might have been something she ate last night. She said she was feeling a bit queasy after we got home from services. I wonder if the milk was fresh? She always puts a lot into her coffee, but I take mine black, and I can't think of anything else she ate that I didn't."

"No one else has complained, or at least not to me. Maybe she just picked up a bug. Again, give her my best."

"Thanks, Rabbi. I will."

Something Phil had said made me uneasy, but I couldn't think of what. I tapped the phone on my knee while thinking, then gave up. If I didn't think about it, maybe I would think of it. Isn't that what always happens with forgotten names or movie titles?

One more call to make, and I wasn't looking forward to it. No, not to my sister. To my niece. Generally, I don't mind talking with her or anyone else in her household, but I had no idea what news I would hear. I figured she would have called if Sherry had been arrested, but she might have been too busy contacting a lawyer, arranging bail, calming Josh. Poor Josh. I wondered what would happen when he went back to school after spring break. At least he would be home for a week, by which time, I hoped, his mother would be exonerated and the real culprit behind bars. And the Easter Bunny was converting to Judaism and drinking from Elijah's cup at the seder. (Easter Bunnies are cute, but I would still prefer to witness Colin Firth's *bris*.)

CHAPTER TWENTY-NINE

I was relieved when Sherry answered the phone. "Boy, am I glad to hear your voice."

"Happy or surprised? Are you still convinced I killed Moorhouse and thought I would have been arrested by now?"

"Come on, Sherry, I never believed you did it. I've spent every minute trying to figure out who did do it. Well, almost every minute, when I haven't been at work or making kugels, and even then I've been thinking about it. I've even recruited some other people to help me. In fact, there will be an article in tomorrow's Philadelphia *Gazette* about Moorhouse's past peccadilloes and questioning why the police haven't looked into the alibis of the women who made those accusations against him."

"What accusations?"

"Didn't I tell you? No, I guess not, since this is the first time you've spoken to me since Thursday night. But I'm sure I told Trudy. Maybe she ... oh, heck, I don't know how she thinks. Anyway, the reason Moorhouse left Walford twenty-five years ago and moved to California is because a group of teens he had been counseling said he had been sexually molesting them. Of course, he denied the charges, and said the girls were angry because he had rebuffed their advances, but he still left under a cloud. My theory is one of them is responsible."

"That's a bit farfetched even for you, Aviva."

"Why? It makes a lot more sense than to think you had anything to do with his death."

"Yeah, but I bet none of them was heard to threaten him, or had punched out a wall."

"How do we know what's been festering in one of their minds for the past quarter of a century? Or how many walls, real or metaphorical, they've punched during the years? We don't even know who they were – as minors, their names weren't reported in the press. But I've got queries out, and someone around here is bound to remember some names. All we really need is the name of one of his accusers still living in the area, and she can supply the rest of the names. Anyway, it will put pressure on the police to look at suspects other than you."

"Oh, right, the *Gazette* is such an influential paper."

"If the Internet version goes viral, it will be very influential. And I intend to send links to the article to everyone on my email list. And Trudy can certainly help with that."

Silence on the other end of the line. "Um, Sherry, Trudy can help, can't she?" I asked.

More silence. Then, "I suppose she can, if she ever comes home again."

"What do you mean?"

"She said she couldn't stand my staring at her as though I thought she thought I was guilty, and she needed a break. She walked out right after breakfast and I haven't heard from her since. She won't even answer her cell phone." Sherry started to cry, "Aviva, what will I do if they arrest me while she's away? Who will take care of the kids? Lynda's leaving for her parents' house tomorrow morning. The kids will wind up in foster care."

"First of all, you won't be arrested." *Maybe.* "And second of all, if you are, you call me and I'll come right over."

"Thanks for the laugh, Aviva. I'm not sure what's funnier – your non sequitur that I'm not going to be arrested, but when I am, you'll take care of the kids. Or the idea that you'll take care of the kids."

"I can be maternal when needed. In the meantime, I'll call Trudy. Maybe she'll answer for me. I'll call you back either way."

I dialed Trudy's cell phone and the call went straight to voice mail. "You know it's me. And you know why I'm calling. You had better get back to me right away or your kids will wind up with me as their guardian. Even better, call Sherry. She needs your support right now, not your avoidance."

I called Sherry back and told her about my message. "Let me know as soon as she calls. In the meantime, is there anything you need? I'll be by later, as soon as the kugels are done."

"Thanks, Aviva. No, we're okay. I picked up some milk this morning and we still have some cereal left, so the kids will have something for dinner. I'm not exactly in the mood to cook."

When Sherry mentioned milk, the elusive connection was made and I realized what it was that Phil had said that had bothered me. I hurriedly said goodbye and sat and thought back to the night before: Sandy had acted out-of-character by getting coffee for Janet. I thought I had seen Sandy put something into one of the cups. Sandy realized when Janet said, "Rabbi Cohen is a lot more traditional in some ways than people realize," that Janet knew Ben had officiated at the Fisher-Rivers intermarriage and was a possible threat to Ben's new job. Phil took his coffee black, Janet with milk. And now Janet wasn't feeling well.

CHAPTER THIRTY

Add another worry now to my list: had Sandy tried to kill Janet? But why would she? Just because Janet had intimated that she knew Ben was the wedding officiant? I knew that, too, but I was feeling fine. Of course, I hadn't had any coffee, but Sandy had other chances to kill me. Hadn't she? And what about Ben? Could he have put something into my hoagie when I wasn't looking? And Steve wasn't looking? And ...

All this speculation was giving me a headache, and I had yet to deal with Steve's news. I checked to make sure my cell phone battery was charged – it was – and then picked up the landline to make sure it was working – the dial tone indicated it was. My concerns for Janet were quickly supplanted by wondering why Trudy hadn't called me back (*Because she didn't want to? Well, what's new? No one wants to talk to me these days.*). Then I obsessed for a bit about what, if anything Leesa had found out. Which reminded me to check my email for the link to her article.

On my way to turn on the laptop, I stopped at the oven to check on the kugels. They were starting to brown on the top, so I turned the oven down to a low heat for the meringue cookies and took the aluminum pans out of the oven. As soon as they cooled, I would slice them. Then they would just need to be reheated.

I took the laptop out of its carry case and put it onto the kitchen table. It would have been easy to go upstairs to use my desktop, but I didn't feel like climbing Everest, I mean, the thirteen steps. Maybe it was time to move to Serenity Acres.

While the computer booted, I began whipping up the egg whites, hoping I hadn't left them out on the counter too long. When they were frothy, I added a small amount of vanilla; when they thickened more, I slowly added the sugar. Then I let the mixer continue at full speed until the whites were standing up on their own. I threw in the chocolate chips, and then scooped out small amounts of the mixture onto parchment paper. After the cookie tray went into the oven, I finished the last task: licking off the beater. The raw dough always reminded me of Marshmallow Fluff.

In the meantime, my dinosaur of a laptop (it was at least three years old) had booted up and I clicked onto my email. Nothing new. Not even any spam. So I wasn't being paranoid. No one wanted to talk to me, even electronic criminals.

In case Leesa had forgotten to send me the link, or had lost my email address, I Googled her name. Nothing new. I tried "John Quincy Moorhouse." Nothing new. I went to the *Gazette*'s website. Nothing new.

I needed to think. I had too many problems, each of which spawned several questions, with no solutions or answers:

Who killed Moorhouse? I knew it wasn't Sherry ... well, probably not ... no, *I knew it wasn't Sherry.* So who was it? Which of his teenage victims was still in the area? Which of those in the area had held a grudge (which ones hadn't?), and which of those in the area who still held a grudge owned a dark-colored SUV with front-end damage?

Who killed the Fishers? Did anyone kill them? Or were their deaths the result of the accident the fire marshal thought it was? Who had something or anything against the Fishers? Was Sandy involved in their deaths? Was Ben? And if it had been Sandy, did she also try to poison Janet? Or did Janet just have a stomach bug? And was there any significance to the car in the garage? And how could a car that had a full tank of gas have been used to pump carbon monoxide into a house?

Where was Trudy? Was Sherry going to be arrested or would Leesa uncover evidence to clear her? Would there be a seder at the Walford jail? Which jail would Sherry be sent to if she were arrested - Walford? County? State? Would she get bail? If Trudy didn't show up in time, would I wind up with the kids? Would Sherry and Trudy work out their differences and get married? Would this whole incident make or break their relationship? Would it make or break our relationship?

Speaking of relationships, what the hell was I going to do about Steve? Would he ask me to officiate at the wedding?

What relationship? And why did I even care?

So many questions, so few answers. As in exactly zero answers.

CHAPTER THIRY-ONE

I was still staring at the computer monitor in a self-induced stupor when the phone rang. My already too wrinkled brow furrowed when I saw on caller I.D. that it was Liz. I couldn't remember the last time she called me at home, probably because she never had. She firmly believed in separation of work and pleasure. Or maybe it was public and private. Whatever, she only called during work hours and only on my cell phone.

During the few seconds it took to realize who was calling and to push the "talk" button, I mentally slapped myself for not having called Liz earlier. Here I had been asking someone like Phil Brauner, who had at best a tangential knowledge of teenage girls a generation ago, and I hadn't thought to call my primary informant.

I activated the phone and said a tentative "Hello," which was answered by an irate, "Did you give my name to a reporter?"

"I, um, might have, sort of inadvertently mentioned your name to Leesa Monaghan. She's looking into John Quincy Moorhouse's background and whether Triple-U had vetted him completely before offering him the job."

"No, she isn't. She's trying to find out the names of some then-underage sexual assault victims who are now on the edge of middle age, married, with teens of their own."

I perked up. "Does that mean that you know them and know they're doing alright, that they put it all behind them?" Oh, wait, why was I happy? If none of Moorhouse's accusers was still psychologically scarred, then Sherry was in trouble. Big trouble.

"No, I don't know their names. After all, it was a long time ago, and I worked in the middle school, not the high school. But I'm an optimist who hopes they got the therapy they really needed and have gone on to have happy and productive lives. Of course," she hesitated, "I could be wrong. Oh! You were trying to find out if anyone besides Sherry had a motive. I'm sorry, Rabbi, I just jumped to conclusions when the reporter called me. I know you're a bit of a busybody, but I should have realized you wouldn't have been trying to dig up the names only for prurient interest. Of course, I have no idea what the reporter's motive is. How well do you know her?"

"Liz, calm down. You're beginning to sound like Janet Brauner, babbling away, saying the first thing that comes to mind."

"I know. I was so upset after the reporter called that I had caffeinated coffee. A whole pot. It's my comfort food. Drink. I'm a bit wired."

"More than a bit. I mentioned your name to Leesa only to explain how I had heard the story. And I know her well – I prepared her for her conversion and then performed her wedding. And arranged for her *get*, unfortunately. She's trying to take the heat off Sherry, but she's also got a good story there about Triple-U's background checks for faculty. Knowing her, she'll get into the whole ethics of whether someone's past should continue to inform their present, especially if a charge was never proven."

"I like Sherry. I find it hard to believe she would do something like that. I wish I could help, but I really don't remember any of the names."

I was trying to recall what Liz had told me on Friday. There was something, some little aside or throwaway comment, that had stuck with me. Obviously, it hadn't stuck with me because I couldn't remember it.

"Don't forget," Liz continued, "I spent my days in the middle school library, and the students knew better than to chat idly when I was around. They were there to study and do research, not to have fun. Oh, dear, I've become the stereotype of the old-fashioned librarian. I didn't mean they shouldn't have fun, just that ... oh, heck, the caffeine is befuddling my brain. You know what I mean. Don't you?"

"Huh? Sorry, I was thinking about something you said. I mean something you said on Friday. Your mentioning that you spent all your time in the library reminded me. Didn't you say you came across a girl hiding in the stacks and crying? Someone who said her mother accused her of lying and slapped her? Do you remember who she was?"

"No, I didn't recognize her. Now, let me think ... No, I'm sure I didn't know her. But I do remember another detail: she looked too old to be in middle school, so I asked her what grade she was in. She said tenth and I asked why she was in the middle school library. She said something about needing to be where none of her classmates would find her, needing to be alone. And then she said something strange – and sad – 'Not that any of them would care anyway. They all hate me.' I wish I could remember if there was anything else I said. I probably mouthed some of those meaningless platitudes that make the speaker feel better than the recipient. Oh, right – she looked like one of those Goths or punks or whatever, with lots of piercings in her ears and her nose and her eyebrow and her lip, wearing all black and too much makeup. Her mascara had run, making her look like one of those racket-makers masquerading as musicians. What was their name? Smooch?"

"Kiss?"

"Right, I think. Anyway, I wanted to but didn't say that maybe if she dressed less absurdly the other kids would like her. She didn't need to hear that from an adult right then. Or, probably, any time. I doubt if I ever saw her again, or not that I remember. Is it important?"

"Probably not, but ... I can't figure out what is and isn't important any more. I just know Sherry's innocent and probably going to be arrested anyway."

"There are a lot of innocent people in prisons. Or ones who claim they're innocent. But in this case, I'm sure it's true. And the optimist in me believes justice will prevail."

"You've definitely had too much caffeine, Liz. You just broke your second rule: never use clichés."

"What's the first?"

"Never call your boss at home. Are you sure it was just coffee you had?"

"Well, maybe a bit of whipped cream, too, but only to disguise the taste of the whiskey."

Huh? Liz Smithers imbibing Irish coffee and it wasn't even Saint Patrick's Day? Although with the combination of Ben's fears of discovery (what a dweeb!), Sandy's anger (what a bitch!), Sherry's troubles (not of her own making; not entirely of her own making, anyway), Janet's illness (deliberate or not?), Trudy's disappearance (where the hell is she?), Steve's abandonment of me (his *what*?), I was ready for a drink. And I don't drink. The only reasonable explanation was that it was almost the full moon.

CHAPTER THIRTY-TWO

I called Leesa, but got her voice mail. "What part of 'Don't divulge your sources' don't you understand? I got a call from my secretary, Liz Smithers. She has a cardinal rule never to call me at home, so you can imagine how pissed she was. In the British sense of the word, too, as she had a few Irish coffees. She doesn't remember any of the names, probably never knew them, so leave her alone. And where's the article? I can't find it on-line. I thought the whole idea of electronic newspapers was almost instantaneous updates. Call me."

That task accomplished, I went back to staring at the list on my computer screen. I was feeling pretty helpless (and hopeless) and not sure how to proceed. I called Trudy's cell phone and didn't bother leaving a message. She had probably already designed an app to read minds. Then I tried Sherry at home, but there was no answer. I didn't bother with a message there, either, especially as the kugels were still too warm to slice and I didn't know when I would drop them off. I then tried her cell phone, and she did answer. Or, rather, Josh did.

"Aunty Aviva, guess what? Bet you can't guess. You're pretty smart, but not as smart as MomT, no one's as smart as MomT, except maybe Einstein, but he's dead. And MomT can never guess what I'm thinking, so you can't. She says she can't figure out what I'm talking about even when I say it. But guess anyway."

"Um, you're answering MomS's phone because she's driving?"

"No. I mean, yes. But that's not the answer I wanted. Give up? MomS is taking us to the movies! MomT's more fun at the movies because she lets me get popcorn and a drink and candy, but MomS only lets me get popcorn and a drink or candy and a drink, but not popcorn and candy. But she said it's a special occasion so I can get both. But Simi can't. She had to stay home with Lynda. She's too little. Not small, young. English is confusing."

"What's the special occasion?"

"I don't know."

"Maybe because Passover starts Monday night?"

"That's not special. It happens every year."

Conversations with kids with Asperger's can be exhausting. "What are you seeing?"

"Some trees, and other cars, and street lights, and ..."

"I meant which movie." Other kids giving that kind of answer would be passive-aggressive smart asses. Josh was just being his literal self.

"I don't know the name. I wanted to see a new animated movie based on a TV cartoon, but she said it wasn't that special an occasion. So she's taking me to a PG-Thirteen nature movie, but I thought it was against the law to take me because I'm only eight but she said not to be scared. They won't arrest her for taking an eight year old to a PG-Thirteen movie and that should be the least of her worries. I don't understand what she means, but then she said she would let me have popcorn and candy if I stop asking questions, so I guess she's going to bribe the movie theater to let me in by buying more junk food. MomT always complains the snacks cost more than the tickets and it's highway robbery, so why don't they arrest the movie theater owner? And where's the highway? Maybe it's Route Seventy-three. The movie place is on Route Seventy-three. But there's a parking lot between the road and the building, so shouldn't it be 'parking lot robbery'?"

"Please ask MomS to call me when she can. Have you seen MomT?"

"Yes."

Silence.

I realized I needed to be more specific. "When did you see her last?"

"This morning."

"Have you talked to her on the phone today?"

"I didn't have to use the phone because she was home when I

talked to her. She went out later, and I haven't seen her tonight. She might be home, but I didn't see her and she didn't talk to me or call me on the phone."

"Are you close to the movie theater?"

"We're on Route Seventy going west and we will be at the Marlton Circle in about two miles. Then we'll turn north onto Route Seventy-three and it will be another two miles to the movie theater. So it's four miles, but we're not going sixty miles an hour, so it won't take four minutes. And we're not going thirty miles an hour, so it won't be eight minutes. And I don't know if there will be any red lights, which last another minute each. So maybe six minutes if the lights are green, but more if they're red."

How do Trudy and Sherry manage? Actually, Trudy probably encourages his eccentricities. It's not as though she doesn't have a few of her own. "Okay, Josh. Nice talking to you. Enjoy the movie. And remember to have MomS call me as soon as she parks at the movie theater."

He recited his "telephone etiquette" social skills training lesson and said, rather robotically, "Thank you for calling, Aunty Aviva. It was very nice to talk to you, too. I will give your message to MomS. I hope you have a nice evening. Good-bye."

He hung up before I could say good-bye, but not before I heard him screaming, "MomS. Call Aunty Aviva ..." Then the phone line disconnected.

I figured Sherry would want to buy the tickets and snacks and then find seats before calling. She would probably come out to the lobby during the advertising to call. It would have to be a short call, though, because I know she loves the trailers for the upcoming movies.

While waiting for her to call back, I checked the meringues, which were now dry to the touch. I took them out of the oven and actually remembered for once to turn the heat off. I wasn't going to be using the oven again as I had decided the chocolate cake was more trouble than it was worth to make. In truth, it's worth every bit of the trouble. I just didn't have the energy. And if I don't have the energy to make something incredibly sweet and chocolaty, then I'm running on fumes.

The kugels were still warm on the bottom, probably because I had left the trays on top of the stove instead of on the counter, and there was heat escaping from my really-should-replace-it oven. I had a feeling I would be delivering the food in the morning instead of this evening. I didn't even feel like collapsing on the couch, but I managed.

Of course, the phone was on the other side of the room when it rang. I groaned as my aging knees creaked. My couch should probably be replaced, too, preferably with a recliner that would automatically raise me up to a standing position.

It was Sherry. "Did you hear anything?"

"Sorry to disappoint you, Sherry, but I was calling to find out if you had. No one is returning my calls – except you, thank you – and I'm left with a million questions and no one to talk them out with. Have the police been in touch again?"

"No. The waiting and the not-knowing are the worst parts of this whole thing. I had to get out of the house. Josh is picking up all the negative vibes and really acting out, so I figured maybe a movie would help. Although I know I'm going to be sorry when the combination of the movie, the sugar, the caffeine, and the sodium make him super manic later. But I figure I pay Lynda to scrape him off the ceiling, so when we get home, I'll hand him over to her and lock myself in the bedroom. Anyway, let me get back into the theater before Josh panics that I've disappeared. I also have to remind him not to keep asking me during the movie what's going on, to remember all his questions, and ask me afterwards. I'm turning my phone off, so leave a message if you have to get in touch and I'll call back when the movie's over."

"I already saw the movie. It's pretty good."

Time to do some serious thinking. Where would Trudy go if she needed to escape? Except when dragooned into taking Josh, movies aren't her thing, unless they can be made into video games and she can design them. She doesn't drink or dance or go clubbing. I can't imagine her sitting in a café reading magazines. But I could imagine her sitting in one using her laptop.

I cut the kugels and covered them with aluminum foil. I wouldn't bring the cookies until Monday night, or Josh would eat them all. I might eat them all, but at least I would know it in time to make more. I changed out of my ingredient (and hoagie) splattered T-shirt and jeans and put on clean ones, found my sneakers under the couch, put some fresh food and water into Cat's dishes, and headed out to the latest internet café in the area, the preciously named Café Wiffie.

CHAPTER THIRTY-THREE

And there she was, with a super extra large cup of something with whipped cream on top and several equally large empty cups scattered on the table. "Have you had anything to eat?"

She looked up at me with, not surprisingly, unfocused eyes. She squinted, "Oh, hi, Aviva. Yeah, I had a couple of chocolate chip cookies. Get yourself some. They're great. And get me one, too. I would do it myself, but I've been staring at the screen so long my eyes won't refocus for distance. I guess I should get new glasses."

"You don't wear glasses."

"Guess it's time to start then." She squinted at me again. "Is it my eyes, or are you pissed off at me?"

"Got it in one. And it's not just me. You've got Sherry so upset she's taken Josh to the movies and is letting him have popcorn *and* candy."

"Uh-oh. That's bad. He'll be bouncing off the walls. I mean, I let him have both, but only at afternoon movies. It is night now, right?"

"Early evening. And Sherry knows what will happen. She said she's going to lock herself in the bedroom and let Lynda deal with him."

"I hope Lynda comes back after Pesach. I think it's time to give her a raise."

"I think it's time for you to go home, lock yourself in the bedroom with Sherry, and don't come out until you've worked things out." She was sitting with her back to a wall, so her laptop monitor couldn't be seen by anyone else. I tried to peer around the side to see what was on the screen. "What have you been doing all day, besides eating and drinking more fats and calories than most inhabitants of Third

World countries consume in a year? And spending more money than they make in a year, too."

Trudy visibly got excited – she sat up straighter, her caffeine-dilated eyes got brighter, and she smiled. "I told you I ran into problems when I tried to find out the names of the girls who accused Moorhouse of abusing them, because of their ages. Well, I decided to check out Moorhouse instead. Too bad there was no Internet twenty-five years ago. Research is so much easier now without having to hack into the ARPANET. Anyway, it seems Johnny continued to be a bad boy after he left Walford. Somehow, he always managed to cover it up, but he left a couple of other towns after allegations by teenage girls under his care. He used the same 'transference' defense and 'revenge' motives to cast doubt on his accusers. But each time he was accused, he relocated. And, each time, his current wife divorced him. He was married four times, and was in the midst of his fourth divorce when an SUV tried to mate with him. Anyway, here's the really interesting thing – there have been a couple of other incidents that could be interpreted as attempts on his life, including another hit-and-run accident, a mugging, and at least two arson fires, one in his home and one in his office. Either he's very unlucky, or someone was after him – or more than one someone. These incidents all occurred on the West Coast, by the way. California was his first destination when he left Walford, San Diego to be specific. Then he began a northward trek – Los Angeles, where wife number one divorced him; then San Francisco, wife number two; Eugene, Oregon, wife number three; Seattle, wife number four, before coming to Walford. The other hit-and-run was in Eugene before he moved to Seattle. It was a compact car, and his only injury was a broken leg. Wife number three was the main suspect, except she was away at the time. And, here's the biggie, in her divorce petition, wife number four accused him of molesting her adolescent daughter from her previous marriage."

"Wow! How did you find out?"

"The information on the divorce was in the Seattle papers, until the judge imposed a gag order. I'm going to do some more snooping (*Hacking, you mean.*) and see if I can find out the status of the case.

I'm not sure if he decamped back to Walford before or after the divorce was final. Once again, though, he wasn't charged with any crime.

"Then I decided to Google adult survivors of teen sexual abuse. There are a lot of sites, most of them from support groups and organizations. I did find some on-line forums where victims told their stories. One of the posters used the initials JQM to identify her abuser. Coincidence? I doubt it. Anyway, a few others responded to her post – a lot of messages in the thread, but from only the same few posters – and their stories are similar: sent to a psychologist by their parents for anorexia; he abused them; they reported him to their parents or another adult; he talked his way out, was never charged, and the girls – young women, rather – were blamed, becoming double victims. It's supposedly a closed group, but the security settings are so feeble anyone could get in – okay, so maybe not you. I left a message apologizing for hacking in and asking if anyone in the group lived in Walford twenty-five years ago and would contact me. So far, nothing, but it's early still. They're probably celebrating Moorhouse's demise – someone posted the news – and planning how to reward the perpetrator. If I don't get any responses to my public posting, I'll try to get the members' email addresses and contact them individually. With some digging, I can probably get their names and home addresses and phone numbers, too, but I figure I'm invading their privacy enough."

"Gee, you think so? You know you're scary, don't you?"

"Yup, but useful, too."

"I can't believe I'm aiding and abetting you like this – or maybe it's just instigating – but it might be even more useful if you do get the names and addresses. Then we can see who's in Walford still. And who's in Walford and also was in all those other cities when he was attacked. If it was one of the group's members, she's not about to incriminate herself by admitting she was in the same area every time Moorhouse was attacked. And if we can figure out who that person was – if there was one – then Sherry's free."

"Or maybe it's a *Murder on the Orient Express* kind of murder, with everyone involved."

"Stranger things have happened. Can you get back into the site and leave another message asking anyone who is willing to be interviewed – anonymously if she prefers – to contact Leesa Monaghan at the Philadelphia *Gazette*? I've got her email address somewhere."

I began reaching for my cell phone, but Trudy stopped me. "It's okay. I have it. I already sent her a note thanking her for the article. And giving her the information about Moorhouse's ex-wife's accusations, so she can contact her directly. She mentioned having found references to Moorhouse on-line, but gave no specifics in her article, so I don't know how thorough a search she did."

"The article's on-line? Great! I couldn't find it before I left the house. Bring it up. I want to read it."

"Let me leave the message on the site for Moorhouse's victims first. I'm sure you would like to read some of the postings, but you'll have to do it on my computer. You can read the *Gazette* article on your own computer, but you'll never be able to get into the JQM-ruined-my-life discussion on your own. Although I guess I could go home with you and hack into it for you."

"No you can't. First, you're going to go to your own home, the one you share with Sherry. Cancel that: first you're going to find someplace that sells flowers or candy, or, better, both, and buy them for Sherry. Cancel that: forget the candy – it's too close to Pesach and she'll probably start to feel guilty and then angry when she eats the whole box before Monday. After you get the flowers, you're going to leave her a voice mail message on her cell saying you'll be waiting for her with an apology after the movie. When she gets home, you're not coming out of the bedroom until tomorrow morning. Or afternoon. Or whenever you've finally settled everything, one way or the other."

"It will have to be by morning. That's when Lynda's leaving."

"Good. It gives you a deadline, so you can't postpone the discussions you need to have. Oh, and before you go home, come with me to my car and get the kugels. It will save me a trip."

"And what is second?"

"Huh?"

"You said 'first' I was to get some candy and flowers. What's second? Going home? Locking the bedroom door, with Sherry and me inside? Taking the kugel for you?"

"No, second is why I don't want you to hack into the support group from my computer. I don't feel like being raided by the FBI."

"Hey, I've been doing this for years and never been caught. Yet."

"Yes you have. You just weren't charged when you agreed to show the University of Pennsylvania how you got into their computers and could have changed those students' grades. You're lucky they didn't report you to the police. The courts might have forbidden you from ever using a computer again."

"That's because the school didn't want any publicity that would make it seem they didn't know how to protect their computer records. Which they didn't. Plus, I never did anything malicious, launched any viruses, or changed any information. And, believe me, I could have become even richer by blackmailing some now very influential, successful, famous, and wealthy Penn grads based on what I read in their confidential files. But, as I said, I'm not malicious. I might make an exception in Moorhouse's case, though, but he's already dead. All I can do now is hope the truth about him comes out and Sherry's exonerated."

"She didn't do anything, so there's no need for her to be exonerated. I keep hoping the fact she hasn't been arrested is a sign the police are looking elsewhere."

"Or they're still amassing the evidence against her. Can't Steve let you know what's going on?"

"He's not involved in the investigation, at least while Sherry's being scrutinized. Besides, he's in Princeton Junction at his daughter's for Pesach." And in his new friend's bed for the Saturday night before Pesach?

"So, call Merino. He questioned Sherry, so he obviously thinks he can be objective."

"He's not likely to tell me anything. He actually came to Mishkan Or last night to question me after services. I used the clergy confidentiality ploy to avoid telling him about your fight with Sherry."

"You mean, Sherry's fight with me."

"From my perspective, it looked like an even match." I checked my watch. I thought it was at least midnight, but it was just after seven o'clock. "Trader Joe's is open until nine. Get over there and buy some flowers for Sherry. They've got some nice orchids, and I know she likes orchids. But first, let me see those postings about Moorhouse."

"Tell you what. I'll leave the laptop here with you while I go to TJ's and then pick it up on my way home. That will give you time to read through them. Just be careful you don't spill whatever drink you get all over it."

"Geez, once, just once, I spill something on your keyboard, and you won't let me forget it."

"And you seem to forget my laptops aren't no-name brands on special deep discount." Trudy always considered it a personal affront that I refused to pay thousands of dollars for a computer with features I would never use or even comprehend.

She set up the page for me while I ordered my drink – a frozen mint chocolate coffee concoction that would probably keep me up not just that night but the next. I made sure she was looking as I put the glass on the conveniently empty adjacent table, far from the laptop, and settled in to read while she picked up her peace offering.

CHAPTER THIRTY-FOUR

The messages on the website were disturbing and painful to read. They had subject headings like "Moorhouse ruined my life," and "I have never been able to forgive my parents," and "I can't trust anyone." They should be required reading for anyone convicted of having taken sexual advantage of young women.

"Consensual?!" one victim wrote. "How could it have been consensual? I was only fourteen. I had no idea what I was consenting to. He said he loved me and would take care of me. He even promised to marry me when I turned eighteen. By eighteen I would have 'aged out' of his system."

Another poster said, "The bastard told me the same thing."

"I thought it would be romantic, like a fairy tale," the first responded. "It was tawdry and dirty and painful. And then he had the nerve to say we couldn't continue because no one would understand."

"He told me I was anorexic because I was afraid to become a woman, which is often true, although in my case, I wanted to be a fashion model and knew I would never make it if I gained any weight. He said he could cure me of my illness by teaching me the 'joys of womanhood.'"

"OMG, he used the same line on me!"

This exchange was followed by a series of short messages which all said the same thing: "Me, too."

Another added: "I went to confession and told my priest. Forget confidentiality – he went and told my mother because he feared for my well-being! My mother didn't go to the police. She went to Moorhouse. He said I was delusional and should be committed for 'observation.' BTW, this same priest was later defrocked for molesting young boys."

"My parents had me committed, too. When the physical showed I wasn't a virgin, they added promiscuity to anorexia, attempted suicide, and schizophrenia. I was in the hospital for two months. It was a good thing they kept me under close watch or I wouldn't have *tried* to kill myself. I would have succeeded."

"How many of us wound up in hospitals and medicated?" asked another. Almost all the women in the group responded in the affirmative, although a few said they weren't in a hospital, but were taken to psychiatrists and put on psychotropic medications.

"My parents took me to a psychiatrist who put me in a mental hospital. When I refused to admit I was making up the accusations against Moorhouse, I was put on drugs. Within a month, I was an addict."

"I know what you mean. I finally 'confessed' just so they would say I was cured and could get on with my life."

"I still can't believe no one would believe us. There were so many of us and he did it for so many years in so many different places. And his lechery was an open secret, around here in CA anyway."

"As an adult, I realize how creepy he was, always getting a bit too close, stroking my arm or taking my hand in his and then running his thumb along my palm. At the time, I thought he was wonderful and sensitive."

The question, "I wonder how many of our mothers he was *shtupping*?" received near unanimous responses of "Ewww." But one speculated, "Not so farfetched ... maybe that's why our mothers wouldn't believe us."

"But our fathers didn't believe us either, and I don't think he was fucking them."

The next posting was a bit longer than the others. "I really hate my parents. They did everything wrong when I was entering my teens. They moved from the Bronx where I could get into NYC easily to the Middle-of-Nowhere, NJ. They wouldn't let me stay in touch with any of my old friends, saying I needed a fresh start. Hell, they even changed our names! Is it any wonder I turned to sex and began to live for punk rock, weed, and coke, both the soda and the drug? When they sent me to Moorhouse for therapy, I thought I had found my soul mate. It was 'our little secret' that he loved sex (with me only), punk rock, weed, and coke. He dumped me when I turned sixteen, so I told my parents so I could get even with him. They said I was a liar. My mother slapped my face and my father refused to talk to me. As soon as I could, I moved as far away from my parents as I could. I hardly ever see them anymore."

I reread that last message. The story sounded familiar, and not just because it echoed all the other postings I had read. I wondered if it had been written by the same girl Liz had found sobbing in the stacks, the girl who said her mother's response had been a slap. But other pieces of what she said reminded me of ... I couldn't remember. I just knew it was something else Liz had said. The writer had opted to be anonymous, so I would have to wait for Trudy to find out whether it was possible to find out her identity. "Middle-of-Nowhere, NJ" was an apt description of Walford.

I was getting too depressed reading these messages, especially when I realized the writers weren't all in their forties. Moorhouse had continued during the years to prey on young teen women, and his most recent victims were still in their teens. I couldn't figure out how he had gotten away with it for so long, especially now when such accusations were taken more seriously than a generation ago. It was no longer a case of "innocent until proven guilty" with sexual predators, but "we don't believe you, and if you are by some chance found innocent, we still won't believe you." Had he become more cautious, targeting fewer teens, moving around more frequently, using aliases, wearing disguises? The secret of his "success" may have died with him.

Trudy hadn't returned yet. Knowing her, she was comparing each orchid to find not just the perfect one for Sherry, but the most perfect, period. If she had her laptop with her, she would have been checking out orchid websites. She probably was anyway, on the extra laptop she kept in the trunk of her car.

I opened up a new window on Trudy's laptop and found Leesa's article. The headline was, "Who Killed John Quincy Moorhouse?"

The subhead was even better: "Did Walford U. Knowingly Hire an Accused Sexual Predator to Head up the Student Counseling Center?"

Leesa's style was a combination of traditional newspaper writing – who, what, where, when, why, how – and breezy, informal, first person columnist blogging. She had all the factual information, but also some speculation.

She wrote:

> "On the surface, John Quincy Moorhouse was a good hire for Walford University. He had a Ph.D. in psychology from Temple University. He specialized in adolescent eating disorders, a necessity in a college environment. He had thirty years of clinical experience, first in the Walford area and, for the past twenty-five years, on the West Coast.
>
> "But those are just the superficial facts. Underneath his seemingly stellar surface was a disturbing series of allegations of sexual abuse. Notice I said "abuse," not "misconduct." For at least the past twenty-five years, John Quincy Moorhouse has been the subject of accusations, in every location where he lived and practiced psychological therapy, that he had sexual relations with his patients. And those patients were all between the ages of fourteen and sixteen. And none of them was believed.
>
> "On Thursday evening, April Fool's Day, John Quincy Moorhouse was killed in a hit-and-run accident outside the Walford University Student Counseling Center. But it is not an accident if someone is specifically targeted. Witnesses reported seeing Moorhouse step off the curb in front of the Counseling Center. A dark-colored SUV pulled away from the curb, sped up, and seemed to aim for him, killing him instantly. Had one of his victims gotten her revenge?
>
> "Lieutenant Joseph Merino, who is heading up the investigation for the Walford Police, refused any comment beyond saying the police team is 'pursuing all

possible leads,' including teens out for a joy ride. He would neither confirm nor deny they have questioned Sherry Finkel. Finkel, forty-seven, of Medford was the director of the Student Counseling Center for the past seven years. She was informed the day before Moorhouse's suspicious death that she was being reassigned – basically, demoted – to a position as a part-time administrator and per diem counselor. The person who informed her was Moorhouse, who, as the newly hired dean of the Psychology Department, would be taking over her administrative and supervisory role. The current dean, Merwin Carruthers, who is retiring at the end of the semester, had no role in the running of the center beyond a yearly performance review. According to sources, Finkel, who has always earned outstanding performance reviews from Carruthers, was so angry she punched a hole in a cubicle wall and was heard to utter threats against Moorhouse's life. The same sources, however, unanimously agreed that Finkel would never have carried out her threats and that she was speaking from anger and disappointment."

(*Not a ringing endorsement of Sherry's innocence. And Trudy wrote Leesa to thank her? I had better read on.*)

"Sure, unemployment sucks."

(*Not a phrase you will find often in the mainstream press.*)

"But is it enough of a motive for murder? Being abused by your trusted therapist when you are a teenager is a far better reason. Being abused, reporting the abuse, not being believed, and being punished for lying are even better motives. But, so far, it is unclear whether the police have even pursued that line of inquiry. They seem to be focused on Sherry Finkel. But is there anyone reading this who has never uttered the words, "I'm so angry, I could kill him"?

"And what of Walford University's hiring practices? Did

they properly check Moorhouse's background and reputation? It is doubtful, as a cursory Google search by this reporter uncovered multiple accusations against Moorhouse. And those were just the accusations that made it into the on-line newspaper archives. How many young women never reported his actions? How many newspapers never publicized the reports?

"The Walford University administrative offices are closed for the weekend. I will be contacting them first thing on Monday for comments about why they hired Moorhouse. I am giving them fair warning that I will not be satisfied with the answer, 'We didn't know.'

"Attempts to identify Moorhouse's teenaged accusers have failed. Because of their ages at the time and the nature of their allegations, their names were never made part of the public record. If any of them is reading this column and is willing to be interviewed, please email me at the address below. I promise anonymity.

"In the meantime, Sherry Finkel is bearing the brunt of the Walford Police Department's scrutiny. It is time they turned their efforts to finding the real culprit. And then give that person an award for ridding the world of this menace to young women."

So, objective reporting it's not. But at least now I understood why Trudy was pleased with the article. As soon as I got home, I would email the link to everyone on my list, including congregants. Trudy and Sherry are members of Mishkan Or, and I wanted to make sure they supported her and understood what she must be going through. And I hoped to stop any unfounded, or even founded, rumors and gossip.

I admit to another motive. It was very possible – or, more likely, probable – that someone in the congregation would know one of Moorhouse's victims. Or even have been one.

CHAPTER THIRTY-FIVE

I wished Trudy would get back. I was getting antsy, or, as we say in Yiddish, had *shpilkes*. I didn't feel like thinking any more about Moorhouse, or Sherry, or Steve. What I did feel like doing was turning off my brain. The best numbing activity I could think of was a movie, but I wasn't sure there was anything I wanted to see.

I put my head back and closed my eyes. Now I couldn't see, but I could hear, and found myself eavesdropping on a cell phone call of a young-sounding woman. She was whining, "But, Mom, I have only thirty-four dollars left in my account. I can't pay my bills." I opened my eyes to see a waif, all large eyes and prominent cheek bones and feathered hair. She looked to be in her early twenties. A five dollar cup of something frothy was on the table in front of her. I didn't see her with anyone who might have treated her to the drink, so I wondered about whether she had started the evening with thirty-nine dollars or if she now had only twenty-nine left. I also wondered about her priorities, and noticed she hadn't touched the drink. It must have been window dressing. It certainly wasn't for the calories. The phone in her left hand was pressed to her ear, and she was so thin that her watch had slid past her elbow and up to her bicep. She obviously hadn't finished many of those drinks, if any.

Power of suggestion: her thinness led to thoughts of anorexia led to thoughts of Moorhouse. It was like the old game: tell someone not to think about something, and they would not be able to think about anything else.

I looked away and then spent a few minutes trying not to stare at the man at another table near me. The guy looked like a Mafioso, or maybe an extra on *The Sopranos*: mid-forties; slicked back black hair shot (pun intended) through with gray; mirrored sunglasses worn indoors at night; buffed and manicured nails; deliberately casual clothes, consisting of a black mock turtle neck topped with a black blazer, pressed jeans, expensive looking leather loafers with a tassel, and no socks. He wasn't wearing any gold jewelry, but when he spoke to his companion, an older man sitting with his back to me, I heard a New York accent that would have made Fran Dresher sound upper-class British.

I stopped filling in a fantasy back story for the guy, who was probably an elementary school principal or a social worker. I was about to check Trudy's computer for movie times and listings at local theaters when I sensed someone invading my personal space. I looked up into the eyes of the mysterious stranger who had been sitting at the table opposite mine. He seemed even more menacing until he grinned, pushed his sunglasses to the top of his head, and, while pulling out the chair, asked, "Rabbi Cohen, right? Okay if I join you for a minute?" I'm not sure, but I think he actually said "youse" not "you."

What could I do but acquiesce? "You have the advantage. You know my name, but I don't know yours."

He grinned again – it was a very nice smile, with a lot of expensive dental work evident in the straightness and whiteness of his teeth – and held out his hand. "I'm Vince Ferrillo. I saw you a couple years ago at Thanksgiving service at Saint Catherine of the Woods." (The actual words were: *Tanksgivin' service at Saint Cat'rin of da Woods.*) When he said the name Vince, I realized why he seemed familiar: his voice was just like Joe Pesci's in *My Cousin Vinny*. I liked Joe Pesci, so I automatically liked Vince Ferillo.

"I'm sorry I don't recall you."

"No, you wouldn't. I saw you up there on the pulpit, but there's no reason you would have noticed me. Nice to see a woman up there. No way that's going to happen in the Catholic Church." (Original version: *"Nah, you wouldn'. I saw you up dere on da pulpit, but dere's no reason you woulda noticed me. Nice ta see a woman up dere. No way dat's gonna happen in da Cat'lic Church."* The rest of the conversation will be transcribed in Standard English.)

I just smiled politely, but wasn't about to get drawn into a discussion about another religion's policies. Not that I don't enjoy a good debate, but I was too preoccupied with other matters at the moment.

"I hope you don't mind, but I overheard you and that other lady talking. My dad," he gestured to the older gentleman at his table, "finally told me to come over here and talk to you." He laughed. "One thing I learned a long time ago is not to disobey Vincenzo Ferrillo, Sr., not unless I want a swat across the head."

I smiled politely again and nodded to the other man, who had turned around in his seat to watch our exchange. I could now see he was a paunchier, grayer (skin and hair), balder, less dapper version of his son. I nodded at him and asked the younger Ferrillo, "Would your father like to join us?"

"Nah, what I have to tell you makes him too uncomfortable. It's kind of a tough topic in our family, pretty much a forbidden one even."

Now I was definitely curious. "What can I help you with?"

"From what I heard, I could probably help you. You were talking about Moorhouse, weren't you? The guy who got himself squished by an SUV?"

"Yes." I hadn't realized Trudy and I had been speaking so loudly.

"What's your interest in him? If you don't mind my asking?"

"My niece's partner – my niece is the other woman I was with – is being questioned in connection with the hit-and-run. I'm trying to find ways to get the police to look for someone else. And, if you don't mind my asking, what is your interest in Moorhouse?"

"First, tell me, what's her motive? I'm guessing it's a woman, or you would have said 'husband' instead of 'partner,' unless, of course, they're just cohabitating. I'm pretty liberal, so it doesn't matter to me either way."

"Moorhouse had just fired her and she was pretty steamed up about it, was heard to utter some threats."

Vince got a faraway look in his eyes and frowned. "Then she wasn't – I'm trying to put this delicately, but there's no way to say it without being blunt – sexually assaulted by Moorhouse?"

Now I wasn't only curious, but excited. Was I about to get corroboration of my suspicions? Were the rumors about to be confirmed?

"No, she wasn't. She had never even met him until that day."

Vince nodded thoughtfully. "From what I overheard you and your niece saying, you've heard the stories about Moorhouse when he was last in Walford, right?"

"Yes. But the police don't seem to be taking those allegations as anything but malicious rumors spread by spiteful teens."

"They weren't allegations and they weren't rumors. Those girls told the truth. I know, because my cousin was one of them, and when no one believed her, she killed herself. And my aunt and uncle died of broken hearts and guilt."

CHAPTER THIRTY-SIX

Wow! I sat there like a dummy whose ventriloquist had abandoned him, my mouth open slackly, my eyes staring, my voice mute.

Vince came to my rescue. "Pretty shocking, huh? Let me explain. When I was a little kid, my aunt and uncle decided they'd had enough of the Bronx and urban life, and bought a farm in Walford. My great-grandparents in Sicily had been farmers, so it wasn't that much of a stretch. Walford was all farms then.

"When I got into my early teens, I started hanging around with some tough, older kids. My parents wanted me to go to college, not be a punk like a lot of the other kids in the neighborhood, and they were worried about the trouble I could get into during the summer vacation without supervision. They both worked long hours in the corner grocery store my grandparents had started, and my older brothers and sisters were already married with kids of their own. They decided I should spend the summers here, with my aunt and uncle and younger cousin. My cousin, a girl, was an only child. In a Catholic family like ours, having only one kid was a sin second only to having a kid without marriage. From whispers, I think my aunt had a lot of miscarriages. I wonder now if the chemicals on the farm caused them.

"So I got shipped out here, to help with the farm and 'learn the value of hard work.' I hated it at first, but then that physical labor put some muscles on my flabby city frame, and the girls started to notice me. I liked that.

"And, after a while, I discovered I had a knack for raising vegetables. My aunt and uncle had a few acres of corn, tomatoes – of course, tomatoes, for Christ sake – oh, sorry, Rabbi, for heaven's sake – how can you farm in Jersey and not grow tomatoes? – um, what else? Oh, zucchini and pumpkins. And some apple and peach trees. They even put in some grapes vines and made their own wine.

"They taught me everything about running a farm, and let me drive the tractor. For a kid from New York, where no one I knew had a driver's license, driving a tractor gave me bragging rights when I got home. I started to look forward to my summers here.

"My cousin was a few years younger. Seeing her only once a year I could see her changing as she got older. She had been a skinny little kid, but then the next summer was getting chubby, then the next was developing curves, if you know what I mean. Then suddenly she was a skinny kid again. More scrawny then skinny. She had stopped eating. If forced to have more than a forkful of salad, she would throw it up. She exercised obsessively. My aunt and uncle, busy as they were, still noticed."

"Let me guess," I interrupted. "They sent her to Moorhouse because she was anorexic."

He pointed his index finger at me. "Got it in one. And if you've uncovered the stories, you know what happened next. But it was worse than no one believing her. She was pregnant by the bastard, and he denied ever touching her. She insisted Moorhouse was the father, that she'd never had sex with anyone else. When no one, including her parents, believed her, she went into the barn one night, took some rope, and hanged herself." He stopped and his eyes filled. "I was the one who found her."

"How awful for you." Stupid words. Too bad he had mentioned that his aunt and uncle had died. If they had still been in the area, they would have been on the top of my suspect list. Talk about a motive for murder! "What happened to your aunt and uncle?" I asked.

"They struggled on for a few more years, but the joy had gone out of their lives. My uncle had always been a heavy smoker. Then he started drinking. My aunt even pulled out the grape vines so he couldn't make any more wine, but there was plenty of other booze around. He died a couple of years ago when his lungs and liver both self-destructed. My aunt, to punish herself, imitated my cousin and stopped eating. When she died, a few months after my uncle, the autopsy showed untreated stomach cancer. Like I said before, I think they both died of guilt and broken hearts.

"By then, they had sold off most of the acreage to developers. They left the house to me. It was in pretty bad shape, so I had it torn down and built a new one in its place. There were too many bad memories anyway in the old place. The good ones just won't come back."

"You live in Walford now?" I asked. He certainly had a good motive, too.

"Yeah. I made a lot of money with a string of fresh produce stores in the New York area. I still own them, and do surprise inspections, but let others do the day-to-day managing. I just watch the finances and my investments, which I can do on-line."

"When did you hear Moorhouse was back?"

He grinned again. "You suspect me, huh? As though I'd have told you about my cousin if I'd had anything to do with the bastard's death. I didn't know anything about his being back until I heard about the hit-and-run. I wasn't sure it was the same guy until the paper said he was a psychologist. Hadn't thought about him in years. But I think about my cousin every day. I named my new house for her: 'Connie's Rest.' When they do find out who did it, I plan to hire the best defense lawyer I can find for the guy, or gal."

He noticed me glancing at his father. "Don't even think it. Not that he wouldn't have wanted to kill Moorhouse, but he's not allowed to drive anymore. Macular degeneration. Besides, his style would have been to kneecap the guy, then shoot off his balls, then let him bleed to death. Sorry." He shrugged. "Pop's not connected, but he still believes in the Old Country ways. Don't you, Pop?" The old man grinned, a partly toothless parody of his son's. "Nothing wrong with his hearing," Vince explained to me. "Just his eyes."

Vince started to stand up. "Before you go, Vince, I have another question. Do you remember the names of any of the other young women who leveled accusations against Moorhouse?"

He shook his head. "Sorry. It's a long time ago, and I'm not sure I knew the names even then. My cousin's friends were too young for me to take an interest in; there were enough older ones around to keep me busy. I just remember my aunt and uncle were concerned because they weren't part of the 'in-group' so they started their own clique. I think they called themselves 'The Pink Ladies,' like from *Grease*. Yeah, I remember now, they even got matching jackets with the name on the front and a motto on the back: 'Too hot to be cool." It was their way of thumbing their noses at the popular kids. Like saying they didn't care if they weren't invited to the prom, they'd make their own fun.

"Listen, I really have to go now. It's late for Pop to be out, and he needs to get home for his meds." He looked rueful. "Me, too, both the time and the meds."

We both stood and shook hands. "If there's anything else you remember, Vince, please call me." I took out my card and jotted another name and number on the back. "Or call Lieutenant Merino at the Walford Police Department. He's in charge of the investigation. Do you mind if I share your information with him? Or would you be willing to tell him yourself?"

He took the card but instead of looking at it, as most people would have, gave me a steely-eyed glare, the kind I hadn't seen since my sister had discovered I'd bought grass – for our mother. "I'd rather stay under the police radar, if you know what I mean."

I didn't, but could make an educated guess. I decided not to pry, for once. "Call me, then. Please. Would you be willing to speak with a journalist? She won't reveal your name."

"Maybe. I have to think about it. But I doubt it. I'd rather not have a journalist know too much about me either. In fact, why don't you tell her without telling her how you found out? She can write about Connie and her parents using their names, if you think it will help. We had different last names – my aunt and mother were sisters – hers was Costello, like the comedian. My aunt was Rosa and my uncle was Antonio."

I waited until Vince and Vincenzo left and then called Leesa. I left her a message to give me a call, and gave her a brief outline of what Vince had told me. Then I sat and thought.

Okay, it was stereotyping, but Vince's not wanting any police or press attention had gotten my attention. He said his father wasn't "connected," but did that mean he wasn't? I only had his word that he hadn't known Moorhouse was back (*Note to self: Had Triple-U announced Moorhouse's appointment as the new dean before he showed up in Sherry's office? If so, when and where?*) Maybe he had told me the story about his cousin because he knew we (*We? I meant the police, of course. Yeah, sure I did.*) wouldn't be able to prove he'd been anywhere near Triple-U on Thursday night. But someone like Vince, as if I knew what he was like based on a ten-minute conversation, would probably have hired someone to do his dirty work for him.

I called Merino's office number and left him a message. Everyone except me seemed to have something to do on a Saturday night. "Lieutenant, it's Aviva Cohen again. Listen, I just had an interesting discussion with someone who doesn't want the police to talk with him. But his cousin committed suicide after Moorhouse assaulted her, and he's convinced his aunt and uncle died from broken hearts and guilt that they hadn't believed her. He says he had nothing to do with Moorhouse's death, didn't even know he was back in town, but I have to wonder. I mean, even if he didn't do it himself, he could have hired someone. I have a sense that he's got the resources to do so. Anyway, it's something else for you to look into instead of harassing Sherry."

I had almost added that I was suspicious about Vince because he's Italian, but stopped myself in time. After all, that would have been as bad as saying I'd thought someone had committed financial fraud because he was Jewish. Besides, with his last name, Merino was probably Italian, and I didn't need to give him another reason to dislike me.

CHAPTER THIRTY-SEVEN

Now I really needed to go somewhere and not think. After a quick look at the movie listings, I decided on a modern remake of a classic movie. I wasn't sure it would measure up to the original. But I figured the star and director were ones I'd enjoyed before, so it should at least be watchable. Besides, it was either that movie or a G-Rated animated one, and even in my most dire junk food deprived state, I would never be that desperate for popcorn.

If Trudy got back soon, I would be able to make it to the eight twenty showing. Otherwise, I'd have to wait until the ten forty-five. But I probably wouldn't be able to sleep anyway, so it didn't matter. The really big question was: did I want to go alone or with someone? And if I wanted to go with someone, the moderately big question was: who would be free this late on a Saturday night to go with me, except someone as pitiable as I am? I had never considered myself pitiable until Steve's revelations of this afternoon. So here was something else to avoid contemplating: why was I so bothered about Steve's life? Which brought me back to the moderately large question with an emendation: who would be available to go with me and to talk with me about Steve? I knew I was contradicting myself, but talking about a situation with a friend wasn't the same as brooding about it. Or avoiding it. Oh, who was I kidding? I needed to talk with Caryn Rozen, the only friend I had in the area who knew me when, who knew Steve, who would commiserate with me and, even better, tell me a few home truths. Trudy and Sherry didn't count; they had their own problems and didn't need to hear me whine about my paltry ones.

Another thing not to think about: why do I have so few close friends? Women in movies and novels and real life all seem to have a group of friends they can rely on for a sympathetic ear and an absorbent shoulder. I had ... Caryn and ... maybe Brenda Fishman. But I really couldn't confide in Brenda the way I could with Caryn: her husband Ron Finegold was Mishkan Or's cantor and religious school principal, so I was nominally his boss. Trudy and Sherry were relatives and had no choice but to be there for me, as I was for them. I had a lot of superficial friends, casual friends, acquaintances, colleagues, congregants with whom I could socialize on a minimal level in a large group, but not one-on-one. So that left me with a close friend count of one.

I phoned that one close friend, and Caryn picked up on the first ring, a sign that she was waiting for someone (not me) to call. Unless she just happened to be sitting at home with the phone in her lap. It was the former.

"Hi, Caryn. Doing anything tonight? Want to go to a movie and then have a postmortem about my dead love life?"

"Dead? You mean dead, buried, rotted into the ground and become fertilizer. Love to, but I'm waiting for Alan to call and let me know what time he'll be done with inventory at the store so we can meet for dinner."

"How many times did you cancel plans with girlfriends because a guy asked you out at the last minute? It's time to come through for your comrades-in-feminism. Dump the date in favor of the girlfriend."

"You're right, Aviva. Knowing Alan, he'll call at eleven, say he got tied up, forgot our plans, had eaten some disgusting wheat grass and raw-milk yogurt combination for dinner, and was too tired to get together. Screw 'im."

"I thought you did. Are."

"In theory. Now and then. When we're both in the mood, which is less and less often. It was just wishful thinking when I told you I'd miss the sex if Alan and I stopped seeing each other. You can't miss what you're not getting. So, what do you want to see, what time, and where should we go afterwards?"

I explained I was waiting for Trudy at Café Wiffie, and couldn't leave until she showed up. I didn't think she would appreciate my disappearing with her laptop.

"So why don't you call her?" I hate it when Caryn makes a reasonable suggestion I should have thought of.

"Um, I don't know. Maybe because it's a good idea and I'm not thinking clearly."

Caryn must have picked up my mood through the ether. "Do you want to skip the movie and go straight to the talking?"

"No, I really need to veg out for a while. And I've been tasting popcorn since yesterday."

"And you'll be tasting it all day tomorrow, too. Call Trudy and get back to me. If she's going to be a while, I'll meet you at the café, we can have our bull ... er, therapy ... er, gabfest first and then go to the late movie. Otherwise, I'll meet you at the Marlton AMC for the earlier movie and we'll go somewhere after."

Once again, Caryn made sense. That was why she was the one I needed to talk to. That plus her being my only close confidante.

I got hold of Trudy right away. As I suspected, after choosing several orchids, she decided to pick up some more things at Trader Joe's, where she was checking out the ingredients and unit pricing on every item in the store. She promised she would be back within half an hour. I called Caryn back and made arrangements to meet her at the theater for the earlier showing. Whoever got there first would buy the tickets. "Don't forget to call Alan."

"Nah, not gonna bother. If he remembers to call me, let him wonder where I am. It's not as though I'm married to him. Even when I was married to him, it wasn't as though I was married to him."

While waiting for Trudy, I looked up carbon monoxide poisoning. I was about to give up trying to figure out if they added anything to it to make it smell, as they do for natural gas, when I finally found an explanation of the difference between the two: natural gas is, er, natural, while carbon monoxide is produced by "the incomplete combustion of the fossil fuels – gas, oil, coal and wood – used in boilers, engines, oil burners, gas fires, water heaters, solid fuel appliances and open fires." It's natural, and it's odorless, and there's no way to make its presence known, except with a detector. And a CO detector won't send out an alarm signal if there's a natural gas leak.

I was still pondering this information – I've no idea why – when Trudy walked in. As I knew she would, she had gone overboard and bought two of every orchid species in the store, plus a two-pound box of Kosher-for-Passover chocolates. "We can always put them out at the seder if she doesn't want to hoard them."

"Have I got news for you." I told Trudy all about Vince's cousin. "He said I could contact Leesa and tell her about his family's experience with Moorhouse. He doesn't want his name used, though. Wonder why? Well, I can guess, but then I'd be stereotyping. Unfortunately, all he remembers about Connie's friends is that they were part of an outsider clique that called themselves 'The Pink Ladies' and used the motto 'Too hot to be cool.' Pretty pathetic when you think about it. I'm sure it only made their outsider status even more conspicuous. They probably thought the other kids were laughing with them, not at them."

"I like it. And it's accurate. Grown up geeks are considered hot, especially after they make their first million. I know from experience."

"You're not a loser."

"You must not remember me in high school."

Trudy was closing down her laptop when I thought of something else. "Remember you said you could find the names and addresses of the posters?"

"Of course I remember. It was my idea."

"Concentrate first on the person who sent the message about Moorhouse's death. She has to be someone local."

Trudy gave me a look that I misinterpreted as admiring. "Good idea, Aunty. I can't believe I didn't think of it. I guess it was just too obvious." She dropped the act. "Of course that's the first name I'm going to check."

I took her comment for what it was worth, nothing, and said my goodbyes. "I'm really busy tomorrow, but call and leave me a message if there's anything to report, about anything, or if you need anything for Monday night."

"The only 'anythings' I need are for Sherry's innocence to be proven and for us to be back to our old selves. And happily planning our wedding."

CHAPTER THIRTY-EIGHT

Caryn must have left her house right away, as she had further to drive but was waiting for me, tickets in hand. Despite the chilly, rainy weather, she was standing at the curb outside the theater.

"What's the matter?" I asked as I approached her. "Don't you have enough sense to come in out of the rain?"

"I'm standing under the marquee and staying dry. After a day in the office staffing the phones and scheduling funerals, I needed to get some air."

"Steve is seeing someone and leaving Walford."

Caryn knew me well enough not to be nonplussed by my non sequitur. "Give me a sec to exchange these tickets for the later show. Then we'll go over to Fridays and talk."

"Not Fridays. Too noisy."

"I know, but it's walking distance and the parking lot will be filled later. I've got a good spot and I'm not about to lose it, even for you. Besides, the babble will make it harder for someone to eavesdrop."

"Right, as though anyone cares what a single, lonely, overweight, middle aged loser has to say."

"Have you forgotten Rule One of girlfriend commiseration night?"

"'No self-pity allowed.' But can't we make an exception this one time?"

"No."

TGI Fridays was crowded and just as cacophonous as I had expected. Most of those waiting for tables either were in a large group or wanted to be close to the bar and the TV perpetually tuned to ESPN. The only time I will sit at a bar is if the TV is tuned to PBS. So I never sit at a bar. A small table in the back, perfect for our needs, opened up and we were seated within a few minutes. Caryn insisted on ordering me a salad and a slice of lime for my glass of water. "If I know you, which I do, you'll get onion rings and fries and top it off with potato skins and fried mozzarella sticks. Plus a bucket of movie popcorn smothered in fake artery cloggers and an extra large Diet Coke."

Damn, she did know me too well.

Caryn waited for the server to leave before leaning forward, staring me in the eye, and saying, "Spill. What did your outburst mean? I understood the words but not the context. And certainly not why you're so upset. The other day at lunch you insisted there was nothing but friendship between you and Steve. What changed?"

"What changed was the realization that he's no longer going to be a presence in my life. I've gotten used to having him in the area, having him as a friend." *(What did it mean,* I wondered, *that I hadn't included Steve on my list of close friends? Oh, right, he's an ex-husband, not a girlfriend.)*

"Tell me about his girlfriend. Is she why he's leaving the area?"

"No, he feels it's time to go back to his job at Crescent State while he still has a job to go back to. And his daughter's expecting his first grandchild and lives up there, in his old house, I think. And I'm not sure she's a girlfriend – silly name for people our age. They've gone out only a few times, but they're meeting each other's families during Pesach."

My throat was dry, so I took a drink of water before resuming. I had to clear my throat before talking. I wasn't sure why as my throat only closes up when I become emotional. And I was being very matter of fact and dispassionate. My eyes were tearing only because of the low light in the restaurant. No other reason.

"There's been absolutely nothing between us except a friendship of sorts." I continued after clearing my throat again. "We still bicker and disagree. Days – weeks – can go by without our seeing each other or even talking on the phone. But, well, I guess I just always figured he would be around if I needed him. I got along fine without him for over twenty years, but have become dependent on him again in just sixteen months. How pathetic is that?"

"Rule One violation! It's not pathetic to be human and want to connect with another human who is simpatico. Are you worried your feelings are more than friendly?"

"I didn't think so. But lately, I don't know, I find myself having strange thoughts about Steve. Then I remember why we divorced and the thoughts go away."

"People change."

I shook my head. "The core issue is still there: neither of us is going to give up our job so we can be together."

"How do you know? Have you asked him?"

"He's going back to Crescent. He answered without my having to ask."

"But he could have returned any time in the past eight months or so. His sabbatical was only for six months, and so was his contract with the Walford Police. But he stayed. Why?"

"It wasn't for me. He just enjoyed the challenge of doing something different and moving from academic theory into real world practice."

"So what has changed now? Is he no longer challenged?"

"What changed is his meeting someone who lives near his old home, and his daughter's pregnancy. And he said Crescent is no longer as understanding about his extended leave. So, nothing has changed. The job is still a primary motive, along with family, of course. And, let's be honest here, I haven't been 'family' in almost a quarter of a century."

"If things don't work out with this other woman, what do you think will happen? Will he ask the Township Council to make his contract permanent and retire from Crescent? Or will he move back to Princeton Junction anyway?"

"I think he'll move back. He'll want to be closer to his grandchild when it's born."

"To do what? Babysit? And what if Crescent decides they got along fine without him for the past couple of semesters and his pension will be cheaper than his salary? I think you need to be patient, Aviva, and see what he has decided when he gets back. Then you can figure out your feelings and what you're going to do about them. If anything."

"When did you get so smart and reasonable, Caryn? You're right. I should stop obsessing about something that might not happen. Besides, I have other things to obsess about."

I updated Caryn about my evening's reading and the conversation with Vince Ferrillo, then filled her in on the Janet Brauner's doubts about the Fishers' deaths and my probably irreparable rupture with Ben Bronfman. By the time I finished, we had just enough time to pay our bill (my treat, to pay Caryn back for her therapy session), walk back to the theater (it was still raining, but we both had hoods on our winter jackets), and buy our snacks (the prerequisite popcorn, Diet Coke, and Junior Mints for me; a bottle of water for Caryn). The movie wasn't great, but was entertaining. It was different enough from the original that it didn't suffer too badly in comparison. And it was just what I needed to put my brain into hibernation.

My oblivion didn't last long, though. As we were leaving the theater, Caryn said, "I have a nagging feeling the three deaths – the two Fishers and that guy from Triple-U – are connected somehow. I'm just not sure how."

"The only way would be if Audrey Fisher had been abused by Moorhouse – that's the name of the guy from Triple-U – and killed him and her parents. It seems a bit of a stretch. I mean, if she had been one of Moorhouse's victims, she would have had a motive to kill him. And maybe would have wanted to kill her parents if she thought they'd been complicit, at least through their silence. But why wait all these years to kill her parents? I'm sure she had plenty of other chances over the years. No, I just don't see it."

"You just have trouble imagining why anyone would want to kill their parents. That's because you grew up with the fun equivalent of Lucy and Ricky rather than stodgy Ozzie and Harriet. Replace your mother with your sister and think again."

"I get annoyed at Jean, but I've never thought of killing her. I've been tempted to stuff her into a box and ship her to a place with no telephones or mail service, but that's as far as my destructive fantasies have gone. You're right, though. It is hard for me to imagine such a toxic relationship that a child would murder its parents. I'm not naïve. I know it happens – look at the Menendez brothers. Just not among anyone I know."

"You mean not in the Jewish community. It happens. I'm sure it does."

"But you said you've never come across a case at the funeral home."

"That just means I haven't, not that my grandfather never did."

"Did he?"

"I don't know. I'll have to ask him, though. Now I'm curious."

On that morbid note, we parted at our respective cars, with my promising to keep Caryn apprised of any future developments.

A lot of people say they get their best ideas in the shower or while falling asleep. I get mine when I'm driving. On my way home, I began to think more about Caryn's suggestion. Was it so farfetched to think that Audrey had murdered her parents? There was only one way to find out: I would have to email Trudy with another "assignment." I'd ask her to find out all she could about the Fishers. Okay, I wouldn't find out if Audrey had killed her parents, but maybe I would get a clearer picture of their relationship. Or maybe not. I was definitely not thinking clearly.

But I was thinking clearly enough to recall the elusive thought that had been niggling at my mind since I had read the post from the woman whose mother had slapped her. She talked about turning to punk rock and drugs. Liz had described the sobbing student in the middle school library stacks as being dressed all in black, with piercings and too much makeup. Liz had even used the word "punk" to describe her. The coincidences were on the increase.

As soon as I got home, I emailed Trudy. "I know – okay, I hope – you're not on-line and are having a romantic night with your beloved. As soon as you get this, check out some names for me: Florence and Milton Fisher (they're the couple that died of carbon monoxide poisoning the other day) and their daughter Audrey. They moved to Walford about thirty years ago from Connecticut; don't know where in Connecticut, but close enough for a pre-teen Audrey to go to New York City with her friends."

I didn't add my suspicion that Audrey and the anonymous poster were the same person. I wanted to see what Trudy found out first.

CHAPTER THIRTY-NINE

The morning arrived too early for my liking, but almost too late for my work. There was no religious school because of the public schools' spring breaks. Some local districts began the Monday after Palm Sunday, which today was, and resumed the Monday after Easter. Others began on Good Friday and started again the week after Easter Monday. So we give the kids off both weeks, calling it the Passover break. No one – parents, students, teachers, principal, even the not-involved-enough rabbi – had ever complained.

The synagogue would be filled, though, with volunteers armed with scrub brushes and scouring pads to clean up the kitchen in time to prepare for Tuesday night's seder. I often stop by at some point to pretend to supervise, but was off the hook this year because of the Caplan-Pinsky wedding. And I had better hurry or I would be late.

The wedding invitation said twelve noon, which meant the ceremony would start at twelve-thirty. The signing of the *ketubah*, the wedding contract, was scheduled for eleven-thirty, and probably would take place at noon. I still had to be there by eleven. The wedding venue was a fifteen minute ride away, and it was only nine o'clock, but I needed to shower and wash my hair, figure out what to wear, wrestle my hair into a presentable state, and try to put some eye makeup onto my eyelids instead of into my eyes. And I really, really, really wanted to check my emails in case Trudy had found out anything.

The first three tasks were easily accomplished. I can take a shower and wash my hair in about ten minutes. I wrapped my head in a towel and opened the closet to get the simple, pearl gray, three-quarter length sleeve, mid-calf length shift I wear for all weddings. I decided to put on the makeup while my hair was still bound up, to avoid getting mascara all over my bangs, an easy thing to do when one has to put one's nose against the magnifying mirror to see one's eyes. I thought I'd done a pretty good job until I put on my glasses and realized the shadow on one eye was several shades darker than the other. It was easier to darken the second eye than lighten the first, and I finally got them even. Sort of.

That just left my hair. I took out a large brush and the hair dryer, and did exactly what my hairdresser did when he styled my hair into a smooth, frizz-free, swingy creation. So why when I did my hair did it look like I had used an egg beater on it? I gave up, smoothed some serum on my hair so the frizz was shiny, and looked for a pair of shoes that matched each other.

It was now ten-fifteen. I had just enough time to check the email before leaving. Of course, it was then that the computer decided to give me some kind of cryptic "cannot come out of hibernation" message. I turned off the power, waited ten seconds, and rebooted, which took another seven minutes. (I'd checked my watch. I really should take Trudy's advice and get a newer computer.) It was a good thing I had to wait, because I had forgotten to feed Cat, who was nipping my ankles instead of rubbing against them. Unless I wanted to have to change my pantyhose, I had to feed him.

The phone rang just as I just finished rinsing off the plastic spoon I had used to scoop out the disgusting smelling cat food I would probably be sharing with Cat in a few years if I didn't do something about my retirement savings. I decided not to answer; if it were important, the caller would leave a message.

It was, and he did. It was my favorite local police lieutenant, Joe Merino. "Rabbi Cohen, what have you gotten yourself into this time? Vince Ferrillo is not one of the good guys. Cross him and you're likely to have another car accident, and this time you won't survive it."

I was able to grab the phone before he disconnected. "Joe, it's Aviva." I figured his message showed enough concern for my welfare to switch to first names. "I've only got a few minutes before I have to leave to officiate at a wedding. What do you know about Ferrillo?"

"Just stay away from him, Aviva."

"But he sought me out, in a public place. We met by accident when he overheard Trudy and me talking about Moorhouse's death. Which Sherry had nothing to do with."

"Nothing with Ferrillo happens by accident. He might be worried that your meddling in this investigation could put him in jeopardy."

"Why?"

"Don't be so naïve. He's here in Walford hoping to distance himself from some nasty business in the Bronx. Let's just say he's under FBI surveillance and leave it at that."

"If he's under surveillance, I should be safe then. Besides, he was very nice to me. Well, until I mentioned that he should tell the police about his cousin. He did look a bit scary then. But I'm sure he wouldn't hurt me."

"Then why were a couple of menacing-looking characters parked where they could watch your house late last night? After I heard your message, I sent a patrol to check. They spotted the car, told the guys a neighbor had reported an unfamiliar vehicle with two guys in it, and politely asked them to exit the car. They sped off. We found out why when we finally stopped them and searched the car. They had several unregistered guns and a brick of crack cocaine in the trunk."

"How do you know they were watching me? There are some teens and young adults on the street who are probably involved in drugs."

"Aviva, these guys are part of Ferrillo's 'staff.' They weren't there to provide goodies for a teen rave. When the squad car drove up, one of the officers thought he saw the guy in the passenger seat quickly lower a pair of binoculars. And, yes, they were found under the seat."

"Maybe they were looking for owls."

"You'd better take this seriously, Aviva. I'm telling you, these are not people you want to get involved with. Stay close to home the rest of the day."

"Are you crazy? I've got to leave in half an hour to officiate at a wedding, and then I've got to ... do other things."

"Then stay in public. Don't take back roads. And watch your rear view mirror."

"Joe, you're scaring me."

"Good."

CHAPTER FORTY

Joe's warnings really had me spooked. But it was hard to think why I would be in danger. Except for having told the police about Ferrillo's motive for killing Moorhouse, that is. But I also suspected, um, no one else I could name. Not yet, anyway.

It was getting late, but my computer had finally booted up and I had just enough time to check it. I clicked onto my email account and found ... nothing from Trudy. I grabbed a jacket and made my way into the garage while phoning Trudy: "Enuf sex already! Get up and answer my email!" To make sure Josh didn't hear the voice message notification buzzer and decide to check the phone for his MomT, I used her office number. Trudy keeps the door locked when she's not working in there. And sometimes when she is working in there.

I hadn't even finished backing out into the street when my phone dinged to let me know I had a message. Sometimes, I lose the cell phone connection when I'm in the garage, and in-coming calls go directly to voice mail. It was Trudy, calling back. "What's the matter, Auntie Mame? Jealous? Don't worry, I'll do it. But I don't know why you want me to check out someone named Fisher. Another of your hunches, Miss Marple?"

Hey, Trudy's a techie. She's allowed to switch her literary allusions. I was impressed she even knew them.

It was then I noticed I had another missed call, one from last night. It was from my mother. "I really hope you're out having a good time. It has to be better than the time I just had with your sister. Why does she insist on treating me like a doddering old lady? Okay, so my eyesight's going, and I'm using a walker more, but my mind is as sharp as ever. Forget the doddering old lady – she's treating me like an infant! I swear, the hospital must have given me the wrong baby. There's no way a sour puss like her could have come out of my body. So, I know you're busy, but do call when you can. I need to hear from one relative who's sane. Love ya."

Love you, too, Mom, I smiled to myself. I would have to find time to get up to Boston soon and see her.

I made it to the hotel in plenty of time. The usual pre-wedding chaos was prevailing – an usher's boutonnière was missing its stem; the clasp on the groom's mother's necklace broke; the flower girl refused to wear anything on her feet except her light-up Barbie sneakers; the bride's uncle, who was to escort her in place of her father, who had moved to the Bahamas with his secretary and wasn't invited to the wedding, was stuck behind an accident on the New Jersey Turnpike. As I said, the usual.

Even though the couple was in their forties and it was a second marriage for each, they were going all out for the wedding. The bride, Amanda Caplan, had explained that her first wedding was at her parents' house, as they did not approve of her fiancé. It turns out their instincts were correct, as her now ex-husband was serving twenty-to-life for masterminding a drug distribution ring in Walford High School and environs. It was his fifth arrest on the same charge, although the first two reports were sealed as he had been a juvenile at the time. Amanda had divorced him after his first arrest as an adult, and had the foresight to have him sign a *get* before his incarceration.

The groom, Michael Pinsky, had gotten married while still in college, and his parents had not approved of his choice or timing either. But his girlfriend was pregnant, so they reluctantly attended a small wedding in her parents' house, with a judge officiating, as the bride was not Jewish. Their suspicions about their daughter-in-law did not abate when she had a sudden miscarriage only a few days after the wedding. The marriage lasted just a few months longer. They got an annulment.

The couple decided that this was their last – and, actually, first – chance to have the wedding of their (her) dreams. They had the financial resources to do what they wanted, and their parents were so happy that they infused large amounts of cash into the enterprise, too. Designer gowns for the entire bridal party, paid for by the couple; out-of-season flowers; the ballroom at a prestigious hotel for the reception; a customized hand-painted *ketubah*; a lavishly catered Kosher dinner; a two-week cruise through the Mediterranean for their honeymoon. And a wedding planner to coordinate it all. Not my taste (except the Kosher food), but beautiful.

The wedding planner took care of all the problems: she found a way to secure the boutonnière, fixed the necklace with some dental floss, convinced the flower girl the Mary Janes were much cooler than the Barbies, gave the uncle alternate directions. The photographer was cued, and the couple and their witnesses gathered around the table to sign the customized *ketubah*, which would be framed and displayed in the couples' home, plus the commercial one and the civil license, both of which would be placed in a safe deposit box with their wills and insurance policies.

"Now, you know, Michael," I said sternly to the groom, "once you sign this document, you're married. No backing out. The rest of the day is just formalities, but the *ketubah* is the real thing. It's a legal document."

He grinned, grabbed the pen, and, channeling Thomas Jefferson, signed boldly in the spot I indicated.

"Gotcha now." Amanda winked. "I knew from the moment we met that you were doomed." She signed. The witnesses signed. I signed. Everyone pretended to sign again as the photographer snapped away. Michael's parents admired the signatures. Amanda's mother and uncle pointed to the illuminated *ketubah*. Everyone applauded.

I gathered the printed *ketubah*, which I would read during the ceremony, and the civil license, and put them in my folder with my notes and my Rabbi's Manual and made a quick potty stop. One of the bride's attendants – they all decided "maids" was a bit silly at their age and various marital statuses – was fiddling with her hair. She didn't have all that much to fiddle with; it was thin and straight, but she had teased it up into spikes and kept the spikes in place with hairspray. It wasn't working; bare patches of scalp still showed through the sparse hair. Her glasses, the kind of nerd ones with thick black frames that look coolly retro on twenty-somethings and dweeby on anyone else, were getting speckled with hair spray. She was wearing the same elegant gown as the other attendants, but on her it looked like an overly long house dress. She was tall enough to carry off the dress, but box-shaped, not willowy. The edge of the cap sleeve was cutting into the flab on her upper arm.

The woman was intent on the mirror and didn't notice me until I emerged from the stall and went to the sink to wash my hands. Her eyes met mine in the mirror, and she did a double-take. "Rabbi Cohen?"

I put on my polite "I-know-I-know-you-but-can't-think-of-your-name" smile and nodded.

"I guess you don't remember me. We only met a couple of times. Audrey Fisher. Well, Fisher-Rivers now."

I wondered how Janet Brauner was going to react when she realized Audrey was in the wedding party. "Of course. Audrey. I was thinking about the wedding and not paying attention. How are you? I'm so sorry about your parents."

"Don't be. I'm not." She looked at me belligerently, as though daring me to contradict her.

"I know nothing about your relationship with your parents, but you need to allow yourself to grieve. They died suddenly and left you an orphan. You must be feeling something." I was channeling my inner-therapist.

"Yeah, relief. I was an orphan a long time ago. They weren't my parents."

I figured she was speaking metaphorically, but had no chance to ask her what she meant or to think about it. The wedding planner opened the bathroom door a crack and gleefully trilled, "All out! We're lining up! It's show time!"

As I joined the cantor – Ron Finegold's presence was mandatory, if the couple wanted any singing – at the head of the processional, I had my first good look at the assembled bridal party. I had heard about brides who deliberately chose tacky outfits for their attendants so no one would outshine them, but I'd never heard of one who had deliberately chosen ones who were uniformly unattractive. The gowns were too expensive to be tacky, but the body types and faces didn't go with the designer couture. Audrey Fisher-Rivers fit right in with the others.

Come to think of it, so did Amanda. The bride made the best of her looks, but the highlights couldn't disguise the essentially nondescript mousiness of her hair color, and nothing short of cosmetic surgery would have been able to disguise her lack of chin and her close-set eyes. But the look in her eyes as she glanced at her groom dispelled any homeliness. She was as radiant as any bride I've ever seen, and Michael returned her look with a rapturous one of his own.

Not that Michael was any prize either – the cummerbund on his tux emphasized instead of hid his pot belly, and he had an unfortunate comb-over and a more unfortunate "soul patch" that might have looked okay on a man two decades younger, but looked like a smudge of dirt on him. As the saying goes, love is blind. And it must have been in their case.

Oh, well. Who was I to judge? After all, I'm the one who had spent Saturday night at the movies with a girlfriend, and then gone home alone to feed my cat.

Ron and I took our places under the *chuppah*, an elaborately beflowered bower made of the same material as the bride's gown, and turned to face the assembled guests. As the rest of the wedding party made its way up the aisle, Ron commented *sotto voce*, "A bit of a rogue's gallery." I suppressed a guffaw and smiled, I hoped, beatifically.

It wasn't surprising that I recognized most of the bridal party and many of the guests from Mishkan Or. Amanda's parents were long-time members, and Amanda had grown up in Walford. The ones I didn't recognize were probably Michael's relatives – he was from Long Island, New York – and friends of theirs from out of the area. I caught Janet Brauner's eye and gave her a nod and smile. She nodded back, and Phil, sitting to her right, gave me a thumbs up. To Janet's left were her sister and brother-in-law, Charlotte and Marty Silver. I spotted Len Krassner and his wife. I guess she had forgiven him for having abandoned her after services Friday night, when he joined me in my chat with the police, as they were holding hands and she had her head on his shoulder. Sweet. Brenda Fishman, Ron's wife, was there, too. I was hoping I was seated at a table with them rather than with the great aunt they had to invite, her unmarried nebbish son and the parents' business associates they couldn't place elsewhere.

Audrey was the first of the attendants to arrive and I nodded to her as she took her place to my right, with the others falling into line in a diagonal behind her and going down the steps that led to the *chuppah*. One of the bright lights set up by the videographer was shining on her, bringing acne scars into bas relief and making her face look even more like a moon map. I couldn't be sure, but four of those scars – one just under the middle of her lower lip, one each on the top and bottom of her left eyebrow, and one on her right nostril – looked suspiciously as though they could be healed over piercing holes.

I thought of Liz's description of the young woman crying in the library stacks a quarter century ago: "She looked like one of those Goths or punks or whatever, with lots of piercings in her ears and her nose and her eyebrow and her lip."

CHAPTER FORTY-ONE

The ceremony went well. No rings were dropped, no wine spilled, no glass splinters escaped from the linen napkin when the groom broke the glass, no attendants were conspicuously drunk, no babies cried, no one fainted, Ron was in-tune, and I didn't lose my place.

I skipped the reception line, made my way through the crowd of well-wishers, smiling and nodding even to strangers, and went back to my car to drop off the paper work and get my purse and an embroidered shawl to dress up my nondescript dress. On the way back into the reception area, I stopped again in the rest room. I was still in the stall, and therefore even more invisible than a middle-aged woman usually is, when I heard the outer door open, followed by a gaggle of giggles.

"Can you believe those attendants?" The voice seemed to belong to a very intolerant teen, the kind who cannot imagine ever being older than twenty-two. "I mean, those dresses! They'd have looked better in brown sacks!"

"I know," said a second. "And why did she ask them to be her bridesmaids? They were so unattractive. And old."

"My mom said they were all Amanda's high school friends and their husbands," a third voice piped up. "They were all in some group together, something like 'The Pink Panthers.' I've no idea what it means. More like 'The Losers!'"

"I think it was 'The Pink Ladies.' Our high school put on the play *Grease*. A bunch of parents picketed outside, said the story was immoral. Anyway, I don't know why Amanda didn't ask us, we're cousins. But, I guess if she'd asked us, we might have made her look bad. Not that she looked so good. But, for her she looked okay."

"I bet the music is old fogies' sixties stuff."

"Worse. It'll be disco. At least the food should be okay."

They finally exited, leaving a fog of cheap perfume behind. I coughed my way out of there, and thought about what they'd said. So The Pink Ladies weren't just a creation of Vince's imagination. Or of his cousin's. I would have to find some way to introduce the subject, casually, of course, and see if I could get any information about Moorhouse, discreetly, of course.

By the time I had picked up my place card, and checked with Ron that we were indeed at the same table, although undoubtedly too close to the band's speakers, the reception line was done and the hors d'oeuvres were being served. I placed myself close to the kitchen doors so I could snag the baby lamb chops before they disappeared, grabbed some sushi, and found a small round table with an empty chair. Fortunately for my sleuthing purposes, the other occupants were members of the wedding party.

"Mind if I sit here?" I smiled sweetly. How could they refuse me, without insulting the rabbi? They couldn't. They could have said they were saving the seat for someone else, but their mothers wouldn't have approved. And I knew all their mothers.

Irma – how could anyone under the age of eighty be named Irma? – hesitated as she squinted at me nearsightedly; she refused to wear her Coke bottle thick glasses and had been unable to wear contact lenses. Once she figured out who was asking, she said, "Please join us, Rabbi. Um, when Nancy gets here she can pull up another chair." She was as gracious as she could be. My presence was probably going to put a damper on all their gossip. I would have to do my best to encourage them to ignore my presence and chatter away. Drink is always a good relaxer of inhibitions.

"I'm going to the bar. May I get anything for any of you?"

Fran, whom I liked because she made me feel both tall and thin in comparison, perked up. "I've a better idea. I'll go snag a couple of bottles of wine for the table. 'A bottle of red, a bottle of white ...'" she warbled off tune. I think Fran had already managed to down a few glasses of something in the short time since the end of the ceremony. Unless she had started before but had managed to maintain her decorum, not to mention balance, until now.

"Let me help you." I got up quickly. "I'm not much of a drinker, so I think I'll just get a soft drink." With a shot of rum, but they don't need to know that. I've an image to uphold. But, if I'm not careful, I'll be on the floor before they will. I'm the original "one drink, one drunk." But there are times, such as wedding receptions where I'm an obligatory rather than welcomed guest, when a drink is a necessity.

Besides, maybe I could get something out of Fran before she passed out.

"So, I understand you and the others have known Amanda since high school. That's a long time to maintain a friendship."

Fortunately, Fran was tipsy enough not to notice my implication they were old, but not drunk enough not to want to talk. "You wouldn't have recognized us then!" She laughed. "What losers we were! Completely uncool. Would you believe we even celebrated our nerdiness by calling ourselves The Pink Ladies? Lame! But we did have some fun together."

We got to the bar and while Fran batted her eyelashes, heavily coated with mascara that was starting to flake onto her cheeks, at one of the bartenders, I asked another one for a Diet Coke with rum. Have to watch the calories if I'm going to raid the Viennese dessert table later.

We got back to the others, where Nancy, the most attractive of the quartet, which wasn't saying much, now sat in an extra chair that had been shoehorned next to Barb, who had an unfortunate resemblance to a crane. The construction machine, not the bird. I said, as though apropos of nothing, "Fran was telling me all of you were high school friends. Have you all stayed in this area?"

"Irma, Barb, Fran, and I did," Nancy said. "But Audrey moved to the West Coast after high school. She really hated her parents, even more than a normal teenager does, and got away as soon as she could. But, she was only a tangential member. She was too weird even for us. I can't believe how she looks now, so mousy and plain. And it's amazing she actually got married. Of course," she looked at the others and giggled, a distinctly uncool thing for a woman in her forties to do, "so did the rest of us."

"Hey," Barb interjected. "Did you hear? Our great nemesis Cindi ..." They all chimed in "... with an 'i'!" before engaging in a group snigger. I noticed the level in the bottles was already greatly diminished. How could they drink so much so quickly? Even though I was sipping my spiked Coke slowly, I was already feeling its effects.

Barb controlled her chuckling and continued, "Cindi got divorced for the third time, and now has five kids from five different men. She just applied for welfare! Her file showed up on my desk. I almost denied her claim, but couldn't find a reason. Oops," she covered her mouth in mock chagrin, "I shouldn't have said anything. Privacy violation." This time she guffawed.

"You didn't say anything that's not public knowledge," Fran was starting to slur her words. "I was behind her in the supermarket the other day, and she was paying with food stamps! Well, a food card, or whatever they call them now. I could tell it wasn't a regular credit or debit card, though. And I made sure she knew I saw it! Hee, she tried to scurry out in a hurry. And she looks like she's seventy-three, not forty-three! Well, we showed Miss High and Mighty Head Cheerleader and Prom Queen, didn't we?"

They all clicked glasses. "To The Pink Ladies! Too hot to be cool!"

When they stopped laughing and high-fiving each other, I asked, "Was there anyone else in the group?"

They looked at each other warily. "Well, there was one, but she was only a sometime member. I think she was more invested in us than we were in her. But we shouldn't speak ill of the dead."

"Dead?" I put on my best innocent face. They were getting so *shickered* by now that I could have said, "Oh, you must mean Connie Costello," and they wouldn't have noticed. "What happened? Cancer?"

"If only," Fran started to shake her head, but immediately thought better of it. "She killed herself."

"How awful," I said. "Did she leave a note? I'm sorry, I shouldn't be so nosy." Yes, I should, but I realized I was treading on delicate ground here. I hoped they would disagree with me, and their desire to speak ill of the dead, despite previous protestations to the opposite, would outweigh their discretion.

Obviously, their love of gossip won out over good manners. Fran continued. "I don't know about a note." She looked at the others who shrugged in agreement. "She had been battling depression for a while, but no one talked about it then or tried to get her any help. We all figured it was just that she didn't like being on the outside. And it didn't make things easier for her in school that she lived on a farm. I mean, most of our parents were professionals. She was the only one of the Pink Ladies who wasn't Jewish, too, so even in our group she felt different."

"Was there anything specific that precipitated her suicide?"

They looked at each other again. This time, it was Nancy who spoke for them. "Well, her parents were sending her to a shrink because she had stopped eating. The guy was supposed to be an expert in anorexia. She accused him of having sex with her, but," she hesitated before reluctantly continuing, "none of us believed her. We thought she was just trying to be the center of attention."

"Did any of you also see this psychologist?"

"No," said Barb, "not the three of us. But Audrey did. Where is she anyway? Oh, there she is, talking with Amanda's parents." Barb lowered her voice even though it was doubtful anyone sitting even at the next table could have heard her over the babble of other voices.

"Audrey claimed this guy had molested her, too, but we didn't believe her either. She was just so bizarre looking then, we couldn't believe anyone would be so desperate for sex they'd bed her. And she and Connie were best buddies, so we thought she just didn't want to be less desirable than her friend. We never heard anything about any of this guy's other patients accusing him of anything, but after Connie's suicide, I began to wonder. I still wonder ..."

They looked down guiltily, not meeting my eyes or each others'. The discussion seemed to have sobered them up. I put on my professional voice, "There's nothing anyone of you could have done to prevent Connie's suicide if she was determined to end her life, especially if she was clinically depressed."

"Yeah," said Irma. "That's what the grief counselors the school called in told us. But, it didn't really help. Maybe if we had believed her, she wouldn't have done ... what she did. Or even if she had, at least we'd have known we tried to help, instead of, I admit, it, laughing at her."

"Did any of you know she was pregnant?" I realized my faux pas a few seconds too late. I hoped no one would notice, but Irma did.

"How did you know she was pregnant?"

I put on an innocent face, as I lied. "I didn't. But I was talking to people about Moorhouse and someone – I can't remember who – mentioned there was a girl in the high school who committed suicide after claiming he had raped her and gotten her pregnant. I think I would have heard if any of his other victims had killed herself, too." Whew. I think I got away with it.

Three of the four of them looked surprised at my question. The fourth, Irma, just looked uneasy. "Yeah, she did tell me. And I'm pretty sure she would have told Audrey, too, but I don't know for certain. I found her throwing up in the girls' room one morning before homeroom, and berated her for being bulimic as well as anorexic. She told me she was pregnant. I'm ashamed now, but I told her she couldn't be, that she was too skinny to be getting her period, and that's why she hadn't had it, not that she was pregnant."

"If she was pregnant, it was probably by that guy – what was his name? – the son of those tenant farmers her parents hired?" Barb asked. "Remember him? He was a year or so older than us, had dropped out of school. We used to tease her about liking such a loser, but she did seem to spend a lot of time with him. One night we were all talking about 'doing it' and Connie said she had. We thought she was bragging. But maybe she wasn't. Maybe she accused Moorhouse to cover up what really happened? I mean, by the time she killed herself, he and his family had moved away. She was really upset because he didn't say goodbye and never wrote or called." She seemed to be thinking as she hesitated, then continued, "Jorge! That was his name. And what was his last name? Something else Hispanic ... Now I remember – Rivera! How could I have forgotten? We asked him once if he was related to Geraldo. He just blushed and turned away."

"Yeah," Fran said, "I remember now, sort of. Didn't some of the kids call him 'Whore, hey'? I can't believe how cruel teens can be. But I never made the connection between that boy and her depression and then her accusations against Moorhouse."

There was a lull in the conversation as they all contemplated their sin of omission – or was it commission? – in not taking Connie's pain seriously. I looked around the room, idly scanning faces. I did a double-take when I saw who was talking with Audrey Fisher-Rivers. It was Ben Bronfman, with Sandy at his side.

CHAPTER FORTY-TWO

What were the Bronfmans doing here? It was too bizarre a coincidence to think this was the family wedding Shoshana had mentioned on – when was it, Tuesday? – at the IRA when Ben was missing in action. I was trying to figure out how I could saunter over to them and eavesdrop. I knew it wouldn't be a problem leaving my tablemates. After all the revelations and the realizations that they didn't know their friend as well as they had thought, they began to talk about inconsequential matters. Nancy had gotten up to get some more drinks, and the others were draining their glasses in preparation.

I excused myself and tried to get close to the trio without attracting their attention. But the room was too crowded for me to get close enough to them to snoop, and was so noisy I wouldn't have been able to hear them without an ear trumpet anyway. I would have tried lip reading, except for one problem: I can't lip read.

The problem was solved when Ben glanced around and saw me looking at them. He gave a slight smile, which I took as an invitation to join them. It wasn't the most welcoming of smiles, but would have to do.

"Sandy, Ben! I didn't know you would be here. And nice to see you again, Audrey." Lame statement. I had just been standing next to her for half an hour during the ceremony. "I see you three know each other." Punch self in head for the most stupid comment since Custer's scout said, "Don't worry. We'll win, easy." That rum and Coke must have been stronger than I realized. Or maybe it was the second one. Or the third. Damn, I should know better than to drink so much in public. Or in private. But every time a Pink Lady got up to bring over more bottles of wine, she brought me another drink, too.

"Hello, Aviva," Ben said with a definite chill in his voice. I guess he hadn't forgiven me yet for accusing Sandy of having spiked Janet's coffee. "We were just talking about Audrey's wedding." I would have thought that was a dangerous subject for Ben to broach, unless he had been trying to convince her not to tell anyone he had officiated.

"Where's your husband?" I asked Audrey, my voice sounding brittle even to my ears. And were my words coming out clearly? "I haven't met him yet."

"Why do you want to know?" Sandy asked, even more belligerently than usual. "Do you think I've done away with him, too, the same as I did Audrey's parents? Or maybe I tried to poison him so he'd have to leave early with an upset stomach, like that old biddy on Friday night?"

Audrey looked back and forth between us, obviously baffled. "Don't worry, Audrey," Sandy said, "I'm joking. But Aviva isn't. She thinks either Ben or I killed your parents to keep them from telling anyone from Temple B'rith Abraham that he married you and what's-his-name, oh, yeah, George." I was beginning to think Sandy had been tippling, too.

"I don't understand. Why would it matter if you married us? Oh," she widened her eyes, "you mean because George isn't Jewish? Big deal, my parents weren't about to broadcast that information. Appearances meant everything to them, more than the truth. In fact, you could say my parents had a very casual acquaintanceship with the truth."

Okay, another avenue to explore. I had no idea when or where, or why besides curiosity, but definitely worth a private chat with Audrey.

Ben, at his most pompous, drew himself up to his full six feet whatever, peered down his nose at me, and said, "I'll have you know, Aviva, that I met with the president of B'rith Shalom this morning and told him about the wedding. He was very understanding, and said it should not make a difference, since it was done unwittingly. So, obviously, Sandy and I had no motive to do anything to keep anyone from saying anything."

Yeah, I thought, no motive now, but what about earlier in the week?

"Why are you talking about murder?" Audrey asked. "My parents killed themselves." She put her hand over her mouth in a caricature of someone who said something she shouldn't have. "I mean, they died in an accident."

But it was too late. Ben, Sandy, and I had heard her say her parents had committed suicide. We looked at Audrey, who turned bright red and looked like she was about to burst into tears. I started to ask if she wanted to go somewhere quieter and discuss it, when George came running over. Or, rather, he loped. He was tall and skinny, with a prominent Adam's apple and an unfortunate haircut. Unless it was an equally poorly designed toupee. He could have modeled for a portrait of Ichabod Crane.

"What did you say to her?" he demanded. In a less angry tone he asked Audrey, "Honey, what did they say to upset you? Let me know, and I'll take care of it. You know I'm here to shield you." Weird guy, totally overreacting to the situation. And he didn't even know what the situation was.

He turned back to us, "Well, what happened here?" He was actually clenching his fists, looking as though he was going to bash us if we didn't answer. Or if we didn't give him the answer he wanted to hear.

Audrey put her hand on his arm. "It's okay, sweetie, they didn't say anything. It was me. I, um, misspoke and told Rabbi Cohen my parents killed themselves. Of course, I meant to say they'd died accidentally." No she hadn't. She had meant what she had first said. The Fishers had deliberately filled their house with carbon monoxide.

George smiled at his wife fondly, but his protectiveness and barely suppressed rage made me uneasy. I was even more uneasy when he scowled at me and said, "Rabbi Cohen, huh? So you're the one who sicced that old guy on us?"

"What old guy?" Audrey and I asked almost at the same time.

He smiled indulgently at Audrey again. "I didn't want to worry you, hon. But some geezer called you yesterday afternoon. You were napping and I didn't want to bother you. He said Rabbi Cohen ..." He glared at me again, and I thought I heard a growl. "... had been asking some questions about that therapist who got himself pulverized the other night. He thought you might remember something about him from high school. Well, I know you don't like to talk about that time, so I gave him an earful and hung up. I told you, dear," he preened, "I'm here to protect you."

Wow, this guy was definitely weird. I was going to have to find out more about him. What about him attracted Audrey? Was she looking for a father substitute? Was she lonely and desperate? Was I practicing psychotherapy without a license? Again.

I also had to look for Phil Brauner. I had no doubt it was he who had called Audrey. I recalled his saying that there was something tickling the back of his mind about Moorhouse. He had obviously remembered what it was. I wish he had called me before trying to question Audrey, and antagonizing her watchdog of a husband.

I was now surrounded by people who were less than pleased by my presence. I had a feeling Ben wasn't going to get together with me for lunch to compare sermon topics, and Sandy wasn't going to invite me to do shopping therapy with her. And Audrey and George were, well, giving me the creeps. I would have to find a way to talk privately with Audrey, though. And hope George was out of the area, preferably in another state, when I did.

"Oh, there's the Pinskys. I haven't had a chance to speak with them since the ceremony. Excuse me, please." They did, too eagerly, I thought, and I headed across the room, squeezing between increasingly inebriated and appetizer-stuffed guests. I suspected there would be a lot of leftover food after the dinner.

As I banged elbows (mostly mine), stepped on toes, and alternated saying "excuse me" and "sorry," I thought about what Audrey had revealed. Suicide did make more sense than an accident, and answered all the questions Janet had raised. But why would Audrey and George have wanted her parents' deaths to be seen as accidental? And how did they know the deaths were suicides if the fire marshal had declared them accidental? And ... I suddenly was left with even more questions than before, including one about suicide clauses in life insurance policies. I had no idea whether the insurance would pay for a suicide. But there was someone here who would know. I looked around for Len Krassner. I had a feeling his wife wouldn't be too pleased with me again, but it wouldn't take me long to ask him about the insurance regulations.

I spotted him and his wife standing in a relatively quiet corner. I could put off talking with the Pinskys and the Caplans until the dinner. It seemed more important that I take Len aside and ask him about the suicide clause. Mostly it was more important because I was afraid I'd forget if I waited until later. And my talking with him now would be more inconspicuous than pulling him away from his prime ribs later.

"Having a good time, Rabbi?" Len greeted me. "I hope you're not doing anything untoward that will show up in next year's job review."

"Sorry, but I have. I freely admit this dress is the same one I've worn to every other Mishkan Or wedding for the past several years."

"I happen to think you look lovely, Rabbi, so ignore all those small minded nitpickers. I love that shawl," said his wife Nora, a terrific woman who designed caftans from beautiful hand-dyed batiks. I owned several.

"Thank you, Nora. Coming from you that's quite a compliment. But I'm going to have to ask a favor of you, and take your husband away again. It's just a quick question, no police interrogation involved this time."

"That was far from an interrogation, Aviva, but I was glad to help. And Nora didn't mind; I got her a nice bracelet as compensation."

Nora jingled her wrist at me to show off a beaten silver bangle. "Keep him as long as you want. Maybe the next one will be gold."

Nora waved to some other Mishkan Or congregants and went to join them, leaving Len and me to talk privately.

"What's on your mind?"

I took a deep breath. "Will a life insurance company pay if someone commits suicide?"

He looked at me questioningly. "You don't think Moorhouse arranged for someone to run him over, do you?"

"No, this has nothing to do with him. It's someone else. The cause of death was declared an accident but the beneficiary (*Was Audrey the beneficiary? Maybe it was a home for wayward gerbils instead.*) let slip that it was suicide. I was wondering why someone would try to make a suicide look like an accident. The surviving family member doesn't strike me as the type to worry about what others would think about her parents. I mean relatives. Damn, it's hard to protect identities."

Len laughed. "Don't worry, Aviva, I won't tell. Besides, I have no idea who you're talking about." He furrowed his brow. "Maybe I do. But, back to your question. It depends."

"Terrific, that's the answer I give when someone asks me about a Jewish belief. Depends on what?"

"Generally, if the policy is less than two years old, the company won't pay, or will try not to. If it's an older policy, they usually will, but sometimes only after a fight. It's not worth the time or expense for them to contest the payment, unless it's a multi-million-dollar payout."

"But what about a specific suicide clause?"

"It's for the first two years of the policy only. They figure that if someone is suicidal, they'll kill themselves before the two years elapse, or they'll get therapy in the meantime and die of natural causes many years later instead. Does that help?"

"Yes and no, since I don't know when the policy was written." I stopped as I realized something else. "Or even if they had a policy."

"Is Walford's very own Jessica Fletcher hot on a case? Or are you Rabbi Small?"

"Neither. I used to be a fan of 'Murder She Wrote' and the Kemelman books, but I haven't been to Maine since I went to camp there as a kid, and never sleep late on Fridays." I noticed his smirk. "Well, almost never. No, I'm just too curious for my own good. Thanks, for your time, Len. You'd better get back to Nora. She's admiring that expensive looking necklace Charlotte Silver's wearing."

CHAPTER FORTY-THREE

We were called into dinner then, not that any of us were hungry. But that wouldn't stop any of us from gorging ourselves anyway. It was a good thing I didn't have a doctor's appointment for a while or I would be on the receiving end of baleful glares about my weight gain and cholesterol levels. And Passover wasn't going to help: it wasn't just the amount of food I would be eating during the seders, it was the immobile character of matzah. I made a mental note to check if I had remembered to buy a box of dried fruit.

I was pleased to see I would be sitting with Ron Finegold and Brenda Fishman; I was less than pleased to see Ben and Sandy Bronfman were also at our table. They didn't seem any happier than I was. Also at the table was a widowed great aunt and two couples who worked with Amanda's father. Since her father sold insurance, I hoped his colleagues wouldn't consider the rest of us prospective clients and the wedding to be a busman's holiday.

After we all nodded and smiled and introduced ourselves, the trumpet player blew a flourish and the band leader, who along with the caterer, is the person who's really in charge of the event, told us to stand and turn toward the doorway to greet the bride and groom. Amanda had either taken off a long beaded jacket she had been wearing over her dress during the ceremony or had changed clothes. She was now in a strapless, backless, and nearly frontless sheath, the prefect dress for someone who was minus twenty in both years and poundage. Michael had taken off his tuxedo jacket and was holding it over his left shoulder, while his right arm was draped over Amanda's shoulder and, I swear I saw him fondling her breast. She didn't seem to mind, as she was laughing and leaning into him. We all cheered and clapped and lifted our glasses to the happy couple, and then gathered around them in a disorganized circle dance as the band segued from "Sunrise, Sunset" to "*Hava Nagilla*." Everyone, that is, except me. I sat down and pulled the small dish of nuts towards me. Brenda joined me, and the two of us just shook our heads. Neither of us is a pomp-and-circumstance kind of person.

After the obligatory hoisting of the couple into the air on chairs held by some guys who probably hadn't lifted anything heavier than a beer glass or TV remote since the last time they had played golf or gone bowling, the band leader asked everyone to sit as the salad was about to be served. He then cued the band to play something softer and slower, like the Macarena. It was going to be a long afternoon, especially as our table, as I had feared would be the case, was close to one of the huge speakers in the four corners of the immense ballroom. Brenda and I didn't even try to talk to each other; why add a sore throat to the earache that was sure to follow?

The salads were served and most people sat down, although a few adults were trying to teach the Macarena to some toddlers, much to the amusement of the doting grandparents. Then I noticed Michael's father, who looked very peeved, go up to the band leader and yell something into his ear, after which the band actually did begin to play some generic easy listening background music.

Brenda was on my right, Ben on my left. I tried to angle my body to the right so I could avoid another argument with Ben. When I turned front to pick up my fork, though, I could not ignore him any longer. It really wouldn't have been polite to disregard someone who is talking to you.

"Sandy and I will be moving into Walford in a few months. You and I will be colleagues. I don't think we should allow all these years of friendship to be disrupted by a misunderstanding."

"You're right, Ben. My overactive imagination ran away with me when I realized the coincidence of your being in town when the Fishers died. I was spinning 'what ifs' and I'm sorry if I gave you the impression I thought you were guilty. If it makes you feel any better, I really didn't believe you had anything to do with their deaths." I hope he wouldn't notice that I had not included Sandy in the "you."

He didn't.

"And I'm sorry I overreacted. But at least now B'rith Abraham knows, so I don't have to keep looking over my shoulder, waiting for the other shoe to drop."

I had heard of a chip on a shoulder, but not of a shoe.

With thoughts like that, I knew it was time to switch to Diet Coke without the rum. "I'm glad everything is working out for you, Ben. I really am looking forward to having you in the community. Now, if you'll excuse me for a minute, I need a drink. I mean, a soft drink." I looked around the table. "Can I get anyone anything from the bar?" There was a collective negative shaking of heads.

I made my way through the maze of tables, smiling and mouthing hello to people I didn't recognize. The problem with being in the public eye, especially in a small town, is that people you don't know think they know you. I couldn't afford to offend anyone by not saying hi.

As I passed the head table, Amanda called out to me. "Rabbi, come over here, I haven't had a chance to talk to you since the ceremony."

I inwardly sighed and took the seat that Michael had vacated for me. "It's great to do a wedding for a couple that looks as right for each other as you and Michael. You both seem very happy, and so do your families."

"Oh, we are. All of us. Our parents even like each other. They're planning a winter trip to Arizona together – the four of them decided Florida is too 'common.' So," she switched topics, "I saw you and the Bronfmans talking to each other. How do you know each other? Or do all rabbis know all the other rabbis?"

"Far from it," I laughed. "Ben and I were classmates. I saw him at a conference last week, and he mentioned he was staying to go to a family wedding, but I didn't realize you were the family."

"Sandy's mom and my dad are brother and sister, but I haven't seen my cousin in ages. She and Ben keep moving around, and never locally. Until now, of course. It will be great to have her back here. I used to idolize her when I was a kid. She was my cool older cousin. She often babysat for me, and I would follow her around like a puppy dog. I was devastated when her parents moved from Walford to Doylestown. But that was around the time she left for college anyway, so it wouldn't have mattered if they still lived nearby. But you don't think of things like that when you're seven. I hadn't expected them to make it to the wedding, but then they got in touch with me and said they would be in the area this week and could they still come. Another couple we had invited – you know them, or knew, I should say – the Fishers – couldn't make it at the last minute, so I was able to say sure, without having to change our order with the caterer."

I was confused. "But the Fishers died a couple of days ago, Tuesday night, I think it was, or Wednesday. But I heard earlier in the week that Ben was staying for a wedding."

"Oh, I didn't mean they couldn't make it because they were dead! Oops, poor choice of words." Her guffaw told me she had been to the bar a few times, too. "No, Flo and Milt canceled a couple of weeks ago. Milt's Parkinson's had begun to progress more rapidly, and he was unable to get out much. Flo was really sorry they couldn't come, but she didn't want to leave Milt alone too long, and it was getting too hard to transport him, even with the handicap van they got. Plus, Flo was still trying to get her head around finding out she had ovarian cancer. And this was after she had survived breast cancer ten years ago. I think, too, Milt was embarrassed to be seen the way he was, all contracted and barely able to speak. Or, maybe it was Flo who was embarrassed. They were really good friends of my parents, and I hate to speak ill of the dead (*No, you don't. No one who uses that phrase means it, especially, it seemed, former Pink Ladies*), but I never liked them all that much, especially her. She was very superficial, always worrying about the impression they made."

Interesting, Audrey had described her mother in the same way. "You were good friends with their daughter, though, weren't you? She is one of your attendants."

Amanda made a face. "I really couldn't exclude her, since I had asked the rest of our high school clique. And since our parents were such good friends. And she had invited me to be her maid of honor, but I was able to get out of it because of the distance. I had figured she'd decline the invitation, using the same excuse I had, but it turned out her parents had been bugging her to visit and had suggested this weekend. I think they wanted to talk to her about their health. So we were stuck with her, and had to do a rush job on the dress fitting, not that six months of alterations would have made a difference. Oops, I really am being nasty today, aren't I? I'm allowed – it's my wedding and I can do what I want!" She grinned broadly at the idea that she was Queen for a Day for the first time in her life.

"It certainly is your day. So enjoy every minute." Since she was in a catty mood, I decided to probe some more. I was curious about her take on Connie Costello, but decided introducing sexual abuse and suicide directly into the conversation wasn't the way to get the information. So I decided to use a back door approach. "How did Audrey get to be a member of the Pink Ladies? Weren't you already together when she moved here?"

Amanda thought for a minute. "I don't think so. We didn't get together as a group until high school, although we had all known each other since kindergarten. I think Audrey moved here when we were about twelve, so we would have been in seventh grade. Or maybe it was eighth. I know it was the middle of the school year, and she was miserable. What twelve year old wouldn't be, moving a couple of hundred miles away from your friends a few months before your bat Mitzvah? And middle school is tough enough without being the new kid, and one who was skinny and spotty and had zilch personality. We only got to know her because her parents sent her to Mishkan Or for Hebrew school. We knew her but weren't friends. The only friend she had then was a Catholic girl, Connie. And we invited Connie to be a Pink Lady, I think it was in tenth grade. It's a blur after all these years. I do remember we had nothing in common with Connie, except she was an outsider, too. She wasn't Jewish, though, and her parents were farmers – there were still a lot of working farms in the area then – and we considered her a Piney. We learned about the Kallikaks in psych course in a unit on eugenics, and the other kids all began to call her Kalli."

With a nod, I indicated my recognition of the reference. In the early twentieth century, a psychologist claimed the pseudonymous

Kallikak family, who lived in the Jersey Pine Barrens, was proof that traits like morality and criminality were inherited. The research was later rejected as pseudoscience, but in the meantime "Kallikak" had become a synonym for "feeble-minded."

Amanda continued, "The only reason we decided to invite her to join us is because she had this hunk of an older cousin staying with her every summer. He basically ignored us – he was three or four years older – but we all had a crush on him. He was from Brooklyn or the Bronx or one of those places with a distinctive accent, and was dark and dangerous looking. Think the young Travolta. Or James Dean in *Rebel without a Cause*. He was the bad boy none of our parents would have ever let us date. Not that he ... what was his name? I used to scribble it all over my notebooks and now don't remember it! In any case, it was pretty unlikely any of us would ever have gotten the opportunity to date him. But we were the unpopular girls, and we had our dreams of showing up the popular ones by being with this older, forbidden guy. So we asked Connie to be part of the Pink Ladies. And Audrey was part of the package. If we wanted access, no matter how remote to ... Vince, that was his name! ... we had to take Audrey, too."

I played innocent, not only pretending I'd never heard of Vince, but that I didn't know about Connie either. I figured the other Pink Ladies wouldn't be comparing notes with the bride about their respective conversations with me. So I asked, "I knew all your attendants. Was Connie unable to make it today?"

"Only if she could have arisen from the grave. Oops, being snarky again. She killed herself our junior year. She and Audrey were having a contest to see which of them could become the most emaciated and depressed. They both got sent to a shrink and then claimed he had molested them. Yeah, right. As if. Wishful thinking on their parts. I think they both got drunk one night and a couple of football players took advantage of them. At least, that was the rumor among the cheerleaders." At my surprised look, she added, "Not that I hung out with the cheerleaders, but I was one of the brains and earned some extra money tutoring a couple of them so they could stay on the squad. They were more than happy to tell tales about the other Pink

Ladies. God, teenagers are insufferable. I'm surprised more of us didn't follow Connie's example." She was quiet for a minute. "I wonder what happened to Vince. He's probably fat, bald, married with a zillion kids, and a numbers runner for the mob. Oh, well. *C'est la vie.*"

We had been talking for so long the band had gone through another set of dances and we were all asked to return to our tables for the main course. "It was nice chatting with you, Amanda, but I don't want to monopolize any more of your time. Again, my best wishes for a wonderful life together."

I still hadn't gotten anything to drink, so I made my way to the bar and then tried not to spill the contents of the glass – too much ice and not enough soda – as I bobbed and weaved my way back to the table. The band had reverted to its earlier decibel level, so I was able to get away with just smiling my hellos to my table mates and didn't have to (wasn't able to) chat with them. For once, I was pleased to be seated so close to the speakers, as I had several new pieces of information to think about, and could be quiet without being rude.

The Fishers had a van. Milt had Parkinson's and Flo ovarian cancer, which might have been the reason for their suicides. I wasn't sure if the reason I hadn't known about their diagnoses was because they never came to services, or any other programs at the synagogue, or if they didn't participate because they were so ill. I have to admit I was a bit hurt they had never confided in me. So much for my abilities as a pastoral counselor. Worse, I had never reached out to them, just to call and say, "We haven't seen you for a while. How are you?" I would have to go through the membership list after Pesach and see how many of the others I had not seen for a while I should contact.

Another thing I had never known was that Sandy was originally from Walford. There was a good reason I hadn't known: I really never cared enough about her to ask about her background. And there was a good reason I had apologized to Ben and not to Sandy about my suspicions: I still wasn't convinced she wasn't guilty of something, even if it was just a lack of manners and personality. Had she been younger, I would have wondered if she had been one of

Moorhouse's patients.

And it was another coincidence in a growing list of coincidences that the Pink Ladies knew Vince. It made sense they would have since Connie had been part of their clique, even if the others had not been wholly accepting of her. I was still intrigued by Vince and his presence in Walford when Moorhouse was killed. "Dangerous" was a good description of him, and not just of his looks when he was a teen. But, damn, he had been charming, and he had convinced me he wasn't involved in the hit-and-run. Would I have doubted him if Lieutenant Merino hadn't warned me to stay clear? Maybe I would have – Vince's insistence on remaining anonymous to both the police and the press tipped me off that he wasn't on the up-and-up even before Merino's call. But maybe he was just what he seemed: a member of the criminal underworld who just happened to have the resources to kill someone but hadn't, at least not in this case. Or had he? I really did need to get Trudy to perform her electronic voodoo again.

I wondered if Trudy had found anything about the Fishers. I had a couple of missed calls on my cell phone from Trudy, from Leesa Monaghan, from Lieutenant Merino and from the fire marshal. Strange that no one had left a message. I would go outside after the main meal – for a breath of fresh air and to get away from the cacophony – and return the calls before dessert. I hoped none of the calls would cause me to miss dessert.

The Fishers' van really intrigued me. I could imagine a scenario in which Flo, wanting to make amends at the end of her life for having doubted her daughter and treated her so poorly, had exacted revenge against the man who was responsible for alienating the parents and daughter even further. I wondered if Flo blamed Moorhouse for Audrey's having moved so far away.

Far away to Eugene, Oregon. Where Moorhouse had lived with wife number two. And where he was a victim – non-fatal that time – of another hit-and-run driver.

So much to ponder, so little time. So many questions, so few answers. Time to eat.

CHAPTER FORTY-FOUR

Dinner was delicious. I was very happy I had worn something loose-fitting or I would have been very uncomfortable. The band leader called everyone up to do the Chicken Dance, which I took as my cue to go outside and return those phone calls.

I decided to call in the order they were received, so Trudy was first. "What kind of game are you playing, Aviva?" Trudy never said hello. Or goodbye. Her phone manners left a lot to be desired, as her mother kept telling her. "I can find no mention at all of a Florence or Milton Fisher in Connecticut. Or in any of the other fifty states, except New Jersey, and that was only from the early seventies on. I even went global – zilch. They seemed to have sprung full-blown from the brow of Zeus when they moved to Walford." Again with the literary allusions? Maybe it was the influence of the stories she was reading to Simi. She hadn't had to read to Josh since he was three; he insisted on reading to her instead. "The only thing I can think of is they were in the Witness Protection Program. I called in a couple of favors and had some, um, colleagues checked it out for me. They found nothing, and if they couldn't, no one can. Not even me, and I taught them all they know."

"Witness Protection? Isn't that for people who are in danger of being killed because they testified against gangs or the Mafia or whoever?"

"You have a great ability to simplify explanations, Auntie, but, yeah, in general, you're right." She stopped. "What an idiot I am. Maybe they weren't being hidden away, maybe they hid themselves."

"Huh?"

"Maybe they created new identities for themselves. Look, I'll get back to you. I need to check if anyone with the name Fisher died about thirty years ago, people whose social security numbers they could have stolen."

"Huh?"

"Don't worry about it. Just keep that sweet naiveté of yours. I'll explain later."

"Huh?" But the phone connection was broken.

Witness Protection? Stealing social security numbers? Florence was a suburban shopaholic lady-who-lunches and Milton was an accountant. What reason would they have to change their identities? I'd have to trust Trudy to figure it out. She usually did.

Next call was to Leesa. "Thanks for calling me back. Have you checked my follow-up story yet?"

"I've had no time. I've been at a wedding all day. Can you give me the gist?"

"The Triple-U administration is threatening a lawsuit, which has no chance of going anywhere but is a good public relations smoke screen. They claim they knew all about the allegations against Moorhouse, but he'd never been indicted, so there was no proof of anything."

"That's not surprising, is it?"

"No, but what is surprising is that I can't find anyone who is willing to talk to me about his having molested her. I mean, allegedly molested. I tried some of the leads that your niece gave me, but no one is talking, even with my guarantee of anonymity for them. They're all on the West Coast, so I can't exactly fly over and try to convince them in person. Not that there are all that many leads anyway. It seems Trudy could only track down two or three. She thinks that website may have been the handiwork of only a couple of particularly vindictive types who wanted to make it seem there had been more victims than there were. Alleged victims. And, Aviva?" She hesitated. "Are you sure there was anything substantive to the rumors here in Walford? Maybe they were just rumors. I can find nothing in any records at all about the incidents — alleged incidents — beyond the couple of newspaper articles and the Google hits. I can find nothing in any police reports or court cases, except his ex-wife's accusation during the divorce proceedings. I called your niece, but she had nothing new to add."

"I do have some information for you, Leesa, but I'm still at the wedding and I don't want anyone to overhear me. My sources are the members of the bridal party."

"Can you give me a quick synopsis? I've got a deadline."

"According to these women I spoke with, two of their friends made the accusations against Moorhouse. No one, not even the friends, believed them. They thought the women – girls then – were trying to be the center of attention. In fact, they think the second one was just a copycat."

"Anything to the first one's accusation?"

"No one knows, or ever will. She's the one I left you a message about last night, the one who killed herself."

"Sounds as though she was telling the truth."

"Maybe. But according to her friends, she was also clinically depressed and anorexic."

"And the second one?"

"Is here at the wedding, one of the attendants. She's the daughter of the couple who died of carbon monoxide poisoning the other night."

"And she's at a wedding? Cold."

"She and her parents seemed to have been estranged for a while, and she carries a lot of resentment against them still. I have Trudy checking into them and, here's the interesting bit, they don't seem to have existed before moving to Walford. Trudy's looking into whether they stole their identities or were in the Witness Protection Program."

"How come I'm the investigative reporter, and you're the one who keeps finding all these juicy stories? Keep me in the loop – a scoop like that will definitely get me set up at the paper, especially on the heels of the Triple-U/Moorhouse debacle. Unless, of course, the university really does have a chance in court."

"I don't know, Leesa. I hate invading people's privacy like this."

"No you don't, or you wouldn't still be prying. Listen, just promise you'll think about giving me the story after everything's resolved.

And before one of the other reporters gets wind of what's going on."

"Leesa, even I don't know what's going on."

Third call was the one I was least looking forward to returning, so I didn't. Instead of calling Merino, I called the fire marshal instead.

Bob Jeffers picked up at the first ring. "Hello, this is Rabbi Cohen returning your call."

"Thanks for getting back to me. I understand you want to talk to me about the Fishers, that you think there are too many inconsistencies between some information you've uncovered and the official report."

"It's gotten even more complicated. I just heard the Fishers may have committed suicide."

"How reliable is the information?"

"I got it from their daughter, although she later said she had meant to say 'accident.'"

"I've got a couple of men out sick, so I'm pulling extra duty this weekend. Gotta be a good role model. So stop by any time today, and we can talk. I'll be here."

"That would be great. I'm at a wedding right now, and will want to go home and change first, so it may be a few hours."

"No problem. I'll be here. And, confidentially, I've had some doubts, too, but there was nothing we could find that pointed to anything but an accident."

I'd put off the inevitable as long as I could. I had Merino's direct number, so I didn't have to go through the switchboard. I was hoping he wasn't at his desk and we could continue playing telephone tag for a while longer. Say, another month or so.

"Merino here." I guess I had used up all my chits with the universe.

"Hi, Joe. Aviva Cohen, returning your call." May as well try for an informal, chummy tone. I was sure it would turn serious soon enough.

I was right. "Rabbi Cohen, I need you to stop by my office as soon as you can. We need to talk."

Uh-oh. "Sorry, Lieutenant, but I'm at a wedding and won't be able to get away for a couple of hours." The truth was I could have left at any time after the ceremony, but he wouldn't know that.

He knew that. "I'm sure they don't need you to help cut the wedding cake. Just get over here. It could be a matter of life and death."

"Whose?"

"Yours."

CHAPTER FORTY-FIVE

"You already scared me enough this morning, Joe, when you told me about Vince Ferrillo. Don't you think telling me again is over kill?" I winced. "Bad choice of words, huh? And is this about Ferrillo or some other boogeyman?"

"Don't make light of the matter, Aviva. We have some new information that makes it imperative we talk to you. If I have to, I'll send over a squad car and put you in protective custody. Or I'll call Homeland Security and tell them you have information about terrorists that you refuse to divulge."

"Can you do that?"

"Probably not, but only because Steve would bust me down to traffic control. You've been at that wedding for hours. It must be ending soon."

"Then you've never been to a Jewish wedding. The ceremony took only twenty minutes. The reception will go for another hour or two." I glanced at my watch. It was already three o'clock. "I might be able to get away around four."

"Is the cake that tempting? I'll buy you a donut instead."

"Wedding cake is often like the pastry on display at a Jersey diner. Looks great, tastes like cardboard and sugary glue. It's the Viennese table I'm waiting for."

"What is a ...? Never mind. We have to talk with you, and it's too sensitive to trust to the phones."

"Are you suggesting the police phones aren't secure? And someone can tap into a cell phone?" I thought about Trudy and her cohorts. "Oh, I guess they can."

"The answers are yes to both your questions. We do need a face-to-face with you."

"Then we'll do it tomorrow. Maybe."

"We need to do it now. Hold on a sec ..." He must have put his hand over the mouth piece, because all I heard was a muffled mumble. (Nice alliteration, but is there any other kind of mumble?)

I then heard a very clear and very familiar voice. "Just get your cute little butt over here as soon as you can."

"Stop lying, Steve. First, my butt isn't cute, unless you mistake cellulite for dimples. Second, it's far from little; never has been, never will be. Third, what would your new girlfriend think about your flirting with your ex-wife? And fourth, what the hell are you doing back in Walford?"

I could hear sniggering in the background. "Aviva," Steve said in the quiet voice I knew meant he was getting to the end of his patience, "I'm on speaker phone."

"Oh, oops. Sorry." No I wasn't.

"Believe me, I'm not flirting. I'm telling you that uncute, cellulite-pocked butt will be in a sling – and the rest of you in traction – if you don't talk to us soon."

"Police brutality?"

"Not from us, from the mob. We need to know everything you know so we can figure out why you're in their sights. You're getting too close to something, and we need to figure out what it is."

"You didn't answer my question. Why are you back in Walford?" What I really wanted to ask was how things were going with his girlfriend, but even I could tell it wasn't the time.

"Joe called me to talk some sense into you. He had a feeling he would get nowhere."

"And you would?"

"I've had more practice with your stubbornness."

"May I go home and change first?"

"No, your house is probably the most dangerous place for you to be. Joe told me he warned you this morning to stay in public view."

"Does a meeting with Bob Jeffers count as public?"

"What are you talking about? Are you still on that supposed case, too? The hit-and-run isn't enough, now you have to meddle in proving an accident was murder?"

"No, it was suicide."

He was silent. "You still there, Steve?"

"Yeah, I am. Shit. Of course, that's what it's all about. No wonder Ferrillo is keeping an eye on you. We were thinking it had to do with the hit-and-run. I had forgotten you were poking your nose into the Fishers' deaths, too. No wonder the FBI wants to talk to you. Just be here by four-thirty."

"What? The FBI?" But the line was dead. People had been hanging up on me a lot lately.

I made my way back into the reception hall. If anything, the band was even louder. They were now into the oldies phase of the day, starting, of course, with Bob Seger's "Old Time Rock and Roll." It used to be one of my favorite songs, reflecting perfectly my views on most musical genres from Disco to whatever the latest permutation was, until it became a staple of every Jewish celebration, along with "Bad Bad Leroy Brown."

Janet Brauner waved to me from her table, and I realized with a jolt of guilt – or was it fear she could get me fired? – I hadn't spoken to her yet. I sat in an empty chair next to her. "How are you feeling, Janet? Phil told me yesterday you were under the weather." It was difficult to speak in soothing, professional tones when I had to yell into her ear to be heard.

"Much better, thank you, dear. I thought at first it must have just been one of those twenty-four hour things, but then I remembered I had succumbed to temptation and had fettuccini alfredo when we treated ourselves and went out for an early dinner before services. All that fat must have been too much for my poor gallbladder." She laughed. "It happens every time I indulge, but I never seem to learn. Anyway, let's go out to the hallway where we can talk without screaming." *Bummer. I guess Sandy's off the hook. At least for now.*

As the heavy double doors closed behind us, we both heaved a sigh of relief. "I feel like I've been swimming," Janet complained. My ears are all clogged up. I hate how loud these bands are. They must be getting kickbacks from audiologists."

"I know what you mean. I feel the same." I spotted a couple of easy chairs down the hallway. "Why don't we sit there?"

As we settled into the chairs – so low and soft, I knew we would be sorry later when it came time to stand up and neither of us would succeed, at least not gracefully – I apologized to Janet for not having come over sooner.

"Oh, please, Rabbi. I know you have a lot of people you need to *schmooze* up. Don't worry about it. But I did have something to tell you. Phil gave me the message that you were wondering if I remembered anything about Moorhouse. At first, I didn't recognize the name, but when he reminded me about the sex abuse scandal, it all came back to me. I seem to recall there was no proof he had ever touched those girls. But here's the thing: one of the accusers was Audrey Fisher! Her mother told me about the incident, and was furious, not at Moorhouse but at Audrey. She didn't believe her and thought she was making it up."

"What do you think?"

"That she was making it up. In fact, I know she was. I told you Florence was one of my dearest friends. She took me into her confidence and told me she had taken Audrey to the gynecologist, who said Audrey was still a virgin!"

"So why did Audrey say it?"

"Why did she do anything in those days? For attention. And revenge. She never forgave her parents for moving from New York to Walford. She was determined to make their lives a misery, with her outlandish clothes and piercings and tattoos and makeup. And she largely succeeded."

"Did you say 'New York'? I thought they were from Connecticut."

"They only lived there for a couple of months. No, they were from the Bronx originally. Florence worked very hard to get rid of her accent, but it would creep in now and then. Milt never bothered. He was proud of his working class background and that he had made something of himself."

"Milt was an accountant, wasn't he?"

"Yes, and a very good one. Until his Parkinson's got too bad, he had his own firm and made quite a nice living at it. I think Milt still had a few clients he kept after closing the company. With computers and the Internet, he said, he could work from home. Janet used to work off and on as a real estate agent both in New York and later in this area, but it was from boredom rather than need. She hasn't worked at anything like that in about twenty years."

"Did they move here because Milt was ill?"

"Oh, no. They moved here ... let me think ... about thirty years ago, I guess. No, he's been ill only for the past five years or so."

I debated whether to ask Janet whether she knew about Florence's illness, but figured she would volunteer the information if she knew. She did, at least in part. "And then Florence started to feel tired and went to the doctor for a checkup. I'm not sure if she got the results, though. At least, she hadn't told me."

Audrey passed us then, heading toward the restroom. I wasn't sure how much, if anything, of our conversation she overheard. She waved at us and continued on without stopping, so she hadn't heard, didn't care, or really had to go.

Janet leaned in closer and practically hissed into my ear. "I cannot, absolutely cannot believe the *chutzpah* and disrespect that girl is showing. She's as bad now as when she was a teen. I even called her yesterday and told her exactly what I thought about her behavior. No funeral, no *shiva*, a cremation – that's all bad enough. But being in a wedding party only a few days after her parents were killed is outlandish! It's beyond, well, I'm speechless!"

Janet must be extremely upset to be speechless.

"How did Audrey react? Did you use the word 'killed' or 'died' when you spoke to her? Did she say anything?"

"I might have said 'died,' but I still think there's something wrong with the deaths. I did tell Audrey that things didn't add up and she should talk to the fire marshal, but she told me to mind my own business and hung up on me! On me, her mother's best friend! She and her husband are a good match."

"Why do you say that?"

"After Phil gave me your message and I told him what I knew, Phil remembered the incident, too, and tried to call Audrey to ask her to contact you, but her new husband was very abusive to him and slammed down the phone, so he never gave her the message."

"Talking about me?" Audrey was standing next to us, and Janet's voice had risen with her indignation.

"Yes, I am. You have no right to be here. Whatever problems you had with your parents when you were a teen, well, you're not fifteen anymore. Grow up already. Learn some respect!"

"You mean, put on a show of grief when I don't feel it? No, thank you. My parents had the corner on hypocrisy and lies. I could never come close to being as good as they were. Or maybe I should say 'bad.'"

"That's a terrible thing to say! Your parents were wonderful people, so kind and compassionate. When I was sick last year, your mother brought over already cooked food for us to put in the freezer and visited me every day when I was in rehab. No one else did. No offense, Rabbi, I know you visited when you could and you had other commitments, too."

Okay, I was put in my place.

"Kind? Compassionate? That shows what good actors they were. They never showed me any kindness or compassion! Want to hear all the lies they told you? No? Well, too bad. I'm going to tell you anyway; maybe then you'll stop idealizing them.

"They told you they were from Connecticut, right? Well, we never lived there. We moved here right from the Bronx. And our name wasn't Fisher. It was Fleischer. They changed it when we got here. Know why? My parents swore me to secrecy, said they were in the Witness Protection Program because my father had testified against the Bronx mob. I doubt very much he ever met anyone from the mob. I think he was embezzling from clients and was about to get caught."

"Your father was very honest." Janet was almost in tears, and I was getting worried she would work herself into another heart attack. "He did our taxes every year and wouldn't let us get away with anything that had the slightest chance of being questioned."

"He was probably afraid if you got audited, he would come to the attention of the IRS. Believe me, that's the last thing he would have wanted. And you can believe me. I'm a lot more truthful than they ever were. Let me ask you: what did my mother say George and I do for a living?"

"She was very proud of you. She said you both worked at a community college."

"Doing what?"

Janet hesitated. "She never really said, but gave the impression you taught English literature, and George was the comptroller."

Audrey laughed. "Typical. I'm the secretary in the English department – I don't even have the lofty title of administrative assistant – and George is the payroll clerk in the comptroller's office. He processes the pay checks, basically just pushing the right buttons so the computer can spit them out.

"And guess what else they lied about? On Thursday, when I was going through their papers to find their wills and the deeds to the cemetery plots and their insurance policy and ... it doesn't matter, just all the official papers I would need ... I discovered my birth certificate. The reissued one, with their names on it. Along with adoption papers. Somehow, they forgot to tell me I was adopted. Imagine being forty-two years old and finding out your parents weren't. It explained a lot: the constant criticism from my mother, the lack of interest from my father. I wasn't the perfect child they had ordered. I wasn't pretty and petite and smart and polite and someone they could show off. Instead, I was an embarrassment and a big disappointment. So tell me, why should I show any respect for such liars? I'm better off without them."

She turned and walked off without another word. Janet and I sat there stunned. Neither of us said another word either.

CHAPTER FORTY-SIX

"Did you believe her?"

Janet shook her head. "I can't. She did not describe the people I knew. Her mother always said Audrey was a pathological liar. I thought she was exaggerating. It looks like she wasn't."

"Unless ... Listen, I didn't know the Fishers, or Fleischers, or whatever their name was, well; and I don't know Audrey at all. But ... well, I asked Trudy to do a computer search, and she could find no trace of them in Connecticut. In fact, she could find no trace of them at all before they moved to Walford. I have to wonder if maybe, just maybe, there's a germ of truth in what Audrey said." I held up my hand to stop Janet's expected protestation. "I know it's hard to think that your friends may not have been who you thought, but, please, just try to recall if there's anything at all that could prove or disprove what Audrey told us."

"Why did you want information about Florence and Audrey?" It was not the protest I expected. "Oh." Janet covered her open mouth. "It's because of Moorhouse, right? You wanted to find out if they could have been responsible for running him over! I know how you think, Rabbi (*I certainly hope she didn't.*). You think they killed him and then went home and committed suicide!"

"Janet," I tried to keep my voice level, "the Fishers died two nights before the accident. And I didn't suspect suicide until Audrey mentioned it. I wanted more information about Audrey, but there were unlikely to be any records of her before she moved to Walford because of her age. When Trudy told me she couldn't find any mention of the Fishers before thirty years ago, she suggested they were either in the Witness Protection Program or had stolen their identities to hide their real ones from the authorities. Audrey mentioned those same two possibilities. That's why I want you to think back on your years of knowing them, especially when they were first here. Was there anything that didn't seem right?" I decided I wasn't above some flattery. "I mean, look at how good you were at noticing the inconsistencies in the evidence that the carbon monoxide leak was an accident. You just knew it wasn't, even when everyone else said it was."

Janet visibly preened. "Well, yes, it looks as though I was pretty astute there, wasn't I?"

"Yes, you were. I'm not asking you to come up with anything here and now. When you get home, sit down with Phil and see if the two of you can come up with anything."

She didn't say no, which I took as an encouraging sign, so I continued, "I just had another idea. I know you want to do something to honor the Fishers' memories, since Audrey's not sitting *shiva*. Why don't you get some friends together and maybe their reminiscences will spark some memory in you."

"I do want to do something, but I'm not sure when. What with the seders tomorrow and Tuesday nights, everyone will be busy, cooking or cleaning or traveling. We wouldn't be able to do anything until at least Wednesday night." She thought a moment. "Quite a few of us are here at the wedding. I'll ask if any of them would like to come to our place tonight. The wedding should be done soon, or at least we can leave without being impolite. I didn't plan to clean the house for Passover until tomorrow anyway, since we'll be at our son's for the first seder and at Mishkan Or for the second. We can stop at ShopRite or Trader Joe's on the way home and pick up some cheese and crackers and fruit." She laughed, "Not that any of us will be hungry, but we need to serve something!"

"That's a great idea, Janet. Thank you. And, please, call me after they leave, no matter how late, and let me know if you learn anything that could help us figure out what's going on."

My brain was about to shut down from sensory overload. Janet went back to corral her friends for the impromptu informal *shiva* and I was headed toward the bar before I remembered, first, I was driving and, second, I had to go to the police station. Either one of those was a great reason not to imbibe, but the two of them together made the reason unassailable. I settled for another Diet Coke. I put the glass down at my place at the empty table – Ben and Sandy engaged in doing the Electric Slide was a sight to behold! – and, ever mindful of the input-output equation, decided to pay a visit to the restroom before drinking any more.

I nodded absent-mindedly at the other wedding guests, exchanged a few pleasantries with members of Mishkan Or, tried to ignore the now feeling-no-pain Pink Ladies (minus Audrey) who were gesturing for me to join them, and noticed Audrey huddled in a corner with George, probably trying to keep him from thumping me. By the time I got to the restroom, the slight urge was becoming an uncomfortable urgency.

After answering my call of nature, I opened the cubicle door and almost closed it again when I saw Audrey at the sink. She was dabbing at her eyes, removing her remaining makeup in the process, and looked as though she had been crying. She looked up when she heard the door open and our eyes met in the mirror. I had to come out and talk to her.

"Are you okay, Audrey?"

"Yeah," she lied. "Just got something in my eye. I'm not used to wearing makeup and rubbed my eye, and got mascara in it. I decided it was easier to just wash it all off."

I let the lie pass. "I'm sorry about earlier. I had no idea what you are going through. I can't imagine not learning you're adopted until after your parents die. And they died so suddenly, too."

She shrugged. "It was a shock – not their deaths – oh, don't look so scandalized, Rabbi! They were dying anyway, Parkinson's and cancer. They took the easy way out. I can't say I blame them. But the adoption – I mean, how could they have kept something so ... so ... so ... oh, what's the word? Vital? Important? No, fundamental! So fundamental to my sense of self, to our sense of family! How could they have never told me?"

"Forty-plus years ago, people weren't as open about adoption. There was something, I don't know, furtive, secretive, almost disreputable about it. People didn't want anyone to know they were infertile; women who put their babies up for adoption were told they were unfeeling and abandoned their children. It was a different mindset." I thought about Trudy and Sherry, and how Josh knew his father was a gynecological turkey baster, how Simi, as soon she was old enough, would know she was adopted when her birth parents died and there were no other family members who could raise her.

"I know all that, but still. At the very least, they could have said something in their suicide note, instead of waiting for me to find the papers. And they must have wanted me to find them because they didn't destroy them. In fact, they left them with all the other important documents where I couldn't miss them."

"So it was definitely suicide?" Audrey nodded. "Why didn't you tell the investigators?"

"George thought it would be better – less paperwork, fewer police investigations, no questions from the insurance company. I just went along." She looked around the empty restroom as though someone might be eavesdropping, and lowered her voice, "George even told me to destroy the suicide note, but I kept it. Don't tell him."

As if I would. I took a deep breath before my next question. "Audrey, I know you've been married only a short time, but are you afraid of George? I couldn't help but notice that he seems, well, overly protective and a bit volatile."

She laughed. "Oh, he's fine. It's all a macho act. He tries to compensate for looking like a scarecrow and having a dorky job by coming across all caveman-ish. He's harmless."

I changed the subject. "What are your plans now? Are you going to stay in Eugene or move back here?"

"Oh, go back to Oregon, definitely. We love it there, and, as lowly as our jobs may be, we've had them for a long time and don't want to look for new ones or relocate. We've got a nice little house in a semi-rural area, not far from the city and the college, but close to woods and lakes." She laughed again. "I just realized how similar it is to Walford! I can't believe now that I was upset when we moved from New York. I could never go back to that kind of urban lifestyle again. As soon as I settle the estate and sell the house, I'll be heading back.

George may need to go back earlier, but I can get compassionate leave from work. And, let's face it, the paychecks George prints out are more essential to the running of the college than photocopying test questions. I'm just worried the house might not sell, what with the traumatic deaths."

"I might be interested in buying it." (*What?!*)

Audrey looked skeptical.

"No, really, I would. I'm over fifty-five, I'm tired of the steps in my townhouse and would love to move somewhere without stairs or neighborhood garage bands." Mr. Sullivan, my eighty-year-old next-door neighbor, had suffered a stroke last winter and his daughter made him move in with her after he left rehab. The new owner was a single mother with a teenage son who thought he was the second coming of Ringo Starr. But at least he was willing to shovel out my driveway, a job I had relied on Mr. Sullivan to do. He demanded a much higher salary than the fresh-baked chocolate chip cookies Mr. Sullivan accepted as pay, though.

"If you're serious ...."

"I am. Could I stop by and see the place, maybe tonight or tomorrow?"

"Um, sure. Either day. Just call first." She searched her bag for a pen and scrap of paper, tearing it off an envelope, and scribbled down her cell phone number.

"Great. Thanks. Tell you what: let's plan on seven tonight. I'll call if I can't make it."

"Sure, that will be fine."

"Okay, I'll see you later, then."

I bet Steve and Joe (and the FBI?) would love to hear what I planned, not that I had any particular plan in mind. Maybe I'd neglect to tell them.

CHAPTER FORTY-SEVEN

I got back to the table in time to get up and fill my plate with all kinds of beautiful looking small pastries. I added a few pieces of fruit for balance, and was able to resist the non-dairy fake ice cream. Brenda and Sandy were chatting together and laughing like old friends, as were Ron and Ben. I would have to make sure I got together with the Fishman-Finegold couple soon to compare notes. Not that I wanted to poison Brenda's mind against Sandy (no, not me), and Ben was going to be a colleague, for better or worse, with Ron and me. But it might not be a bad idea for me to add a few of my own observations and experiences.

I took a few bites from each piece – as usual, I took more than I could eat – and wondered whether it was time for me to investigate medications for my lack of impulse control. Why had I ever decided to go to see the Fishers' house? Yes, the steps were getting a bit much for my creaky knees, and the drum practice next door was destroying my few remaining auditory cells, but I couldn't afford to move to Serenity Acres. When new, the houses cost almost double what I could get for my townhouse, and the resale price would be even higher. And did I really want to live across the street from Charlotte and Marty Silver? They were nice enough people, but Charlotte was Janet's sister, assuring me a complete lack of privacy. Besides, there is no way I could pack up and move all my books from my home study. And my bedroom. And my living room.

It was now four o'clock. I had half an hour to get to the police department, then I needed to go to the fire department, to the Fishers' former house, and, finally, home (if my overly protective ex-husband would let me) to check emails, answer emails, check phone messages, return phone messages, and wait for Janet to call back. Not necessarily in that order. At some point, sooner rather than later, I needed to get out of my long dress, heels, and pantyhose and into a pair of jeans or, even better, sweat pants. An already long day was about to become even longer. In fact, it was about to become a long night.

People were starting to leave, clutching their napkins wrapped around slices of wedding cake that would probably never be eaten. I went to the table where the new in-laws were holding court. "Rabbi, aren't you going to stay until Amanda throws her bouquet?" Mrs. Caplan asked.

"After two failed marriages, I think I'll give someone else a chance." Not a particularly appropriate comment to make at a wedding. The Caplans and Pinskys laughed politely; little did they know I wasn't kidding.

I said my goodbyes and made my way through the room waving and nodding to others. When I finally got to my car, I took off my shoes and reclined the seat back. Five minutes, that's all I needed, just five minutes to rest my eyes before facing the Inquisition.

Fifteen minutes later, I awoke with a start, feeling even more tired than before. Now my eyes were gritty from the mascara that had started to flake off, my feet had swollen so much I had trouble stuffing them back into my shoes, and I was not going to get to the Walford police station by four-thirty. I just hoped Steve didn't decide to send his minions after me. Or worse, that the FBI didn't put my picture on the walls of the post office. I always look terrible in pictures.

Being that it was a late afternoon on a Sunday, traffic wasn't too bad. I figured if I got caught speeding, I would invoke Steve's name. As I pulled into the driveway and waited for a break in the cross traffic so I could turn left, I glanced into my rear view mirror. I wasn't surprised to see a couple of cars behind me. After all, people were still leaving the wedding. I idly noticed the front windows of the car directly behind me were tinted, though, which was illegal in New Jersey, but figured the car was from out of state.

I pulled onto the road, and the two cars behind me followed

closely. I still wasn't suspicious. It was only after I had driven a few miles – and switched lanes a couple of times to get around slower moving cars, that I realized those two cars were still there. I decided to experiment. I slowed down. So did they. I sped up. So did they. I switched lanes. So did they. I put on my turn signal. So did they. I didn't turn. Neither did they.

I know back roads and debated taking them instead of the main road to the Walford police station, but taking a back road had gotten me into trouble sixteen months ago. I decided to stick on roads with witnesses in case the drivers did have nefarious plans against me. What bothered me the most was the presence of two cars. Were they planning to flank me on either side and force me to stop? I stayed in the right lane, so they wouldn't be able to do so without going into the emergency shoulder.

I could have called nine-one-one, but by the time they responded, I would be at the police station. I drove at a steady speed, just above the speed limit so as not to tip off the pursuers that I was on to them, as if my earlier maneuvers weren't evidence enough, and pulled into the municipal building's parking lot. The other two cars braked, but the drivers must have realized where I was going, because they peeled off so quickly the lead car went into a fishtail.

It had seemed as though I had been driving for hours, but I was only ten minutes late. From the greeting I received, though, it might have well been an hour.

"What's the matter?" Steve was waiting for me outside the police station, in the lobby of the Municipal Building. "Is your watch broken? Or have you forgotten how to tell time?"

"Hey, I'm not all that late. Besides, you set the time and then hung up before I could confirm. So don't blame me. Besides," I paused, I thought, dramatically, "I was followed."

Steve laughed, and my anxiety turned to anger. "I was in danger, and you laugh?"

"We know. Didn't you notice a second car? It was the FBI. They were following the car that was following you."

"I thought the two cars were together. Wait a minute – what do you mean? The FBI is tailing me? Why?"

"Don't be so egotistical. You're not important to them, except for what you might know that you don't realize you know. They were following the other car. It was just coincidental the other car was following you."

I must have been more tired than I realized, because I had trouble following what Steve said. "Huh?"

"Just get in here. All will be explained. Well, some will be explained. We need to talk. I don't know how you managed to get yourself into this mess, but we've got to figure out how to get you out."

"I have no idea what you're talking about."

"And that, my dear, is the problem in a nutshell."

CHAPTER FORTY-EIGHT

Instead of heading to his office, Steve led me to a conference room. Sitting around the table were Joe Merino, his sidekick, the newly minted Sergeant Ryan, an older bald man, and a younger man and a disgustingly fit middle-aged woman with the distinct button-down look of Federal agents (Steve's right – I do watch too many cop shows on TV). Steve made the introductions. "You know Joe Merino and Marc Ryan. This is Bob Jeffers. We thought it would make more sense for him to come here for the meeting rather than you going to see him later." The younger guy stood to shake my hand; so much for stereotypes. He looked too young to be the fire marshal, but these days my dentist and gynecologist look like they should be worrying about the SATs, not the condition of my teeth or nether regions. "And these are Krista Conover and Brad Johnson from the Organized Crime unit of the FBI." The older bald guy and the middle-aged, humorless-appearing woman just nodded their heads.

"Wow," said Ryan. "You look great, Rabbi."

I hoped my smile of thanks made up for the glare he got from Merino because of his unprofessional comment. Steve helped, too, by adding, "Yeah, she always did clean up nice." I ignored his left-handed compliment.

As I sat at the table between Steve and Bob Jeffers, Krista Conover started right in with no preliminaries. "We understand you have been going off on your own and investigating Vincent Ferrillo. Not only are you putting yourself into danger, but you are interfering with an on-going surveillance operation."

"Hold on, now. I'm doing no such thing! I didn't even know Ferrillo existed until last night, when he approached me!"

"Let me guess," Brad Johnson had a patronizing smile I didn't like even if he was older than me. "Vince – he told you to call him 'Vince,' right?" He smiled condescendingly as I nodded. "Vince told you he owned a string of produce stores in New York and dabbled in ... what was it? Real estate?"

"Financial investments."

"Right. That's this week's cover story. Well, it is accurate, if you consider hiding the proceeds from drugs, prostitutes, protection, and gambling in off-shore accounts to be investing. What else did he tell you, Aviva?"

"Well, *Brad*, nothing that would pertain to any kind of FBI investigation, unless you care about who besides my niece's partner had a reason to kill a pedophile therapist."

"I think you mean 'pedophilic.' Unless the therapist was treating pedophiles." I really wanted to wipe the smirk off his face, but I didn't think Len Krasner would enjoy defending me on a charge of striking a Federal agent, no matter how justified I was.

I sneaked a look at Steve, who was trying very hard not to laugh. I gave him my version of the evil eye, the narrow-eyed stare that could quell a disruptive class of twelve-year-old students at fifty paces, and he laughed out loud. At the moment, I had no idea why I had ever married him.

"Sorry," he said, "but I do enjoy seeing Rabbi Cohen put in her place."

"No one has 'put' me anywhere. And you," I looked back at Brad, "can address me properly and respectfully, or this meeting is over. I have absolutely no idea why you dragged me in here. I have no information for you at all. I know nothing about organized crime, except what I read about in the papers or watch on TV shows. And I really don't think Efrem Zimbalist, Jr. would have treated a civilian with such contempt. Especially an innocent civilian who came here of her own free will. And whom you wanted to see."

Not to be outdone, I sat back with a satisfied smirk on my face. Looking around the table, I saw Ryan mouth to Merino, "Who's Efrem whatever?" Joe just shook his head. I was sure he was trying very hard not to laugh. So was just about everyone else, with the exception of Johnson. He was turning beet red. Even his partner, whom I had pegged as the "bad cop" until Johnson opened his mouth, was biting her bottom lip in an attempt to keep a straight face.

"After all these years, I should have known better than to think you could be intimidated, Aviva. Um, I can call you Aviva, right?"

"Sure, Steve."

He grinned and then addressed the others sitting around the table. "As I told you before the meeting, Rabbi Cohen doesn't intimidate easily. In fact, the more you argue with her, the more stubborn she becomes, even when she thinks she might be wrong. Not that she ever thinks she's wrong."

"I admit I'm wrong. When I am."

"If that's true, then why aren't we still married? If you'd admitted you were wrong to be so stubborn about your job ... Sorry, we need to get back on topic here. Let's start again. Rabbi Cohen, we know you were worried when Sherry Finkel was questioned in the hit-and-run death of John Quincy Moorhouse. We know that you uncovered certain rumors about him that led you to believe that the driver of the SUV could have been any one of a number of women who, as teenaged patients of Dr. Moorhouse, had been sexually abused by him. One of those women was the cousin of a known crime figure, Vincent Ferrillo, who came up to speak to you at an Internet café. Don't look surprised. I told you, the FBI has had Ferrillo under surveillance for some time. An agent witnessed your discussion. (*Surely not that skinny, whiny, spendthrift?*) We know, too, that a congregant of yours had raised questions about the accidental deaths of Florence and Milton Fisher, a seemingly unrelated case to that of Moorhouse's death. But what you don't know is that Fisher and Ferrillo had a business relationship. We have reason to believe Fisher was helping Ferrillo launder money and hide it in accounts in the Cayman Islands. It seems now that you have other information, too, relating to whether the death was an accident or suicide. Or, as we first suspected, murder."

"Murder? Oh, never mind. This is all too much for me to take in right now. Especially on top of everything else I learned – or heard –

today. The women telling me were drinking and I'm not sure how accurate their generation-old memories were. But there seems to be another connection, too, between Fisher and Ferrillo – the Fisher's daughter Audrey Fisher-Rivers was Connie Costello's best friend. Both of them accused Moorhouse of molesting them, but Connie also claimed he had impregnated her. When no one believed her, she killed herself. She was Vince Ferrillo's cousin; he used to spend his summers on his aunt and uncle's farm here in Walford. He now lives in a new house on whatever acreage remains of the old farm, and named it 'Connie's Rest' in her memory."

"And you know all of this how?" Krista Conover asked.

"Some of it Ferrillo told me at Café Wiffie – hey, don't look at me like that; I didn't name it. The rest of the information I got from the Pink Ladies."

Brad seemed to have recovered from my embarrassing him. "What does *Grease* have to do with any of this? Are you deliberately trying to make a mockery of these proceedings?"

"What proceedings? I'm just here telling you what I know. If I may continue without being interrupted by your insults, I will explain. The Pink Ladies was the name a group of high school outsiders called themselves. Their motto was 'Too hot to be cool.' Today's bride was a member, as were Connie Costello and Audrey Fisher. The other members of their clique were in the bridal party. After a few glasses of wine, they were more than willing to tell me everything they knew about Connie. And before you ask, the only thing they knew about her cousin, who was just old enough not to care about his cousin's friends, who were jail bait anyway, was that he was a hunk. They all had a crush on him. I think they described him as dark and dangerous and compared him to James Dean or the young Travolta. End of information."

"So these, er, Pink Ladies corroborated what Ferrillo had told you."

I nodded.

"Interesting that he told you all that information. Another question: how did he find you at the café?"

"He happened to be there with his father and overheard my niece

Trudy and me talking about Moorhouse. I was suspicious when he said he didn't want to talk to the police or the press about his information. It made me wonder if he was trying to defuse any interest I might have had in him by coming forward with the story about his cousin. But I had never heard of him, or of his cousin, so I'm not sure what was going on."

Brad Johnson got back some of his bluster. "You really think it was coincidence he 'happened' to be there? Ferrillo leaves nothing to chance. He knew you were there, and arranged to meet you 'accidentally.'"

"But how? And why?"

"We're not sure yet how he knew where you would be. But as to why – maybe he miscalculated, although that would be unusual for him, and thought you knew more than you did, in which case you might be right that he was trying to direct you away from suspecting him."

Maybe it was my long day and resultant fatigue, not to mention the overeating I did at the reception, along with four rums and Diet Coke, which was three more than my capacity, but I was getting more and more confused. (*Damn! Should I have been driving? Well, too late to worry about it now.*)

Before I could reveal the extent of my bafflement, Bob Jeffers chimed in with a change of topic. It was hard to take seriously someone who looked as though he should be at home studying for his geometry final, especially when he spoke in a high pitched voice. It sounded as though it hadn't changed yet. "If I may change the topic slightly, Rabbi Cohen, what did you mean when you told me earlier that the Fishers' deaths were suicides?"

"I was talking to their daughter, Audrey, at the wedding, and she said 'suicide' instead of 'accident' when talking about her parents' deaths. Later, she told me her husband had found the bodies and a suicide note and convinced her to cover it up as an accident. He didn't want the insurance company to refuse to pay." I shrugged. "I guess he didn't know that in New Jersey the suicide clause is in effect for only two years. Of course, I have no idea when the Fishers took out their policy, or if they even had one, but her husband has to have known, since Audrey found all the insurance papers." I stopped and thought, holding up my hand so no one would interrupt me. "No, that doesn't make sense. Audrey wouldn't have looked for the papers until after the cover up. So I really don't know if the insurance is the real reason her husband didn't want the deaths to look like suicide. Although I can't think why else he would have gone to such lengths to hide it."

"And what lengths are those, Rabbi?" Jeffers asked.

I was startled to realize I had no idea. "I don't know. I just figured he had to clean up the evidence of the suicide and then rig things to look like an accident. He's probably the one who stuffed the leaves and twigs into the dryer vent and then turned on the dryer."

Jeffers nodded. "We had wondered. The debris in the vent looked more like someone trying to build a nest than a bird building one. Not that starlings or house sparrows build particularly neat dwellings. Also, there didn't seem to be enough to clog up the vent."

"Then why did you declare it an accident?"

He grinned. "We didn't. No official papers have been filed. We just released that information to the press so Ferrillo wouldn't know we were on to him."

"I'm confused. Why would Ferrillo want to kill his accountant? Unless he was also his lawyer? Sorry, bad joke. Some of my best friends ... I'd better shut up now."

"Good idea, Rabbi, especially since Brad and I are lawyers," Conover said. "And a good question. We're not sure why Ferrillo would want to do away with Fisher, unless he was worried about a death bed confession. We were wire tapping the Fishers – yes, before you protest, we had a warrant – and we know Ferrillo was trying to get Fisher to turn over the access codes to the accounts in the Caymans." She saw me open my mouth and forestalled my objection. "I know: why would Ferrillo allow only one person to have the data about the bank accounts? It seems Fisher and Ferrillo were squirreling away some excess monies for themselves. Ferrillo had full access to those accounts, but then he found out, we're not sure how, Fisher had opened a couple of additional accounts which Fisher had 'neglected' to tell Ferrillo about. Yes," (she was definitely a mind reader), "we know Fisher's embezzling monies from the mob was a good way to ensure his death. But he was safe as long as he didn't give the account numbers to Ferrillo, who had to be worried Fisher would die of natural causes, and the codes would be too well hidden to find. But now ... if the daughter is telling the truth and Fisher killed himself, who has those codes?"

CHAPTER FORTY-NINE

"Maybe Ferrillo tortured Fisher to get the information from him, and then killed him." I shuddered at the memory of Ferrillo's description of what his father would have done to Moorhouse.

"Good idea, Rabbi, but the autopsy showed no evidence of torture. It showed no evidence of anything except carbon monoxide poisoning." Now Brad was back to sarcasm.

"Oh." I thought for a minute. "Wait – I just remembered – Audrey told me her parents left a suicide note. Her husband found it, showed it to her, and told her to destroy it. But she didn't. I wonder if they left some clues about the bank accounts in the note. They left things they wanted Audrey to find in obvious places."

"Like what?" Brad still sounded quarrelsome.

"Like adoption papers filed away with the insurance papers and house deed and cemetery plot deeds. Audrey had no idea she was adopted," I added, "until she found the papers. She was understandably hurt that they never told her, not even in the suicide note, but just left the papers for her to find."

"Did she say there was anything unusual about the note?"

"No. The only thing she said was that her husband told her to destroy the note so they could pretend the deaths were accidental. And that her parents could have told her in the note she was adopted. Actually they should have told her as soon as she was old enough to talk."

"So you don't know if it was typed or written?"

"I think we're thinking the same thing, Brad," Krista said.

"Wouldn't be the first time," he grinned. Oh, my, was there some more-than-collegial fraternizing going on between Agents Johnson and Conover?

"How about cluing in us peasants, then?" I was getting impatient and tired. And my feet hurt, I had a headache, and I could feel a run beginning in my pantyhose. Two runs, one in each leg.

"If the note is printed from a computer, they may have saved the file and linked it to the bank account numbers and access codes. If it's handwritten, there could be notes that look like doodles, but can be interpreted by someone in the know. In either case, there may be clues embedded in some of the words. How am I doing, Brad?" Conover was definitely flirting.

"You got it in one. I've taught you well."

"If you two would stop patting each other on the back, maybe we can finish up here? I haven't been home in hours and have a very hungry cat that is probably shredding the toilet paper in revenge."

Johnson smirked again. "Yeah, it figures you have a cat."

I tried not to rise to the bait, but couldn't stop myself from staring at him before deliberately turning my back and addressing the rest of the participants. Not that Merino or Ryan had contributed anything to the discussion. "I'm going to the Fishers' tonight. I'll see if I can get Audrey alone and if she'll show me the note." I made a face. "I'm certainly not going to ask her husband any questions. He has serious anger management issues."

Steve used the quiet but steely voice that told me he was really ticked off. "What do you mean you're going to the Fishers'?"

"Um, I told Audrey I might want to buy the house, and she told me to stop by tonight and she would show it to me."

"And," Steve continued in the same tone of voice, "what did you mean about her husband?"

"Oh, at the wedding, he was about to blow a gasket when he thought someone had said something to insult Audrey. And then he had a fit when he realized I was the one who had raised questions about Moorhouse and implicated Audrey. Turns out Phil Brauner ... one of my congregants," I added for the benefit of the others, "had called yesterday and asked George to have Audrey call me to talk about her accusations against Moorhouse. He hung up on Phil and never gave Audrey the message. Wait a minute – if you have the

Fishers' house bugged, you should know all of this."

"We, um, deactivated the bugs after the deaths. We didn't think we'd need them. But now – wait, did you say her husband's name is George?" Johnson and Conover exchanged a significant look. Well, significant to them. I had no idea what it meant.

"Yes, George Rivers."

Johnson and Conover nodded at each other. "That explains who George is. We may have removed the bugs too soon." Conover said.

Johnson asked me, "Do you know what George does for a living?"

"He works in the comptroller's office at a community college in Eugene, Oregon. Audrey described him as a glorified payroll clerk. I think he's got an accounting degree of some kind, but it might be an associate's degree, not a bachelor's or master's."

"So," Johnson looked at Conover. "What do you think? Was Fisher grooming his son-in-law to take over the family – pun intended – business or was Ferrillo double-crossing Fisher?"

"Maybe a bit of both."

"I'm confused." I was getting peeved at repeating that phrase, but it was true. "What does George have to do with any of this? The guy looks like Jack Skellington's son. And his doting wife doesn't think too much of his accomplishments. She's the one who told me all he has to do is punch the right buttons so the computer will spit out the paychecks. I can't imagine him as a criminal mastermind."

"We weren't sure who he was, either," Johnson said. "His name was mentioned in a couple of phone calls between Fisher and Ferrillo, but there was no other identifying information, not even a last name. In fact, we weren't sure if George was a first or last name. And we thought he was someone already in the mob, someone either Fisher or Ferrillo was grooming to take over after Fisher's Parkinson's would become too severe for him to continue. There was some discussion between them about Fisher giving the codes to this George, but Ferrillo wanted them himself. If we had known George was Fisher's son-in-law and had access to his house, we wouldn't have removed the bugs. Of course," he said after a moment's thought, "if they used cell phones instead of the Fishers' land line, it wouldn't have mattered."

"You didn't have the whole house bugged?" Merino sounded surprised.

"No need. Fisher's only contact with Ferrillo was by phone, and always on his land line."

"But cell phones can be bugged." I regretted my words as soon as I said them, and tried to backtrack. "Um, can't they?"

Conover was very suspicious. "And how would you have come across that information?"

"I read it somewhere?" Everyone at the table, even Ryan who had been very unobtrusive, looked at me skeptically. "Okay, um, my niece is a computer genius and she, um, sort of has some, um, skill in that area."

"You mean she's a hacker?"

"Well, no. I mean, yes, she knows how to hack into all kinds of systems, but she doesn't. Any longer."

Johnson was flipping through some papers in a very thick binder. "We're slipping, Conover. Why didn't we notice that Trudy Meisner is the rabbi's niece?"

Now Conover was puzzled. "And who is she when she's at home?"

Johnson sighed. "And your generation is supposed to be so computer-literate. Trudy Meisner has been advising the Bureau on computer hacking and security for the past twenty years or so."

"Trudy is an FBI agent? And she never told me?"

"No, Rabbi, she's a consultant. And she was not allowed to tell you. It was part of the plea bargain agreement."

"Oh, you mean after she broke into the computers at U. of P.? I thought the agreement was that she beef up the university's computer security. But that was a lot longer than twenty years ago."

"That was just a minor prank compared to her next stunt. But I've already said too much." Johnson closed his mouth firmly and crossed his arms across his chest, looking like a petulant toddler. A bald, sixty-year-old petulant toddler.

I burst out laughing. "The FBI! Trudy broke into the FBI computers! Good for her!"

Johnson broke his self-imposed silence. "The Bureau didn't think it was a laughing matter. And neither did the courts."

I was still chuckling when Merino brought us back to reality. "So what are we going to do next about Ferrillo? Do you think this George will flip?"

"Know what I think?" Ryan raised his hand and spoke in a barely audible voice, the smart but shy kid in the last row who knew all the answers but was too scared of the older, bigger kids to say anything. "I think George has the codes and is keeping them for himself."

We all turned to look at the pipsqueak. "And how did you come to that conclusion, *Sergeant*?" Johnson was back to his condescending self.

"It's not a conclusion, sir. Just a guess. I mean," and here his voice got a bit stronger and more confident, "let's say Fisher did put the account numbers and codes into the suicide note. And George found the note. If the information was on a second page, he could have just kept it and given only the first page to his wife."

"And if the note said 'Check out the next page for access to a couple of million dollars,' wouldn't his wife have been suspicious?"

"Maybe the explanation was on the second sheet. Or maybe the note was printed from the computer, and George edited out the bank information and reprinted just what he wanted his wife to see. And," he rushed on before more objections could be raised, "he then forged the Fishers' signatures. How hard could it be to write, 'Mom and Dad' in someone else's handwriting?"

"Not bad thinking, kid. There's not a shred of evidence to support what you're saying, but it is creative."

"I wonder ..." I hesitated before continuing. Oh, well, they all think I'm an interfering fool anyway. I can't do any more harm to my reputation. "I wonder if Ferrillo has thought of the same thing? And if George is in danger?"

"Or," said Merino, "if George has made a deal with Ferrillo."

"Same thing. How long do you think Ferrillo would let George live even if he turned over the codes? Or especially if he turned over the codes? Ferrillo wouldn't take a chance that George hadn't changed some numbers or held some back. And do you really think Ferrillo would honor a deal with a low-level bookkeeper like George? He probably has a Wharton MBA waiting in the wings to take over. In fact, I'm not sure why he employed Fisher anyway."

Conover piped up then. "Fisher used to do the books – rather creatively – for Ferrillo, senior. When Fisher, named Fleischer then, was about to be indicted for defrauding some other clients, the elder Ferrillo called in some favors from his fellow countrymen and got the Fishers, or, rather, Fleischers, new identities and relocated them."

"Huh. So both Audrey and Trudy were right." To their questioning looks, I answered, "I had asked Trudy to check on the Fishers, so I could decide if Audrey did have a grudge against Moorhouse. Remember Moorhouse? The reason I started looking into this whole thing? Anyway, she couldn't find any record of them from before they moved to Walford thirty years ago. She thought they had either fabricated their identities or were in the Witness Protection Program."

The FBI agents snorted in unison. Yeah, they were having an affair. They wouldn't be echoing each other's body language so well just from being partners.

"Then Audrey told me her parents had told her they were in the Witness Protection Program," another simultaneous snort, "but she didn't believe them. She thought her father was hiding from clients he had ripped off. I wonder now if she had overheard her parents talking, didn't understand it when she was younger, and her subconscious made the connection when she was old enough to understand that something about her parents' stories weren't kosher."

After a moment of silence, Merino asked, "So, what's our next step?"

I spoke up in a chirpy (me, chirpy?) voice, "Next, I go to the Fishers' tonight, as planned, wearing a wire."

CHAPTER FIFTY

"No way."

"It is highly irregular for a civilian to be put into that position of danger."

"That's an absurd suggestion, but it might work."

"Are you out of your mind?"

"I forbid it."

That last was from Steve, and the only one of the concurrent statements that I heard clearly. "You forbid it? You have no right to forbid me to do anything, Steven Goldfarb. How dare you? Even when we were married, you had no right. Who do you think you are, my mother? No, scratch that. My mother never forbade me to do anything. She usually joined me. Who do you think you are, my sister?" The adrenaline from my anger was dissipating my fatigue.

"Aren't you the one who said the more you oppose Rabbi Cohen, the more stubborn she becomes?" Merino was definitely enjoying himself too much at his boss's expense. If he weren't careful, his prediction would come true and he would be stopping speeders and ticketing drivers who parked in fire zones at the strip malls located on every commercially zoned street in Walford.

"Why not? They won't suspect me. They're already expecting me. Well, Audrey is anyway. It will give me a chance to snoop and ask questions. My cover is that I'm thinking about buying the house, so I'm expected to open doors and peek into closets. And if you guys are nearby and ready to swoop in at the first hint of danger, then there won't be any danger. And I don't see how it would be dangerous anyway. Who knows? I might get some more information to help you. And maybe I can finally exonerate Sherry. She is still under suspicion, isn't she?" This last question was directed to Merino.

"So far, she's our only viable suspect. But I have to admit the evidence is becoming increasingly circumstantial."

"Nothing on her car?"

"Not yet, but the forensics lab is running more tests. Or they will, when they get around to it." Walford didn't have its own lab and had to send out evidence to the State Police. A hit-and-run case probably didn't have high priority in an area that was a prime dumping ground for dead bodies. There's a downside to having one-point-one million acres of ecologically sensitive and protected undeveloped land in the southern counties of the most densely populated state in the Union. Forget about the rumors that Hoffa's buried under the end zone at the Meadowlands. I'm convinced he's at the bottom of the Blue Hole or fertilizing some sphagnum moss.

"So Sherry could still be arrested for a murder she didn't commit? That gives me even more motivation to find out what's going on. Maybe I can tie Ferrillo into Moorhouse's death. Isn't murder a better charge than extortion or whatever it is you're hoping to arrest Ferrillo for? What was it that finally brought down Capone? Tax evasion? These days, you'd be lucky if that would get him more than a fine and a slap on the wrist. But murder ..."

Merino shook his head. "I agree with Dr. Goldfarb. I don't like it. You said this George Rivers has a volatile temper. There's no knowing what he might do if the wire is discovered."

"He won't find it, unless he looks in my bra." There was a collective laugh from the law enforcement professionals, which was everyone at the table except me. "What? Aren't these things hidden in underwear? They are in movies. Although in movies they often short out. I'm not sure I'd want an electrical burn on my boobs. Or anywhere else."

Conover had been looking thoughtful. "We could use one that looks like a beeper. If you wear a pair of jeans, you can put it in your pocket and it's unlikely to be detected. We'd be listening in on two people who probably know even less about undercover work than you do, if possible. No insult intended; just a reality check here. Now, if Ferrillo should happen to be there, too ... but there's no reason to expect him to be. We do need to prepare for the unexpected, though."

I realized the comment about the absurdity but workability of my idea had been made in a woman's voice. Conover was the only other woman in the room. Ergo, she hadn't dismissed the suggestion out of hand.

"Why don't you come with me?" I asked her. "Listen to my reasoning first, then raise objections, if you still have them." I shifted in my seat so I could speak to her directly. Besides, the seats were hard and my *tuches* was getting sore. "They've never met you, right?" She nodded her assent. "I could say you're a friend who decided to come with me to look at the house. Even better, a friend who's a real estate agent. I don't suppose there's any time for you to print up some business cards, is there?" I looked at my watch. "It's already after six, and I told Audrey I'd try to be there by seven. I still have to go home and change, and feed Cat. I can check voice mails on my cell on the way home to make sure Audrey didn't call and cancel. In the meantime, Krista – I think we should call each other by first names if we're supposed to be friends, right? And I don't want to slip up and call you 'Agent Conover' by mistake. Anyway, what was I saying?" I had lost my train of thought.

"You always did babble when you got nervous, Aviva."

"You know me too well, Steve. Um, oh, right. I'll go home and change. Krista, come by and pick me up around quarter to seven – Serenity Acres is only a few minute drive from my place. And you should probably change, too," I eyed her plain black slacks, white shirt, black blazer, and sensible old-lady laced shoes with distaste, "into something not quite so, er, FBI-ish."

"I told you, Aviva, I don't want you going home by yourself. Not while we think Ferrillo has his goons watching you."

"So, what are you going to do, Steve? Stay overnight with me? How will you explain that to, what's-her-name? Ditzy? Oh, sorry, Mitzi. Besides, I thought the FBI was following the guys who were following me." Steve looked irritated, while Merino and Ryan exchanged knowing looks.

"Tell you, what, Rabbi." Krista said. "I've got a bag with some clothes in my car – I didn't have time to check into a motel yet. I'll change clothes here, and then drive you home. Maybe there's a woman officer who could drive the Rabbi's car home for her, taking any tail on a merry little jaunt first and losing them on one of those dirt roads in the area?"

"No one's driving my car on a back road. I don't need it to get stuck in the sugar sand."

"Sugar sand? Never mind. In any case, a police officer is better trained to misdirect and lose a pursuer."

I didn't have to think long. "I like it."

"So do I," said Johnson, obviously pleased with his protégé/lover.

"I don't suppose I get a vote in the matter?" Steve was sounding more and more annoyed.

"No. It's a Federal investigation. We consulted with you as a courtesy. And the Bureau is not known for being a democracy." Johnson's smirk was back.

"I'll get my bag and change in the restroom. In the meantime, Rabbi, I mean, Aviva, check your voice mails and be ready to go when I finish."

"What about a wire?"

"Don't worry. I don't want you to be involved more than you already are. I'll have a transmitter in my pocket, and Brad here can set up a van near the Fishers' house with the receiving equipment. It won't take long. The technology has gotten more sophisticated but simpler to use over the years."

"So it shouldn't be a problem for Brad to use, then." Okay, I'm a coward and just thought but didn't verbalize my sentiment.

"I still don't like any of this," Steve added. "We just asked the rabbi to come in here and tell us what she knows. The plan was not to get her to go undercover for us. But I can tell when I've been outmaneuvered. Ryan, go check the roster and see which woman officer is on duty and can drive Aviva's car home. Tell her I'll meet her in the dispatch area."

As Ryan left to do his boss's bidding, Steve stuck out his hand to me. "Your car keys."

"Have you forgotten how to say 'please'?" I dug my key ring out of my bag and handed it to Steve. "This one opens the door between the garage and the house. Here," I tore off a piece of paper from a legal pad on the table and scribbled a number on it, "this is the alarm code. I'll change it when I get home." I probably wouldn't, mainly because I couldn't remember how, but I didn't need the assembled troops to think they knew the number. "The garage door opener is attached to the sun visor. Oh, and ask her to fill the tank and put it on the department's account." I smiled sweetly.

"One more thing. I'm guessing she'll be there a while until Krista and I get back and Krista can drive her back here. Please explain to her about Pesach and ask her not to bring in any food. She's free to take whatever she wants from the fridge. There are paper plates and plastic utensils on one of the kitchen countertops."

I turned my back on Steve. I knew it would infuriate him, but I was beyond caring. I looked at Bob Jeffers, who must have been feeling like a fifth wheel. "While we're waiting for Agent Conover to return, could you tell me how you think George was able to make the suicide look like an accident?"

"If it was a suicide. But unless Ferrillo got the access codes from Fisher, there doesn't seem to be any motive for him to kill him. He was more valuable to him alive. It depends on who put the debris into the vents, if it was done as part of the deception or if Fisher did it."

"It would have to have been his wife. Fisher had Parkinson's and was wheelchair dependent. But I can't see her ruining her manicure. She'd want to look good for the undertaker. And I'm not joking about that."

"I'm inclined to think it was done afterwards. As I told you earlier, it bothered me that there didn't seem to be enough of a clog to cause a fatal backup of carbon monoxide in the house. It would have been more efficient to close the garage door to the outside, open the door between the house and the garage, and leave the car engine on."

"But there was a full tank of gas in the car."

"Right, but George could have filled the tank afterwards to divert suspicion away from suicide. All he would have to do is close the door from the garage to the house, open the one from the garage to the outside, and let the gas dissipate."

"That's just what he did! Remember I said a congregant was suspicious because some things didn't make sense? She said the Fishers had their dryer checked and had bought a detector the same time she did. They never complained to her about not feeling well. Well, they did complain, but it had to do with Milt's Parkinson's and Florence's cancer, not with headaches and flu-like symptoms; that story only came from Audrey. And the night the Fishers died, my congregant was staying at her sister's across the street. She woke up in the middle of the night, looked out the window, and saw a car in the Fishers' garage."

"And that tells you ... what?"

"Let me finish. The Fishers, according to Janet ... Janet Brauner is the congregant; it was her husband, Phil, who spoke to George Rivers about Audrey's connection to Moorhouse ... so, according to Janet, the Fishers never put their car in the garage. They used the garage for storage instead. And why was the door open in the middle of the night? Walford is a safe area, but people, especially seniors, are still security conscious, especially with Triple-U nearby. Never know what those fraternity boys will get up to during pledge hazing. I wonder if the car's still in the garage. It would be natural for me to check out the garage while I'm looking at the house with an eye to buying it."

"And looking at the car will tell you what?" Steve asked. I had forgotten how much he disliked being kept out of a conversation.

"Um, nothing. I'm just curious."

"I wish you'd leave that quality to Cat." Steve was definitely not pleased with me. Too bad. That's what he gets for thinking about leaving Walford. Huh? Now why was I still obsessing about something so irrelevant to my life? Or was it? Maybe my subconscious was trying to tell me something. I decided to pull a Scarlett O'Hara and worry about it tomorrow.

CHAPTER FIFTY-ONE

Krista came back wearing jeans and a bulky sweater topped by an even bulkier multi-pocketed fleece vest. I wondered if the bulky vest was hiding a shoulder holster, but decided I'd be better off not knowing. I made my goodbyes and followed her out to the parking lot. Brad had preceded us so he could set up the equipment van and be in position before we got to the Fishers'. Some members of the FBI taskforce were called in to supplement the team of Brad and Steve, who insisted that he and Merino come along. And where Merino went, so did his puppy dog, I mean assistant, Ryan.

"What, no Crown Vic?" I asked when I saw the royal blue Honda Civic Krista was driving.

She grinned. "It's a rental. I was hoping for a cherry red Stingray, but our expense account was only large enough to stretch to a Civic. I think Brad was as disappointed as I was."

"I didn't get a chance to listen to my voice mails yet. Mind if I do it while you drive?"

"Be my guest. I know how to get to your house." She grinned again. I must have misjudged her and she did have a sense of humor. "Nothing nefarious. I got the directions from the dispatcher after I changed my clothes."

Leesa Monaghan had called again. As I dialed her back, I filled Krista in on my relationship with the journalist. Krista nodded. "Merino showed us the article. He was sure you were the source of Monaghan's information. He wanted us to know what we would be facing when we met you. I read her updates, too. Looks like the university is in CYA mode, threatening to sue her."

"Yeah, well, they would try to cover their asses, wouldn't they?

Leesa told me about it, said they wouldn't get anywhere." I held up my hand as Leesa answered. "Nelly Bly, crusading reporter here."

"What happened to Brenda Starr?"

"I decided I'd rather be historical than cartoonish. Listen, I found out something really interesting about Moorhouse's appointment to the deanship. I can't tell you my source ..."

"No," I interrupted. "The only source you reveal is me."

"Hey, I apologized. I didn't tell your secretary it was you. She guessed. Now, let me finish. It turns out Triple-U had received a very sizable donation, contingent on their hiring Moorhouse either to a new position or to fill an empty one."

"Wait, I need to put you on speaker phone. I'm with someone who needs to hear this story. And, no, I won't tell you who it is. Not yet anyway." I looked over at Krista's grim face. "Maybe not ever." I pushed the speaker button. "Can you hear me, Leesa? Please repeat what you just told me."

As she did, I looked over again at Krista. She was listening with a frown. "I'm not sure that information is relevant."

"It is," I said, 'if the donor was a certain crime boss with a grudge against Moorhouse, someone who wanted to lure him back to Walford so he could wreak his vengeance."

"Crime boss!" Leesa was so excited her voice squeaked.

"Patience. All will be revealed. Maybe."

"Grrr. Okay, answer me this: why wait twenty-five years?" she asked.

I shrugged before remembering she couldn't see me. "Maybe because he just recently moved here and his cousin has been on his mind."

"Cousin?"

"Leesa, I've said more than I should have." I snuck a peek at Krista who agreed. "I can't tell you more or it could jeopardize a Federal investigation, not to mention me. I promise, when it's over I'll tell you whatever I can."

"You had better, but if I find out anything on my own, I'm going to print it."

"Just be careful, okay? I'm in enough trouble with Steve as is."

"So what's new? Call me when you can."

"What do you think?" I asked Krista. "Did Ferrillo want the university to make Moorhouse an offer he couldn't refuse?"

Krista groaned. "Do you have any idea how tired I am of hearing that old chestnut? Who knows? Maybe. Or maybe the donor was someone he really had helped."

"But why anonymous?"

"Why not? A lot of people give anonymous donations."

"Not around here. Ever hear the old joke?" No, she probably hadn't. "A guy stands up at a fundraiser and in a loud voice says, 'I, Moishe Pipik of 123 Main Street in Yahupitz, hereby pledge one hundred thousand dollars – anonymously." I waited for a laugh. None was forthcoming. So much for her sense of humor. "There are two reasons people donate to Triple-U: to get their slacker kid into the school or to see their name emblazoned on a building. An anonymous donor shouts 'Vince Ferrillo' at me."

"When we arrest him, we'll ask. Maybe it will help with the tax evasion case." Krista made a joke! I wondered if she got tired bouncing between being a professional and a human being.

I went back to my messages. There was another one from Trudy, rather succinct: "Call me. Use the house phone." She was sounding more like her mother all the time, but I valued our closeness – and my life – too much to tell her.

"Get me out of here! No, get *her* out of here!"

"Hi, Trudy. What's the problem now? Is Sherry on a cleaning and cooking tear?" Whenever stressed, Sherry cooked. She had a lot to do for the seder, but her sisters were all chipping in with some dishes, so she was probably experimenting with whatever recipes she got from friends or her myriad cookbooks.

"No, you idiot, it's my mother! Your sister, in case you've forgotten!"

"I thought she was coming tomorrow."

"She convinced Larry and Karen to come today instead, so they wouldn't have to worry about traffic. It made sense, but it also means an extra day with her. She's driving me crazy! She walked in and immediately began to criticize: 'Why didn't Sherry use celery in her chicken soup?' Uh, maybe because no one in her family likes cooked celery. 'What do you mean you're using paper plates? What's wrong with Great-Grandma Tilly's dishes?' Um, half of them are chipped, they were probably decorated with lead paint, and there were never enough of them for forty people anyway. To make matters worse, she decided to surprise us and just show up. And they arrived while Sherry was out – giving a formal sworn statement to the police. So I had to fill her in on the past few days. At least now, she's also pissed at you. But I could kill Larry for not warning us. I swear, he's such a wimp. Forty-eight years old and still intimidated by his mother."

I heard a muffled laugh and realized I still had the speaker on and Krista could hear every word. "Glad you're enjoying this," I hissed.

Krista guffawed. "Even computer geeks have mother troubles, huh?"

"Who's that?"

"Long story, Trudy. But if everything works out the way I plan, Sherry will be totally exonerated by the end of the evening."

"No, Aviva! Don't be busy tonight! I need you to take Mom off my hands!"

"Sorry, I'm too busy catching a ... I don't know what I'll catch. But don't you want to have the family together tomorrow night and not worry about whether Sherry will be with us?"

"At least talk to her."

I sighed for the umpteenth time. "Okay, put her on."

As I waited for Jean to pick up the extension, I asked Krista if she really needed to hear all this. "Oh, yes," she answered. "I haven't enjoyed myself so much since I heard the surveillance tapes made when that fruitcake in Montana who wanted to run for president tried to convince a stripper to pose as his society fiancé."

"So, you can't call your only sister?" Jean was sounding more peeved than usual.

"Hi, Jean. I had no idea you were coming today. I've been busy all day, with work. I officiated at a wedding."

"Who gets married the day before Pesach?"

"You know, Trudy asked me the same question. You two are more alike than you want to admit."

"We're nothing alike. I think the hospital switched babies."

"Gee, Mom said the same thing about you."

"What? And you didn't answer my question."

"Which one? Oh, I didn't call because I didn't know I needed to. And someone who honeymoons on a cruise ship with a seder gets married just before Pesach. Sounds like a nice gig, being a rabbi on a cruise ship. I think I'll check it out for when I retire."

"Why do you 'need' to call me? You should do it because you want to. And you knew I was in Boston first."

"Yes, and I knew I would be seeing you tomorrow. Jean, what's really bothering you? You're being more unpleasant than usual."

"Don't get snide with me, young woman. I really do not know how Mom raised you. She never would have let me behave the way you do."

"That's because you never did behave the way I do. So, answer my question now. What's bugging you?"

"What's going on with Sherry? Could she have really done what she's been accused of?"

"First of all, she's being questioned, not accused. Second, no, she could not. Third, I'm trying my best to prove she didn't."

"Oh, no, Spring, not again. Wasn't your last escapade enough? I don't want to go through that trauma again."

"Believe me, Jean, I don't need the trauma either. My shoulder never did heal properly. And, please, don't call me Spring. I've used Aviva for years now."

"It was good enough for Mom and Dad."

"Mom was zonked out on pain killers and Dad was drunk. Okay, he claims he had only one glass of schnapps, but Mom swears he was drunk. And even Mom calls me Aviva."

"And you can't ask how your own mother is doing?"

"I know how she is. She left me a message on my phone last night after you left. That's when she told me she was sure the hospital had given her the wrong baby. I gather it was not a good visit."

"It was fine. But Mom is insisting on doing too much."

"No, she's refusing to act like your conception of how a ninety-four year old should act. Let her enjoy herself. And you should try to enjoy yourself, too. Your visits with Mom and with Trudy would go a lot better if you would learn to relax and let people be themselves. Not everyone wants to be a clone of Donna Reed like you."

"Maybe if you took on more responsibility for the family, I would be able to relax."

"In case you haven't noticed, Jean, the family consists of adults. Well, except Josh and Simi. Even Larry's kids are in college now."

"Yes, well, that's another thing. I don't understand that Josh at all. And as for Simi – well, what will she be like with the parents she had?"

"The parents she *has* are terrific, and she will be, too. As for Josh, he's ... unique. Didn't you read the material I sent you about Asperger's?"

"Yes, but it didn't give me much hope for his future."

"He'll be fine. He had an early diagnosis and lots of interventions. Just accept him as he is. And enjoy your granddaughter – it doesn't matter who her birth parents were, her *real* parents are your daughter and daughter-in-law."

Oops. Wrong choice of word. "Sherry is not my daughter-in-law. I'm still not used to her being Trudy's whatever."

"Yeah, you've only had twenty years to get used to her being a part of your daughter's life. An integral part. How many of your friends' kids have been with their opposite sex spouses that long?"

"That's not the point!"

"Then what is? Listen, Jean, we could continue this conversation *ad infinitum*, but I need to go now. I'll see you tomorrow. Good night."

I hung up before she could add anything, and leaned back in my seat. "My sister is exhausting," I apologized to Krista.

"And I thought my family was dysfunctional."

"Oh, we function okay. It just looks weird to people who don't know us."

Krista pulled up to the curb a block from my house and looked around. "I don't see any suspicious cars, but I want to circle around first to make sure. You gave Dr. Goldfarb your key ring. Have you another way to get into your house?"

"Now you think of it? Yeah, I have an extra key I keep tucked into my wallet."

Neither of us noticed anything that seemed out of place, so we went into the house. Cat greeted me at the door with a very loud meow, and I told Krista to make herself comfortable in the living room while I fed him and then changed. It didn't take long – I dumped the pantyhose into the trash, put the dress into the laundry hamper, put on fresh underwear, jeans, a sweater, and sneakers, brushed my teeth, and ignored my hair. When I got downstairs, Cat had finished his meal and was sitting next to Krista, purring loudly and grooming himself.

"That's a good recommendation," I said. "He likes you."

"Licking his rear is a sign of affection?"

"Yup, it means he trusts you not to attack him while he's vulnerable. Ready to go? We're off to see the Wizard."

As we walked to the car, Krista started whistling "Follow the Yellow Brick Road." I was beginning to like her. Besides, Cat's assessments were seldom wrong.

After driving aimlessly for a few minutes, Krista said, "It looks as though we were right. Ferrillo's guys are watching your car, not your house. There's no sign of anyone following us."

"Maybe they gave up. They have to know they're being followed, too, after the FBI car following them following me continued to follow them."

She gave me a bemused look. "Lose your thesaurus?"

"Sorry, I lose command of the English language when I'm overtired." To emphasize my point, I yawned.

"Want to stop for some caffeine? You will need to be alert."

"No, thanks. I'll still be tired, but I'll also be jittery. Once we get there, I'll be okay. It's just being a passenger that is lulling me."

Serenity Acres was within walking distance of my townhouse, so we got there quickly. There was one car in the driveway. I wondered if there was one in the garage, too.

The house was typical of the burgeoning numbers of new homes in age-restrictive neighborhoods: pale stucco, high roof line, manicured front lawn, narrow patch bordering the front of the house planted with hollies and spiral evergreens, a small portico, no side yard because of the zero lot line. Audrey had probably been watching for us, as she answered within seconds of our ringing the bell – Big Ben chimes. She invited us in, looking curiously at Krista.

"I hope you don't mind, Audrey, but I took the liberty of inviting my friend to Krista to come along. She's in real estate and knows the right questions to ask."

"It's okay, but I wasn't sure you were all that serious. I don't even know what price to ask."

"Don't worry. I'm not in any hurry to move. The house is very nice."

In truth, it could have been nice if it hadn't been so cluttered. It was obvious the Fishers had moved from a much larger place and had brought their furniture with them instead of buying new. The eat-in kitchen to the left of the front door contained too many counter top appliances and a round table too large for the area. Ahead of us was the dining/living room, with an overstuffed sectional sofa, a mahogany dining room set better suited for a separate room, and a huge console TV. One of the two bedrooms, to the right of the main area, was large enough for a queen-sized bed, but had a king-sized one; the other had been converted into an office, complete with computer equipment, recliner, couch, and another large TV. There was a set of stairs leading upstairs to a second-floor loft and a second bathroom, presumably for visiting grandchildren, but being used instead as a storage area. Returning to the main room, I noticed there was a sun room straight ahead of the living room, fitted out with exercise equipment and wicker furniture. The Fishers may have been living in this house for only a year or so, but they had filled it with forty-five years of accumulated possessions.

Did I mention the flocked wallpaper and garishly colored Persian rug in the main room? And the table lamps complete with fringe? I guess they liked the look of early bordello.

Krista played her part well, asking questions Audrey couldn't answer about homeowners' fees and monthly utility bills and maintenance schedules. In the meantime, I poked around. Checking out the laundry room with the offending dryer, I noticed the door to the garage, and opened it. Turning on the overhead light allowed me to see what the dark hulk was.

An SUV. A dark colored SUV. A dark colored SUV with a dent in the front. A dark colored SUV with a dent in the front that could have been made by the impact of a body.

CHAPTER FIFTY-TWO

"Krista, come here for a minute, please. I have a question." I didn't take my eyes from the car, afraid the dent would disappear if I did.

I head a thud from the direction of the kitchen. "Krista?" I called, and a nanosecond later heard Audrey scream, "George! What are you doing?"

I ran – well, waddled as fast as I could – into the kitchen. Audrey had backed up against the refrigerator, her hand over her mouth. Krista was face down on the floor. George, a frying pan on the floor next to him, was bending over her, trying to turn her over so he could prop her up against the dishwasher on the opposite wall. Her fleece vest fell open, revealing her shoulder holster. "Well, lookie here. Why would a real estate agent be carrying a gun? I guess Vince was right about the cops watching us."

"Who's Vince? George, what has gotten into you? Is that a gun?" Audrey was on the verge of hysterics. I guess I would be, too, if my husband had just brained a real estate agent who was carrying a gun.

"That's right, George," I heard a familiar voice behind me in the foyer between the front door and the kitchen. I turned and saw Vince, looking a lot less friendly and more menacing than he had in Café Wiffie. The gun in his hand added to the impression. "I'm always right. Hello, Rabbi. We meet again, under less pleasant circumstances. Why don't you go stand next to your official friend there?" It was a command, not a request. "And, George, be careful with that. I have a feeling you've never used a gun before. In fact, give it to me."

"I'll have you know, Vince, that I grew up around guns. You need them on a farm."

"What, a peashooter to scare off the crows? Oh, go ahead, keep it. Just don't take off the safety. I don't want you to shoot yourself, at least not until we finish our business."

"Would someone explain to me what's going on?"

"Ah, yes, Rabbi, your legendary curiosity. Maybe we'll tell you all about it before we dispose of you and the officer here. Isn't that what the bad guy always does in movies? Tell the hero all the details of the crime, showing off how clever he was, giving the good guy the time he needs to get away? Well, sorry, but even if I do decide to tell you the whole story, you still won't be able to get away."

"Dispose of?" Audrey squeaked. "George!" He was still on the floor trying to lift Krista. Audrey grabbed him by the neck of his shirt and yanked him to his feet. I was glad she did; it prevented him from finding the transmitter in Krista's pocket. "What is all this? Who is this ... this ... this man? Why did you kill Krista?"

"She's not dead. Not yet, anyway. Just stunned. Which is why we'll need to find some good, sturdy rope so we can tie her up before she comes to." I can't believe I ever thought Vince was charming. Maybe if I were a cobra, I would be charmed by him.

George couldn't talk because Audrey had the front of his shirt bunched up against his neck, cutting off his breath. "You might want to let go of your husband, wifey. Oh," Vince held out his right hand, transferring his gun, much larger than Krista's, to his left, "we haven't been introduced yet, although I heard all about you from your late, lamented father. Vince Ferrillo. I'm sure your dad spoke to you about me. He was my accountant. And he had some bank account numbers that belong to me. I have reason to believe he gave them to you. I would like my property back."

"My father never mentioned you. I've never heard your name before. I have no idea what you're talking about," Audrey said. And, much to my surprise, I believed her.

"Are you telling me your father didn't give you the information? I find it hard to believe he wouldn't leave the means to access his nice little nest egg to his only daughter. And, frankly, I'm insulted you don't remember me, even if your father did keep the identity of his biggest client a secret. You called yourself Connie Costello's best friend and don't remember her cousin? The guy you followed around with your tongue hanging out?"

Audrey just stared. "You're *that* Vince? It's been a long time. I'm used to seeing you looking less ..."

"Professional?"

"Um, yeah, that's it. You used to wear work clothes all the time."

"I still do, but now I work indoors and wear thousand dollar designer suits. I don't get my hands dirty."

I must have snorted in derision, because Vince turned back to me. "You know, if you hadn't stuck your nose in where it didn't belong, we wouldn't have this problem. I'm not sure what to do with the two of you. I can't shoot you here. It will be the first place the cops will look when you disappear, and blood does have a way of showing up no matter how carefully one cleans it up. No, I think we'll have to take the two of you somewhere else. Good thing the Pine Barrens are so close. It will be a good place to dump that SUV, too."

"You ran over Moorhouse?"

He chuckled. "Don't be naïve. Of course not. Why would I when George here was only too happy to do it for me."

"George! How could you?" Audrey was sounding like a stuck record. She was getting on my nerves.

"I told you I'd take care of you, hon. I knew how much you disliked him, how he had come between you and your parents, so I took care of the problem for you. I tried before, in Eugene, but all I had was that dinky, light-weight compact, and didn't do anything but break his leg. I figured your parents' SUV would do the job, and it did." George was proud of himself. "Besides, he deserved it, after what he did to Connie."

If this were a cartoon, a light bulb would have gone off over my head. "George Rivers! Why didn't I realize it before? You're Jorge Rivera, aren't you? Florence had mentioned that you and Audrey had known each other in high school. You were Connie's friend, right? The one whose family worked on her parents' farm. The other kids called you 'whore, hey' and asked if you were related to Geraldo."

"Yeah, I'm him. Don't look so surprised. I know I don't look

Hispanic. My father's family was from Mexico, but my mother's grandparents left the Dust Bowl for California with the rest of the Okies. I look like her side of the family. They were all tall, raw-boned, gawky."

"George has put his past behind him," Audrey said proudly. I decided not to ask her where else he would put it. "He's a different person now. He's got a white collar job and kids and grandkids."

"And I do admire a man who betters himself, George," Vince said, "but you know what we talked about earlier. If you want me to get rid of the evidence for you, and you want a cut of your father-in-law's ill-gotten gains, you have to get those access codes for me. If wifey here doesn't have them, then all I can think is that you lied, and you have them."

"What if I do? How do I know you'll honor your part of the bargain and give us one of the accounts?"

"Bravado doesn't become you, George. You don't have the heft to back it up. The truth is, you don't know. So, tell you what, there were five accounts. Give me the numbers for four, and keep one for yourself."

While all of this was going on, I was wondering where the cavalry was. Krista's transmitter must have stopped sending. But wouldn't that have made Brad suspicious enough to rush in? I bent over her to see if I could figure out what was going on.

"What are you doing, Rabbi?"

"I'm just checking to make sure she's still breathing, Vince. Can I get an ice pack or something from the freezer? She's got quite a bump on her head." She didn't, but I needed an excuse to get closer to the kitchen entrance. Maybe I could run out the front door while they were distracted. I had no idea how I would distract them, but I did want to be closer to the door in case something occurred to me.

He chuckled again. "Don't bother. Her head will be the least of her worries in a while. Or yours."

I was getting scared, but tried not to show it. "Well, she's not dead yet, and neither am I, so I'm going to help her." I could out-bravado the likes of George any day.

I positioned myself to block Vince's view of Krista. She must have sensed what I was doing, because she opened one eye, just slightly, and winked. She was faking unconsciousness. I had to figure out what she wanted me to do, though. "Um, Vince, couldn't we take her into the living room, make her more comfortable on the couch or something?"

He shook his head. "You're really something. I guarantee you'll be a lot less comfortable when we truss you up and throw you in the back of the SUV. But, sure, go ahead. I don't care. George and I have some business to finish discussing. You and wifey can take her into the other room. The cop's in no position to escape and, no offense, Rabbi, but I can't see you overcoming anyone and running out the door before I shoot you."

"Gee, thanks," I muttered, lifting Krista under the arms. She might have been slim, but it was all muscle. "Um, Audrey, give me a hand, please?"

Audrey looked like she was in shock. Too many revelations all at once. Her father involved with organized crime, her husband a murderer. But at least her husband and father shared a predilection for changing their names and identities. "Audrey! Snap out of it! I need your help!"

Audrey moved like an automaton, but at least she moved. I again picked up Krista, who was doing too good a job of acting as though she were still unconscious, by her arms, while Audrey got her legs, and the two of us managed to get her into the living room and placed her on the living room couch. "Thanks, Audrey. Please get some ice wrapped in a towel from the kitchen."

As soon as she left, I whispered to Krista, "What the hell's going on? Why hasn't Brad stormed the house yet?"

"Because," she whispered back, while massaging her arms – I must have held her too tightly, "he knows we're not in immediate danger, and won't be until they herd us into the garage. Chances are, if they broke in now, we'd be dead before they got through the bedroom door."

"Bedroom?"

She grinned. "There's a sliding glass door to the deck. While pretending to check out how easily it slid opened, I unlocked it. I'm sure they're already inside, just waiting for the chance to get to Vince and George without endangering us. And, I think the chance is now." She held up the transmitter that had been in her pocket and pushed a red button. I sensed before seeing several armed officers, complete with the kind of riot gear I'm used to seeing on the evening news, come out of the bedroom. They rounded the corner into the living room, and Brad, leading the charge, if something so stealthy could be called a charge, put his finger to his lips. As though I was about to blurt out, "Hey, look who's here to rescue us!"

George was yelling at Vince, Audrey was crying, and Vince was being his icy menacing self when, within seconds, the kitchen door was blocked by a cordon of officers with more firepower than many Army units have. "FBI. Put down the gun, Vince. You, too, George. It's over."

CHAPTER FIFTY-THREE

The next two days went by in a kind of blur. Or maybe a dream. All I know is that none of it seemed real, I was missing chunks of memory, and the more I tried to think about what went on, the more elusive it became. But some things were clear.

Brad ordered Krista out of the house to get her head looked at by the paramedics called in as a precaution. "Don't be ridiculous," she scoffed. "It takes a lot more than a cheap aluminum pan to dent my skull. I'm fine. Barely even stunned. I just figured I'd learn more if they thought I was unconscious. And I did."

"But why did George hit you?" I asked.

"I'm not sure, but I think it's because Audrey wasn't around when he came in and all he saw was a stranger poking around in the kitchen drawers."

"Did you discover anything?"

"Only that the Fishers were disorganized slobs."

"Get out of here, anyway, Krista," Brad went into superior commander mode. "I want you to be checked before I write you up for insubordination. And, Rabbi, get out, too. We don't need a civilian to compromise any evidence."

"Compromise the evidence! You wouldn't have any evidence to be compromised if it weren't for me."

"Just get out."

"It's easier to listen to him than argue when he gets like this," Krista said. "Come on. I think we both can use some fresh air."

I walked out directly into Steve's outstretched arms. I have to admit his hug felt good. Familiar. Comforting.

"You have to stop getting yourself into these situations, Aviva. I'm not sure my blood pressure can take much more stress."

"Then stop eating fries."

"Don't you start in, too."

Too? I wondered who had been nagging him about his execrable eating habits.

"Besides, you're not exactly a paragon of healthy eating," Steve added. We just grinned at each other, and then I leaned in for another hug. Definitely comforting.

"You think you can come down to the station and make a statement tonight, while everything's fresh in your mind?"

"No, I'm exhausted. Besides, I don't have to rely on my memory." I pulled a small recorder out of my pocket. "Voice activated. I've had it for years. Use it in the car when I get a brilliant idea for a class or a sermon or suddenly remember I'm out of milk. I decided to take it with me in case Krista's bug didn't work or something. It's all here, including the time I was with Krista in the living room."

"I doubt the device is that powerful."

"It's not. When I convinced Audrey to help me take Krista into the living room, I managed to leave the recorder on a small table just outside the kitchen. It was covered with unopened junk mail, so I just tucked it under a catalog from the Cherry Hill Mall. I retrieved it when the troops arrived."

"Clever girl. We may need to recruit you."

"Nah, not me. I'm retiring from sleuthing."

"Yeah, right."

In the end, I did go to the station and give my statement. It was easier than going the next day, when I would be busy finishing up paper work before the office closed for the first two days of Passover. Also, I had a feeling I would be dealing with my sister for a lot of the day. Oy.

I eventually got home, and found a slew of messages on my machine from reporters who had police scanners. I deleted them all. There was only one journalist I was going to allow to interview me. I dialed Leesa, but got her machine.

"Hey, Watson, it's Holmes. How would you like to have an exclusive that will guarantee you will never again write an obituary or wedding announcement? Let's meet tomorrow for breakfast at the Walford Diner at ten, and all will be revealed. Don't call unless you need to reschedule our meeting. But not on my home number – I'm not answering it and am deleting all messages unheard. Most of them are from other reporters. And anyone I want to talk to, I'll call. Use my cell instead, If I don't hear from you, I'll see you then. Oh, and don't come over tonight either. I'm exhausted, and going to collapse soon. As soon as I finish prattling."

My next call – I know, it should have been my first – was to Trudy and Sherry. Unfortunately, my sister answered. "Hi, Jean. I have some great news for Sherry. Put her on the phone please."

"She's busy watching the news. You are featured. Is that what you were so busy doing you couldn't see me tonight? Getting yourself taken hostage by the mafia?"

"I wasn't a hostage. Oh, maybe I was. Anyway, I was with an FBI agent who was wearing a wire, the house was surrounded by other agents, and I was never in any real danger. And, best of all, the real murderer confessed to me and I have it on tape, so Sherry has nothing to worry about."

"I gathered that from her reaction to the news. And your niece is doing whatever it is she does to get more information." I just knew my sister was shaking her head in despair. "Why couldn't she have taught math and married a nice, conventional man?"

"Because she's a technological genius and a lesbian. And, so far as I'm concerned, Sherry's my niece, too. Now put her on the phone. Please."

"At least you said 'please,' but I could have done without your sarcastic tone of voice. Before I get her, though, I have one favor to ask – don't let Mom know. Please."

"Now who's being snarky? I have every intention of telling Mom. It will give her tons of street cred among her peeps in the facility."

"I give up on you, I really do. And the problem is, you're probably right. Not that I'm sure what you said, but I get the idea."

I was still chuckling when Sherry picked up the phone. "I can't believe it! You did it again – found the real culprit. What can I ever do to thank you?"

"You can't. You're family. You don't need to thank me. But if you insist, I'll come over for pizza – real, homemade pizza, not that mass-produced chain *drek* – after Pesach."

"Deal."

"Oh, and one more thing. You and Trudy have to go see a marriage counselor. If you promise you will, then you can announce your upcoming nuptials tomorrow night."

"We will. I promise. It means so much to us to have you on our side."

"I'm being selfish. I can't wait to see my sister's face when you make the announcement."

There were two other messages, too, but I didn't need to return the calls right away. They were both from Janet. The first was an apology: "We had a lovely time reminiscing about the Fishers – I'll never think of them by any other name – but none of us had ever noticed anything suspicious. Sorry I can't help." The second was congratulatory: "You did it again, Rabbi! *Mazel tov!*"

The next morning, I met with Leesa and filled her in on the details. Her article was posted on-line by early afternoon, and was quickly snapped up by a syndicate and reprinted in papers, both hard copy and virtual, under her by-line. By late afternoon, Leesa's editor had given her a promotion, a raise, and a new permanent assignment: investigative reporter. She left me a voice mail message: "All debts are paid in full. In fact, I owe you."

I knew Steve had probably left to go to his daughter's for the seder, so after breakfast with Leesa I put in a call to my favorite temporary acting police chief, or maybe he was the acting temporary chief. Whatever his title, Joe Merino actually took my call.

"I figure I've been promoted from disinterested civilian to, um, interested party. Or some such. Could you let me know what's going on?"

Joe actually chuckled, which may have been a first. "You do need to curb that curiosity of yours, Aviva. But you've caught me at a good time. And I'm in a good mood. I'm about to take a break. Why don't we meet at Café Wiffie and I'll fill you in? I'll even treat you."

"Are you sure your macho image won't suffer from being seen in a place with a name like that?"

"I'm secure enough in my manhood to chance it. Besides, there's a rumor the Triple-U students are getting their highs there from more than caffeine. I want to check the place out unofficially."

"I doubt if it's a hotbed of drug activity early on a Monday afternoon, but maybe we'll find a collection of pot plants under the fluorescent lights in the bathroom. See you there in fifteen minutes."

Maybe I was being hypersensitive, but it seems to me that several students made hasty exits and the barristas tensed up when Joe walked into the café. Even out of uniform, he still looked like a cop. Or ex-military, both of which he was.

After we got our drinks – black coffee for Joe, another peppermint mocha blended frozen pseudo-milkshake topped with lots of whipped cream for me – Joe kept his word and filled me in. "Vince, true to form, has lawyered up and is claiming entrapment. He says he fired his first lawyer, but I think the guy quit after he heard the tapes we had from Krista's transmissions. He's now refusing to talk.

"George, on the other hand, has confessed everything. He had found the access codes with the suicide note. Your conjectures with Jeffers about how George masked the double suicide to look like an accident were right – he aired out the garage, took the car, which hadn't yet run out of gas, and filled up the tank, then stuffed the vent with sticks and grass. He removed the CO detector and then bought a new one so he could claim they didn't have one."

"What about Audrey? Is she being charged with anything?"

"That's up to the DA, but she seems to have been an innocent bystander, except maybe in trying to defraud the insurance company. But since the company would have paid up anyway, it wasn't really fraud. But she thought it was." He shrugged. "And get a load of this: she's standing by her man. She says she forgives him, that he did it all for love of her, not for greed."

"I guess love really is blind. Or delusional." Or maybe just desperate. I thought about the research that never-married forty-somethings have only a two point six percent chance of getting married. Their chances of being killed by a terrorist are less than that, but people are still terrified of being caught in a plane hijacking.

ABOUT THE AUTHOR

Rabbi Ilene Schneider, Ed.D., one of the first six women ordained as a rabbi in the US, hasn't decided yet what (or who) she wants to be when she grows up. In her current incarnation, she is Coordinator of Jewish Hospice for Samaritan Hospice in Marlton, New Jersey, near Philadelphia.

She is the author of two other books. The first, the cozy mystery *Chanukah Guilt* (Swimming Kangaroo Books, 2007), was nominated for the Deadly Ink David Award for Best Mystery of 2007; was named as one of 2007's Top Ten Read by My Shelf; and was chosen as a Reviewers Choice Book, by the Midwest Book Review.

The second, the non-fiction *Talk Dirty Yiddish: Beyond Drek* (Adams Media, 2008) was praised by The Jewish Weekly Forward, the oldest and largest independent national Jewish newspaper: "Such a breezy, engaging book, I should be so lucky to write. Ilene Schneider, *mazel tov.*"

You can read about *Chanukah Guilt* and Ilene's other writings at www.rabbiauthor.com. Contact her at rabbi.author@yahoo.com.